A River
too Deep

a novel of loss, love, and faithfulness

Sydney Tooman Betts

Waterfall cover photo by Don Paulson
Cover sketch of Jay Tavare by Anita Thubakabra Mihalyi

ISBN 13: 978-1-7329079-0-4

For my husband,

who inspires my male protagonists

and supports all of my dreams

The People of the Book

A River Too Deep
Light Bird's Song
Straight Flies the Arrow

Chapter 1

How to recount the strange events that led to my present life is something of a quandary. My orderly father would have advised me to start at the beginning—but as much as I loved and respected him, starting in the middle is the only way to make sense of it.

ESCAPING HENRY WAS so effortless I could hardly believe I had succeeded. Earlier in the week, I learned that the public coach made its circuit on the very day Henry had arranged for me to see the dress-maker. Layering two suitable mourning dresses over my most durable muslin petticoat, I tucked the one possession I could not leave behind into my deepest pocket and prayed the Captain would cross my path in town. He did. We nearly collided, and he eagerly came to my aid, paying my fare and detaining Henry's hired man until the coach to the outpost pulled away.

The afternoon was sweltering, but the speeding horses produced a welcome breeze, and a glance around the coach's dark compartment calmed my fears. The only other traveler was a slight, bespectacled man possessing little of the vitality so characteristic of the region. He withdrew even from me, which was just as well. I wished to speak with no one.

What would Henry do when he discovered that I had fled? Would he send someone after me? Praying that nothing would delay the Captain, who was due at the outpost the next day, I pulled the Bible from my pocket and took refuge in my favorite Proverb.

> Trust in the Lord with all thine heart,
> and lean not unto thine own understanding.
> In all thy ways, acknowledge Him,
> and He shall direct thy paths.
> Be not wise in thine own eyes.
> Fear the Lord and depart from evil"[1]

I had certainly departed from evil, though not in the way the last verse meant. A lifetime with Henry would have been unbearable.

EARLIER THAT SPRING, shortly after Grandmother had died, my father received an astonishing letter. It was from his stepbrother, who had run away as a youth. The family had not heard from him in eighteen years and presumed him dead. I knew him only through stories, and few of those, as his name provoked sorrow and frustration. Aunt Louise, whom I had never heard speak unkindly of anyone, called him incorrigible; and whenever he was mentioned, Grandmother's eyes grew dull with pain. The letter invited Father across the Alleghenies to see for himself how his wayward younger brother had changed, so as soon as Father's business affairs allowed, the two of us left our village north of Philadelphia.

"What shall I call my mysterious new uncle?" I asked my father as our boat wended down the Ohio. "I always called your sister Louise, but I'd known her all my life."

"Well," replied Father, rubbing his chin. "He's grown too much a stranger for me to guess what he might like, Alcy. You'd better call him Uncle Callen until he has invited you to use his given name."

"I wish he'd written before Grandmother died. I often suspected that she blamed herself for his failings."

"That she did," my father agreed. "She indulged him far too much as a lad and disciplined him far too little."

"Then she must've changed greatly with age!" I loved my grandmother dearly, but she managed her household with a firm hand.

"You were half-grown when we moved in with her, and she was not about to repeat her mistake. Your Uncle Callen was only six when she married his father. His mother had died when he was four—old enough for him to feel the loss keenly but too young for him to cope with it well. You remember, of course, that my real father died during the War for Independence."

"Yes—the battle of Yorktown."

"Mother remembered how hard Louise and I had grieved for him and felt a great deal of sympathy for her new little stepson."

"How old were Aunt Louise and you?"

"About nine and six."

"No, I meant when your mother married your stepfather."

"Oh, I was fifteen, or nearly so. Louise was about twelve."

"Did you mind them marrying? I've asked myself how I might feel if you married again."

Father shook his head. "Not at all. I'd been clerking in his accounting house for about a year prior to the wedding and admired him greatly. They married the same day the Federal Convention assembled to revise the

Articles of Confederation in Philadelphia. I thought it fitting—both our nation and family had hope for better days."

"What was he like—Uncle Callen, I mean?"

Father leaned against the rail, watching the river lapping against the shore, but as he considered his answer, an affectionate twinkle brightened his eyes. "He was willful and mischievous, but disarmingly charming. I've never known a child to possess such a knack for talking his way out of trouble— you certainly didn't."

"I've never been good at hiding anything," I laughed. "Were you fond of him?"

"Yes—very, and he of me. He followed me everywhere. I taught him to whittle whistles, skip rocks—the things little boys love to do. The War had been hard on his father's shipping business and the trouble between England and France kept it hard. The Royal Navy constantly harassed our ships—seizing cargo, conscripting our sailors. It was the primary reason we declared this last war. My stepfather worked long hours getting the business back on its feet and hadn't any spare time for a young boy."

"Is that why Uncle Callen left?"

Sighing deeply, Father turned again to consider the river. "I've long thought I played an unwitting part in that. I was by nature the sort of son your grandfather wanted—eager to join in his enterprises and quite proud to take his name. As the hours I spent with him increased, your uncle began resenting us both—me for taking his father's attention and your Grandfather Callen for taking mine."

"Couldn't Uncle Callen have joined the two of you?"

"Shipping never interested him. He was more inclined toward adventure than commerce. Of course, that irked your grandfather, but the harder he pushed, the harder your uncle resisted. Eventually, the distance between them grew so wide they hardly spoke."

"Do you expect he's changed much?"

"'To him that is joined to all the living there is hope...'"

"'For a living dog is better than a dead lion.'"[2]

"I quote it that often, eh?" he chuckled.

"Every time Uncle Callen's name is mentioned."

"Not a day has gone by that I haven't prayed for him—and to think, after all these years, he's alive! I'm determined to give him every benefit of the doubt, Alcy, and want you to do the same. It takes little intelligence and no compassion to recognize a man's faults, and if he hasn't yet turned over his life to Jesus, we can't expect him to act like a saint. These new territories have few churches, and I'm afraid we might find him quite a rough fellow. Do your best to love him as he is."

AFTER WE FINALLY reached the Mississippi, we traveled north by steamer and then by coach the rest of the way. Father's excitement mounted with every docking or change of carriage, reminding me of a boy eagerly marking off the days until Christmas. As forests gave way to cultivated fields, he began restlessly checking his pocket watch. When we arrived at our stop, however, neither of us was prepared for the handsomely attired man who met our coach.

Mid-thirty and quite attractive, Uncle Callen looked like neither the unruly youth I had imagined nor the hardened character Father expected. I might have thought him an imposter had he not so closely resembled my memory of Grandfather. The likeness faded, though, as I peered into his eyes. They were not warm blue but cold pewter and held none of Grandfather's humor. More surprising was his similarity to Father. As the two embraced, I reminded myself that Uncle Callen shared none of our blood. He had our Scots-Irish coloring, though his chestnut locks were untouched by the silver that nearly covered Father's head and was a good deal lighter and straighter than my own. Most striking were his familiar gestures and inflection of voice: quite natural, I supposed, since we had all been raised beneath the same roof.

"Horace!" he exclaimed while turning in my direction. "Is this young woman my niece? From your letter, I thought she was a child. Come, Alcy, let me look at you." Firmly pressing my outstretched hand, he twirled me halfway around. "Your father wrote that you were lovely, but I assumed he was expressing the bias all men harbor for their daughters. Now I realize he's as prone to understatement as ever. You've inherited my stepmother's large, expressive eyes. 'Changeable as the color of the sea,' my father used to say—only her lashes were neither so long nor so black."

I tried to draw my hand away: his tone was as silky as his waistcoat, and I wasn't used to such familiarity from strange men. If he noticed or took offense, he hid it graciously, for which I was grateful. Father's obvious delight with his assessment made me recognize how childish I was being.

"I'm sure the last thing either of you would like is another carriage ride, but we'd best be going before it gets dark."

We didn't argue. The sun had already begun drifting toward the distant, gently sloping hills. As we drove down the settlement's main avenue, we noticed typical buildings that heralded new growth, some boasting shingles that revealed their owner's trade. A white stag identified the tavern for several of our fellow travelers, and a smithy beat his rhythmic pattern from the livery to which the coachmen headed with his horses.

Two women chatting pleasantly over the whitewashed pickets surrounding their gardens glanced at our carriage as we approached, but when I nodded, they turned away. I thought it odd. In a community this small, they must've recognized my uncle; but before I could ask if he knew them, he began pointing out a partially built brick structure.

"When it's complete," he explained as we turned onto the river road, "it will serve as our town hall. "Did you see the cornerstone?"

"Yes," answered Father. It was inscribed: Monroe, 1817.

"We laid it last month. As I'm sure you've guessed, we chose the name to honor our new President. All this area needed was a firm, managing hand," he added, a bit of frustration edging his voice. "But by turning most of this land into farms, they've shortsightedly lost the opportunity to harness the river close to town. What remains is so far north or south that the distance and terrain become prohibitive. What will they do when they lack mills to grind their grain, make cloth, or cut timber?

"I'd hoped to buy this parcel of land we're passing for that very purpose, but a man named Lawson grabbed it up before I raised the capital. Just this morning, I offered him nearly twice what he paid for it, including the cost of his house, but he refuses to budge. Says his wife loves the view of the river from that hill."

He nodded toward an immaculately kept white cottage built on a small rise overlooking the river. Chickens roamed freely in the yard, darting between the feet of a slender, golden-haired woman taking down freshly washed clothes from a line.

"I'm considering buying the land over there—on the western side of the river." He pointed to a spot beyond the bank. "In addition to owning the mills, I thought I might make a tidy profit ferrying materials to be processed across and back, but this river isn't easily navigable. Its bed is full of rocks and the snow melting off those mountains to the north swells it treacherously each spring. By the early fall, it becomes too shallow. A bridge would be the only realistic solution, and I could offset the construction cost by charging a toll. It would serve Lawson right for his stubbornness—what would his pretty wife think of their view then?"

Father shifted uncomfortably. "Sounds like you've planned it out well. Your father thought very highly of your intellect. He'd hoped to send you to Princeton before offering you a place in his business."

"Yes...he told me. It was one reason I left. I still love learning new things, in fact, I dare say I own the most complete library in the territory, but he and I could never agree on my vocation. He continually tried to squeeze me in to his own dreary and dignified mold."

"Grandfather, dreary?" I blurted out. Grandfather had been dignified, but I could not imagine anyone finding him dull. "I don't mean to contradict you, Uncle, but I thought he had a wonderful wit."

"Had you been an energetic boy of seventeen," he smiled, "you might have felt differently. He wanted me to be Alexander Hamilton—without the dueling, of course—I preferred Daniel Boone. Ah, here we are."

We had ridden about five miles from town to reach a long lane curving gradually uphill to a well-built pale gray stone house. It was larger than I had expected and looked as if Levi Weeks, the architect from Philadelphia, had designed it. A high-pitched roof over-hung a wide veranda running along all four sides, punctuated by windows of surprising size. To the south stood several other buildings outlined against a pink and coral cloud: an ample looking stable with an adjacent paddock and a smaller structure that likely housed hired men. A number of them milled about it, gawking as we alit from the carriage.

Father nodded in their direction while a manservant, Pinckney, engaged Uncle Callen. "Alcy," he whispered, "I'd prefer you didn't wander far from the house unaccompanied."

I agreed readily, gathering up my skirt to ascend the wide steps. Our host took them two at a time, ushering us through the tall entryway into a gallery running through the center of his home. Spacious looking rooms flanked both sides: one a well-furnished parlor framed by an open double doorway and the other, I guessed, a dining room. I caught only a glimpse as the pocket doors were partially closed and Uncle Callen's pace was brisk. When he reached the far end of the gallery, he held out his hand toward the smaller of two bedrooms.

"This one's for you, Alcy, and the other just beyond it is for you, Horace. I hope you'll find them comfortable."

Before we had a chance to answer, a woman about Father's age stepped into the hall.

"Ah, Mrs. Hodgetts," my uncle called. "Let me introduce you to my brother, Horace Callen, and his daughter, Alcy. Please see to it that she has everything she needs and assist her in any ways she desires."

"Mr. Pinckney will carry your trunks in presently, Miss," she nodded, "though if you don't mind, I'd like to unpack them on the morrow. Supper is waiting to be served, and he'll be needing to drive me home before dark."

"That will be fine," I smiled, enjoying her candor. "I can easily find anything I need for the evening."

"If you'll excuse me then, I'll be fetching your father and you some hot water for washing up after your long journey."

My room had been considerably outfitted to suit a feminine taste, containing not only a dressing table, a full-length mirror, and several wardrobes, but also a canopy bed draped in rose-colored silk. The effect was beautiful and the furnishings fine, quite unlike the simply constructed bed and chests I expected. More surprising still were the grand portraits that hung in the gallery where I found Father waiting. They could have been Van Dykes had their dress been correct for his period.

"Who do you think they are?" I asked Father, tucking my hand in the crook of his arm.

"I've no idea, I'm sure. I've never seen either of them before."

A door opened opposite us and Uncle Callen stepped through.

"That dusky green becomes you, Alcy."

"Thank you, Uncle Callen. Your home is lovely."

"I hoped you would like it."

"Alcy and I have been wondering about your paintings. They look like old family portraits, but I can't identify the subjects."

"They are the Mahans, a couple for whom I worked when I first left home. They passed away many years ago."

"They must've looked upon you as a son to have left you such fine likenesses."

"Yes. They hadn't any children of their own."

"Did you work for them long?" I asked, wanting to discover all I could of my uncle's history.

"Only a few years. Their horse unexpectedly bolted, throwing their buggy over the side of a bridge and drowning them both."

"Oh," I murmured. "I'm sorry. You must have cared for them deeply to have kept their portraits."

"Were it not for them, I wouldn't have amassed the wealth I enjoy today—you could say they gave me my start. I keep their portraits as a reminder, not of the Mahans alone but also of how easily life can be snuffed out."

"Yes," Father nodded. "'The grass withereth, the flower fadeth, but the Word of our God shall stand forever.'"[3]

"Still quite religious, Horace?"

"Religious? No. It's always struck me as man's attempt to placate God— but they have it upside down, don't they? The Almighty, Himself, settled our debts."

"Well then," replied my uncle, "shall we go pray over supper? I'm afraid Mrs. Hodgetts will become quite put out if the dinner she prepared grows cold."

As Pinckney pushed back the dining room doors, I hoped that neither he nor his master caught my expression in the huge gold-leafed mirror. Hung atop a marble fireplace, it reflected an elegant crystal chandelier that would have looked at home in an ancestral mansion. How Uncle Callen had obtained them, I wondered, perusing an expansive table full of Old Paris china; but as I listened to my uncle during dinner, I concluded there was little he could not do. He seemed an expert on subjects as varied as curative herbs and politics and divulged his ambitions to enter the latter field when the area's population increased sufficiently to set up a government.

After dessert, he suggested, "If you'll indulge me, Horace, I'd like us to retire to the library instead of the parlor. I've recently received a volume that I suspect Alcy might enjoy."

Father had no objection, so we followed him again to the far end of the gallery and entered a room that I liked best of the entire house. Rich, dark paneling and stuffed leather chairs declared it the retreat of a manor lord, and the enchanting view put me entirely in sympathy with Mrs. Lawson. Two large windows splayed the waning light over bookshelves that reached the ceiling, while a matching glass-paned door opened to a garden that sloped down toward the water. Opposite this was a closed wooden door that I assumed led to Uncle Callen's private quarters.

His collection of books was outstanding. In addition to the expected classical Greek and Latin works, he owned Shakespeare's plays, Shelly's and Byron's poetry, and the works of two important American authors: Washington Irving and Hannah Adams. As he withdrew a petite, nicely bound volume from a high shelf, he suggested, "This should be of interest to you."

To my delight, it was *Sense and Sensibility*, authored simply by "A Lady" according to its title page. "I have wanted to read this," I smiled, "but Grandmother would not permit a novel in her house."

"Yes, I can well imagine. She used to tell Louise, 'They put unseemly ideas in young women's heads.'" His imitation of her tone was so exact that I began to giggle, and, pleased with his success, he offered, "Keep it. It's not much to a man's taste."

My father's blue eyes twinkled as he nodded in assent.

"It's very good of you, Uncle. I look forward to devouring every word. Would either of you mind terribly if I retired? I'm rather fatigued from the journey."

"I mind very much," my uncle answered, caressing my hand as he had when we first met. "Rarely has anyone so lovely ornamented my den, but I wouldn't want to ruin such beauty by depriving you of rest."

"Thank you, Uncle," I answered, fighting hard against the urge to pull away. This man was my father's beloved brother, and I wasn't only a new acquaintance—I was his niece.

"Go ahead, dear," Father added. "Your uncle and I have much catching up to do."

"Good night then, Uncle Callen, and thank you again for the book. Good night, Father."

Finding my room with ease, I changed into my nightclothes and climbed beneath the covers to read my very first novel. As the characters unfolded, however, I began to feel ashamed. Each time the cold-hearted John Dashwood spoke, I imagined my new uncle playing his part. The two could not have been less alike. John Dashwood deprived his young sisters of their home and restricted them to a meager income. Uncle Callen had made clear that his home was ours and had provided for our every comfort. Still, ever since alighting from the coach, I kept feeling as I had last winter during Mrs. Schumacher's fancy dress ball. My partners had each worn elaborate masks, but none were able to prevent occasional hints of their identity. Of course, I, too, had worn both costume and mask, and my fancies now were likely as silly as they had been then.

It would take a little time to become accustomed to his lavish compliments. I had thought my face and figure tolerable and had received a fair share of attention from suitors, but I certainly did not consider myself a beauty. My friend Allison was far prettier with her chocolate eyes and ready smile. Otherwise, Uncle Callen had been a gentleman in every way. Resolving to both like and love him, I closed my book, prayed for a kinder heart, and drifted off to sleep.

LIFE IN MONROE PROVED pleasant. Uncle Callen had thought of our every need, even obtaining an eastern saddle for me so I could ride with Father and him every morning. When the two of them were busy with their own pursuits, I curled up in one of the stuffed chairs in the library, stitched on the veranda, or sketched under an enormous shade tree in the garden. On the steamer, I had feared he might consider me an intruder since his original invitation addressed Father alone; but if he did, he hid it well and paid me an embarrassing amount of attention. I could easily see why Grandmother and Louise had found his charm irresistible. He pursued what he wanted with such confident grace that Father and I soon found ourselves swept up by the current of his enthusiasm.

"This country becomes more beautiful with every passing day," I sighed. We had reined in our horses to watch a flock of geese landing on the pond.

"I certainly understand, Uncle, why you love it out here."

"Don't you miss the luxuries of civilization: the dances and soirées?"

"You've made us so comfortable, we have hardly anything to miss—and I've always preferred a few close friends to a multitude of acquaintances. I've been surprised, though, that no one has called on us."

"I miss hearing you play," Father joined in. "Alcy is quite an accomplished pianist."

Uncle Callen turned his horse until he faced me. "Don't you miss it?"

"Sometimes," I confessed, "but I didn't expect to find the opportunity." Moving his horse close to mine, his voice took on that silken tone. "Then we must do something about that. When we return to the house, I will ask Pinckney to find one."

"I'm grateful for your kind intentions, Uncle, but surely such pieces can only be built back East, and I doubt we will impose on you long enough to warrant such expense."

With mock horror, he replied, "You aren't planning to leave me already? I've just regained my brother—would you take him away?" Before I answered, he slipped his gloved hand over mine and murmured, "Would you deprive me of a niece of whom I'm growing quite fond?"

I lowered my eyes, unsure of how to respond. "I wouldn't willingly grieve you, Uncle. It's of Father's business interests that I was thinking."

He squeezed my hand affectionately. "You've made me happy saying so. Horace," he called, turning toward my father, "can't you delay whatever it is at least a few months longer? I've a man in town that does banking for me. I could arrange for him to act on your behalf."

"It's possible," shrugged my father, "but I need to return by November at the latest. Would you consider coming back East with us?"

"Certainly—if I had sufficient incentive to do so."

When they both became quiet, I glanced up to find their eyes fixed on me oddly, as if I'd missed a cue.

"Alcy," prompted Father, "I believe your uncle is waiting for the lady of our house to issue him an invitation."

"Oh! Yes, of course," I blushed. "You'd be most welcome."

He gave my hand another squeeze. "Then it'll give me the greatest pleasure to accept."

As we returned to the house, I felt we had turned some sort of corner but could not quite figure out how or to where. Afterward, though, Uncle Callen asked me to "do him the great favor" of running his household while in residence. I readily agreed, happy to make myself useful and glad for a way of thanking him for his hospitality.

His housekeeper, Mrs. Hodgetts, was a marvelous cook and as plump as my grandmother said all cooks should be. While seeking a replacement for old Lisbeth last summer, Grandmother had sternly warned me, "A thin cook is not to be trusted. She either has too little love for good food or doesn't like her own cooking—and neither is desirable."

My new responsibilities would frequently take me into the kitchen, so I hoped this might allow Mrs. Hodgetts and me to become better acquainted. Since Grandmother had gone to be with the Lord and Allison had gone to be with John—both their hearts' desires respectively—I had missed a woman's company. Mrs. Hodgetts was apparently of a different mind. Although she was always kind, she engaged only in the briefest of conversations, asking me which meat to serve or about supervising the gardener, and then hurriedly left when she had finished her duties.

"ALCY," UNCLE CALLEN called from the library door one early afternoon. I was sitting beneath a shade tree, sketching a beautiful bevy of deep pink azaleas with the sparkling Monroe River in the background.

"I'm here, Uncle," I answered, but before I had stopped drawing to show him where, he seated himself on the lush grass beside me.

"Don't let me interrupt," he urged, looking over my shoulder. "You're quite good. Do you also paint?"

"Yes, but I'm rarely satisfied with the results."

He looked as handsome today as I remembered Grandfather looking, though I still felt startled by the coolness of his eyes.

"I suspect you're too modest to praise your own work."

"No—honestly. Ask Father. I can never shade with colors as well as I do with charcoal, and then my paintings look flat."

"Well, perhaps I'll soon be in a position to judge that for myself. I'm taking a steamer down the Mississippi to New Orleans come August. While there, I will buy you the finest supplies available."

"Thank you. I'd like that," I told him, pleased but no longer surprised by his generosity.

"It's nothing." He grinned; absentmindedly stretching out one of my dark ringlets and watching it spring back into place. "I look forward to seeing my garden on canvas. I've been searching for the right painting to hang above the small table next to the front door."

"I'll do my best, Uncle, but you mustn't have high expectations."

"Anything it lacks in quality will be made up by fond memories it will evoke."

I kept drawing, at a loss for a reply and keenly aware of my heightening color.

"Horace has kept you engagingly innocent, Alcy. I find it enchanting."

"Do you go to New Orleans often?" I asked, hoping to redirect the conversation.

"Yes. About once a year."

"I've often wondered how you furnished your home so elegantly this far from New York or Philadelphia. Did you have many things brought upriver?"

His eyes so unexpectedly hardened, I regretted asking, but then his lips curved into an affable smile. "Yes again. You have a discerning eye. I had many of the finer pieces—the mirror over the dining room fireplace, the mantel itself, and the chandelier—shipped up. I have a penchant for quality craftsmanship."

"The mantel is my favorite," I confided. "I've heard New Orleans is a fascinating city with its French and Spanish roots."

"Would you care to see it for yourself? Your father would like to accompany me if I can persuade you to join us."

"To New Orleans? Yes, I'd like that very much."

"You may find the heat unpleasant," cautioned Uncle Callen. "The summers are horrible so far south."

"I wouldn't miss it. I want to see where Jackson defeated the British. May we?"

"Alcy," he chuckled, "you astound me. You're much too young and graceful to be interested in wars."

"Not wars, exactly," I smiled, recalling the never-ending tactical discussions in which Father and his friends engaged during this latest one, "but of history. Battles are an integral part of it, don't you think?"

"Yes," agreed my uncle, "and New Orleans has seen her share. Like anything that offers riches, power, and beauty, many have wanted to possess her. I will enjoy showing you her finer sites, as well as introducing you there to many of the more stimulating aspects of life."

Uncertain of his meaning, I concentrated again on my sketch, which wasn't easy. His fingers brushed my neck each time they captured and released another curl. "What is the occasion?"

"Business—which leads to another reason I wished to speak with you. Horace tells me you're wealthy in your own right."

"I suppose so. My mother left me her estate, and I inherited her brother's recently. He was a naval officer, killed in the battle of Baltimore."

"I remember him well—a fine man. My stepmother, your grandmother, also left you a stipend, I believe, from the money my late father left her." When I glanced up with surprise, he quickly added, "Horace mentioned it. As you can see from my home, I've become quite prosperous. Would you allow me to invest a portion of your inheritances? I'm considering a cotton venture in a growing settlement downriver called Natchez. We'll spend a few days there en route to New Orleans, and you already know about my plans for a mill."

"I appreciate your wish to include me, but most of my assets are held in Trust. Father invests those that aren't."

Uncle Callen shrugged. "That need not hinder me. Your father wants to invest your fortune where it can make the best return. How much capital do you have all together and in what allotments do you receive your living?"

"I'm sorry; I can tell you only the latter." My conscience pricked me; I wasn't sorry but relieved. "You'll have to ask Father about the rest."

"I didn't mean to make you uncomfortable, Alcy. Your future is important to me. Like anything fine, a genteelly raised woman needs careful tending. Your father is getting older, and I wish to give you every advantage of my experience."

"Thank you for your consideration, Uncle Callen, but my father is not yet fifty. I don't expect to be deprived of him any time soon and hope to long be married before that dreaded day."

"These past 18 years on my own have taught me never to discount the unexpected. God forbid anything should happen, but if it does, wouldn't you wish to be prepared?"

"Yes," I nodded. "I suppose so."

"Good, then it's settled. Come inside soon. The sun will spoil your lovely complexion. Your father and I are in the library finalizing the particulars of the trip."

"But, I thought it wasn't yet decided."

He rose to his feet and smiled at me indulgently. "As I said, your father has kept you engagingly naïve. What did he read to us the other day? Ah, yes: 'Man was not made for woman, but woman for man.'[4] Men make their plans and ask their wives—or daughters—only out of courtesy."

Lifting my hand to his lips, he held my gaze until I looked away; but as he turned to cross the lawn to his study, I tossed my paper onto the grass. I no longer felt like drawing.

AFTER DINNER THAT evening, Uncle Callen was called away by urgent business. Father let out a slow, satisfied sigh as he watched him ride down the lane.

"My stepfather would have been proud of the man his son has become. Your uncle has managed to combine his love for adventure with the

17

stubborn determination that used to drive his father mad and has turned them into useful characteristics."

Offering me his arm, he guided us down toward the river.

"Does he never give you a reason for misgivings?"

Father paused for a moment before he answered. "He's a man of the world to be sure, Alcy, and perhaps too driven by ambition, but I have hope that the Word is affecting his heart. Don't you think the questions he is asking during our Bible readings show thought?"

"Yes," I answered honestly, "but..."

"But what, dear?"

"I'm not quite sure how to put it into words. This afternoon he made me exceedingly uncomfortable."

"Why? What did he do?"

"For one thing, he asked me some very pointed questions about my income."

"Oh. I'm to blame for that, sweetheart. I suggested you might be interested in supplying capital for investment. Was there something else?"

"Well... first, he invited me to go to New Orleans with the two of you, and then, after I'd accepted, he told me you'd already settled it."

"Alcy, as grown-up as I consider you, I still claim the right to make decisions on your behalf."

"That's not what I mean. It was his manner. I found it—demeaning."

"Why? What did he say?"

"'Man was not made for woman, but woman for man.'"[5]

Father looked at me uncertainly. "Aren't you being a little sensitive? He is quoting Paul, or nearly so. If anything, that shows how closely he attended to our reading."

Put that way, I agreed my concerns sounded baseless and wished I hadn't brought them up.

"Is there anything else?"

I hesitated to say more, unsure I could justify my feelings. His improprieties were subtle, more in tone or length of touch than anything clearly objectionable.

"I can tell there is something. Let's hear it."

"He kept touching me."

Father stopped and looked at me quite gravely. "Exactly what did he do?"

"It wasn't anything much—he was just tugging at a stray curl, but it seemed an excuse to stroke his fingers against my bare neck."

Father's eyes dropped to the ground as if he searched for a response. "He is a man, Alcy, and you have grown lovelier than you realize. I

18

wouldn't be at all surprised if he finds you attractive, though that doesn't give him an excuse to take liberties. Would you like me to speak with him?"

"No, Father—please don't!" I'd be mortified. "It lasted only a few seconds. Perhaps I'm making too much of it."

"Do you remember our conversation on the way out here—how we agreed we should give him the benefit of the doubt? In every way, he has far exceeded our expectations, and we've spent the better part of two months in his home. What you describe sounds like an uncle demonstrating a growing affection for a niece, nothing more. Has he done anything else?"

"No," I mumbled, hating the look of disappointment that had crept into his eyes. His reaction made me question my own, which seemed petty once I put it into words.

"What's that?" Father pointed to an unnatural amber glow silhouetting the northern slope.

As the smell of smoke wafted toward our nostrils, we saw three or four dark figures galloping over the top. One of the riders saw us and veered in our direction.

"Go inside quickly" yelled my uncle, clearly recognizable now. "There's trouble at the Lawsons'—the whole house has gone up in flames. We've come to rouse the others to help put it out."

"I'll get my horse," my father shouted.

"No, I've plenty of men. Stay with Alcy. If it's Indians, I don't want her left alone."

Counsel in the heart of a man is like deep water, but a man of understanding will draw it out.

Proverbs 20:5

Chapter 2

OVER THE WEEKS, Father and I had heard about savage attacks and other misfortunes that plagued the town since its inception. Some of the original homesteaders had returned east, many selling their possessions to pay their fares. My uncle thought it his Christian responsibility, he had told us, to purchase the most costly items, additionally explaining his acquisition of so many fine heirlooms. As the two of us ascended a hill for a better view of the countryside, we could just make out the charred remains of the Lawsons' clapboard house. The fire had burned it to the ground, killing the entire family.

"What a terrible waste," Father groaned while we rested our horses in the shade of a small clump of trees. "I had occasion to speak with Lawson in town. He was a hardworking and sensible fellow."

I remembered the lovely woman taking clothes from the line the day we arrived and could not help but wonder: "Doesn't your brother think it odd so many tragedies have befallen a town this small?"

"He tells me it's typical of new settlements; not arson, of course—but people coming west with more dreams than plans and a high percentage of them failing."

"Do you honestly think Indians started that fire? Why would they do such a thing?"

"I don't know, sweetheart. Maybe Monroe has unwittingly impinged on their hunting grounds. I met with the solicitor in town yesterday and he mentioned then that they have made various sorts of mischief. Speaking of our meeting, Alcy, in addition to the proposal about Natchez, my brother has been urging me to use a good portion of my inheritance from your grandmother to invest in this territory. He thinks that with a little guidance Monroe could become a booming city and has worked out a way to build those mills."

"Father, you aren't thinking of living here?"

"No, but I've been considering his ideas. I would put up the capital for the mills, and he would manage them as my partner. Frankly, Alcy, I'm contemplating deeding half of her estate to him outright. My business holdings provide us with plenty, and after all, my mother derived far more than half of her fortune from his father. She excluded your uncle from the Will only because she believed him dead. What do you think? You realize, of course, it would affect what you eventually inherit."

I saw Father's point and thought it only right that Grandfather's own son should receive a fair share. "I think you should do as your conscience dictates. My income from Mother and Uncle Daniel's estates is already more than I can use without drawing on Grandmother's stipend. When I come into the whole of them, I cannot imagine needing your half."

Father leaned over and kissed me. "I hoped you would feel that way, dear. Your mother would be quite proud of the sensible young woman you have become. Soon you'll have a husband to take care of you anyway, though your inheritance, even at the lesser level, will afford you the luxury few women have of being choosey. I don't know how I'll do without you when the time comes."

"I don't imagine we will cross that bridge for a long time, Father. I've yet to meet a man whose company I'd prefer over yours for an afternoon, much less a lifetime."

"No one? I thought perhaps that had changed."

"No one—not even the illustrious Joseph Schumacher; though Grandmother would've had you think differently. I was relieved when all his mother's invitations to tea came to nothing. Anyway, whoever takes my hand will have to take you in the bargain."

"No, child. Scripture says a husband and wife should leave their families and cleave to each other,[6] but thank you for wanting me. When you marry, your heart will be full of pleasing your husband, as it should be. Your mother and I met when she was just your age, though we didn't marry until she was twenty.

"With your small bone structure and feminine ways, I've always thought you her replica, and watching you grow into a woman has confirmed that opinion. I disagree with my brother, you know, about your eyes. They are hers, not my mother's. She had the longest, darkest eyelashes I've ever seen. He wouldn't remember her well. We had been married scarcely a year when he left."

His voice grew so wistful that I could barely hear him over the wind that gently rustled the leaves.

"The first time I saw her, she was kneeling at the altar, praying for her father. He was at sea, and they hadn't heard from him in some time. I was enchanted and determined to know who she was and why she'd come to Skippack. She was a devoted wife, a precious treasure—and you'll be just like her. When the time comes, you can keep me company by sending my grandchildren around to visit. Meanwhile, I'll race you to the stable."

21

He beat me handily, as usual. We entered the house, laughing and breathless, and almost stumbled into Uncle Callen. He barred our way but not quickly enough to hide the hired hands depositing something into his room. I consciously thrust it from my mind, scolding myself for being suspicious, but when we heard a slight commotion from the gallery during supper, I shot a questioning glance in his direction. His expression revealed nothing, but my father's eyes were all a twinkle.

When we had finished dessert, Uncle Callen carefully folded his napkin, rose from the table, and held out his hand. "Come, Alcy. I have something to show you."

Father grinned widely, as he had the day Grandfather surprised me with a pony, and his brother tucked my fingers securely within the crook of his arm.

"Close your eyes and do not open them until I say you may. I will try not to bump you into any walls."

Bursting with curiosity, I shut them tightly and let him guide me through the dining room doors. Halfway down the gallery, he stopped and turned me toward the wall.

"Now, you may open them."

I did and was astounded when I saw what stood before me: a petite and well-fashioned pianoforte.

"Oh, it's beautiful!" I crooned, stroking the well-polished cabinetry.

"You like it?"

"Oh, yes, Uncle Callen—who wouldn't? I've never seen such an exquisite instrument—and you thought of sheet music!" Sitting down on the matching bench, I sorted through page after page. "This is my favorite minuet, and I've long wanted this nocturne."

He reached around me and lifted the cover off the keys, bidding me to test my skill.

"The quality is superb. How can I thank you?"

"For one thing, you can stop calling me Uncle Callen. You're a grown woman who has lived under my roof for several months. I'd like you to call me Henry."

I preferred the respectful distance between us that his family name emphasized but how could I refuse such a small request? "All right," I smiled. "I'll call you Uncle Henry."

"Just Henry," he whispered, leaning quite close to my ear. "This pianoforte is only the first of many ways that I intend to please you."

Something in his tone set me ill at ease, but I did not want to repay his generosity with my childish aversions. "The first, Unc...Henry? You have been open-handed with me from the start. If we searched from here to

Philadelphia, I doubt we'd discover another man who so indulges his niece. Where did you find it?"

Rather than answer, he ran his fingertips down the back of my neck. "Play to your heart's content. You can show your gratitude to me later."

His caresses dampened my delight and eroded the fragile trust I'd been struggling to sustain since that day in the garden. Looking for Father, I found him leaning against the dining room doorway—out of both earshot and a clear view. He would only have witnessed my exuberance, disarming any objection that I might raise and leading me to suspect my uncle timed his liberties with care. As the latter sat down upon the settee beneath the portraits, Father walked over and took his place.

"Alcy, you look pink with happiness," he observed. "Henry has certainly made his fondness for you clear."

"Indeed, Father, he has," I responded. Any protests I voiced this evening would just seem unappreciative. "My uncle's feelings are becoming clearer by the day."

EARLY JULY WAS dreadfully humid. Father and I were sitting on the veranda, catching what little breeze we could, when we spotted a sorrel trotting up the lane. The crown of a huge elm hid all but the rider's white britches, but as he emerged from its shadow, brass buttons marching up a high-collared blue military coat glinted in the bright afternoon sun.

"I believe he's a Captain," remarked Father, pointing out the three bars on the man's saddlecloth. "And see the single epaulet over his right shoulder?"

I nodded that I did.

When the stranger caught sight of us he removed his crescent-shaped hat, revealing a thatch of unruly auburn hair. "Good afternoon," he called, tucking the hat under his arm as he sidled up close to the porch. Lively amber eyes anchored in a sea of freckles leaped from me to Father and back again; and within minutes, Father had invited him to dismount and come up the steps. "I am Horace Callen and this is my daughter, Alcy."

"Nathaniel Anderson," the stranger introduced himself, offering us a brief bow.

"We are visiting my brother, Henry Callen. What brings you here?"

"I'm on a month's leave from the outpost and am considering settling in Monroe when my term of duty has ended. This area suits me well, I like its varied terrain—full of challenges and possibilities. My native Boston seems dull by comparison and, frankly, drawing rooms and dainty manners have always bored me. My mother had quite a time trying to turn me into a proper gentleman."

I found this hard to believe. He radiated good breeding, and though he was not handsome, he was attractive in a way that eludes many men with more perfectly formed features.

"Sir," he addressed Father. "What do you make of the townspeople? I have found them singularly unreceptive and can't account for it. My mother did manage to instill me with at least a few social graces."

"We have found the same," replied Father, "but we can't offer an explanation. I understand their lack of interest in a middle-aged man like me, but

I can't imagine why they ignore Alcy."

"That's very odd, indeed!" agreed the Captain, merriment dancing in his eyes. "I would've thought Miss Callen particularly welcome—if not for her obvious elegance then for her connection with your brother. He appears to hold a prominent place in the district."

Father nodded. "He's the largest landholder and owns several of Monroe's businesses."

"Our neighbors back east would've been eager to make his acquaintance," I added, "and felt him socially obligated to reciprocate. However, during the entire two months we have stayed here, he has neither entertained nor have we had a single caller. You can help us remedy that today by joining us for dinner."

The Captain accepted without hesitating. "They can't be ignorant of his position. The end of every avenue I travel is the same: talk to Henry Callen. It's why I've come. I'm interested in a parcel of land to the north of his. You must know it. The house recently burned to the ground."

"Yes," Father shook his head. "A frightful business, that. Do you know if they've apprehended anyone?"

Our new acquaintance's brow pinched together, forming a deep crevice. "No," he replied, "and I hardly know what to make of the fantastical things they are saying. No Indians live within a hundred miles of here, and if they did, I can assure you they would attack the most outlying properties. I thoroughly searched the place shortly after the fire and couldn't find a single unshod hoof print. How do you suppose a war party sneaked in and out without leaving even one? No, something is amiss, and I should like to find out what."

"Perhaps my uncle has learned something. That's his carriage coming up the lane."

"Henry!" called my father once his brother alighted. "Come [...] new friend, Captain Anderson. Alcy has invited him to dine with [...] evening."

My uncle looked displeased but couldn't rescind the invitation. As I listened to their dinner conversation, I was struck by the sharp contrast between the two. Henry bothered little to hide his indifference—he was eager only to dismiss our new friend's suspicions—but the Captain's open and friendly manner was irresistible. He listened keenly to everything Uncle Henry had to say, responded with grace where a man of lesser character might have shown offense, and thanked us so warmly for dinner that Father asked if he'd join us the next morning for our daily ride. To our surprise, he declined, citing a previous engagement that he admitted, when pressed, was with his Maker.

"Then don't let us deter you," replied my uncle. "I'll send word to you at the outpost if that land becomes available."

"Not so hasty, Henry," my father interrupted. "We pray and read the Scriptures every morning, Captain. We would welcome you to join us, though you'll have to ride out from town rather early."

"I'd be happy to, sir, providing your daughter doesn't mind."

As he looked my way, I could not suppress a smile. I was delighted to have a change of companion and had already begun regretting the short duration of his leave.

ONE EVENING, AFTER listening to me execute an intricate sonata, Captain Anderson remarked, "I'm amazed at your good fortune, Mr. Callen. This pianoforte is exceptional—as fine as any I've seen in Boston. How did you come by it?"

"Yes, Uncle Henry," I chimed in, "you never did tell us."

My uncle, who had imbibed a little more sherry than was his habit, shrugged his shoulders. "Miss Callen wanted it, and I ordered it. Do you want me to procure one for the outpost, also?"

Where, I asked myself, could he have ordered it made and delivered in such a brief time? Scarcely three weeks had passed between the morning Father mentioned that I enjoyed playing and the evening of Henry's surprise. Craftsmen who made such specialized pieces lived in areas where the demand for their work was high, which surely meant New York, Boston, or Philadelphia. Perhaps, I supposed, he could have had it sent up by some connection in New Orleans.

overheard a clerk in the general store speaking
at the fire. "Wasn't what those murderous savages
knew her say Mrs. Lawson sang like an angel and
all evenin' long. Lawson lugged it out in the wagon
nt'n."

replied the customer. "I didn't think she'd last out here—
but never thought she'd be burned in her bed."

t doesn't feel safe no more!"

"My and doesn't believe it was savages," added the customer. "He thinks that Mr. Callen had a…"

When I heard our family name, my head naturally spun in her direction.

"Shush, Beatrice," the clerk cautioned. "That niece o' his is over by the piece goods. D'ya wants me to lose my job?"

What, I questioned, had she been about to say? Uncle Henry lacked moral fiber, but I could not see how he could have been connected to the fire—he had been among the first men trying to put it out. As I recalled the way he tore over the slope, though, my spine began to tingle. Not only was the ease with which he found my pianoforte odd, but I'd been puzzled by its rich patina. Such gloss develops only with age and care. Gripping hold of the counter, I stepped toward the door.

"What has happened, Miss Callen?"

Glancing up, I saw a dark military coat framed by the noonday sun.

"You were your usual bright self when I saw you alight from your uncle's carriage. Now, you look as though you've seen one of the town's phantom Indians."

Should I tell the Captain what I had overheard? His friendly tone had already dispelled some of my doubt and to relay such a serious implication simply because Mrs. Lawson owned a pianoforte might be irresponsible. I was likely allowing my imagination to run away with me—perhaps the couple was in financial difficulty, and Henry had bought it from them.

"Nothing's wrong. I overheard something unsettling but do not think it credible and prefer not to repeat it."

"Very well. I won't press you. I was heading to your uncle's estate when I saw you arrive. Are you finished shopping?"

"Yes. I didn't find what I wanted."

"Ah. Here comes your father. May I call on you later?"

"Certainly, but only if you'll stay for dinner."

My spirits had picked up in his company, but when Father told us the solicitor needed him in town for the rest of the afternoon, they plummeted.

"Then I think I'll walk home. It's such a beautiful day; I want to think and pray about a few things." Riding alone in the carriage with Henry was undesirable on any day—unendurable after what I'd just heard.

"Walk? Alcy, it's over five miles!" protested Father. "I prefer that you do not wander about by yourself, particularly in light of recent events. Oh, there is Asbury; I have to go. Talk some sense into her, will you Anderson?"

"Yes, sir." The Captain turned toward me with an agreeable grin. "You just invited me to dinner. Am I to dine without you?"

I looked awkwardly at the ground, lacking the art of successfully concealing my feelings, and he dropped his playful banter.

"Something's wrong; I can see it. Was what you overheard about your uncle?"

"It was conjecture only but of a very unsettling sort."

"What if I accompany the two of you on my horse?"

"Would you?" I brightened. "That would make all the difference."

"Then it's decided."

Together we fetched his mount and met my uncle who, for once, seemed unperturbed to see him.

"Anderson," he smiled, "join us in the carriage. Pinckney can take you back to town when he collects Horace."

"It'll be my pleasure, Mr. Callen, but if it's not an imposition, I'd like to stay until Horace arrives."

"Suit yourself," replied Uncle Henry while he helped me mount the step. He took the seat next to mine, leaving Captain Anderson to sit opposite me after he tied his horse at the rear.

"I heard something in town about that land you want: it has been sold."

"Sold? This morning I was told it wouldn't be offered until they completed an inquiry."

"The transaction was concluded about half an hour ago."

I noticed a vein pulsing at the Captain's temple as he clenched his jaw. "May I ask, Uncle, who purchased it?"

"That, I can't say, but as you are already aware, Alcy, I prefer for you to call me Henry."

"Can't say or won't?"

My friend's question made me wonder if he, too, distrusted my uncle. His tone was uncharacteristically sharp.

"May I remind you, Anderson, that you'll be dining at my table tonight and that we have a lady present? I've given Alcy free run of my house, but I'm your host."

"You're quite right," murmured the Captain. "Please accept my apologies—both of you."

Uncle Henry looked satisfied, even smug, but he dropped the matter and was soon engrossed in letters he had retrieved in town. Captain Anderson had a greater struggle recovering his composure, but as the tension abated, he leaned forward, pleasantly increasing our intimacy.

"What are your hopes for the future, Miss Callen?"

"I suppose the things most women want—a loving marriage and children. Truthfully, though, I want my life to count for something more than I feel it has so far. Back East, I belong to the typical charitable societies but am kept so sheltered I rarely meet anyone with whom I can share the Gospel or be of real benefit. Reading Acts for these past weeks has stirred my heart. I want to serve God without reserve, whatever the cost. Sometimes I wonder what I would do if my faith were truly tested."

A rut in the road jostled Henry's letter just enough to reveal both his avid attention and clear disdain, but Captain Anderson looked at me with a wholly different expression, tender and contemplative at once.

"Your sentiments are admirable, but you're still very young—not more than eighteen or nineteen, I imagine."

"I turned seventeen in May."

"Your poise gives belies your age. I thought I'd erred on the younger, not older side. Even Jesus was sheltered at home before beginning His ministry. Trials will come—they're an unavoidable part of life—but the Lord, not your strength or even commitment, will provide the grace for you to endure them. As for a family," he smiled, "what higher calling could a woman have than raising children in the nurture and admonition of the Lord?"

As we had come to the lane leading up to the house, our conversation ended, but it marked a distinct turn in our relationship.

OVER THE NEXT FEW weeks, I realized what I had told Father under the tree was no longer true. My eagerness for Captain Anderson's company far surpassed anything I had felt toward previous callers. He was full of integrity, intelligence, and warmth—and a man in whose care I could safely entrust my future. In many ways, he reminded me of Father, who had always been like a pillar, portraying well the steadfast dependability of our Father in Heaven. This, and their obvious regard for each other, recommended the Captain highly.

Uncle Henry also changed that day. The more persistently I withdrew from him, the more he sought me out, discovering solitary places I retreated for escape.

Father unwittingly became his accomplice: frequent stomach pains often sent him to bed. While walking in the garden, I was about to mention what I'd overheard during my last visit to town, but before I had a chance, he let out a disgruntled sigh.

"Henry seemed impatient to rid us of the Captain. I think, my dear, he considers your young man a threat."

"Captain Anderson? He is the most pleasant man I've ever known."

"And his high opinion of you is obvious, but have you ever considered how that makes Henry feel?"

"I do not catch your meaning. The Captain is a fine, well-educated man from an excellent family. Why should our regard for each other trouble your brother?"

"I think Henry desires your good opinion for himself."

"He will certainly not do so by insulting my guest."

Father stopped and took my hands in his. "You miss my point, child. Do you remember the conversation we had by the lake, just before the fire?" I nodded.

"You sensed something that day of which I was unaware, and I have been watching to see if it's true. I suspect Henry is hoping to win your affections."

For a moment, I felt too stunned to reply. I had felt Henry's interest but thought it quite unlike courtship. "Do you consider that proper? He is my uncle and twice my age."

"Only a step-uncle, dear. You are not truly related, and Captain Anderson must be twenty-five or six to have obtained his rank. Henry is less than a decade older. Mature men often make the best husbands and marrying a younger woman appeals to many of them."

"I doubt it appeals to their wives."

"Alcy, I can't understand your aversion to him," Father chided. "I've sometimes thought your opinions of others too charitable but never before too sparing. Henry has been nothing but kind to you—and exceedingly generous."

"You don't wish me to consider him seriously as a suitor?"

"Not at present, but if he embraces our Savior, the match presents many advantages. I certainly approve of your Captain, but he's a seasoned soldier and one whom I doubt is given to whim. His leave is short—barely enough time to secure either of your hearts."

"He's assured me the outpost is no more than four hours by coach, less by horseback, and he plans to return as soon and as often as feasible."

"Well, I'm delighted to hear it and believe he indicates his intentions by telling you so. Has he made you an offer?"

"No, but now that I know you approve, I'm inclined to accept if he does."

"Do you love him?"

"I hardly know… I dread his leaving. He's genuinely devoted to Jesus and, insofar as I can tell on a short acquaintance, quite worthy of my trust and respect. Both are vital, don't you think?"

Father nodded. "Yes, my dear. Love takes time, but you have already the essentials of a very fine marriage. I just wish he would settle the matter more quickly than I fear he shall. It would give me peace of mind to know you are cared for well if I don't recover. The pains I've been having refuse to relent."

"Father, don't talk like that. If something happened to you I couldn't bear it."

"Oh, you would bear up well enough. You're strong and resilient, and don't forget who holds you in the palm of His hand. Trust Him. I know you love me dearly, and we've been great friends all these years since your mother died. Honestly, I couldn't have borne them without you."

I had not thought Father's illness serious and supposed he would soon recover with increased rest. Remembering Henry's eerily prophetic notion that I might need him someday, I shivered.

"Are you cold, my dear?" asked Father. Rather than waiting for a response, he drew my hand beneath his arm and placed it in the crook of his elbow. "Let's go inside."

We returned to the house linked closely together but were soon lost in quite separate thoughts. While he felt so ill, I did not see the point of pressing my misgivings about his brother. Father wanted so badly to believe he had changed, but his older age was the only transformation I could detect.

All the following morning, Father lay in bed, and though he came out of his room for the noon meal, he returned to it quickly with sharper pains than before. He did not take supper with us, and the next day he did not get out of bed at all. The liveryman, who acted as the town's doctor, visited him but could not adequately explain his decline.

"I guess he just wore himself out," he suggested to Henry and me as we stood in the gallery.

"But his health was robust on our journey here, which was long and often exhausting, even for me. I would have supposed him to become ill then, not now while we're comfortably situated."

"Sometimes it happens that way—as if our bodies' sense they have the ease to give way to an illness they have kept at bay. Give him time and send for me if the laudanum does not help his pain. Good day."

While Pinckney showed the man out, Henry ran his palms up the backs of my bare upper arms. "Alcy," he murmured, "we must be thankful Horace did not begin this on your trip; I wouldn't have been there to care for you or offer comfort."

Comfort was hardly what he gave. He reminded me of old Lisbeth's grandson gazing at a pie he wanted to devour. As I resolved to wear long sleeves in the future, regardless of the weather, the gallery clock chimed noon, and Pinckney opened the door for our punctual guest.

The afternoon passed by slowly. Concern for my father dampened my spirits, and Henry dropped all pretense of civility toward the Captain. The latter excused himself early, explaining he had errands in town, and I withdrew to Father's bedside. Indeed, I began a constant vigil there, relieved only when Captain Anderson came to call.

The window had a breathtaking view of the valley and distant, thickly forested hills to the north that ascended into tall mountains. I longed to discover what adventures they held, but they were much too far to hazard alone, and asking anyone to take me there was out of the question. The garden would suffice for exercise and reading for stimulation, but my love for books soon placed me in peril.

AFTER SEVERAL DAY'S CONFINEMENT, I slipped into my uncle's study to browse the shelves for a new book. Father was sleeping peacefully, and Mrs. Hodgetts told me Henry would be out until supper; so rather than returning to the sickroom, I sank down in a large, well-stuffed chair to read by the open window. The warm breeze billowed the drapes in gentle undulations, lulling me into a drowsy haze until my eyelids became as heavy as my book.

I remember nothing else until hooves trotted up the lane. Eager to speak with my friend, I marked my place and was about to jump up when footsteps hurried past the open window. They were not the Captain's: he would have waited in front for Pinckney. Shrinking back into the tall, winged chair, I tucked my dress about my ankles and pulled up my legs beneath me while the latch clicked in the garden door.

Henry's light footsteps crossed the room toward his desk and a key turned distinctly in a lock. Heavy boots clumped after him, but no one spoke. I was glad; I had no desire to eavesdrop and much less to be caught doing so. I began to think they might get what they came for and leave when a snicker that I recognized sent my heart into my throat. It belonged to Henry's foreman, Stump, for whom I had developed a marked dislike.

I had never learned his given name or what happened to the fingers on his left hand, but their loss did not impede his cruelty. He particularly enjoyed tormenting a wiry young man who followed him around like a lonely pup. The youth was apparently slow-witted, often requiring additional instruction; but rather than reward his loyalty with friendship, Stump made him the butt of his jokes.

"Let's have it," demanded Henry as he thumped two glasses down on his desk. Paper crackled in answer as if it were being unfolded. "Asbury recorded it this morning, boss, all legal like."

"Good," replied Henry. "I don't want anyone questioning its legitimacy. My niece's suitor has been very persistent." I heard him pouring twice, likely from the cut-glass decanter he kept on a bookshelf behind his desk. "You're to be congratulated for your success—on both ends. To Callen's Mill!"

The two laughed conspiratorially, and after a pause, Henry poured another round.

"What about that brother o' yers?"

"Horace is of no concern."

I could not hear Stump's muttered reply, but Henry answered him sharply. "No, we can't have the Army snooping around here. His leave is almost up, and until then Alcy is keeping him quite occupied."

"Seems Lawsons' land's not the only thing o' yers he wants."

"He can want her all he likes, but I'll have her—and I don't much care if she is willing or not. But if he doesn't watch his step, I'll take you up on that offer."

"Her, too?"

"Regretfully, yes, unless she makes quick peace with our arrangement. She would make an excellent politician's wife—pretty, well educated, genteel. Hold off until we return from New Orleans, though," he huskily chortled. "I intend to enjoy myself while we're there."

The foreman laughed, though I did not understand why, and I again heard the click of a lock.

"What about the other documents? Did Asbury give those to you, also?" asked Henry, adding as paper began to rustle, "Good. My patience is at its end."

Heavy boots clumped over the garden threshold and the lighter ones stepped through to my uncle's private rooms, but fear kept my limbs frozen as they were. I don't know how long I listened, but when all became still I slipped across the hall into Father's room and silently shut the door.

This time, I was determined to tell him everything I had overheard, both in the study and in town. When I turned about to face him, however, I saw he was not alone. Both Henry and Pinckney were standing beside his bed.

Father smiled at me weakly. "Alcy, I was just going to ask Pinckney to look for you."

"If you need me no longer then, sir," said the manservant, "I will see about serving supper."

Henry nodded and Pinckney brushed past me, barely glancing my way as he opened the door. On Father's bedside table lay an imposing set of documents, clearly bearing three signatures.

"I'm sure you realize the gravity of your father's condition, Alcy," my uncle asserted, "and anxiety for you can only hinder his recovery. Therefore, I have advised him to amend his Will, entrusting you to my care until you are of age. He has also named me the executor of his estate."

I looked to Father for contradiction, but instead, he nodded. "My brother will take good care of you, my dear."

"I trust this arrangement pleases you as much as it does me," added Henry, crossing towards the opened door. Grasping its edge, he leaned forward, half-hiding father from my view. "You've lived in my home a little more than three months, Alcy, but I daresay strong feelings have already formed between us. Should what we most dread happen, I will treat you as if you were my own—in fact, I feel already that you are."

The horror I felt must have shown on my face, for his eyes brightened. All at once, I understood how far I had misjudged him. He had never meant to charm me with his intimate tones and touches. Like the green-eyed tabby in his kitchen, he enjoyed tantalizing the prey he intended to devour and was succeeding staggeringly!

"I will leave the two of you alone, Horace. I am sure Alcy is deeply thankful for your prudent planning and would like to express her gratitude privately."

"Alcy, dear, please don't look so stricken," pleaded Father once Henry had closed the door behind him. "You have no idea how I've struggled with this decision. Life for a single young woman is more perilous than you can appreciate, and I have no one else to whom I can send you."

I lay my head upon his bed, too aghast to speak.

"Is he so odious to you?" he murmured, lightly stroking my hair. "I hoped you'd grown to like him at least a little."

Should I tell him now what I had overheard? Even if I had drawn a wrong conclusion about the shopkeeper, there was little to mistake about the foreman's conversation. Father might be able to amend the documents or draw up altogether new ones.

"When must your Captain return to his post?"

"Four days—this coming Thursday."

"If I am not here when he asks you to marry him, as I believe he will, Henry assures me he will consent. Alcy, please don't look at me that way; it troubles me to grieve you, but we have to face the inevitable. In the meantime, Henry promises to engage a companion for you. It would be indecent for a man and woman of your ages to reside alone together."

"You speak as if you're already dying."

"Frankly, I don't think I can tolerate this pain much longer. I'd rather be at rest with our Lord and see your mother and grandmother again. Oh, please don't cry, darling; you're breaking my heart."

Lifting my head, I saw that he looked very pale.

"Alcy, I'm too tired to discuss anything further tonight. Please, be a good girl now and let me get some sleep. I'm thoroughly worn out."

"Yes, Father. Good night."

My mind was awhirl with emotions. His high forehead felt moist to my lips and his thinning hair like goose down beneath my fingertips. As my gaze wandered over plentiful freckles and silver-black brows, sprouting in random directions, I felt unspeakable pain.

We had grieved the loss of all those closest to us together; how was I to grieve him alone? He was correct: he had no one to whom he could send me. When he died, there would be no one left.

"Money answereth all things." I could not remember which Testament held the verse—I had paid it little attention—but while I watched him sleep, wondering what to do if he passed away, I pondered the obvious sense of the verse.

Henry would control my father's estate, but I still had the fortunes my mother and her brother left me. As for his newly bestowed guardianship, his arm did not reach across the Alleghenies, and he knew nothing of Allison and John.

He would search for me in Pennsylvania, if at all. Nor was I truly alone: I would run to the Lord.

I lift up my eyes to the hills. From whence does my help come? My help comes from the Lord who made heaven and earth.

Psalm 121:1-2

34

Chapter 3

FATHER WAS NOTICEABLY worse in the morning, so rather than pester him about the Will, I brought him relief in the only way I could: singing cherished hymns printed in a small book he had once given to my mother. I nearly skipped Christ the Lord Is Risen Today—we normally sang it only at Easter—but upon consideration, I thought a reminder of the resurrection might offer hope. During the first stanza, his ragged breathing became peaceful, and by the end of the second, it stopped altogether.

Captain Anderson called as soon as he heard that Father had gone home and wanted to ride with me the next afternoon to the small cemetery, but Henry excluded him from the carriage. I remembered little by the graveside but a blur of faces and the Captain's clear voice repeating Jesus' words to Martha when Lazarus had died: "I am the resurrection and the life. He that believeth in me, though he were dead, yet shall he live: and whosoever liveth and believeth in me shall never die." [8]

Staring numbly out the carriage window, I wondered how the sun could shimmer so brightly over the passing countryside. Rain would have been far more suitable.

"I am thankful," murmured Henry, "for your father's timely execution of our new arrangement."

He pressed my limp fingers to his cool lips, but I jerked my hand away and moved against the compartment's farthest wall. I was certain his gratitude was feigned, and his mention of the Will left me wondering if the short space between its ratification and Father's death could be coincidental.

"When will you engage a companion for me?"

An air of self-satisfaction crept into his carefully fashioned appearance as he leaned back against the opposite corner. "Whom would I hire, Alcy— the tavern girl? I promised that to Horace to soothe his priggish sensibilities."

His eyes once more reminded me of the kitchen tabby, only the time for toying with his prey was over. How I longed for Captain Anderson's buffering presence, but Henry insisted I not receive callers for several days. "Mrs. Hodgetts is with us during the day and Pinckney at night. Lock your door, if that makes you feel more comfortable."

As soon as the carriage stopped, I ran up the steps, down the hall, and into Father's room. I hoped absurdly to find him there as if the day had been a bad dream, but his bed was as empty as I knew it must be. Taking my usual place in front of his window, I watched the weary sun clothe the hills in gloom and did not turn around when I heard the door handle. I wanted solitude and hoped my posture conveyed as much, but I was ridiculously naïve to think my desire mattered. When Father had departed, so had Henry's restraint.

The buttons of his waistcoat pressed against my back as he stretched his arms around me to rest his hands on the window ledge. "Come, Alcy," he mumbled against my ear. "I wish to comfort you."

"I want to be alone, Uncle."

"Uncle?" he snickered. "Ah yes…Horace wanted us to be family; and I, for one, intend to grant his dying wish."

I felt sick but struggled to maintain my composure. "Uncles and nieces are family."

"You've long realized I want more than that and, in point of fact, that relationship doesn't exist."

His lips began wandering over my neck, so stunning me I could not move until I heard the door handle turn.

"Supper is ready, Miss…Sir," called Mrs. Hodgetts.

"Leave us," spat Henry, twisting sufficiently toward her that I could duck beneath his arm and flee to my room. What she thought I do not know, but I heard Henry cursing.

"Go ahead and lock it," he sneered as I fastened the latch. "Judge Abbott will be here Saturday. I've asked him to marry us then." He paused as Mrs. Hodgetts bustled by toward the kitchen, and then continued in a low, emphatic tone. "If you know what's in your best interest, Alcy, you'll offer your consent freely. Failing that, I'll gain it by other means. No one will come to your aid. Anderson leaves Thursday—and if he delays, I'll have him shot in the head and tossed into the river. How would you like to have that on your tender conscience?

"I see that you refuse to answer," he continued, "but hear me clearly. How well you enjoy your life from this point on will depend entirely on your efforts to please me, both in public and in private. You're a sensible girl and know I can be generous. I will give you one night to contemplate your response, but tomorrow Pinckney will remove this lock."

Having barricaded the door with the heaviest furniture I could manage, I pressed my forehead against the jamb and listened to his tread snapping angrily down the hall. Faint clangs, as Pinckney lifted the lids from serving dishes, assured me that Henry had reached the dining room and was likely seating himself at the table. Supper would occupy him for a while.

Perched on the edge of my mattress, I contemplated all he had said. A thousand nights could not persuade me to marry him, but neither could I take his threats lightly. I eyed my windows, which opened on the farthest side of the house from the dining room, and considered slipping across the lawn to the stable. The drop from the sill was not deep nor the building far, but several hired men were ever-present in the small, enclosed yard it shared with their lodgings. They reminded me of the malcontents Absalom gathered around him[9] and were apt to offer more trouble than aid. At least my door was bolted tonight, and in the morning, my presence in the stable would arouse less suspicion.

"Lord, help me!" I whispered, flopping back under the tall canopy, but the room seemed hollow and vague uncertainties began tormenting my heart. God knew how the journey would affect Father's health. Why had He not somehow warned us? We had sought His counsel each day before leaving. How could He strand me with this...this...vile scoundrel or let Henry force me into a marriage His Word expressly forbade?[10]

The answers that sprang to mind distressed me more than the questions: perhaps He was not there at all or did not care what happened to me. Maybe I believed the Bible only because my parents had, like Lisbeth clinging to her "dear old Grammy's" fairy stories. Feeling like a battered ship fighting desperately to regain safe mooring, I tried to thrust the doubt from my mind.

"Lord, I know You are real. You have to be. Help my unbelief! My whole life has been built on You..." Some snatch of a Psalm about nature proclaiming the existence of God wafted through my memory, soothing me a little—until I heard Mrs. Hodgetts calling for Pinckney to take her home.

As the manservant tightly shut the front door behind them, and the cart crunched down the gravel lane, I grew cold with fear. Pulling the covers up around my neck, I listened to Henry's steps coming up the hall, but though he paused briefly outside my door, he crossed to the library.

I let out a sigh, sank back into my pillow, and lay alert to every sound, inside and out. I had been living in Henry's home for months, yet I knew Pinckney no better than I had the day we arrived. He seemed a vacant man, devoid of emotion or any hint of humor or warmth, but he surely would not stand by while Henry...while...my fears were too horrid to put into words.

Hours seemed to pass before the cart scraped into the stable yard again, and many more until the manservant leaped up the steps to the servants' entry, walked briskly through the kitchen, and thrust all the heavy bolts into place for the night. The gentle thud of an interior door reported he had retired for the evening, and then the muffled sounds of two male voices announced that Henry had entered the servant's private quarters through the adjoining door. When, at last, nothing but the chiming clock disrupted the silence, I finally drifted into a fitful sleep.

THE NEXT MORNING, I awakened with a headache and recoiled when I caught sight of my reflection. My skin was pale and the dark circles beneath my eyes looked huge and ghastly. After listening at the door for a moment, I peeked out to make sure the hall was empty, crept down the gallery, and paused before the pianoforte to listen for voices from the dining room. Happily, there were none, but I jumped when Mrs. Hodgetts bumped the kitchen door open with her hip.

"Good morning Miss," she greeted me. "I did no' mean to startle you. You must be starved after going t' bed like that without your supper." As she carried a full breakfast tray across the hall and laid it on the table, she caught my eyes darting toward Henry's chair. "Mr. Callen is already in town."

She could not have missed my relief, and I wondered what she made of it after discovering me in his arms last evening.

"He says, Miss, that I am t' give you my best wishes for a happy marriage."

My cheeks felt hot with shame. It was indecent to marry so soon after Father's death. "My uncle is unable to engage a companion for me," I explained. "Without the benefit of marriage, I could not continue to share his home."

"Ach! There's truth in that," she declared, setting down a plate full of eggs and ham. "My Bess would gladly be a companion to you, but if you do not mind me saying so Miss, no respectable family will let their daughter live with 'im.' I'll just go and fetch your tea."

The whole town must suspect him. No wonder they had cut a wide path for Father and me; and as Henry's wife, they would wash me with the same tainted brush. Dropping my head into my hands, I waited for her to return.

"You poor dear," she cooed, handing me a warm cup, "and your fine father not yet cold in his grave. I would not o' come back this mornin' 'cept for you, Miss, and had a hard sleep—as I can see you did; but I will stay on as long as you are in this house. A sorrier situation I never seen—you a good God-fearing girl and him the son o' Satan hisself. But eat your breakfast, dearie. I'll no' have you missin' no more o' my meals. You must keep up your strength to fend him off."

She was full of surprises. I had no idea she was so aware of what went on outside her kitchen, nor that she harbored such kind and motherly feelings for me.

After breakfast, I went to the stable, which was empty of man and beast, but someone had taken my saddle and hung it over a high rafter, well out of my reach. The carriage was also gone—which brought to mind yet another difficulty. The town was small; how was I to go there without Henry spotting me? Sinking onto a bundle of hay, I would have cried had I not noticed a shadow move. Someone was watching me.

I left the barn quickly and walked toward the hill where Father and I had viewed the Lawsons' burned home. From its high vantage, I could see if someone followed me from the outbuildings. He did. He never showed himself well-enough for me to identify him but lurked at the outskirts of every place I went. Henry had planned well, though he did offer me one kindness: he stayed away the entire morning, most of which I spent praying in my room. The Lord had once sent an angel to usher Peter out of prison.[11] He was able to send me help also.

"PINCKNEY, SET MISS Callen's place beside my own from now on," said Henry upon entering the dining room at noon. "We marry on Saturday and I intend to keep her within reach."

I questioned whether he truly aimed to instruct his servant or keep me mindful of his threats last evening.

"My congratulations, Mr. Callen," replied the servant while moving my place setting, "and my felicitations to you, Miss." His manner was so glib, so unlike Mrs. Hodgetts' outrage, that I began to suspect he was complicit in Henry's plans.

"Alcy, you look forbiddingly prim in that high collar," declared Henry as he pulled out my chair. "I have made you an appointment in town today with the dressmaker. You will need a trousseau for our honeymoon, which we will combine with our trip to New Orleans. You may wear black out of respect for your father, the color sets off your complexion nicely, but I want them décolleté." He leaned over my chair as I took my seat, drawing an indecently low line across my bodice with his finger. "I'm sure you have noticed that I have a fondness for displaying the beauty I acquire."

I could not help stiffening but did not bother to reply. A single phrase had captivated all of my attention: "in town today." Today was Wednesday; the day, according to Captain Anderson, the public coach made its weekly circuit to the outpost. Once there, I could join a party returning east.

"Thank you, Henry," I replied, hoping I had kept the excitement from my face. "At what time does Mrs. Trent expect me?"

"Four o'clock."

I looked down lest my eyes betray my glee. The coach left at five. I would have time to withdraw funds from Mr. Asbury and board before Henry returned to retrieve me—unless, of course, Henry had business in that office. All would be lost if he did; I had only a few coins in my purse.

"Will you accompany me?" I asked, attempting to instill my voice with a note of pleasure.

He looked up immediately and with such intense scrutiny, I feared he could read my thoughts.

"I would enjoy nothing so much as watching Mrs. Trent fit you, my lovely, but I need to inspect a new property. I've always thought you rather intelligent. I hope you are coming to terms with our union."

As he lifted my hand to his lips, I shuddered involuntarily, furnishing him the evidence he sought. "Do not forget what I told you last night. Whether or not your Captain returns alive to his post depends entirely on you. Farley will drive you in to ensure your good behavior."

After dessert, I hastened to my room; three holes in the wall had replaced the latch. They would not matter if my plan succeeded. Should I include Mrs. Hodgetts, so she would not worry? No, the less she knew, the less she could tell Henry, and the less he could accuse her of helping me. I pulled a second black dress atop the one I already wore, glad that I had earlier put on my most durable muslin petticoat. Glancing around the room, I considered what I might take. It must appear as it always did, offering the illusion I planned to return. I decided to leave all but two items. No one could expect me to go to town without my purse, and happily, the small Bible Father gave me for traveling fit neatly in my deep dress pocket. Only one item pained me greatly to abandon—Mother's little hymnal.

Henry had selected my escort well. Farley was a brawny man with an observant eye and sharp wits. My primary hope of evading him lay in his penchant for the tavern at the opposite end of Main Street. I entered the dressmaker's establishment directly, canceled my appointment, made certain Farley was not within sight, and ducked across the alley to the solicitor's foyer.

Miss Callen, is that you?" asked Mr. Asbury when I knocked at his half-open door. He was dressed as usual like the gentlemen back East, and I wondered what had brought him to Monroe. "Come in, sit down."

"Thank you, sir, but my business is brief."

"Please, allow me to express how sorry I am for your loss. Your father was a fine man. I had hoped he would have a...I had hoped to know him better."

"Thank you. He spoke well of you as well, and thank you for coming to his funeral."

"It was the least I could do. Captain Anderson did a fine job. I think he's missed his calling."

"Yes. I can't have imagined burying my father without someone reading the Scriptures."

He nodded. "And what can I do for you, today?"

"I would like to withdraw some money."

He stared at me blankly for a moment, as though he had not understood my words, and then slowly shook his head. "Your uncle has not told you? You cannot access your account without his permission until you turn twenty-one."

"I refer to my personal account—not Father's estate. You have withdrawn money from it several times on my behalf."

His eyes fell to the papers on his desk, which he began to shuffle.

"Miss Callen, I wish I could tell you differently. When your father was alive, he allowed me to advance you anything you requested; your uncle has instructed me otherwise. I cannot give you as much as a penny."

"Then sir," I murmured, tottering against the chair he had offered me earlier, "would you consider personally advancing me a small sum? I will repay you speedily and with any interest that you ask."

"How I wish I could," he muttered. "I have a daughter just your age."

"Please, sir...I only need enough to..." I did not finish. Stump said he had retrieved the Lawsons' deed from this very office. Henry had been right: no one would help me—no one could but Jesus.

"I am truly sorry, Miss Callen."

"I understand," I mumbled, "and bid you a good day."

Unsure what to do, I leaned back against the door I closed behind me. Mrs. Trent might still be able to give me a fitting, forestalling any questions Farley might ask when he called, but as I staggered out the dark foyer Captain Anderson and I nearly collided.

"Miss Callen! Are you all right? I wanted to call on you today, but your uncle told me I was not welcome."

"I know; that was nothing of my wish."

"I was over in the General Store when I noticed you come in here and couldn't miss the chance to say goodbye. I leave in the morning."

I nodded, tucking my lower lip between my teeth as it quivered.

"You look ill."

"I'm well enough, thank you, but it will not bode well if anyone sees us together."

"Come inside, then," he suggested, ushering me back into the foyer I had just left. "Whatever is wrong? You look nervous as a mouse."

Keeping my voice quite low, I confessed, "I was hoping to take the coach to your outpost, but Asbury can't advance me the funds. Father made Henry my guardian."

"I expected he had, but don't you think running away is rash? As the primary law of the territory, my commander might be forced to return you."

Shaking my head, I explained, "I hadn't thought of that, but I can't stay with him another night."

The Captain's expression grew dark. "He has not…harmed you in any way, has he?"

"No, but he—I will tell you all if you promise first that you won't go anywhere near him and will leave for the outpost tomorrow as planned."

"Very well, I give you my word."

"He intends for Judge Abbot to marry us Saturday and then will take me to New Orleans—but another matter is more pressing. Last night I locked my door to him; this morning Pinckney removed the latch."

The Captain exhaled sharply through clenched teeth; "I presume, in addition to the impropriety of marrying so soon after your father's death; that you do not consent?"

"Most certainly I do not! Aside from the fact that I don't like him, I have grave suspicions about his character and believe the townspeople do also. Father and I watched several men, Henry at their head, galloping across the ridge from the Lawsons' the night their house was set ablaze. The next evening he gave me the pianoforte."

"You think there is a connection?"

"In the General Store, I overheard the clerk saying Mrs. Lawson played a 'little piano.' You came in afterward and remarked about my pallor."

"I remember well. You were determined to walk home."

"The woman she addressed brought up my uncle but stopped talking when I turned my head."

"So that is what you wouldn't tell me?"

"Yes, but there is more. The night before Father died, I overheard Henry talking with Stump in the library. Stump handed him the deed to

Lawsons' farm and Henry congratulated him on a job well done. Henry had long wanted the place."

"I suspected so, but that's not proof of a crime. You know I can't keep this information to myself?"

"Yes," I nodded. "I only ask that you do nothing before returning to the outpost."

"Agreed. Here," he turned my palm upward and filled it with coins. "This is more than enough to cover the fare."

"Thank you," I smiled, as warmed by the tender way he kept my hand as I was by gratitude. "I'll repay you as soon as I'm able."

"There is no need. I'd give far more to insure your safety. Before you leave, though, I want to write you a letter of introduction to my commander. His wife will welcome your company."

"I'll be glad to have a friend in the place."

"You have one already."

"I know. Please come to the outpost straight-a-way. I'm afraid of what Henry might do to you when he discovers I've fled."

"I will—this evening, perhaps. Is there anything more I can do to help?"

"Would you purchase the ticket? I prefer to keep my plans hidden."

"Yes, good point. Anything else?"

I was about to say no but then thought of Farley. "Do you know Henry's man with the scar through his left eyebrow?"

He nodded. "Stocky, light-haired?"

"Yes. He's to bring me home. Would you keep him occupied until the coach has left? I suspect you'll find him in the tavern."

"Gladly." With a reassuring smile and brief bow, he let go of my hand and trotted toward his lodgings. I slipped into the dressmaker's to make certain Farley had not checked on me and then leisurely strolled to the livery stable. Captain Anderson met me along the way, ticket and letter in hand, and said his farewells before setting out to detain my guard.

Keeping my head low, I handed the ticket to the driver and climbed into the coach's dark compartment. My double garments made the afternoon heat oppressive, but I dared not raise the panel hanging over the window to let in air. Instead, I sat alert to every passerby, daubing up beads of perspiration and stealing glimpses at a fellow traveler. He was a timid little man who seemed more afraid of me than I was of him. Not until the horses pulled away did I inhale deeply, and when we picked up speed, I lifted the curtain to relish the breeze. Escaping had been remarkably easy, and I was grateful to the One who made it so.

"EXCUSE ME, SIR." I addressed the little man when he consulted his pocket watch several hours into our journey. "Would you please tell me the time?"

"Half-past seven, Miss."

Nodding my thanks, I closed my eyes and listened to the horses' steady hoof beats. The light had grown dim and I felt exhausted, more from apprehension than effort. The coach's flat cushion offered little in the way of comfort, compacted from years of transporting passengers, but I didn't care. I was free of Henry.

Father's dead body, so yellow and waxy, buffeted my memory. When his breathing had stopped, it had been obvious that his spirit was gone. His lifeless form reminded me of a peanut hull, devoid of the essential part. Although I thought the analogy vaguely disrespectful, the impression refused alteration. Grandmother had often told me that God disguises mercy as suffering. I now had a glimpse of what she meant: had it not been for his pain, I would never have been able to let him go. I missed him dreadfully.

A gun blast roused me from my reverie and as the driver cracked his whip, the coach lurched forward at a faster speed. A quick questioning glance at my companion's frightened face told me he would be little help.

"It must be the savages that whole town was talking about!" he whined.

I knew this couldn't be, as Captain Anderson was not a man to make false assertions and had been quite confident of his facts. Anyway, Indians this far west owned no guns and we heard two distinct sets of gunfire.

"Sir, quiet your fears on that account—whoever is chasing the coach possesses firearms; they can't be savages."

"Highwaymen, perhaps—wanting to rob the coach?"

"Very likely," I replied, though I feared it was Henry.

"Well then, if we give them our valuables, they may leave us alone."

I would have greatly preferred highwaymen to Henry. Without money or possessions to yield, they could have little interest in me; but the sun had nearly set and the coach moved too swiftly to afford us a glimpse of the assailants.

The driver whipped his team to such a speed that I slid against the little man as we rounded a bend, and when the coach abruptly halted it pitched me onto the floor. Before I could get up, a man flung open the door, shot my pitiful companion in the chest, and began rummaging through his pockets. I was aghast, unable to fathom why he would do such a thing—the harmless fellow would have willingly given up anything he had! Silently pressing myself into the shadows, I hoped the rancid smelling thief could not see me. He stood framed in the waning light, giving me the advantage, but he struck a flint and exploded with raucous laughter.

"Look at who we got here!" he called to a companion. "It's d' boss's fine lady from Pennsylvany." Leaning inside, Stump's slow-witted underling grabbed for my arm.

"Get your hands off of me!" I cried. "Henry won't take your rough treatment kindly." My uncle was sure to exact revenge but would do so himself and in private.

"Drag her out here," ordered a chillingly familiar voice, followed by some unintelligible command. This was too horrid. Of all the men Henry might send to retrieve me, why had he sent this one?

"No Stump—we can't!" the slow-witted man replied. "We could'n 'show up home ag'in if we did. D'boss 'ould kill us fer sure."

What they couldn't do, I had no idea, but the older man slowly shook his head. "We was jus' wait'n' 'til after their trip. She's made it a mite easier by runnin' an' we get some fine dainties tonight 'stead o' hoecake."

"What'll he say when he finds out?"

Stump grinned. "He won't. We'll take'r bloody dress t' old Judge Abbott 'n he'll say she was kilt by a savage. Callen's next o' kin. He still gets the prize—jus' not the frilly wrappin'. Hold her tight. She's scrappy and I don't want no tell-tale scratches."

"Jesus, help me!" I whispered, trying to wrench free.

"Sorry missy," the foreman snickered, "Jesus ain't here."

Unexpectedly, he fell backward, a blast from his flintlock flaring boldly against the darkened sky. A "whump" sounded behind my head, knocking the simple man into me, but before he slumped to the ground, someone hoisted me off my feet onto the back of his mount. I could barely breathe, he pinned me so tightly, and though I twisted my head this way and that, I could only see him slicing through the team's leather harness and slapping their rumps to send them running. He did all this so swiftly I never glimpsed his face, but after my initial panic, I knew who he was. Rough rows of braid and hard brass buttons kept pressing uncomfortably into my back.

For the better part of an hour, we hurtled over rugged terrain, which felt exhilarating after so many hours in the coach. As we slowed to a steadier pace, though, I began to question why he had veered so far from the road.

Perhaps he knew a shorter route to the outpost or left it to evade Henry's men. The thought of that "whump" made my stomach turn. I was thankful the blow released me but sure it killed the slow-witted man.

What had sent Stump toppling backward? I could not figure it out. His gun fired the only shot. Whatever the cause, I was glad the Captain had decided to leave Monroe early!

"Do you think Henry will come after us?" I asked him. "Unless he proves I am dead, he can't inherit."

He mumbled something I could not understand. We were climbing steadily upward, probably through the hills and into the very mountains I had longed to explore, and he was likely absorbed in choosing our way. It did not matter; I would wait until we stopped to receive my answers.

As I reflected on the tenderness he showed me earlier, I felt awash with relief. Except for Father and Grandfather, Captain Anderson was the finest man I had ever known; and though I did not feel the passion Marianne Dashwood[12] expressed for Willoughby, I could easily grow accustomed to the feel of his strong arms. Life was not a novel, and the Dashwood sisters were not real. Had they been flesh and blood, however, I would have chosen Elinor, not Marianne, to advise me. Guided firmly by good principles and reason, her esteem for Edward led to a happy outcome. Marianne's infatuation with Willoughby only plunged her into disgrace. Besides, Father already approved the match and Grandmother would have also—though I doubted she would condone the way he was holding me. I did not care. His actions had made his intentions clear, and I felt blessedly secure for the first time in weeks.

As we weaved slowly through densely growing trees, more disjointed questions began creeping into my thoughts. I had distinctly heard horses following us earlier and occasionally thought I heard them still. At the slow pace we now traveled, they would surely overtake us, but the Captain seemed unconcerned. When at last I worked out the answer, I felt quite foolish: they were the horses he cut loose. Why, I asked myself, had he done so—to allow them to find food or water? He was the type of man who considered everything.

Heavy with exhaustion, my head kept dropping forward only to jerk me awake again. I lay it back against his chest, too weary to consider propriety, and felt something warm oozing into my dress below the collar. It felt tacky and too thick for perspiration, but while I tried to think what it might be, my jaw sagged, and I sank into a deep, much-needed slumber.

Light rain awakened me to a night so black that I could barely see, but I surmised from the sound of crashing water that we approached a wildly flowing river. The horse's gait had slackened, and the Captain no longer held me tightly. I began to suspect he had fallen asleep. He leaned so heavily against me, I doubted I could bear up much longer and was quite relieved when the horse decided to stop. High above us loomed a dark formation, more the height of a massive castle than an outpost, but not a single candle burned in a window or illuminated the way to the gate.

"Captain Anderson, I think we are here." My whisper sounded raspy after hours of disuse and oddly amplified by the lonely silence. "It must be quite late; everything's locked up."

The Captain did not budge.

"Captain Anderson, wake up. We are at the fort."

When he still did not answer, I reached behind me and jostled him gently, but rather than stirring, he slid to the ground like a heavy sack.

"Captain!" I cried, jumping down onto wobbly legs. I feared the fall might have broken his neck. He lay on his side, not moving at all. Kneeling on the wet grass, I attempted again to shake him awake, when all at once my hair stood on end. What I touched was not a uniform, and this man was most definitely not the Captain!

Behold, the eye of the Lord is upon those who fear Him, upon those who hope in His mercy, to deliver their soul from death.

Psalm 33:18-19

Chapter 4

I JERKED MY HANDS away and staggered to my feet, but as I tried, palms to mouth, to keep from retching, my legs buckled and gave way.

"This cannot be!" I stammered. "It simply cannot be!"

Graphic tales of torture flooded my memory while the collected tears of the past few days burst their dam and flowed freely with the rain. Scalping and mutilation, captives burned alive or having their hearts cut out while beating—not once had I thought I might be exposed to such dangers. Eastern Pennsylvania was both well-populated and defended, and in Monroe, Captain Anderson had dispelled my fears.

"Why, God? Are you punishing me? First Father's death, then Henry and his men, and now this… this…savage! How could you let this happen? Surely, it would've been better had Stump killed me."

After I'd spent myself sobbing, I tried to assess my situation rationally. The savage posed no threat at present—he was unconscious—but neither could I climb down this mountain. The drizzling had stopped, but dense clouds now covered the moon, depriving me of sufficient light to see my fingers. Even so, I might feel my way far enough from him to keep hidden should he revive.

A deep, guttural moan interrupted my plotting, stirring my conscience in ways I did not welcome. He was in obvious pain. How would he fare if I left? Wolves, bears, even mountain lions roved this territory. If one happened upon him, it might tear him to shreds. The possibilities were horrid, bringing to mind the half-dead man the Good Samaritan had aided.[13]

"Oh!" I groaned, wishing I had never read the story. It cast the savage as my neighbor and goaded me towards the unthinkable.[14] Surely, God would not expect me to tend him. How would I defend myself if he woke up? Yet, if I left him to die, how was I different from the heartless priest or Levite? Trapped between fear and conscience, I recalled my conversation with the Captain in the carriage and broke into near-hysterical laughter. I had questioned what I might do if my faith were truly tested. Now I was finding out!

Crawling back to the savage, I felt along his exposed arm to see if it was sound; the fall had pinned the other beneath him. A breastplate of hard ribbing lay across his torso, mucked with the same tacky substance, I supposed, that had seeped into my dress. Following its trail over the tightly woven staves, I found a splintered hole and grasped at once what had happened: the discharge from Stump's gun had shattered them.

The vivid memory of his brutal face drove away all lingering plans to flee. I might prefer death at his hand to this savage's, but I suspected the preamble Stump planned would have been far worse. I could still see his greedy, grabby hands and smell his alcohol-drenched breath. If the savage had not come to my rescue…

My stomach painfully contracted while my cheeks grew hotter than his fevered flesh. He had swept me up as if I were a straw doll, and not only did I revel in his strength, I also leaned familiarly against his half-naked chest. What must he have thought? At least the pressure of my body likely helped his blood to clot.

I felt sick from shame and queasier still as I considered how to proceed with his care. If the ball had lodged inside him, I would have to cut it out. Otherwise, the wound might fester and refuse to heal. Steadying him against my chest, I ran a hand behind his shoulder and found a spot where his flesh was torn. He jerked sharply when I touched it, but I felt weak with relief.

"Thank You, Lord, for small mercies," I sighed. "It must've gone clean through."

I was sorry to have hurt him and astounded by his fortitude. He had ridden vigorously for hours with the ball's exit uncovered. I did not wonder that he had lost consciousness, but as I thought of the man's grit and determination, my heart began to race.

"Lord," I rasped, trying to quell my reviving panic, "I'll do all I can to mend him, but when he improves, I'm trusting that you'll offer me a way to escape!"

Fearing I might faint, I drooped my head toward my knees and inhaled slowly, but with each deep breath, I grew more lightheaded. The dark seemed to close in, begging me to give up, until I remembered something my father often said.

"You are borrowing trouble, Alcy. Obey God and commit to Him the things you can't control."

Father was right. I would give my charge the care he needed and leave the rest to God. He was faithful and would deliver me—whether in life or by death.

Raising my head, I saw the clouds had abated in patches, providing enough starlight to see an occasional outline. The roaring of the river was unmistakable, so I headed toward its sound and smacked right into one of Henry's horses. Apparently, the hoof beats I had heard belonged to them, and, though they startled me for a moment, they proved a gift. Each bore a blanket rolled in oilcloth and a saddlebag packed for an extended excursion. No one would be alarmed tonight when Henry's men did not return. Feeling their contents, I found a cup with which I ported enough water to wash the savage's wounds.

I had touched few men in my seventeen years and never one without proper clothes. Besides the knotted ribbing I had mistaken for the Captain's buttons and braid, my patient wore only buckskin leggings and a breechcloth; but though I found his nakedness disconcerting, I was grateful I need only remove the breastplate to cleanse his wound. It felt as if it were made of small bones woven with leather strips and edged with coarse strands that hung loosely from each side. My imagination took off wildly as I fingered them, my hands so shaking from the grisly possibilities I could barely maneuver it over his head.

Unsheathing his knife, I cut the hem from my petticoat and used a portion to bathe the dried blood from his chest and back. The rest I meant for a bandage, but the wound lay in an awkward position. I could cover it neither by looping the muslin around his collarbone and below his arm nor by wrapping it around his chest, so I did both, tying it off on one side of his neck. Afterward, I gently eased his back onto the blanket I had taken off Stump's horse and covered him with the other. The night air felt wonderfully refreshing to me, but his condition would make him susceptible to a chill.

Now I had only to wait for the sun to rise. From the look of the sky, the hour might be anywhere between ten and five. I guessed it somewhere in the middle. It depended on the length of my nap, which was impossible to tell.

Curling up on a patch of thick grass, I reflected on the Proverbs I had read in the coach. The Lord had shown Himself repeatedly faithful and His hand had been obvious during the entire wretched day. Not only had escaping Henry been astonishingly simple, but also my rescue by the savage had been perfectly timed. I would have greatly preferred Captain Anderson, of course. As it was, I felt a fearsome wolf had snatched me from a mangy cur. Nonetheless, God had provided an escape, and trusting His plan had been the verses' point.[15]

"Lord, I want to do just that—trust You, I mean. Please glorify yourself in me and provide me courage, whatever happens. I can't face this—any of this—without Your help."

My heart wandered over Father's advice in the garden shortly before he died. "Don't forget who holds you in the palm of his hand." He had also confided he thought me strong, but I felt miserably weak. As I had always deemed myself fearful by nature, two verses had long been my favorites: "The Lord is my light and my salvation, whom shall I fear?" and "The Lord is the strength of my life; of whom shall I be afraid?"[16] Repeatedly reciting them, I fell into a deep slumber until a penetrating howl abruptly awakened me from sleep.

I sat up, thoroughly chilled and shaking. Assuming it came from a wolf, I contemplated ways to defend us should the animal attack. God gave King David victory over a lion; surely, a wolf was smaller and less ferocious. Snapping twigs from a fallen branch, I fashioned a rudimentary weapon, but though I listened alertly, I could not hear any discernible difference in the creature's call.

Why, I pondered, did dread make time pass slowly? Waiting for Pinckney's return last night had seemed interminable. Was it only last night? It seemed much longer and felt like weeks since we buried Father. Tucking my knees under my chin and my arms about my legs, I laid the limb aside and stared at the savage's dark form.

He was sleeping so peacefully on the makeshift pallet that I half regretted my giving him both blankets. The grass had felt pleasantly cool when I first lay down. Now it was so damp that I could not stop shivering, and an irritating couplet kept skipping through my head.

"If two lie together, then they have heat: but how can one be warm alone?"[17]

I was quite certain Solomon had not written this to encourage the idea I was entertaining, so when my head became too heavy to hold up, I lay back on the grass, tucked my feet beneath my skirt, and pulled my hands inside my sleeves.

Unable to get warm, I wondered if I could remove the top blanket without awakening my patient but dismissed the idea for the reasons he had needed it in the first place. Dare I move a little closer? I had ridden against him for hours with no ill effects. What if he were Captain Anderson? Would I have any qualms moving nearer? Yes, I concluded, but I might do so anyway to survive; and while I was certain the Captain would not take liberties, the savage was unconscious and could not.

Another howl sent me creeping closer to observe his breathing. It was heavy and regular and did not alter as I lightly lay down on the excess blanket; but though I now felt drier, I was still so cold that I could not stop shivering. Gently scooting beneath the cover, I edged in close enough to grow wonderfully warm without actually touching him and felt decidedly silly that my fear of the wolf instantly subsided. How could an insensible savage protect me? For all I knew of doctoring, he might be near death; and if not, he would likely pose a greater threat if he awoke and found me under his blanket. I was glad, nonetheless, not to feel so alone.

Staring at a star peeking over a treetop, I thought about Father's Will. He had been quite right. I had not grasped the vulnerability of a woman alone in the world, and I understood now why he had made me Henry's ward. Praying that the savage would not awaken before morning, I slowly drifted down into an exhausted sleep.

THE ILL-MANNERED SUN insistently awakened me the next morning. My bed felt unusually hard, my back unexpectedly stiff, and my mind entirely unwilling to cooperate. Turning over on my side, I burrowed beneath my covers to escape the offensive light; but an unfamiliar scent coaxed my eyes to open. Memories of last night tromped through my head like a red-coated regiment, defying resistance and demanding I give them quarter.

Poking my head out of the blanket, I glanced at the savage, then quickly away, refusing to peruse his facial features. They were too personal and made him too real—like a farm animal given a name—and I was too groggy to face the possibilities they evoked. He lay so still I thought he was dead, but when the blanket atop his chest gently rose, I could not say which I felt more: disappointment or relief. I did not wish him ill, but what would become of me if he revived? Carefully edging out from under the covers, I resolved to heed Jesus' admonition to take "...no thought for the morrow: for the morrow shall take thought for the things of itself. Sufficient unto the day is the evil thereof."[18]

In the bright sun, he appeared younger than I had imagined, easing my fears a bit and arousing more of my natural compassion. The blood he had lost had drained much of his color, but otherwise, his health seemed excellent. As I touched the skin around his wound, the corners of my mouth moved slightly upward. He felt markedly cooler, and now that my brain was awake and the morning's initial shock was wearing off, I was glad.

Assuming he continued mending at his current rate, he could soon fend for himself, and I could slip off without denying my conscience.

The looming formation that I had sensed in the dark was a steep cliff jutting over this side of the river. Opposite, it curved southward, forming a high wall that sheltered us from whatever lay above it or on its other side.

After plunging down the cliff face, the river flowed south and somewhat east. Taller mountains rose to the north. They were doubtless the ones I saw from Father's bedroom, but since I knew neither how long I had slept nor how much farther the coach would have traveled, they could not help me determine the direction or distance to the outpost.

On my way to further explore the saddlebags, I spotted an unfamiliar roan with a woven bridle nibbling a clump of grass beside the river. He eyed me warily when I tried to approach him and repeatedly evaded my grasp. Leading the others downstream lest they foul our living space, I discovered a simple enclosure fashioned from limbs and brush. The stage horses entered it readily, as did Henry's bay, but his dapple-gray mare was less cooperative. Retrieving sugar from a saddlebag, I enticed her into the pen, and the half-wild stallion followed, apparently liking her company.

In addition to sugar, the well-stocked bags held the flat cornbread Mrs. Hodgetts called hoecake, beef jerky, coffee, a pan, and a small flask of whiskey. I thought the last possessed medicinal qualities but was unsure if I should apply it to my patient's wound or dribble it into his mouth. Hoping to ease his pain, I decided to try the latter and discovered he had a pouch of his own fastened to his belt. It held a small supply of something I deduced was pemmican. Miss Whitney, my governess, had read about our soldiers eating it during the War for Independence, so I tore off a tiny piece. It was surprisingly palatable, but feeling like a trespasser, I put his bag down quickly and resolved to use none of his supplies. He would need them when I was gone.

Returning to the saddlebags, I found a comb—though I did not want to guess whose it was—and the greatest treasure of all: a small sliver of soap with which I thoroughly washed the comb and my dresses. The savage's blood had saturated the latter, hopelessly staining both. Had they not been black, anyone seeing me from behind would conclude I had been shot. More unnerving was the quantity of blood that had dried in my hair, matting it into a thick clump. While my head lay against his chest, my upswept curls had sopped it up like a rag.

The only sounds were rushing water, which soothed my tattered nerves, a few twittering birds, and a squirrel crackling leaves in the branches. Though the river moved swiftly over the cliff, an overhang stuck out so sharply that a shallow pool had formed behind it, worn smooth by the volume of water flowing back over the rock. I eased down into its cool recesses, laying back to soak my hair, and found the gentle rise and fall of the water so calming that I began almost to enjoy myself. Indeed, I would have, had I been entirely able to forget my patient.

Wonderfully clean, I retreated for privacy to a grove of cedars tucked partly under the overhang. The desire was absurd of course, considering the savage was unconscious, but his foreign looks and dress underscored that wish. For the first time in weeks, I need not listen vigilantly for Henry's footsteps, avoid his lingering touches, or puzzle over his enigmatic statements. What was it about his very tone that could make a simple word sound indecent?

Would anyone connect my disappearance to Captain Anderson? I hoped not, nor could I see why someone would. After all, the Captain had been with Farley at the time the coach had departed. No doubt, he would come across the wreckage when he traveled to the outpost—might already have done so judging by the sun's height in the sky. What would he do when he did not find my body? Even now, he might be searching these woods.

"Lord, help him find me before the savage wakes up."

When Mrs. Hodgetts discovered my bed made and my belongings intact, she would probably think an Indian crept in and made off with me. The near accuracy of this conjecture made me chuckle, so startling a squirrel that he leaped to a farther tree. The Captain must have been wrong concerning their whereabouts, provoking another dreadful notion: might more savages be nearby? The pen was large enough for a dozen standing horses. If I succeeded in fleeing from this one, I might find myself in the hands of…

"No!" I chided myself, repeating, "'Take no thought for the morrow,'"[19] again as I sat down against a smooth-barked tree to dry my hair in the sunshine. "Lord, none of this would have happened had my father not died; yet I know You are perfect in all Your ways. You're worthy of my trust and have never failed nor forsaken me."

Opening to Genesis, I chose the story of Joseph,[20] whom I imagined felt much as I did. He had been tossed from one horrid situation into another even worse, first when his brothers sold him as a slave and then when he was imprisoned for a crime he did not commit. Still, as the story neared the end, Joseph saw why God had allowed his enemies to succeed: He saved his whole family from starvation!

I was particularly struck by the timing of Joseph's two dreams. They quite clearly announced the Lord's plan before his brothers ever plotted their part, bringing several other Scriptures to my mind. One, I knew by heart: "All the days ordained for me were written in Thy book before one of them came to be."[21] The other, whose location I could not remember, said something about God knowing the end from the beginning and what was from what is yet unseen. I found it impossible to imagine how God might use my predicament, but neither, surely, could Joseph while the slavers carried him away.

The savage looked less ashen when I returned to him, causing me to question how many days he might remain asleep. His lips were becoming dry, steering my mind toward the hired hands' whiskey, but the thought of dabbing it over so private a spot made my insides cringe. Cradling his head lest he choke, I rested the flask on his chin and trickled the scantest drop on his bottom lip.

His tongue began seeking the much-needed liquid, a response I anticipated, but my reaction took me by surprise. I felt repulsed by so forced an intimacy; and yet, I also felt sharp fascination. It shattered my resolve to hold myself aloof, and my eyes—as if possessing a will of their own, darted up to his.

They were deeply set beneath a broad, surprisingly well-formed forehead, and flanked a masculine but not overly large nose. Their edges lacked the creases that revealed Captain Anderson's age and disposition, but whether this was due to fewer years or a less pleasant temperament was impossible to say. A scar followed the length of his right hairline, and his pronounced cheekbones formed flat planes that extended down to his firmly set mouth and chin. Unlike Captain Anderson, he had not one freckle, only a flat black mole above his left eyebrow that I initially mistook for dirt.

Noticing the sun had sunk low enough to give accurate bearings, I left my charge and followed the horses' trail of hoof prints. They were quite clear at first, leading me downhill well over an hour through the deep wood, but the earlier, heavier rains last evening washed away all prior traces. Only one path looked wide enough to accommodate large animals, so I took it, choosing broader offshoots whenever it divided until I could no longer ignore my stomach's cries for food.

I turned and retraced my steps, feeling confident I was making the right choices, but after far more than sufficient time had passed to come upon the hoof prints, the woods instead unexpectedly opened onto an unfamiliar glade.

"Lord, help me," I murmured, my heart sinking as I glanced up to locate the sun. Either clouds obscured it from view or I had grossly lost track of time. I looked for something—anything—that might offer a clue to the right direction, whipping my head around sharply when I heard a distinct snap. Fearing a bear or another savage, I took off across the meadow, refusing to stop until I gained a massive trunk standing like a tower just inside the tree line.

Slipping around to its other side, I doubled over, trying to calm my ragged breathing; but as something rustled in the brush, I pressed my back flat against the rough bark. I do not know how long I stood there, listening for signs of a pursuer; but when the pounding in my ears subsided, I heard the faint, unmistakable sound of crashing water.

"Sufficient unto the day is the evil thereof,"[23] I repeated for what seemed the hundredth time, asking Jesus to help me take courage and concentrate on what was vital. If I wanted to give in to hysterics, I could do so later; for now, I needed to find my way back.

Trudging through the dense undergrowth, I headed as directly as I could manage toward the crashing water, urged on greatly by the fading light. At last, I came upon the river, turned upstream, and nearly cried when I caught sight of the pen full of horses. While considering throughout the day how I might escape the savage, I never once imagined I might welcome his presence; but seeing his blanketed form brought surprising relief.

Dribbling water through his lips with a dampened bit of petticoat, I began to wonder what kind of man he was. Not all of the Indians Miss Whitney and I read about were the murderous lot of popular lore. Samson Occum received Christ and became a missionary to his tribe—and what of Mary Jemison, an English girl captured by Shawnees during the French-Indian War? Given the opportunity, she refused to leave them! I thought her choice unfathomable, but it surely showed she had not found life among them repugnant.

Once I had tended my patient and satisfied my hunger, I curled up on a patch of warm grass and slept until cold urged me to avail myself of last night's warmer accommodation.

BIRDS, SINGING PLEASANTLY in the trees overhead, awakened me early the next morning. Feeling almost well-rested, I lay drinking in the salmon-colored sunrise until my charge's deep breathing tugged for my attention.

Our isolation and his need for my care colluded to stir up companionable feelings, but I knew I dared not trust them. They reminded me of Old Lisbeth's youngest grandson. While napping in our kitchen on cold afternoons, the tot looked like a painted cherub. His cheeks were plump, his tiny mouth rosy, and his hands often lay folded as if praying—but he spent his waking hours terrorizing the servants or our neighbor's cat.

How well closed eyes concealed a man's true character. Shakespeare had called them windows of the soul. Would my patient's eyes look like Father's: loving and kind, or would they be cold and mocking like Uncle Henry's? Perhaps they would share the Captain's twinkle. More likely, they would be cruel and certainly quite dark. His silky hair, woven with several large feathers, was as shiny and black as a raven's plumage.

As I rifled through a saddlebag for hoecake, he kicked his blanket down around his knees, exposing more of himself than I had seen before by daylight. I stopped mid-action while pulling it back up. A ghastly scar rode the edge of his breechcloth across his abdomen. Already, I had noticed small nicks on his chest, but this one's pallor showed it had been deep and clearly announced its probable cause. He was no youth, but a seasoned warrior. I let the blanket drop. The warm sunshine would prevent any chills and his scar the construction of treacherous illusions.

His uncovered form declared much about his life. It was obviously full of rigorous activity. Veins snaked along the surface of his arms, extending over rough broad hands with short, calloused fingers. He wore a band on each arm, midway between shoulders and elbows, accentuating his strength with each hill and valley.

As I examined the hard collar about his throat, the tightly woven strands that held it together brought to mind the ones that hung from his breastplate. Both were hair, I was certain, provoking a sudden shiver, but at least they were black, not golden or ginger or even my own dark brown. They might have been his own or from his roan's tail. Whatever their source, I needed to squarely face my future should my plan to leave him fail.

He had not wished me dead, else he would not have saved me from Stump—but why had he? Were women scarce in his village, or had my helplessness aroused his pity? The latter was out of keeping with all I had read about his kind. More likely, I was a commodity to barter, provided God gave me the strength to survive the initial tortures.

Thrusting aside that horrid thought, I pulled out my Bible but was unable to quell the primary question: to whom might he sell me? New Spain was too far, and though Frenchmen still trapped beaver along this river, their defeat in Lower Canada last century had stopped that sort of trade. One possibility remained, and that was most revolting: he might sell me to another savage.

While thumbing through Paul's letters, a verse in Second Timothy leaped from the page. "Therefore, endure hardship as a good soldier of

Jesus Christ. No man that warreth entangleth himself with the affairs of this life; that he may please Him who has chosen him to be a soldier." [24]

In my present circumstance, I was loath to apply it. Was God assigning me to a harder life? The thought was barely credible, so I pushed it away. God had not made me run from Henry, the decision was my own—yet, there was no other choice. I shuddered as I thought of my door's missing lock. Between it and Stump's comments, I could easily guess how Henry intended to gain my consent. I could no longer stand his presence, much less his touch.

I found the passage I sought in Colossians. "Slaves, obey in all things your masters according to the flesh; not with eye-service, as men-pleasers; but in singleness of heart, fearing God." [25]

This, too, I found difficult to apply. I kept picturing servants in cleanly starched aprons, but I would more likely be digging for roots, wiping sweat and snarled hair from my eyes. Worse yet, I might be forced to…to…the possibility was too hideous to put into words. I shoved it from my mind and returned to the Scriptures, locating another pertinent verse in Titus.

"Exhort slaves to be obedient to their own masters, and to please them well in all, not answering again, not pilfering, but showing all good fidelity, that they may adorn the doctrine of God our Savior in all things." [26]

I could easily avoid talking back to him—I had no idea how to speak his language—but what had Paul meant by "adorning the teaching of our Savior?" Asking the Lord for insight, my mind turned towards my patient's wounds. The heat and swelling around them were obvious, but they alerted me to an inner condition that I could not see. Respect, faithfulness, and honesty were much the same—the outward evidence of what lay within a heart. By living in a manner consistent with his faith, the lowliest slave could proclaim the beauty of our Savior—even if his masters forbade him to speak! Unexpected joy bubbled up in my heart: even while facing this loathsome prospect, Jesus showed me purpose and hope.

"Lord, I beg You to help me escape, but if I am unable, help me be like Joseph—faithful to both You and my master. My foolishness may have brought me here, but You knew this would happen before knitting me together in my mother's womb." [27]

Tucking my Bible back into my pocket, I drew water from the river and contemplated my charge while eating a second piece of hoe-cake. My Grandfather had said Indian tribes varied as much from each other as the British do from the Spanish. While the Oneidas had kept Washington's troops from starving at Valley Forge, the Iroquois had fought us fiercely. To this, I added the accounts of Lewis and Clark's expedition: far more

Indians helped than hindered them. Of course, their journey took place long before Tecumseh's uprising.

The sun still hovered below its zenith, proclaiming the way east, so I headed in the direction I had walked yesterday, but this time I carried the savage's knife to mark my way. In what felt like no time, I had already reached the forest glade and a few hours later came to the end of my previous exploration.

Looking this way and that, I searched for some indication of a path but could not detect even the smallest. I decided to head south, assuming I would eventually rejoin the river or, failing that, follow the X's I had made back home.

Home? I shook my head at my use of the word. The waterfall was picturesque, but a spot in a clearing could hardly be regarded a home, especially when shared with a savage stranger.

Perhaps, I mused, "savage" depended mostly upon whose side a person stood. Could I fault someone for fighting for his home and land? The brutality reputed to many, however, went far beyond protecting their families. Then again, a man of Father's acquaintance frequently bragged about his exploits against Tecumseh. Little boys in Skippack deemed him a hero. Father and I thought his cruelty indefensible, and he was not the only one of his kind. General Jackson slaughtered a whole village in retribution for an attack by an altogether different tribe. Had he been nicknamed Ol' Hickory for his tough constitution, I wondered, or for the hardness of his heart?

I certainly knew white men I would call savage; the warrior had saved me from two of them. Mulling over the events of the past month, I grew convinced that Henry and his men had burned out the Lawsons. Would they blame Indians, as well, for killing my fellow traveler and the coachman?

Even when I had left his scars exposed, my patient had looked so peaceful in the waning light that I had trouble imagining him heartless. Lord willing, I need never find out, but if not, this savage might be kinder than the one from whom I had fled. Lisbeth had often quoted Taverner's proverb, "Better the devil you know than the devil you don't," but I could not agree. Life with Henry held only horrors; my fate with the warrior at least held an element of hope.

When the forest abruptly gave way to a ravine, I peered through the treetops to locate the sun. It still hung overhead, providing plenty of light, but between struggling through the dense brush, finding safe ways to descend the slope, and becoming lost in my thoughts, I was no longer certain of my way.

Pivoting completely around, I attempted to return by following my markings, but this proved more difficult than I would have predicted. I expected X's on trees where there were none and came across others where I had not expected to find them. When the sun finally sank low enough to offer directions, I abandoned my markings altogether and headed east.

Thankfully, I did not travel far before coming across a small, clear brook. I drank my fill and followed it upstream, assuming it would connect with the river, which it did, but not until the sun had sunk so low, I had begun again to panic.

How far I was from the falls I could not determine; I just prayed that the way upriver would be navigable. It was, but by the time I had reached the makeshift pen, the sky had turned from coral to purple.

Scurrying over to my patient, I bent down to trickle more water through his open lips, but what I felt while laying my palm to his bandage threw my emotions into turmoil.

His fever was gone, for which I was thankful; but a return to health meant a return to consciousness, and I desperately needed him to sleep through the night. The sun was already slipping away, robbing me of any chance to flee.

I packed up one of the saddlebags. At first light, I would take Henry's bay, but rather than make a third attempt to return to the outpost road, I would head downriver.

If the forest thinned high enough to afford a good view, the fort or a homestead might be visible in the distance. If not, I was not certain what I would do. I dare not follow the river too far south. We were surely in the mountains above Henry's valley, and it would lead me directly back to Monroe.

The last thought gnawed at my resolve. So much depended on things I could not predict: the aforementioned view, even the weather. On the clearest day, I might not spot the outpost; I had only the vaguest notion where it stood. If clouds obscured the sun, I could attempt nothing. The river might turn in unexpected directions, and then God alone knew where I would end up.

No settlements lie west or north. If I did not die of starvation or exposure, I would probably become the wolf's next meal—and what of those verses that had leaped out at me? They, along with something from the conversation in Henry's buggy, nibbled at my heart. I had told Captain Anderson I wished to serve God whatever the cost. Perhaps He was answering my prayer.

"But I'm scared, Lord—scared to stay and scared to go—and I don't know how I can do either! If the savage awakes…"

Once more, I imagined myself filthy and worn, my back breaking beneath a heavy burden or in some savage's longhouse, expected to breed his…

"God, I can't do it," I groaned. "You've got to help me get away or else show me—in a way that I can't miss—what You want!"

Anxiously eyeing the savage, I decided to dress his wounds before entirely losing the light, so I ripped a fresh strip from my petticoat's hem, lathered up the soap, and knelt beside him to cut his soiled bandage—just as his eyes fluttered open.

Thou art my portion O, Lord; I have said that I would keep thy words. I entreated thy favor with my whole heart; be merciful unto me, according to thy word.

Psalm 119:57-58

Chapter 5

BEFORE I COULD OFFER a timorous smile, the savage knocked me backward, crushing me beneath his weight while banging his knife from my hand. It flew a foot's distance, but he instantly snatched it, pressing the blade into the pliant flesh below my jaw. I could feel my pulse throbbing against its edge as eyes so black that I could not distinguish their pupils bored into mine. I had imagined them many ways, but never so chilling.

Frantic, I searched for a way to explain why he found me bending over him, knife in hand until a scarlet splotch began seeping through his bandage. He followed my eyes to the spreading color and appeared rapidly to grasp my intentions, for he sheathed his knife and shifted his weight onto his own limbs. Air filled my lungs in sharp, painful gasps as I lay still, trying to subdue waves of overwhelming panic.

When he, at last, loosened his grip on my wrists, my eyes prickled with tears. I shut them tightly, afraid to elicit his scorn; but when his fingertips touched my face, I flung them open. Gently, tenderly, he wiped away each trickle, muttering indecipherable sounds unmistakably intended to soothe. This unexpected gesture unleashed so many of my overwrought emotions, I longed to sob uncontrollably.

Rocking back onto his heels, the warrior let me up, offered me his knife, and pointed to the soiled cloth. I felt awkward touching him while he was awake and more so because his eyes refused to leave my face. I guessed he searched for signs of treachery, but he apparently found none, for he soon grew so curious about his uncovered wound that he seemed not to care that I still held his weapon. While reaching for the muslin and soap, I thought I might slip it into my pocket, but a swift, almost indiscernible, sweep of his eyes showed me he was taking in my every move.

He accepted the knife's return as though I followed the natural, expected course, then watched inquisitively as I lathered up the bit of soap and daubed it over the wound. It must have stung, for he flinched and his eyes grew wary; but he stood stock-still until I finished. Washing the ball's exit wound proved more difficult. Each time I tried to move behind him, he twisted to keep me in front. After several unsuccessful attempts, I arose, thinking I could reach over his shoulder, but he stood up also.

I staggered backward—his stature was far more imposing than I had realized—but he quickly closed the gap, motioning again to his wound and uttering a command. Everything in me cried out to flee, but even if I could move my feet, I knew running would be fruitless. He probably knew these woods well, and I had twice managed to get lost in them during daylight. Furthermore, savages were reputed to torture captives who showed fear.

Asking the Lord to calm my trembling, I slipped my arm beneath his and gingerly ran my fingers up and across his shoulder blade. My cheek lay so near his chest that I felt its heat, and though I abhorred the ways he might misread such intimacy, his posture indicated nothing. When I found the tender spot, he kept himself so immobile that only an upward glance told me he had felt it. His eyes noticeably widened and his jaw tightly clenched.

Having bathed his wounds, I had only to bandage them, but this proved even harder; I needed to nearly embrace him while winding around the muslin. Securing it over his shoulder proved even worse. Reaching up to tie it around his neck brought our faces disturbingly close, and only the dusky sky offered hope he did not see my change in hue. I felt as if my cheeks had been set on fire.

Looking for an excuse to draw away, I remembered he had eaten nothing and drunk little for two days, so I headed to the river to fetch clean water. The savage stayed in the clearing, his tired eyes carefully trailing me as I rifled through the saddlebags. When I knocked the flask out, I eyed it speculatively. It might induce a longer and deeper slumber, and if he slept past dawn, I could slip away. This time, I would follow the river, but as I thought of the place it inevitably led, my stomach knotted up. Henry had become nasty on the evenings he had imbibed too much sherry. I could not take that chance with the savage, not after the terror I had just experienced.

When I offered him the tin cup, he drank from it eagerly and then motioned that I should fetch him more water, but he seemed uncertain about the hoecake. He sniffed it cautiously before breaking off a morsel and putting it into his mouth. Afterward, he drew pemmican out of his pouch, ate a portion, and then offered some to me. I accepted it gladly after two days of meager rations; and when we both were satisfied, he walked directly to the roughly made enclosure.

I followed at a distance, unsure what to do now that he was awake, and watched as he inspected each horse. His hands roamed over their legs, haunches, bellies, necks, and spines, and he thoroughly checked the condition of their muzzles and hooves. When he openly admired the dapple-gray mare, I felt ridiculously pleased, as if I had presented him a valuable gift. This evening had been full of inconceivable emotions, but just now, I was too weary to sort them out.

Obviously fatigued, the warrior returned to the clearing and began pulling the makeshift pallet into the grove. I assisted his efforts, aware too much exertion might reopen his wound, and then returned to the bed of grass I had occupied most of our first night. Stretching out upon it, I let my mind wander over this whole bewildering evening.

My patient's unpredictability had kept me entirely off-balance. One moment, he terrified me; the next, he offered me comfort. He expected me to obey him and then offered me his food. The effect on my emotions was maddening! I longed desperately to escape, but I also felt ridiculously forlorn outside the cedars—like a dog put out for the night.

The constant peril of the past weeks must have addled my senses. His eyes, upon awakening, had been more savage than even my fears had painted them. Still, the portrait I had formed while he slept had been much like a child's drawing: flat, inaccurate, and out of proportion. In only a few hours, he had surprised me with qualities I admired: intelligence, keen self-control, and even compassion.

The grass felt uncomfortably damp, shifting my mind to the warm blankets and wonderful security I had felt last night. Why did my patient have to awaken? Tonight, no doubt would be cold, lonely, and sleepless. Perhaps, I should slip away now. I need not stay for conscience's sake. He was quite able to fend for himself, even against the wolf; but remembering the latter, I decided to stay put.

Oh, Lord! I prayed silently, closing my eyes. Why didn't You keep him asleep just one night longer? Uneasily, I recalled my request as the light was waning. Could the warrior's waking be God's answer? I could not deny the possibility but set it aside, rolled over, and tried to sleep.

Within moments, my eyes startled open. The savage was standing over me, uttering commands as he motioned with his chin toward the cedars. When I failed to obey, he hauled me to my feet, pulling me into the grove, and nodded to his pallet. I could guess what he wanted but did not move—sleeping next to him now was unthinkable. Reiterating his command, he lifted the top blanket and signaled emphatically that I should crawl beneath it; and when I shook my head, he dragged me there himself.

"Jesus, help me!" I mumbled.

The last time I had breathed those words this very man had been the Lord's answer, and he could surely assault me as easily off the pallet as on. Throwing him a wary glance, I lay as close to the edge as possible, turned my back, and stayed still as a rabbit in a predator's view. I knew he had sat down when the bottom blanket moved, and when I felt him pull the top one up over my arm, I stopped breathing altogether. Leaning lightly against my back, he wrapped the cover around my shoulders, as my mother had when I was little, and securely tucked it under my chin. Then, after mumbling something into my ear, he rolled over and began the slow even breathing of sleep.

Exhaling deeply, I thanked God for His faithful protection. Clearly, the warrior demanded I obey him; and yet, he had insisted only that I sleep between warm blankets rather than on the cold ground. He had been firm and determined, using force when words did not suffice, but he had not hurt me since our initial encounter. In fairness, and I could not fault him for that: I, too, would feel alarmed to find a stranger kneeling over me with a knife.

"Lord, I'm so confused. He is so wholly unpredictable that from one minute to the next I cannot guess what to expect."

Letting go of an anxious breath, I realized there were only two things I knew for certain: God held me in the palm of His hand, and none of this had taken Him by surprise. Relaxing in that grip, I thanked Him for His faithful care and drifted into a surprisingly peaceful sleep.

THE WARMTH OF THE morning coaxed me out of a deep and satisfying slumber. I rolled onto my back and drowsily stretched, but as my eyes gradually pulled open, I grew suddenly alert. The warrior squatted above me, studying my face as I had his. He must have seen my alarm, for he began gently stroking my cheek, murmuring his words of comfort.

As I recalled what I had thought of his sleeping form, I wondered what he thought of mine. Was I the first white person he had encountered?

Now that I saw them in daylight, his eyes were finely shaped and held none of last evening's hostility. What did he make of mine, so light in color compared with his own? As I cautiously curved my lips in greeting, he echoed the motion, his black eyes conveying more warmth than Henry's had while smiling broadly.

Tapping his fingers against his chest, he made sounds that I haltingly repeated, taking them as his name. They were difficult to pronounce and he corrected me several times before I passably said them. In return, I imitated his gesture, slowly saying, "Al-see," but he shook his head and uttered a blunt sound I took to mean, "No." Covering my fingers with his own, he articulated several new syllables, which I mumbled indifferently.

I found his touch disquieting, and though I had never particularly liked my name, I did not want him to give me a new one. It unpleasantly underscored my loss of both freedom and status. As if he read my thoughts, he enunciated them a second time, pressing his fingers against my collarbone. I mimicked them more clearly, suspecting I had no choice but felt little reward when I saw his eyes smile.

He rose, apparently satisfied, and walked directly toward the enclosure. Since he had not motioned for me to follow, I hurried in the other direction for some much-needed privacy. Glancing over my shoulder, I saw that he was watching me, but he did not show any concern: I could not get far on foot. I was beginning to think escape might be impossible unless God provided some extraordinary means. The warrior's awakening had indeed changed everything. At least, he did not seem cruel.

When I returned, I found him leading the horses out of the enclosure and into the woods, taking the very path I had traveled over each of the previous days. He had not indicated anything I should do, so I pulled out my Bible and headed to the smooth-barked tree.

Flipping through the pages, I came to the Book of Esther, who, when she was about my age, had also come into the power of a fearsome foreign man. As I thought of her, my mind naturally drifted to Allison, whose middle name was Esther. How different were our lives from what we had planned. We had intended to stay in Skippack, caring for our children together as we had our dolls. The winter before Father and I came to Monroe, a handsome surveyor, tall as a tree, married and carried her away to his farm in the Shenandoah Valley. I had received a letter from her at Henry's last week announcing that she was with child and asking me to act as godmother, but between funeral arrangements and dodging Henry, I had not taken the time to reply. What would she conclude when she did not hear from me? I could not bear for her to think I took her request lightly, and she would certainly want to know that Father was gone.

His death had left a gaping hole in my heart. He had been my sole parent for several years and in many respects my closest friend. As I pictured his ashen face, the words he quoted to me so often began ringing again in my heart. "Take no thought for the morrow...."

Returning to the Book of Esther, I read that her parents had named her Hadassah, but her foreign lord called her a name in his own tongue that meant Star. I questioned whether the odd syllables the warrior pronounced meant anything. Perhaps they were not a name at all, but the word for slave. Settling down to the narrative, I wondered if Esther grew to love the king she was forced to marry. The text said that he found her pleasing, but she could see him only if he called for her, and he had not done that for thirty days!

Reapplying myself to my reading, I came across Mordecai's question, "Who knoweth whether thou art come to the kingdom for such a time as this?"[29] Esther had been afraid to intervene for her people, yet she had entrusted herself to the Lord, saying, "If I perish, I perish."[30] Through humble submission, she not only influenced her earthly master but also the course of history. Had she sought safety instead, she would have lost everything. Satan's plot, of course, was obvious: through Haman he intended to kill all Jews everywhere, nullifying God's promise to use their lineage to bear the Messiah.

The Lord knew everything. Might He, for His own purposes, have arranged my predicament? Unlike Esther, I had no people to save, but God's ways are not our ways. Grandmother must have reminded me of that hundreds of times, but only now did its significance sink into my heart. During my whole life, my parents had instructed me to trust Him, but this was easy while under their care. Our home was full of love and our life pleasant. Now though, like Esther and Joseph before her, I faced a possibility opposed to any of my natural desires. Did I trust God enough to follow Him if He led me there?

"Lord, help my unbelief."[31]

The Holy Spirit reminded me of some verses from John 12. "He who loveth his life will lose it, but he who hateth his life in this world, shall keep it unto eternal life."[32] I flipped there, wanting to examine the surrounding context.

"If any man serves Me, let him follow Me; and where I am, there shall My servant be."[33]

How backward I had remembered them! They did not say Jesus would go wherever His servants did, but that His servant would follow Him wherever He went. Tears of joy mixed with gratitude streamed down my face. God's ways were amazingly upside down from my own, and yet, He was gracious enough to stoop down and explain them to me.

"I am willing to do anything, Jesus, even become a slave if You intend it, but if that isn't something You have planned, please show me how to get away."

God's will or not, I felt frightened by the thought of going alone to a strange, uncivilized people. I would have much preferred to go as Captain Anderson's wife or in company with others of my own kind. Yet, the Lord Himself would go before me, as He had before Joseph when the slavers took him into Egypt.

"And if I perish, I perish." Closing my eyes and leaning back against my tree, I quietly began singing my mother's favorite hymn.

> Be Thou my Vision, O Lord of my heart;
> Naught be all else to me, save that Thou art.
> Thou my best thought, by day or by night,
> Waking or sleeping, Thy presence…

A shadow blocked the sun. Opening my eyes, I saw the warrior standing in front of me and stopped singing. He made gestures that were difficult to make out in the shadow that he cast, but grasping this impediment, he squatted down. Uncertain of his aim, my heartbeat quickened while he smoothed a calloused hand up my throat, over my chin, and then launched his fingers from my lips; and when I did nothing in response, he repeated the gesture on himself and started rhythmically chanting. I imitated the sounds, guessing he wanted to teach me these also, but he shook his head and returned his hand to my neck and mouth. When he had done this a few more times, I finally saw that he wanted me to continue the hymn. I shyly began to do so, having finished only one stanza, and knew I was correct when I saw his pleased expression.

As I sang the last verse, he thumbed quizzically through my Bible, which I had laid down on the grass, and then, finding nothing of interest, tossed it aside. It landed on the water's edge, where a little eddy picked up and swirled it out into the rapidly moving water. Crying out, I sprang to my feet and lunged straight into the river. I had lost my father, my fortune, all hope of returning to my friends or even familiar surroundings. I was not going to lose this, my only consolation and most precious treasure!

The warrior plunged in also, swimming so strongly that he reached it in seconds. Standing stiffly against the current, he waved it over his head, grinning like a school-boy who had won a prize.

I ran to meet him as best I could, slipping on moss-covered rocks and stumbling as the river dragged against my dress. When he placed it in my hands, I could hardly contain my joy. It poured out in a torrent of grateful English and in smiles so wide and irrepressible that my cheeks began to ache.

As he silently listened, his eyes displayed a series of expressions: bewilderment, perhaps, that a seemingly useless object inspired such passion; relief that I was no longer miserable; delight with my babbling thankfulness—evidently plain, despite my foreign words; and something else that I could not fathom. Up to my waist in rushing water, I began to understand that my happiness somehow mattered to this man. He held me securely against the current, ensuring my Bible did not become lost again, and steered me toward a section of the bank where I could easily emerge.

As we climbed onto dry ground, I realized I would soon need to clean his wound, but my petticoat was soaked. I tapped the hilt of his knife, and he handed it over without hesitation. Turning my back, I raised my skirt only enough to cut off a fresh length of muslin, but he became unexpectedly inquisitive about the process. He bent down, determined to discover the source of the clean bandage, but modesty forbade me to reveal it.

Hastily pushing my hem down into place, I squeezed out the strip and hung it from a branch to dry in the strong afternoon sun, then cut his wet wrappings. I was concerned his efforts might have irritated his wounds, but though both were noticeably redder, neither had split open. Standing as still as he had last evening, he proved a most cooperative patient; but my control over my responses proved much weaker. His glistening black hair and coppery skin called vivid images of King David, my romantic girlhood hero, to mind, suddenly and persistently coursing color up my neck.

On so bright an afternoon, I was sure the warrior noticed. Indeed, though I did not lift my eyes, I suspected he began purposely to provoke and deepen the hue. Once I had cleansed his chest wound, he kept twisting around as he had last night, forcing me to repeat the same embarrassing embrace to reach his back. That was not all. While I was trying to swathe him in muslin, he leaned his head so close to mine that I could feel his breath on my ear.

He did the opposite as I tried to tie the bandage off, drawing himself up to such height that I strained on tiptoe to reach my arms around his neck. Then, while my face was closest to his, he brushed his cheek against my hair, inhaling deeply, as if he were taking in my fragrance. This unnerved me so completely, my legs gave way. Before I could catch my balance, I stumbled against his chest, and his broad hands promptly encircled my waist. He meant only to steady me, but as I drew away, crimson from head to toe, the unmistakable smile twitching about the corners of his lips provoked an instant, unfamiliar contracting in the pit of my stomach.

Mercifully, the warrior ended my discomfort by signaling for me to follow him to the river's edge. Pulling me down to squat beside him, he drew back the leaves of a low-lying bush to show me a throng of wild berries. He plucked one, grinning playfully, and popped it into my mouth. It was cool and tartly delicious after several days of hoecake and jerky, but the feel of his fingers on my lips was so unsettling, I was once more lost in awkwardness. Eating several and indicating he wanted me to gather the rest; he rose abruptly and walked to another part of the woods.

In a surprisingly short while, he returned to the clearing and handed me two dead rabbits. I smiled, thankful that we would have fresh meat to eat, but had no idea how to answer his expectant look. Seeing my confusion, he led me to a tree stump, slit one's throat, and hung it over the edge to drain. I was aghast when he bade me follow his example, but my sentiments—I knew—were born of privilege and would serve me ill as a slave. Homesteading girls all over our burgeoning nation performed such duties daily; surely, I could also. Besides, the warrior clearly expected it, so unless the Lord speedily answered my prayer to escape, I would have no choice.

Having spent the larger portion of the day together, the word *escape* sounded oddly off the mark. It seemed unappreciative of the kindnesses he had shown me and almost disloyal. I could not relish the thought of servitude, much less to a people of different custom from my own, but he had been far too agreeable to consider an enemy.

Gripping the rabbit, I held my breath and resolutely did as he showed me, all the while keeping my dress as far from the stump as possible. I wished the poor creature was neither so warm nor soft, but I felt an absurd amount of satisfaction when I glanced up and saw his look of approval. My pleasure was short-lived. When he slit his rabbit's underbelly, peeling back the pelt to expose its bloody muscles, I felt so sick that I eyed the tree line. Were it not for the damage to my pride, I would have dashed there for relief, but I conscientiously imitated his actions, instead, paying careful attention to the words he used. Their gist was simple to understand. Retaining the sounds seemed impossible, except for rabbit and skin or fur. He had repeated each many times. The more I tried to remember them, though, the less I thought of the task I was performing, making it a bit less odious.

While roasting the rabbits over a small fire, he cut green branches from a young sapling and formed them into a drying frame. Over this, he stretched their pelts and placed them in an open spot to cure, and then led me down to the river. He splashed up so much water that I shook my head, pointing to his bandages, but he just splattered me playfully in reply.

We returned to the clearing in companionable silence. The evening grass was damp, so I perched on a fallen log a short distance from the fire. The warrior followed suit, sitting so close that his arm brushed mine while we ate our suppers. The natural, untamed confidence with which he held himself was so different from Father's dignified manner or Captain Anderson's military straightness, I wondered how they would react to him. In the flickering firelight, he looked fearsome, even while unthreatened, but his conduct throughout the day had certainly not been savage. He had been thoughtful and reassuring, even endeavoring to please. Looking up quickly, I caught him studying me as well and wished I knew what he was thinking.

Thoughts of Father brought with them thoughts of Henry, reminding me of the date: Saturday, August 2. Judge Abbott had been due to arrive in Monroe this morning, and I—had I not fled—would soon be enduring a ghastly wedding night. I shuddered at the thought. The more I considered Stump's conversations, the surer I became that my uncle meant for him to kill me. He had said my stained dress would provide the necessary proof to obtain what Henry was after. Since it was not me, it could only be my money.

The warrior must have felt my brief tremor. He stopped eating to search my face, bemused curiosity flickering in his dark eyes; but when he could not find the trouble, he softly stroked my cheek. I smiled, hoping to convey he was not the cause, and he flashed me a grin so agreeable it revived that peculiar feeling in the base of my stomach. This time, he openly acknowledged my blushing, enclosing my burning cheek in his hand and running a thumb over the edges of the color.

70

Who was the strange young woman I had become—so uncertain and so shy? Even Grandmother used to remark on my poise, which had not faltered with wealthy or handsome men. I had found Captain Anderson's company endearingly comfortable.

As the warrior walked away, my odd stirrings quieted; but his parting glance renewed them so instantly, I began to think he posed an entirely different threat than the one I had first feared. Too shocked to even give it voice, I tried to picture the Captain's earnest face, but my mind kept drifting helplessly back to the man who had shared the log. Had he awakened only last night? It seemed long ago, my feelings were so altered.

Beckoning me to join him, the warrior drew me from my musings, coming over to grasp my wrist when I did not immediately respond. Gently tugging me into the grove of cedars, he lifted the top cover and gestured for me to crawl beneath it, which I did. Still, knowing neither his customs nor the expectations he might form, I again turned my back.

Tucking the blanket around my neck as he had last night, he was soon lost in heavy slumber, while I lay listening to night sounds, reflecting on the past day. I felt deeply ashamed of the distaste I had felt for him simply because of his ancestry and was sorry that I judged him savage before knowing his character. Asking the Lord to forgive my arrogance, I added another request to my prayer. I hoped the Lord would prevent the warrior from selling me and, in doing so, realized I had abandoned my plan to flee.

I am God, and there is none like Me, declaring the end from the beginning, and from ancient times things not yet done.

Isaiah 46:9-10

Chapter 6

THE WARRIOR WAS SLEEPING quite soundly when I awoke, so I eased myself from between the blankets and scampered off to bathe in private. What an extraordinary place this was. The freshly rising sun streamed in dapples through the trees, and when I pulled off my dress, several doe drinking downriver lifted their heads.

As we stood staring at each other, I thought better of removing my shift. The warrior's footfalls were noiseless. Yesterday, his shadow alone warned me of his presence. Folding my garments over a low-hanging branch, I tested the temperature with my toe and then eased down into the pool behind the fall. I lay suspended in the undulating water, listening to birds while I followed the antics of a squirrel. He leaped playfully in a nearby tree, chattering to some hidden brother or sister.

A deep sense of peace settled about my heart, and as the ripples gently, soothingly, swirled my loose hair about the pool's surface, the past months' troubles seemed to float away. Could any place but Eden have been this lovely? I wished I could stay here forever.

I had felt happier during the past day than I had for a very long time, with nothing more than two badly stained dresses, a much shorter petticoat, my Bible, and a stranger who stirred unfamiliar feelings in my…in my what? They were so unparalleled in my experience that I was not sure how to determine their origin. He made me feel like a woman encountering her first man, enlivening me in ways I was unaware existed. Oddest of all, he made me feel unaccountably safe, profoundly so, as if I had come home. This, I mused, must have been how Eve felt when she met Adam.

The last thought gave me a jolt. I thrust it away, shocked that my mind had wandered into such an ill-chosen avenue. Why were perception and reality often so exasperatingly at odds with one another? Henry had not owned me, but he made me feel as if he did. This warrior doubtless deemed me a possession to keep or sell at will, and yet, he made me feel…

"Oh—what am I thinking?" I sputtered aloud, finding myself treading down the same improper street. "At most, I can allow myself to hope he does not sell me." As I recalled his pleasure in the dapple-gray mare, however, I began to fret. I had seen many men sell horses they liked when offered sufficient incentive—he might sell me just as carelessly.

Though the morning warmth was increasing, I felt suddenly chilled. If only Father had not...gone. I longed to lay my cheek against his freshly starched shirt, to smell the familiar fragrance of his cologne, to hear his resonant voice saying everything would turn out right...

Refusing to yield to fear, or at least give way any further than I already had, I fled to my Heavenly Father. If slavery were my lot, I prayed that I would make the Gospel appealing through my willing obedience, and while doing so recalled a passage Mother insisted I memorize. I could no longer recite it perfectly, but I remembered the gist well:

"Wives, submit to your husbands so that even if they do not obey the Word, your respectful and chaste behavior will win them—just as Sarah obeyed Abraham, calling him lord. You are her daughters if you do well and let nothing terrify you."[34]

I was struck by the last few words. My circumstances had changed, but God had not. He still had me, as my father had said He would, in the palm of His hand and promised never to fail or forsake me.

As I saw the common thread woven between the passages I read yesterday and the one I now recited, I felt a growing sense of awe. Each portrayed someone who was subject to another and prescribed the same means for gaining influence. They reminded me of something my Mother said on a day I felt Father had treated me unfairly: "Willing submission opens hearts."

Her words had meant little to me at the time, and I now saw why. I had misunderstood them. She had meant for me to open Father's heart, not my own! Looking back, I recognized she was right. When I was stubbornly willful, I created only strife, frustration, and guilt. My respectful obedience always ensured the opposite: goodwill, cooperation from parents and grandparents, and agreement with any sensible requests.

As I hazily imagined how I might apply this to my future, I thought of various events in both Grandfather's business and Grandmother's household. Captains, clerks, or servants who worked hard and showed respect earned advancement, privilege, and trust. Those who did not benefitted no one, least of all themselves. How wonderfully like the Lord to illumine the way through unfamiliar terrain!

I wished Mother could know how her advice still helped me, even after many intervening years. As I closed my eyes, trying to call up her face, I remembered several other things she often said. "God doesn't give instructions so He can test our obedience. They show us the straightest highway through trouble," and, "Happiness is not a reward for obedience any more than milk is a reward for squeezing udders—it's simply the natural consequence."

I missed her intensely. What would she think of my scandalous feelings? Doubtless, she would be appalled, as any civilized woman would and should be. The warrior was of not only a different kind but surely also a different faith! Yet, I did not choose to react as I did when I was near him. Until he awoke, I was unaware such feelings existed. They sprang forth, unbidden, as if they had been lying dormant within me all the while; and now they were awakened, they refused to return to their slumber. He was so vital, so unlike any man of my acquaintance. They seemed as pale compared with him as their skin would be next to his.

"Oh, what am I doing?" I muttered, swishing the suds out of my hair. "Surely, even pondering such things is improper! I may not be able to quash my feelings, but I needn't submit to their rule. Lord, please forgive me if I've unwittingly sinned against You and help me guard my heart."

As I began to rise from the water, a pebble disturbed the placid surface. I looked up, trying to find from where it dropped. The jutting cliff formed a natural ceiling that protected the pool from falling debris. Another fell, then another and another, forming a deliberate arc to my right side.

Glancing over my shoulder, I saw the warrior squatting on the bank, pebbles in hand, and quickly sank beneath the water. How long had he been watching me, and could he tell what I had been thinking? The question was nonsensical, of course, but he seemed so easily able to discern my thoughts.

When I turned around to face him, he glanced at my dress, hanging nearby, and a mischievous smile spread slowly across his face. He had apparently been too polite to take me unawares but was not averse to having fun with my predicament. Then, to my horror, he slipped off his moccasins and began unstrapping his leggings! I hid my eyes, praying he would keep his breechcloth on.

As the water began lapping against my neck, I peeked cautiously through my fingers and spied him skimming bubbles from the edge of the pool. He acted like a little boy, capturing and popping them repeatedly until they floated out under the falls.

Deprived of this new diversion, he waded toward me, setting my heavy hair adrift on the moving water. I modestly clutched it back in place, but when I glanced up; his face looked like a dark squall gathering off a rocky coast.

What could I have done that made him so suddenly angry? As he grasped my forearms and narrowed the space between us, my heart pitched into my throat. I was scared to look up, so I kept my eyes on my floating locks, uneasily watching them swirl around his waist and entangle his breechcloth.

Encompassing my wrists within his broad hand, he carefully matched each finger to the black and blue marks my dress sleeves had hidden and then searched my face so intently that my eyes rose against my will. His expression had softened to regret, but as he slipped my clinging hair behind my shoulders, the black clouds assembled more violently than before.

Following his gaze, I found purple and yellow splotches poorly concealed beneath the ripples of the pool, contrasting harshly with my pale shoulders. He gently rubbed them like a drawing he wished to erase from sand, but with a tenderness that told me Henry's man, not I, was the object of his ire. Uncertain of what to do, I offered a shy smile, kindling such a warm response I could no longer hold his gaze.

I dropped my eyes once again and, noticing his knife bobbing in the water, remembered that I had not yet dressed his wounds. When I pointed to his bandages, he promptly cut them off, so I lathered up his hand and motioned for him to wash his chest. With a teasing grin, he shook his head, smeared the suds onto my palm, and sank down so I could reach his upper body without exposing myself.

I appreciated his consideration, but this brought his ever-searching eyes so close to my face that he ruined my concentration. Hurrying through my task, I slipped beyond the reach of his gaze to tend his other side; and when I was done, he disappeared beneath the pool, erupting a few arm-lengths away, and shook his hair like a spaniel. Reaching the bank in a single stroke, he splashed me playfully, clambered up several rocks, and abruptly strode into the woods.

When I was certain he was out of sight, I emerged also, listening all the while for signs of his return. The horses were nickering pleasantly, so I guessed he had gone to the enclosure and was likely to stay there long enough for the sun to dry my shift. I was enjoying the warmth of its bright rays as I wrung out and combed my hair, but once the birds stopped chirping, I knew he had left the pen.

Hastily retrieving my dress, I pulled it over my head, catching the hem on a low prickly shrub. I was still struggling to free it without tearing the fabric as the warrior appeared with the dapple-gray mare.

Squatting to cut away the clutching thorns, his attention fell to the bottom of my petticoat. He fingered the torn edge, recognizing the cloth and satisfying his curiosity about the place I found such endless supplies of muslin. It was scandalously short now, exposing more than half my calf, and very ragged looking. Embarrassed, I tried to cover it with my dress, risking his disapproval by using his word for "no." He refused to let go. Flashing me an impish grin, he pointed to his shoulder and began ripping away the next length. If he did not consider me his property, he clearly thought my petticoat was his.

While I wrapped his chest, he amused himself with my half-dried tresses, exploring them as he had the bubbles: lifting and squeezing the waves and allowing them to spill through his fingers. I tugged them away, briskly pushing them behind my shoulders, but he simply reached around me to continue his play.

Encircled in his arms, his warm hands skimming my back now and then with his efforts, I felt awash with that same unfamiliar weakness his nearness so often engendered; but at least I need not stretch up to tie off his bandage. My knees would not have held.

Relieved when he straightened up, I shrank away, supposing he would set about his business; but he leaned against a tree instead, watching me twist my hair into a thick coil at the nape of my neck. He shook his head, gravely frowning his disapproval while reaching behind me to jiggle it loose. Dividing it into equal parts, he drew the sections in front of my shoulders and wove each into thick braids, starting behind my ears, and tied the ends with a strip of fringe he cut from his leggings.

As he stepped back to admire his handiwork, I awakened to his goal. He was transforming me into a woman of his kind, first by denying my name and now by insisting I wear my hair in their fashion. His tone conveyed satisfaction and pride—as if this altercation had elevated me to a superior people. Adding insult, he looked expectant, as if he thought it was natural for me to return his pleasure.

It took conscious effort to respond with grace, but I knew he did nothing more than my grandmother would have done. Had she brought a woman of his tribe to work in our home, she would have called her by a name that was easy to pronounce and attired her like a proper servant.

Looking down at the braids, I forced myself to smile. Submitting was much easier for me to read about than to do; and had my eyes met his, they would likely have revealed the mutiny I felt. I mumbled thanks as honestly as I could, hoping my tone made clear what my words obscured, and apparently it did. When he coaxed up my chin so I would look into his eyes, they held such approval that my heart turned over. How could I remain annoyed with such a man?

With a warm parting smile, he let me go and led the mare away from the river. I was curious to see where he was taking her, so I followed them to the glade I had stumbled upon the first day I had become lost. Watching as he stroked her hair and muzzle, murmuring soothingly all the while, I began inwardly to laugh. He was gentling her as he had gentled me; letting her grow used to him as he drew closer. It was working just as well with her also, for though I knew she was temperamental, she soon allowed him to swing up onto her back. Perhaps he would keep us both.

He looked wild and magnificent atop her, man and beast working in unison so seamless it appeared without effort. Bareback, he indicated his wishes by the pressure of his legs rather than the reins, and I wondered if the ancient Greek myths about centaurs arose from such a sight. Glancing my way, he shot me another of his disarming smiles, and I retreated hastily into the trees. I had not meant him to catch me watching.

Settling against the smooth-barked tree, I flipped to the book of Daniel, who had been taken captive as a youth to a foreign land. As I was reading the first chapter, the ground started quivering and a twig crackled. Assuming the warrior and mare were returning, I closed my eyes quickly to pray, only to open them again seconds later. The sounds were coming from above the cliff.

Had Captain Anderson found us? I did not know which stirred in me more—hope or disappointment—but each began vying for supremacy. As I looked up and all around me, fear replaced both. Three unknown warriors broke into the clearing, encircling me repeatedly from atop their horses. Their faces held curiosity but not alarm as I mustered my courage, shoved my Bible into my pocket, and quietly stood up.

While they briefly continued their circuit, I saw they were no older than the warrior who had rescued me. The eldest hung two dreadful-looking strands of enormous curved yellow claws from his neck; and his hair, pulled back from his face, revealed several ugly slash marks. One was so near his right eye, I was amazed he had not lost it. By comparison, the other two were less intimidating. The first looked about my age and the second much younger, perhaps thirteen or fourteen.

They talked animatedly among themselves, noting aspects of my appearance, I supposed, until the eldest began demanding answers to several indecipherable questions. Unable to give them, I lowered my eyes, hoping to hide my increasing unease.

My warrior returned within moments, leading the dapple-gray, and the four forgot my presence in a hail of greetings, questions, and answers. While they were admiring the mare, I slipped away, praying for courage and considering escape; but seeing they were obviously his friends, I proceeded to treat them as I had Father's visitors, offering them our remaining food supplies. Afterward, I fetched fresh water from the river and, now able to identify the berry bushes by leaf, scurried down the bank to find them in abundance.

My warrior's pleased expression paid me well for my efforts, and he seemed suitably impressed that I had labeled each correctly in his tongue. His friends neither spoke to me nor smiled, but nonchalantly accepted the refreshments as one would from any servant. After refilling the cups, I retreated a little ways off, as our maid would have done at home, but my warrior motioned for me to come back and sit beside him.

All four talked at length and with much energy, but I understood nothing until my warrior began imitating the shot through his shoulder. Turning to me, he outlined the damaged breastplate on his bare chest, thrust his chin towards the cedars, and held out his hand. I guessed what he wanted easily and when I had retrieved it, his friends were suitably amazed. They fingered the splintered hole and congratulated him heartily—all but the youngest, who simply beamed.

Soon, I guessed, my warrior had introduced me into the conversation. His gestures took in my presence, the bandages, and the food, and his friends' indifferent expressions changed to nods of approval. Afterward, they proceeded to the pen, where they enclosed their horses and admired the new ones the warrior had acquired.

As I observed them from a distance, melancholy descended on my heart like heavy rain. This place had become a refuge: a haven from Henry and his home's constant reminders of my father's painful death; a break from the normal routines of life that grief had rendered tedious; and a buffer from the formidable prospects my future might hold. The addition of these new warriors awoke me from all fanciful wishes and made facing my uncertain future painfully unavoidable.

When they returned to the clearing, two carried saddles from Henry's horses, and my warrior ducked into the cedars to retrieve the leather bags. He displayed their contents for his friends, passing around the unfamiliar items.

As he pulled out the flask, though, I grew concerned. I could not know what to expect from the group while they were sober, much less if they became drunk. Telling myself that divided between four it held too little whiskey to pose a threat, I watched each cautiously sniff then taste the burning liquid.

Lastly, my warrior drew one of the rifles from its long pocket. He looked puzzled, as did his friends, while examining the first, and then he took out its twin and cast both aside with the whiskey flask. Why had I never thought of them? It was just as well; I would not have done him harm.

Pulling the nearest saddle towards him, he began cutting the leather into strips that his friends wove and knotted to form a long rope. I watched curiously, noting that he enjoyed some standing among them. Even the fierce man did as he bade without question. As I observed the latter, I concluded his clawed appearance belied a jovial temperament, for he, of the four, most often provoked his companions' laughter. The one about my age, by contrast, was serious and silent. He took in everything but responded rarely and less affably. I instantly liked the youth. His warm disposition and admiration for my warrior were as obvious as the bright epaulet Captain Anderson wore on his shoulder.

They were all industrious, contrary to what I had heard about men of their race. Indeed, I was beginning to think few of the deprecating things said of them were true. They were likely no different from any group of people, containing sluggards and savages as well as men who strived for a higher standard.

Would I be able to embrace their people—and would they welcome or reject me? I suspected, earlier, that my warrior deemed his people as superior to mine as my people thought they were to his. Of all the women in Monroe, I was probably the least prepared for manual labor, and from all that I had read or heard, harsh treatment was the usual lot for slaves unaccustomed to hard work.

While a child, my mother had taken me to visit friends on the eastern shore of Maryland. I will never forget the beating their foreman gave a Negro woman who had not kept up in the field. Mother and I both felt ill and found an excuse to cut our visit short. When I asked her how these hospitable friends could allow such conduct towards another person, she had said they believed their dark-skinned slaves were of inferior intelligence. Their language, her friend had told her, consisted mostly of unintelligible grunts, and they could only understand the clearest means of reprimand.

I wondered if my warrior's people would regard me likewise and determined to make every effort to learn both their language and any required skills. I already recognized phrases that designated meals and bedtime and could say their words for knife, sing, wild berries, eat, drink, come, no, rabbit skin or fur, and possibly slave and master.

"Let nothing terrify you,"[35] I repeated to myself, unaware I mumbled it aloud. My warrior must have caught my concerned tone, for he gently turned my face toward him, searching my eyes as he did last night. When he warmly caressed my cheek, I feared his friends might misinterpret his familiarity and dropped my eyes; and when I next looked up, they were taking apart the second saddle. Disappointment drove my eyes back downward. I had assumed he would keep it for my use. I doubted I could ride bareback as they did, but I had formed the question too late. Perhaps he intended me to walk.

Aimlessly perusing the pile of discarded items, I was surprised to see the guns. Had he misidentified their purpose or failed to connect it with his wound? Picking up the nearest rifle, I knelt in front of him, and in the sudden silence, I felt all four pairs of curious eyes. I had grown up around firearms, though I never needed to use one. Without words, I was unsure how to indicate their purpose.

Supposing a demonstration offered the best method, I loaded the barrel with powder and ammunition and stuffed down both with the attached rod. My observers were attentive but obviously perplexed, especially when I rose and took aim at a dead pine.

The sudden blast sent them jumping off their seats, but their cries of alarm quickly changed to deep, unrestrained belly laughter. Swiftly turning their heads to meet the threat, they found my feet flung into the air by the gun's sharp kick and my backside unceremoniously hitting the dirt. I was scarlet with shame, but as my warrior hauled me to my feet, his companions began motioning toward the tree.

"Wagh!" shouted the youngest, staggered by the damage the ball created.

While they jabbered excitedly, the warrior snatched the gun from my hand, examined the trigger mechanism, noted the place I had shown him for the ammunition, and adroitly reloaded. He aimed, bracing himself against the kick, and discharged the weapon.

As birds scattered, he stared with awe at the hole he blasted through the rotting bark and then tossed me a most appreciative grin. The others glanced my way also while clamoring to take their turns, and though none of them offered me the slightest smile, each managed to convey his approval. They spent the rest of the daylight perfecting their aim, choosing increasingly more difficult targets until I reminded my warrior I needed to change his bandage.

Nodding agreement, he tossed them some comment or command and, grasping my arm, guided me to a place well out of their view. His wounds, we found, were scabbing nicely, neither one tearing open from the active afternoon; but as I daubed them with soap, he began openly trying to provoke my discomfort. Employing all his previous tactics, he sought ways to increase our intimacy, and each time he succeeded, an infectious grin parted his handsome face. My earlier resolve to remain unaffected took flight like the birds when they had heard the gun blasts, and my unbridled reciprocation of his smiles served only to intensify his efforts.

When, at length, he allowed me to tie the fresh bandage, he firmly encircled my waist with his hands. Deliberately, tenderly he brushed his smooth cheek against my ear, making my already weak limbs feel as liquid as water; and when he began to whisper impassioned words, every nerve in my body sprang to life. I could tell by his inflection that he was leading to some point, laying out reasons, and seeking a response. His speech sounded persuasive and full of dignity and pride as if he thought he offered me a great honor.

Earnestly I tried to fathom his meaning. It was quite evidently important to him, but when he drew his head away to read my eyes, I am sure he found little but bewilderment. At once, frustration replaced his eagerness, and his mouth set into a hardened line. He put me away from him abruptly and strode off briskly into the dusky woods.

I longed to chase after him, to offer him at least a smile, but how could I set our relationship aright when I did not understand how it had gone wrong? I felt miserable, and more so when I rejoined the others in the clearing. Time passed by agonizingly, and his obvious absence roused questions from them that I had no words to answer.

After waiting a good while, the clawed man set out in the direction my warrior and I walked, and caution replaced acceptance from the younger two. Then, when the clawed warrior returned alone, my inability to understand their language excluded me from all his answers. Had my warrior abandoned me to them? I felt wretched but did not see how I could have reacted any differently.

LATER THAT EVENING, he strode into the clearing but did nothing to ease the tension between us. His face looked fierce, compared with the unguarded warmth to which I had become accustomed, and though his eyes followed me incessantly, they revealed nothing of his thoughts.

I was thankful he wanted to retire earlier than usual, but while I was relieved to avoid a wrong impression on his companions, I felt forsaken as he separated our blankets. He kept one and placed the other an arm's length away, indicating I should fold myself within it. His companions slept on his farther side, but I wondered if I would sleep at all.

Fear battered my thoughts. Although our trip west had held uncertainties, I had known roughly what to expect in terms of customs and living conditions. Little had turned out as anticipated, but how was I to sketch any inward picture of life with a people about whom I knew almost nothing? I felt I had already failed the Lord in the task He set before me, though I could not say precisely how. I had made peace with my diminished station in life, submitted to the warrior's authority, and accepted his transformations; but these gains now seemed lost, and the distance he placed me from him made me certain he would sell me.

Something rustling in the tree overhead sent me edging a little closer to him. It was most likely a raccoon or opossum, but tonight the smallest thing appeared threatening. Making certain first that all of them were fast asleep, I inched as near him as possible without touching.

"Lord, I know You made no promises about my new life, except that You would never forsake me; but if You don't object, please let this man keep me. He is kind and I think he'll keep me safe."

As I listened to my petition, I realized I was not being honest. The relationship I desired was far more intimate than servitude, and, unless I was willing to disgrace my Lord, led to an impassible end. For all I knew, my warrior might already have a wife, and even if he did not, marrying him was still out of the question. The Lord forbade believers to mate with unbelievers;[36] and the ramifications of such a union would be permanent and profound. Every way I tried to work it out ended wrongly; yet, remaining his slave was surely preferable to purchase by a stranger who might beat and torture me.

Once I had voiced the desire, I felt deeply shocked, not only by its indecency but also by my fickle heart. Had not I wished to marry Captain Anderson less than a week ago? He had been a suitable match in every way, yet somehow this intense black-eyed warrior had swept him from my thoughts and thrown my heart so off guard that it had become entangled before I knew it was under siege.

Perhaps these were the feelings Willoughby aroused in Marianne. If so, I had a great deal more sympathy for her now and understood why she had not wanted to settle for a more reasonable alliance. Could not marriage engage both my heart and reason? My father certainly loved my mother passionately. Perhaps the truer form of love came only with time.

"Lord, please set my heart aright. Rid me of all illicit intentions and give me the grace to face whatever You set before me."

It was good that the warrior had withdrawn. I felt like a traitor to everything I embraced dearly, but in His kindness, my Friend and Redeemer brought to my memory several cherished verses from several Psalms.

Like a father pitieth his children,
So the Lord pitieth them that fear him.
For He knoweth our frame.
He remembered that we are dust.[37]
When I said, "My foot slippeth;
Thy mercy, O Lord, held me up.
In the multitude of my thoughts within me,
Thy comforts delight my soul.[38]
O, give thanks to the Lord, for He is good;
For His mercy endureth forever![39]

Were I to rely on my own righteousness to save me, I would be utterly destroyed.

Turn thee unto me, and have mercy on me, for I am desolate and afflicted. The troubles of my heart have enlarged; bring me out of my distresses!

Psalm 25:16-17

Chapter 7

JUST BEFORE SUNRISE, I awoke to find my warrior contemplatively watching me. He caressed my cheek to answer my timid smile, and I hoped the uneasiness between us was over. His reserve returned, however, as the first hint of sun crept stealthily into the morning sky, and he engaged in none of his former games while I changed his bandages.

Once he packed our limited belongings, including the two guns and saddlebags, he stowed the remainder within the grove of cedars as if he thought they might be useful later. The other three warriors tied the string of horses to the youth's pony without indicating which I should ride. While waiting for instructions, I watched the warrior circle around me once on the dapple-gray and then disappear into the woods. The others quickly mounted and followed. Was I to run behind them, or was he abandoning me? Perhaps the Lord had decided I was not fit for the assignment.

How irritatingly changeable I found my emotions! Only one week ago, the warrior's departure would have brought me great relief. Now I felt so desolate, my face began to crumple and tears began stinging my eyes. Before they spilled over, however, the dapple-gray trotted back into the clearing, and his rider leaned over and pulled me up firmly against his chest.

As we wound around the cliff under which we had camped, he wheeled his horse to overlook the fall, but I could make out only its uppermost regions. Mist, wafting in and out of the trees, cast enchantment through the barely dawning light, preventing a glimpse of the cedar grove and any hint that a river valley stretched from there southeast. Monroe surely lay there somewhere in the distance, causing me to wonder if he had noticed it on an earlier, clearer day and was allowing me to say goodbye.

Bringing his heels down into the mare's sides, he urged her to the head of the line of horses that were following a tributary north. We rode in silence, keeping near the river until the mist cleared, and even then, we did not stray too far. Sometimes he chose a way nearer and sometimes farther, but he always kept it within sight.

As we crested a high ridge, we spied a small herd of deer below us, which had come to drink while the sun was still yawning. Pulling the mare to a halt, he gently pressed me down over her neck, holding his splayed hand on my back long enough to convey that I should stay still. An arrow, drawn silently from his quiver, whizzed past my ear on its rapid flight and was joined by several belonging to his companions. Each felled a deer from the rear of the herd, keeping it from scattering before they achieved their object. I was sad to see such gentle and graceful animals, their lovely black eyes still open, meet such a violent end, but it happened so swiftly they could not have felt much pain. Afterward, he gently tugged me upright, urging the mare forward to the place they lay, and his companions hoisted them atop the horses in tow.

For many hours, we traveled higher into mountains above breath-taking valleys the river had cut through the woodlands. They looked so untouched, I wondered fleetingly if we were the first to lay a foot there but dismissed the idea, as the warrior seemed well acquainted with the way. Amazed by the beauty around every new turn, I began to understand why some men left all things familiar to go wherever the next hill led. This demonstration of God's unspoiled creation was more splendid than anything I had ever conceived, leading me to wonder what heaven was like. Unsullied by sin, it was surely more splendid, though I simply could not imagine how.

The contrast between my bleak prospects and God's magnificent handiwork coaxed my memory back to the horror I felt before the warrior woke. I expected torture but received companionship. Each day I encountered new, exhilarating experiences and discovered much about myself—both painful and pleasant—of which I was formerly ignorant. I had crystallized my concept of what truly mattered and had come to a vastly greater understanding of God's love and faithfulness. Far from forsaking me, He had blessed me at every turn, supplying me the courage to face each day.

Why was I so slow of learning, so hesitant to greet what lay ahead with cheerful anticipation? I had already witnessed His power to save and even had an inkling of His unfolding plan. Indeed, I had good reason to believe He was directing my way. Instead of dreading life among the warrior's people, why should I not look forward to the adventure—knowing that the same Jesus, who had given me such grace over the last week, went ahead of me? Remembering He once called the disciples, "O ye of little faith,"[40] I prayed He would increase mine. I had no other source from which to gain it. If I drew comfort, though, from this warrior's presence and hope from his kindness, how much more could I rest secure in the eternal God who promised me His care and protection? My earthly master might sell me tomorrow, but my Heavenly Lord had already amply proven His love. He not only died to redeem my life but also prepared a place for me to dwell unfettered in His presence forever. Upon Him, all things hinge.

My heart bubbled with several Scriptures that underscored what I had just been thinking, and I inwardly recited each in succession. "Neither death nor life, nor angels, nor principalities, nor powers, nor things present, nor things to come, nor height, nor depth, nor any other created thing shall be able to separate us from the love of God which is in Christ Jesus our Lord."[41] "Since God is for me, who can be against me," and "What can man do to me?"[42]

The Holy Spirit's timing was impeccable, as always. He led me to this sustaining joy just minutes before the warrior halted, whispered something in my ear, and pointed to a sheer cliff sticking out from a mountain in the distance. I gathered this was our destination.

We had been traveling at a steady pace without stopping until the sun was full in the sky, slightly past its midpoint—somewhere, I guessed, about two o'clock. Captain Anderson had been right after all, at least about the distance between Monroe and this warrior's tribe. If he did mount a search for me, I doubted he could find me this far away.

After dropping me to my feet and alighting himself, my warrior surprised me by drawing out his knife. His wounds would not need to be dressed for several hours, but I did as he signaled, cutting through the unsoiled bandage. He stood immobile, stiffly leaning forward only enough to improve my reach; but when I was about to turn my back to retrieve more hem, he firmly clasped my shoulder and shook his head. I understood and did not argue, especially as his assessment was quite correct, but I would miss the daily closeness.

ROUNDING THE TOP OF the promontory, an awesome sight unfolded. A huge mass of tall asymmetrical cones, all leaning slightly in one direction, stood in concentric circles. They were vibrantly colored, painted with varying designs, and wholly unlike anything in appearance or quantity I had anticipated. Miss Whitney and I had read of longhouses and small clusters of thatched huts. These tall tents, which I later learned were simply called dwellings, numbered in the hundreds.

Someone must have seen and announced our arrival, for people came eagerly to greet us before we reached the village edge. A middle-aged woman with striking bone structure and regal bearing caught my attention. She greeted our party with warmth and my warrior with relief, which grew to concern when she noticed his scab. It had not occurred to me that someone might be worried about the long time he took to come home. Surely, she was his mother.

All around was noise and excitement, for his return held obvious significance for many. Once he set me down, a group of small black-eyed children—mostly naked—engulfed me. They shyly touched my dress, braids, and skin, as fascinated with our differences as I was, and several whispered to each other while gaping at my face. More than anything I had experienced thus far, their open incredulity and intrusively exploring fingers made clear I was entering a foreign land. They were unlike any children of my acquaintance.

Looking up from the tops of their dark heads, I saw the regal woman glance inquiringly in my direction. I dropped my eyes instinctively, but the warrior called his sounds for me and motioned for me to come to him. I disentangled myself as quickly as possible, but when I reached the place he had been standing with the woman, they were gone. Looking around, I spotted him striding purposefully toward the middle of the encampment and hastily trotted to catch up.

Passing women stared at my long black dress, and their own calf-length doeskins jolted my sense of propriety. It was hardly surprising they would expose their ankles, though; their men were mostly unclothed above the waist and many wore only breechcloths. I smiled timidly, hoping to conceal my fear, and prayed that God would help my legs to hold. According to Miss Whitney, these same women would soon form two lines and beat me so frenziedly as I ran between them, I was likely to collapse. The ordeal reputedly killed many, maimed more, and left few unscathed.

Halting before a large tent near the center of the grouping, the warrior called something to its occupants inside. I assumed the answering call was an invitation to enter, for he grasped my wrist, pulling me in behind him after the older woman. Just before lowering the entry flap, he issued an order to the youth in our party and then took a seat.

The structure, about twenty-five or thirty feet in diameter, was constructed of very tall poles encircled with hides that had been sewn together. It took a moment for my eyes to adjust, for the late afternoon sun, filtering through a hole near the top where they had fastened the poles, offered the only light.

Most of the occupants were men, many middle-aged or older. They all greeted my captor with warmth and enthusiasm, and a man who seemed to be in charge invited him to sit to his left, which I later learned was a place of honor. I remained standing where he left me, unsure what would happen until the regal older woman beckoned me to kneel with her a little ways back from the men.

The youth called at the entryway, and, upon hearing the man in charge reply, another young captive ducked inside. At least, I assumed she was a captive. Her hair was more coppery than Captain Anderson's. Her dress, however, was much like the one worn by the regal woman, and the sun had deepened her abundantly freckled skin to a soft shade of brown. She looked about my age, though her petite frame and bone structure might have lent an appearance younger than her actual years, and she seemed, as she came to kneel beside me, almost as unaccustomed to this company as I was. First reticently glancing from our host to another older warrior, she looked astonished when her eyes came to rest on my face. Her mouth readily curved into a shy but warm smile, and I liked her instantly.

When my warrior uttered the sounds that he used to identify me, I looked up and found the men were all staring in my direction. He motioned me forward, gesturing that I should stand before the group, apparently on display.

My stomach began churning. Surely he would not begin bargaining over me already, but if he did, the presence of the red-haired girl made sudden sense: they intended to auction us both.

The men were unmistakably appraising, particularly the middle-aged host, who directed the majority of the discourse. At the invitation of my warrior, he lifted my braids and seemed to assess their weight, and then nodded in response to the younger man's assertion. Afterward, he rubbed the fabric of my gown between his thumb and forefinger, frowning while he raised it slightly to peer at my feet or shoes.

I dropped my eyes lest they show my profound disappointment. All along, I had been aware that my warrior might sell me but had not expected anything like this so soon.

Confirming my suspicions, the host called the red-haired girl forward, but instead of assessing her as he had me; he began speaking to her in his tongue. She quite obviously understood him but began to stammer uncomfortably when she turned toward me. Employing more gestures than words, she managed to convey that I should keep my chin up and raise my eyes from the floor.

Doing so, I found a scrutinizing but humane face that suggested he was pleased with what he saw. His exceedingly familiar looks and manner nagged at some part of my brain, though we could not have met before. As he uttered the sounds my captor always used to call me, holding my gaze while nodding with the others, the girl answered one of my unspoken questions.

"You," she motioned toward my chest and then my eyes, "Eyes…"

The next part was more difficult to grasp, but as she pantomimed waves and held out her arms to form in a wide circle, I began to guess what she might mean.

"Lake?"

She shook her head, frowning as she searched her memory for the correct English word. Apparently, she could not find it, but she cupped her hand and lifted it to her mouth as if she were drinking.

"Water?"

Her face brightened as she nodded emphatically.

"My eyes are like water?"

"Yes," she answered. "Eyes-Like-Water."

I wondered again if this was a name or if she merely recounted my warrior's description. At least the familiar sounds did not mean slave or simply woman. Waiting until we fell silent, our host dismissed us to our places where the girl, as best she could, began translating the continuing conversation. Little of it made sense.

My warrior spoke at length, showing them the guns, his scabbed wounds, and the ruined breastplate—by which they were suitably impressed. After listening with avid curiosity, they began nodding affirmatively and making sounds I took for sanction of his choices. Toward the end of his tale, they threw approving glances in my direction, leading me to conclude, coupled with his actions, that he was describing my part in his recovery.

I breathed a little easier. No bidding had begun, and as I watched them come to a consensus about something, I began to hope I had mistaken their aim.

"Old men talk," the girl confided. "Horses and Eyes-Like-Water—his." She pointed to my warrior. It was what I expected, but stated aloud it sounded demeaning.

My warrior became pensive for a few moments, deliberating over what he was about to say while the others patiently waited. When he spoke, they nodded heartily, donning pleased expressions that underscored their agreement.

The girl smiled, looking genuinely happy as she explained, "Preying Eagle," I recognized the syllables as the ones my warrior had called himself, "make Eyes-Like-Water…"

Here her English broke down again. First clasping her hands close to her chest, she then offered their invisible contents to me.

"Gift?" I asked, and she again brightened.

"Preying Eagle make Eyes-Like-Water gift—to Running Deer."

When she said the last, clearly indicating our host, I felt as if the floor had given way. My warrior continued speaking, perhaps explaining his reasons, for the men punctuated his statements with more nods and smiles. Sensing my dismay, the girl fell silent, for which I was thankful. I was struggling too hard to control my emotions to pay her any heed.

Reminding myself that the warrior, not the Lord, had forsaken me, I listened while they decided my fate. The elegant woman looked pleased, congratulating me for my good fortune with abundant smiles and nods. Perhaps she considered the gift evidence of my value or simply thought it an honor to be given to such a great man. My new master appeared to be highly respected among them.

In concert, both my former and new masters turned to look at me. They held their faces so conspiratorially close and wore such similar expressions that a sudden realization broke through my dull senses: our host was my warrior's father or uncle. Their features, though obscured by differing ages and weights, were too alike for any other explanation.

While the elder asked the regal woman a question and gained her answer, the girl resumed her taxing attempts to translate. The words for which she searched appeared beyond her memory's reach, but as I strained to piece them together with her gestures, the conversation took a turn both surreal and repugnant.

"Two Doves," the girl indicated our companion, "she woman of Running Deer." She then angled her chin toward our host.

I suspected as much. As she imitated a woman nursing an infant, I guessed, "Baby?"

Again, the girl nodded. "Two Doves," she held up four fingers, "baby— all boy," and then she pointed to Preying Eagle.

"Two Doves has four children," I offered, "and all of them are sons?"

The girl beamed. "She want girl-baby. Preying Eagle give Eyes-Like-Water to Running Deer. Make girl-baby."

The color must have drained from my face, for I felt quite faint. She proposed my worst fear—something I had known was a possibility but assumed the Lord would not allow.

Lord, I prayed inwardly, *please say this isn't so!* I tried to choke down the panic I felt to keep my new master from seeing my horror. *Did Hagar feel this way when Sarah gave her to Abraham?* I knew my warrior had been angry last evening, but this was a cruel way to punish me. It was too horrible to bear!

Lifting my eyes, I saw they all expected something—as if the warrior had granted me a privilege for which I must express great thanks. The girl, apparently assuming I had not caught her meaning, tried several other avenues to convey it until relief broke across her face.

"Daw-tar!" she pronounced haltingly, at last able to recall the correct word. "Eyes-Like-Water daughter…daughter for Running Deer and Two Doves."

As a grain of hope tentatively pierced my horror, I asked, "Am I to be a daughter to this man and woman or bear a daughter to him?"

Her eyes grew wide and she adamantly shook her head, but I could not tell which proposition so obviously appalled her. Seeing my unease still lingered, her head stopped shaking and began nodding. "Yes, daughter. He father, she mother, he brother. You daughter; you sister."

Enormous relief flooded my heart, and though I felt overwhelmingly shy under so much scrutiny, I smiled happily at my warrior and his parents. Within minutes, I had moved from expecting my worst fear to a role far better than anything I had imagined. How like God to outdo my greatest hopes!

Our host told the girl his expectations of me, which she translated with grave simplicity; and though she grew quite visibly fatigued, every remembered word seemed to unlock another. I was to obey him, his wife, and their four sons without question, work hard for his people, and avoid bringing any of them shame. All this I was glad to do. I had already resolved to do so as a slave, only now I was elevated to adoption.

When he asked if I understood his requirements and would comply with them, I nodded in assent and asked her to thank him for his kindness and for that of his generous son. The entire room full of people seemed pleased that I was sensible of so great an honor and thought it fitting that I was grateful to its giver.

"Old men say," the girl interpreted when they resumed their discussion, "white men no good. Good warrior make dead. Good he take woman."

Running Deer turned to question Preying Eagle, whose brief answers appeared to be what his father expected. He met them with reserve, however, as did most of the others present. What either man said, I could not tell. The elder man told the girl not to translate, but the many eyes that turned my way were full of speculation. A few had nodded when Preying Eagle spoke, as if what he said seemed reasonable and good, but others looked unsure, perhaps even wary. All approved his father's response— except Preying Eagle. Thunderclouds, as fierce as the ones I had seen yesterday, began brewing in his eyes.

"White family—where?" the girl haltingly asked for Running Deer.

"They are all dead," I replied. "My father died last week."

"He give you to man?"

I had hoped to avoid such a discussion—it had too many twists and turns—but I endeavored to answer simply and succinctly. "Yes, to his stepbrother, but he only wanted my father's wealth. He ordered another man to kill me."

This took much and strenuous discussion back and forth, as did all our discourse until frequent interpreting stirred more of her memory. Only considerably later did I discover how she translated any of my replies, and for that I am grateful. Had I understood her better, I might have doubted she was sane.

"Her father's false brother was a trickster who wanted to steal her father's herd," she explained to them. "He ordered a coyote to drop her in a ravine so her head would burst open."

"Did he give your father horses?" she translated next.

I could not fathom why he asked this and thought at first that the girl misspoke, but she insisted she did not. "No," I answered, using their word, and many of the men looked inexplicably relieved.

"Where is this warrior?" Running Deer continued.

"In the valley below the waterfall."

They discussed my answer for a few minutes, and Preying Eagle filled in details about the location.

"Men say," the girl continued, "where is killing man?"

"Dead," I told her. "Preying Eagle shot him."

"Not say name," she whispered sharply. "He here. Say brother."

I did not understand why this mattered, but whatever she rendered caused a commotion and another lengthy discussion, followed by questions about Monroe, its location, and its inhabitants. I related the Captain's estimate of the distance and tried my best to assure them the settlers had no interest in the hills or the mountains, only in protecting themselves. The last thing I wanted was to incite an attack. The people of Monroe would not stand a chance.

"Your brother," she nodded toward Preying Eagle as she touched my pocket, "asks, 'What...?'" Pulling it open, she looked in.

I pulled out my Bible, delighted the Lord had opened a way for me to speak of Him so soon, and told them it was the Word of God. My joy was tempered, however, when this caused a great uproar, threatening my already fragile standing. I did not see what else I could have answered; it was the truth and the very reason, I was certain, the Lord had brought me to the place. Instantly, a look of comprehension dawned across Preying Eagle's face, and he animatedly related the incident at the river.

The oldest warrior, whom they simply called Old Man, spoke. "When I was a boy, a grandfather told me the Creator gave our brown-skinned people a book and the white man a bow and arrow. The white man stole the book and left the bow and arrow for us. We have lived this way to this day. Perhaps this daughter has come to return it. Is this His book?"

The red-haired girl and I talked at length before she told him, "She did not hear about the bow and arrow, but this book was given to a brown-skinned people who lived toward the rising sun. They followed it and became great warriors. Their people were few, but the Creator handed them victory over their enemies."

"How do you know this?" Old Man questioned. "You have lived few summers. Have you seen these things?"

"The Creator tells of it in here." Again, I held up my Bible.

"Go on," he replied.

"People killed the men who spoke the Creator's words." They looked astonished and dismayed to hear this. "The Creator sent man after man to turn their hearts to Him. They killed them all, so He sent them His son, thinking they would listen to Him. They killed the Son, too, but death could not keep Him because He had no sin. One day, He will return for those who love Him."

Another man, whom the girl called her father, chimed in excitedly, "We have heard the Creator would return. Is this Him, or some white man's god?"

"There is only one true Creator," I answered, "and He has given the book for all who will listen, brown or white."

This seemed to ring true to them for they nodded in agreement.

"All you have said, my heart says is so," replied Running Deer, my warrior's father, turning to address the others present. "I would like to hear more of this book. Perhaps the Creator kept the white men from shaming this woman so she could restore it to us.

"I am happy to give her a place in my woman's dwelling. You have heard her promise to work hard for our people and not bring shame upon the heads of her family. I ask you to be patient and look the other way if she offends out of ignorance. No one is to hurt or molest her. Her heart is large with gratitude, but she may find our ways strange and unpleasant. What does she know of us, except that my son kept her from shame and death? She does not know the emptiness of stomach when the hunt is not good or heartache when a brother dies in battle.

"Until the Moon of Yellow and Falling Leaves, she will live as we live—only then can she know where her heart rests. When she forgets the trickster and his coyotes and she sees only dark eyes all around her, she may long for people of light skin and eyes like water. At that time, she may choose to become one of the people. If not, my son will return her to her own people as he took her away from them. Now you may go," he told me. "You have much work to learn."

Two Doves, my warrior's regal mother, immediately ducked out of the tent's opening and the red-haired girl gripped my wrist to pull me through it also. Within moments, however, we heard soft footfalls trotting after us and turned to find her son. He exchanged meaningful glances with his mother, who nodded briefly and continued without us, and then guided both the girl and me to a secluded space between several of their cone-shaped dwellings.

"Say to this woman," he commanded her, "my blanket wants you."

Although deeply appreciative of his recent benevolence, I felt ill at ease hearing such odd, tenderly intoned words expressed through a stranger and could not sustain his gaze. He grasped my chin firmly, insisting I look into his eyes, and I discovered there the same earnest expectations they had held last night. My determination to be unaffected by him evaporated just as swiftly as it had then, making me grateful for our interpreter's sobering presence.

"Your generosity overwhelms me," I murmured.

The red-haired girl cocked her head, so I simply asked her to thank him; and once she did, he narrowed the gap between us until our bodies nearly touched. Affectionately caressing my cheek, he smiled so warmly that my breath caught in my throat, and the intimacy in his touch made me question exactly what the girl had said. Before I could ask, however, his mother beckoned us sharply and he strode away, leaving my heart a torrent of emotions.

The Lord maketh poor and maketh rich; He bringeth low and lifteth up. He raiseth up the poor from the dust and lifteth the beggar from the ash heap.

I Samuel 2:7-8

Chapter 8

"PREYING EAGLE—he own many horses," my translator shyly smiled. "Old men make him good talk. He…"

Stray red wisps, gloriously illumined by the afternoon sun, escaped her braids and encircled her head like the halo of a Renaissance angel. I returned her smile, patiently waiting for her to finish; but she shrugged instead, unable to give words to her thoughts. Clearly, the exchange she had just witnessed had put her in sympathy to my feelings, but I wondered why she, like my warrior's father, so pointedly mentioned horses.

"What did you say to him?" I asked.

Her freckled cheeks turned a warm shade of pink. "You want…" She stuck up a finger on one hand and wrapped the other hand around it.

"In? Inside?"

She nodded happily. "You want in his blanket."

My face burned. I supposed she thought this a proper response to Preying Eagle's parting sentiment, but her translation was exasperatingly off the mark. Not only had she said nothing of my gratitude—including me in his family was far more significant than keeping me warm—but she also left me vulnerable to a horrid misinterpretation. Indeed, I knew well the base meaning Uncle Henry would have given her words! Suspecting, however, that I would make little headway trying to correct the misimpression or might even make it worse, I let it drop.

"What is your name?" I asked, hoping I had freed my voice of irritation.

She spoke some syllables, which I repeated with less trouble than I had while first pronouncing Preying Eagle's name. However, while she was still struggling to call up the correct English words to translate it, we became engulfed by a group of women asking Two Doves, his mother, what had taken place in the large tent.

Many of the women gawked at my clothing, my face, and hair, but they seemed disposed to be kind—all but one. This woman stared severely, her mouth drawn down by harsh suspicion, and muttered something the girl did not interpret. Two Dove's reply was unmistakably curt, giving me the impression it had not been flattering.

As the small crowd began dispersing, Two Doves asked my red-haired companion to show me where I might gather sticks for her fire in case the night became cold. The sun was beginning to sink, lengthening the triangular shadows cast by their dwellings, and my new friend pointed to one along the way. "This."

"Shadow?"

She smiled again and nodded, "I...and Shadows." She placed her pointer fingers side by side, indicating the second word came after a word she could not express. Ironically, this part of her name perfectly suited her current occupation—or rather, it suited mine, as I was to follow her everywhere.

We picked up light twigs that had fallen onto the nearby forest floor. It was neither difficult nor unpleasant work, and the setting was almost as agreeable as the waterfall had been. The village was surrounded on three sides by tree-covered slopes and the fourth by the precipice my warrior had earlier shown me.

After we had bundled sufficient sticks and thrown them over our backs, we climbed to its top. Sentinels manned their posts, explaining the advance notice of our arrival; but though they regarded me with open curiosity, they said nothing.

The views were spectacular and vast in all directions, and from this height, we were able to watch all of the activity in the village. When the girl spotted Preying Eagle carrying something toward his mother's dwelling, she suggested we descend; but by the time we delivered the firewood there, he was gone.

Taking a path through the trees, we came upon a lake so placid that I could scarcely believe its water was the same that flowed down into Henry's valley. We, alone, disturbed the golden-pink sun reflected in its mirror-like surface by dipping in our families' water skins. These, once filled, were surprisingly heavy. My arms so shook from the effort to carry them that I could barely breathe, much less talk. This suited me well. Although I was delighted I had someone with whom I could speak English, I felt exhausted by the strain of deciphering her meanings. Within minutes, I grew lost in thought, rehashing the scant elements I had grasped of Running Deer's pronouncement. They had shown him to be farsighted as well as magnanimous: accepting responsibility for my welfare and yet essentially setting me free—though I would not be at liberty to leave for several months.

I felt horribly conspicuous while walking through the village, and my back began to ache as much as my arms. At home and in Monroe, my duties consisted of managing the household staff, engaging in social correspondence, and mastering needlework. Although I had been here only a few hours, I was already performing tasks Grandmother would have assigned to male servants. Perhaps God placed that specific time in Running Deer's heart, knowing I could not stand living here for longer. The leaves usually turned yellow during October in Skippack and had fallen by November's end.

I still planned to go to Allison and John, providing Captain Anderson had not yet left the outpost and would lend me the fare to Virginia. How would he react when I showed up there in a few months? Very likely, he would discontinue his suit. Most gentlemen would consider my reputation irreparably damaged by the days Preying Eagle and I had spent alone.

"My love, you are borrowing trouble," declared my father's memory, and he was right. I was fretting over events several months away and missing the essential point. God had not created me to gratify myself, but to fulfill His purpose, and this was my desire, too.

"Lord, do as You wish with my life, whether here or at home, and thank You for giving me an opportunity to speak to them of You. Please make me sensitive to Your voice so I will know what to do and say."

In answer, the Holy Spirit gently nudged my heart, reminding me that He had told me this already. The same principle applied while serving a master, a husband, or a parent. I needed to work hard for Running Deer's family, doing more than asked, without complaint, and leave decisions about my future for the time they would be required.

As I followed the shadow girl into Two Doves' dwelling, I was surprised to find the clawed warrior and his two younger friends talking with Running Deer. Watching their warm interaction, I suspected they were also his sons and, therefore, Preying Eagle's brothers. My translator confirmed this, conveying to me as much as she was able about each.

The youngest, Elk Dog Boy, guarded the family's horses. His quiet brother, Little Turtle, a hunter of eighteen summers, preferred spending time alone. Two Bears, who wore the bear-claw necklaces, was a warrior, a class distinct from hunters, admired for his bravery and sought after for his amiable nature. She also added that he caught even more smiles than Preying Eagle did, but Two Doves called me away before I could ask her to elaborate. Each treated me with consideration and respect, but I developed a special affinity for Elk Dog Boy, whose infectious warmth put me at ease.

After sharing a simple meal of wild turnips, berries, and freshly roasted venison, my interpreter led me to an open area in the center of the dwellings where we knelt with other women in the outer of two circles. Several warriors took turns in the center, regaling the group with stories of courage. Some were of their own and some were of others; some were recent and some from the distant past. This was a favorite pastime and an integral part of their lives, as they had no written history, and it soon became a favorite part of mine.

Although the shadow girl interpreted for me, I understood only when her words and the speaker's gesture combined to make them clear. My warrior spoke at great length, apparently going into more explicit details than he had in the council about our week away, and though I felt awkward as the object of so many eyes, previous experience assured me of a pleasant outcome.

Afterward, we returned to Two Doves' dwelling, where she guided me to a bed made of willow branches. One of Henry's saddlebags sat on it, filled with the cups, soap, comb, and my other dress, and underneath that lay the better of the two blankets I had shared with her son.

I held the latter to my chest, hoping to catch something of him lingering there while pondering his strange words between the tents. Tenderly, I ran my hands over its folds and reddened when I chanced to glance up. His mother had been watching, and I wondered if she had discerned the trend of my thoughts. She offered me a lovely smile, warm and gentle, which I naturally reciprocated, surprised she was so willing to accept a foreign woman into her home.

Gazing at the small ring of embers in the center of the lodge, I gave thanks to God, who had lifted me out of the miry clay and set my feet on a rock, and soon drifted into a sound and happy sleep.

AS THE SUN CREPT out of its bed, the shadow girl crept over to my pallet and shook me awake. I was loath to get up, but the morning felt delightfully crisp, more like early fall than the last full month of summer. Two Doves was already cooking breakfast outside, chatting pleasantly with a small and vivacious, bright-eyed woman.

"This is mother," my companion addressed me. "She is wife …to father, old brother of Running Deer." Her face lit up when she found the right words. "She is called…" She launched her fingers from her lips, as Preying Eagle had to indicate singing, but she pretended a lively guffaw.

"Laughing?"

She shook her head, looking a bit disappointed with herself, uttered some sounds, and then only afterward began to laugh.

"Joking?" I asked. "Her name is Joking?"

The red braids bounced merrily. "Yes—Joking. She is Joking Woman—mother."

I had already met Wooden Legs, her father. He was one of the members of the council who questioned me about the Bible. While we walked toward the lake with our empty water sacks, I asked for how long and for what reason she had come to live with this people. The former she could answer readily: ten summers. Our lack of language rendered the latter was obscure.

"Were you afraid?" I asked, imagining how I might have felt.

"Yes," she nodded, "but..." She shrugged, finding her feelings hard to convey. "Old White-Hair—he gone."

I did not know what to make of her answer, but as the passing weeks incrementally improved her English, she filled in the few details she could. She vividly remembered her family and even dreamed of them in English— redheads every one, though her mother's eyes were like mine rather than amber like her own.

At some point in her childhood, a man with long white braids and a wrinkled brown face had found her wandering dazedly through the woods. He shared his food and water, offering her toothless grins, and then lifted her onto his small bay mount and headed off, she assumed, to take her home. They traveled far, though she could not say if it were one or many days. She kept fading out of consciousness. When she woke, cradled against a smooth, firm chest, she looked up into eyes that were black, not amber.

The old man was Joking Woman's grandfather. Although he lived with a different band, he had heard a raiding enemy had killed her young daughter; so in keeping with their custom, he brought her the wandering girl as a replacement. When my new friend cried for her parents or asked to be taken home, she received unintelligible answers, plentiful smiles, caresses, and tender care. Eventually, she grew to love the black-eyed couple and their teasing sons; and by the time she mastered their language, no one remained who could answer her questions. The old man had died shortly after returning to his home.

Wanting an idea of what to expect, I asked if she liked living here. She replied that she did, but her tone was unconvincing. When I pressed her a bit, she confessed everything had changed the year she entered womanhood. Warriors traditionally began assessing a young woman's potential as a wife during this time, but not one had even hinted that he wanted her.

"Many men die. Many women to pick. No man ask for me. No man want this." She touched a red braid and her freckled cheek. "Summer come; summer go. I make no man-child to hunt food when I old. How I eat? How I get skins, make dress? Where I sleep?"

Her story broke my heart. In addition to an enchanting face full of dimples, she had a sunny and practical disposition that any man should deem an asset.

"You are lovely," I replied. "The Creator made your red hair and freckles, and He can bring you a husband who will love them."

"You think He bring?"

"Yes, He..." A little boy running past us nearly knocked the empty water skins out of my hand and hid behind a tree.

"Look!" she cried. "My name."

I knew her name was not boy. "Hide?"

"Yes," she nodded eagerly. "Hides-in-Shadows."

"Why did your parents call you this?"

"When I woman-child, all call Hair-Like-Fire, but I much...hide in shadows. Not like men women look at me. Brothers laugh," she shrugged. "Call Hides-in-Shadows."

DURING THE NEXT few days in the village, preparing my brothers' prey became the most loathsome of my responsibilities. Hunting provided the tribe's primary source of nourishment, and butchering fell to women. Before I had to do it myself, I never considered whether our servants found the task unpleasant, but doing so now exposed a well-hidden arrogance. I had eagerly eaten the meals Two Doves prepared—I was hungry from a week with little food and the sharp increase of manual labor—but I felt revolted by the thought of bloodying my lady-like hands.

As I slit a doe's throat under Two Doves' tutelage, the stench of my heart repulsed me more than the carcass's foul odor, but this time pride could not keep me from rushing into the brush. I was glad Preying Eagle was nowhere about to see my disgrace. I had seen neither him nor his brothers in days.

When I returned, his mother graciously made no mention of my weakness but persisted in teaching me the quickest, least objectionable methods of skinning the creature, guiding me to clean the hide according to its intended use. Preying Eagle, she told me, had kept the rabbits' fur intact so she could sew me a pair of tall moccasins with the fur turned inward. She would use the doeskins for clothing, so she taught me how to scrape off the hair before I pegged them in the sun to dry. The work was hard, but I strived to do it well, mindful of the purpose for which God called me: to adorn the Gospel through faithful service.

By the time the sun showed signs of setting, Hides-in-Shadows once more escorted me to the lake so we could replenish our families' wood and water. As we rounded a clump of apple trees, a tall splendidly dressed warrior barred our path. He had an air of superiority that brought to mind several sought-after men I had met at balls in Philadelphia, and I wondered for whom he was waiting. As I returned his friendly smile, Hides-in-Shadows yanked me away.

"You not make," she admonished. "He speak uncle—get you for woman."

Her English had been rapidly improving as if she only needed conversation to stimulate her mind. Although she often left out words or substituted incorrect ones, such as small for few, she delighted in expressing her thoughts. This time, however, she had surely chosen the wrong words or I had misunderstood them.

"I am not certain what you are saying. I only smiled, assuming he was your acquaintance."

"He think you want his blanket."

"I cannot work out what you mean at all."

"You see. Sun goes to sleep—Kicking Horse stand by Two Doves' dwelling. Make his blanket…"

When she cupped her hands together, I guessed she meant, "Around? Why?"

"He want you make blanket warm in night."

I felt quite taken aback. "Would Running Deer make me do this?"

"You smile—ask warrior make blanket around you," she replied.

Her manner was somewhat scolding, somewhat teasing, leading me to think she might not be entirely serious, but I resolved to avoid this man regardless. Scouring my memory, I sought other instances in which I might have smiled at a man but found only my adopted brothers. Surely, they were safe, but it might explain why they were markedly freer with me in their mother's lodge than they had been by the falls.

"Had you not told me, I would have given many wrong impressions. I am grateful for your help. What should I do?"

"Make no smiles and wait."

Straining under the weight of my filled skins, my feet trod the path to the village but my mind strayed back to the waterfall. If a warrior's smiles indicated their interest, had Preying Eagle invited me to accept his suit? I had reciprocated plentifully, even initiating many exchanges. Perhaps this explained his odd parting sentiments and warm response to the girl's translation of my thanks.

As I considered his impassioned speech by the falls, my sacks began to feel lighter. Perhaps he, not that warrior, Kicking Horse, might come to his mother's dwelling this evening. I sorely missed him.

"Stop!" I chided myself aloud. "You mustn't let your heart run away like this!" What had Hides-in-Shadows said that warrior wanted me to do—warm his blanket? He might intend something illicit, something I would never engage in, even with Preying Eagle; or perhaps he referred to a courtship ritual I would equally need to reject. Whatever he meant, it could lead to no good end. Any intimate connection with one of their warriors was out of the question.

My spirits plummeted as quickly as they had risen, and I was again glad my companion toted her skins at a quicker pace than I did. Being sensitive by nature, she might perceive my dejection or ask why I had become so quiet—how could I explain such conflicting feelings?

Setting our water in place, I carefully combed and plaited my hair before stitching a rip in Elk Dog Boy's doeskin pouch. His mother highly prized sewing skills, and Aunt Louise had made me practice with such diligence I could make a quick, neat stitch with my eyes closed. Discovering my skill this afternoon, she quickly gathered up the family mending and promised that she would teach me how to weave their intricate chokers and breastplates.

When coral tinged the clouds above our smoke-hole, I could stifle neither the excitement nor apprehension I felt each time I heard a male voice approaching. As coral changed to purple, disappointment overtook relief; and as purple turned to darkest blue, weariness completely vanquished both. I only half-woke when Two Doves gently removed the mending from my fingers, my shoes from my feet, and lowered my shoulders onto my bed.

MY LIFE SOON settled into a steady rhythm spent mostly in the company of women who lived in adjacent dwellings. Although they did not know the Scriptures, they practiced the admonition "look not only to one's own interests but also to the interests of others" more purely than I had ever seen it practiced, sharing each other's chores as if they were members of one large family. All the while, they chatted about many things, few of which I understood, but I caught a word here and there and occasionally an entire phrase. Each of them was friendly and helpful, except the suspicious woman I had met on my first day and her beautiful daughter, Swallow Woman. Both watched me disapprovingly, but as they bore no relation to Running Deer, their lodge was not close enough to ours to share often in each other's labors.

"Pay her no mind," Hides-in-Shadows advised me when she noticed Swallow Woman's malicious looks. "She wants Preying Eagle."

My stomach dropped. "Does he want her?"

"She owns much skill and pleasing to the eye. Most think he will ask for her."

Though I have lived in his village over twice the days we spent by the falls, he had not once waited for me with his blanket. Perhaps he spent his evenings with her. Memories of his smiles, his attentions, and his words between the dwellings assaulted my heart, but I had clearly misinterpreted them. It was just as well. His absence lessened my struggle, and my longing would surely eventually fade.

Swallow Woman was remarkably pretty, and it was fitting that a woman of his own kind should gain his affections. I only hoped their union would not take place until he returned me to the outpost, as seeing them together would bring me agony. Asking God to rid me of all unseemly feelings, I resolved to repay evil with good by finding ways to be of service to her.[43]

Two Doves also watched me intermittently and, to my satisfaction, seemed very pleased with my efforts. I wanted to bless her and her husband for so readily opening their home to me and prayed earnestly for God to make me worthy of their trust.

Each night, I went to bed sore and exhausted, my back aching and my knees scraped and bruised, but as these and my hands became accustomed to hard labor, new muscle replaced my soft flesh. Remembering that the ideal woman of Proverbs "girdeth her loins with strength, and strengtheneth her arms,"[44] I was determined not to complain, trusting the Lord would supply what I lacked in the way of fortitude. I wanted nothing about me to sully the reputation of my Savior.

ONE AFTERNOON EARLY in September, Two Doves included me in a small group of women who were sewing inside to escape the August heat. The dwelling belonged to Quiet Woman, the pleasantly plump wife of Many Feathers, Two Doves' elder brother, but though she welcomed me, I did not think she liked me. Joking Woman always responded readily to my smiles, but Quiet Woman returned them only with nods. Among the elders, her husband appeared to hold a place of honor, though whether he was esteemed more for good judgment or a ferocious war record, I could not tell. This, combined with his fierce looks, intimidated me greatly; but their eldest daughter, Red Fawn, was quickly becoming one of my favorite companions.

She was ever patient, ever willing to repeat a word or phrase as often as I needed to hear it. I had difficulty wrapping my tongue around their unfamiliar sounds, but between my two young friends' efforts, I was soon able to take part in rudimentary conversations and readily recognized frequently repeated commands.

A fearsome blast, which I recognized as gunfire, startled us from our sewing. Laying our garments aside, we followed the curious throng to a sparsely wooded area.

My heart leaped. Preying Eagle stood within a group of warriors less than twenty feet away. During the weeks since we had last spoken, I had forgotten how handsome he was. He could not have missed the women gathering to watch, but not once did I see him look for me among them, confirming with a mixture of relief and loss the conclusion I had drawn about his feelings.

He had ceded the second rifle to Running Deer and decorated both with feathers and leather strips, making even these ordinary items from my former life appear foreign. The warriors, clustering around Two Bears and him, took turns shooting targets suspended from a long tree limb.

The tall warrior, whom Hides-in-Shadows had called Kicking Horse, unerringly hit his mark, provoking loud bursts of approval from the gathering crowd. All at once, he turned to look straight into my eyes, grinning as if he had been exhibiting this skill just for me. Seventeen years of habit undid me: my lips curved up before I could think, and the face just beyond his made me flush with shame.

Preying Eagle was staring at me intently, looking sorely displeased. Glancing sideways, I noticed his mother and Quiet Woman and knew at once that they had also witnessed the exchange. I quickly dropped my eyes, well aware of what they were thinking.

When we returned to Quiet Woman's dwelling, I kept my head down, wishing I could spend the afternoon anywhere but under their scrutinizing gazes. Hides-in-Shadows had told me a little more about this warrior, and I had found none of it appealing.

He had singled out Preying Eagle from their childhood, trying fiercely to establish his own dominance. He had not succeeded. While the people regarded Preying Eagle as honorable and restrained, they thought Kicking Horse was ruthless and rash. These same qualities, however, made him an aggressive and valiant warrior, often counting coup against their enemies. I could not understand how I gained his notice but was afraid he would be trouble.

In Thy book, they all were written, the days fashioned for me when as yet there were none of them.

Psalm 139:16

Chapter 9

RED FAWN'S EYES SPARKLED as she asked Hides-in-Shadows to translate something for me during our evening chores. "Kicking Horse's uncle visited Running Deer yesterday."

My heart sunk. "Must I receive his attentions?"

"Yes," nodded my red-haired friend, "if Running Deer consents."

"Do you think he will?"

"Kicking Horse's family is strong, and you already made your willingness known. If Running Deer withheld his permission, they might be offended. Everyone will be nearby—you can duck out of his blanket when you wish."

"Do not duck out too quickly," teased Red Fawn. "He will think you do not want him."

"I do not!"

Red Fawn cocked her head, making me wonder if I'd used the correct expression.

"You will not convince her," smiled Hides-in-Shadows. "She cannot imagine that an untouched woman might want to turn him away."

"He is my brother's friend," Red Fawn protested. "If you do not want him, why did you smile?"

"I am not used to your ways," I sighed. "My people would have thought me rude had I ignored him."

"Then be sure to hide in Two Doves' dwelling when warriors from other bands visit us. My cousin smiled at one last summer and now dwells far away, to the north."

"Augh," moaned Hides-in-Shadows, "I would hate to leave our people."

"So did she," confessed Red Fawn. "She cried for days."

Now it was my turn to be confused. "Why did she not tell her father she did not want to marry him?"

Both friends gaped at me. "A worthy daughter," answered Red Fawn, "trusts her father to wisely choose a husband for her and grows to love his choice."

Choose for her? Certainly fathers back East refused objectionable callers, but none forced a daughter to marry a man against her will—particularly a veritable stranger. The concept seemed medieval!

"Why did your cousin invite his attention," asked Hides-in- Shadows, "if she did not want him?"

Red Fawn shrugged. "He is a splendid warrior, and she liked to collect smiles the way a warrior collects tokens of valor. My mother was glad. Given more summers, my cousin might have shamed our family. She wanted a different warrior—Stomping Buffalo. He is very handsome."

"This did not matter to her father?" I asked.

"Her life would have been hard with him," replied Red Fawn. "He is lazy and all know his temper. My uncle chose better. My cousin now belongs to a worthy warrior who will provide well for her, and our people gained a close tie with another powerful band. I just wish they lived here."

Hoisting my sticks onto my back, I prayed for an escape from the tall warrior's attentions or at least the presence of mind to ignore them. I paused outside my adopted parents' dwelling, considering how, without Hides-in-Shadows' help, I might make them understand my mistake.

When I ducked beneath the flap, Two Doves smiled warmly and Running Deer nodded his customary greeting. Both watched me contemplatively while I served supper, but, by God's grace, Kicking Horse did not call at any time that evening. I finally relaxed as Two Doves prepared for sleep and suspected she sensed my relief and felt pleased.

On my bed, I found a beautiful pair of moccasins, perfectly sewn to fit my feet. Their fur lining promised warmth for the coming winter and their height promised protection from briars and burs—both qualities my ankle boots sorely lacked. Beaming at Two Doves, I slipped them on and showed Elk Dog Boy how well they fit and then folded them into my saddlebag.

I lay awake, relishing the scent of his oldest brother still faintly clinging to my blanket and thanking God for keeping Kicking Horse away. While asking Him to reward Two Doves' kindness, I realized I was not likely to need her gift. If all proceeded as hoped, I would be at the outpost before the weather grew cold. Surprised that I felt this loss acutely, I listened to my adopted father's gentle snoring, matching my breathing with his until weariness towed me under.

WITH ONLY ONE MATTER was I truly dissatisfied during that first month, and I did not know how to remedy it. There was woefully little time to read my Bible. I rose with the rest of the family and was expected somewhere every waking moment. While working or at night before drifting to sleep, I had time to pray; but for study, I needed both adequate light and solitude. Ever faithful, God provided a way.

Running Deer, as true to his word as time always proved him to be, desired to know what was in the Creator's book and; once he was certain I had settled in, bade me read it to him in the evenings. I was delighted, and even more so when his four sons came to listen. Whether they did this voluntarily or by their father's bidding, I could not tell; but though the eldest two only exchanged normal courtesies with me, Preying Eagle's presence filled the room. I had grown so unused to seeing him that I colored deeply when he ducked into the dwelling and felt grateful that reading required me to constantly look downward.

Running Deer's parents, Old Man and Red Woman, also joined us, along with both his and Two Doves' brothers and their families, making the lodge quite crowded. I recognized his father and the brothers from the elders' council and all the women from the river, but the younger warriors were largely new to me.

Unsure where I should begin, I did as Father would have done and started with Genesis. Hides-in-Shadows and I still had limited speech between us, so I was glad the Scriptures gave a straightforward account of the creation. Their tradition was similar, as we discovered many to be. The Creator, they said, had made all things and then taught their people how to use them, and when they explained they pictured him as an old man, I read Daniel's description of the Ancient of Days.[45] Their normally impassive eyes became filled with cautious wonder.

In the evenings to come, we read about The Fall, which deeply grieved their hearts, but they were not surprised by the following verses that foreshadowed the Messiah. Their traditions had announced He was coming. They also felt it natural for the Creator to kill an animal to clothe Adam and Eve—as hunters, they frequently did the same. Indeed, I was astounded by God's careful preparation of their hearts and minds to receive His Word. They seemed to have been waiting for someone to bring it.

During the days that followed, so many invited others to hear the Creator's Book that we needed to move our readings outside. Night after night, week after week, they soaked up the Scriptures as dry bread soaks up gravy, asking me to read or reread whole chapters by firelight. Poor Hides-in-Shadows did the more difficult part, exhausted herself by translating texts and a multitude of questions. Worn out but never happier, I went to sleep every night deeply convinced that God designed my arrival here and astounded by His perfect plans.

A HEAVY RAIN RELENTLESSLY pummeled our dwelling on the late September Tuesday that marked the ninth week since I buried Father, and unbidden images of his dead or dying form persistently battered my heart. They were as confining as the downpour, driving away all happier recollections until I felt engulfed by melancholy. Even the company of my closest friends did nothing to alleviate it.

While we sewed, Two Doves showed my two friends, their mothers, and me a lovely doeskin dress she had almost completed. She had dyed it the color of the spruces that grew near the lake. Confiding it was a special gift, she wove porcupine needles around the neckline in a clever pattern that would have thrilled Aunt Louise.

If the Lord ever blessed me with children of my own, I hoped to follow her fine example. She epitomized the qualities I aspired to possess someday, offering steady guidance and encouraging warmth though I am sure I tried her patience. Afraid to denigrate my mother's loving memory, I took a long time to call Two Doves by that tender title. Her gracious care, however, gradually eroded my resistance, though I still felt too shy to voice my attachment. She opened her heart to me as a daughter, not as extra hands to lighten her labors, and I, in turn, worked eagerly at anything she set before me and many tasks she did not. It was easy to see why her sons adored her.

As my thoughts inclined toward her eldest, I sunk deeper into misery. "Hope deferred makes the heart sick," I repeated silently, "but when the desire cometh, it is a tree of life."[46] The first part expressed my feelings perfectly, but the last made me feel all the more disheartened. My hope was not only postponed; it was entirely futile.

Only once since our goodbyes between the dwellings, had Preying Eagle paid me particular notice. His youngest brother had wanted to teach me to ride, insisting, "Your feet will become sore when we journey to the winter place. If you straggle behind, you will be a coyote's supper." Seeing the sense in his warning, I never mentioned that I had been riding most of my life. Besides, his womenfolk straddled bare horses like the men.

While Elk Dog Boy was showing me how to mount the gentle, old horse he had selected for my use, Preying Eagle led a pony across the field. Her coat was a lovely brown, covered here and there with white splotches that looked like spilled milk. Acknowledging me with a cursory nod, he placed her grass rope bridle in his young brother's hand, telling him emphatically, "She rides this one." Then, taking hold of the old horse, he turned and walked back to his herd.

The pony had a charming, intelligent face and calm nature; and as she was petite, I could easily hoist myself onto her back. Riding astride was far easier and more enjoyable than riding sidesaddle, though her bare spine made me unexpectedly sore. We raced wildly through the meadow and sparser timber that bordered it, dodging low hanging branches, leaping fallen logs, and laughing until our sides hurt.

Elk-Dog-Boy was an amazing horseman, showing off acrobatic stunts that people would have admired at any fair back East. While seated, he could flip from forward to backward or stand while galloping at top speed; but when I gushed with admiration, he merely shrugged and said any village youth could do the same.

If the past couple of months had made Preying Eagle's indifference to me painfully obvious, the past few days had shredded all my remaining hope. Running Deer and the other elders had included him, as they did a number of leading young warriors, in some crucial discussions held in our dwelling. One of the Allies, as the confederation of villages called themselves, had noticed a formidable enemy migrating along the colder side of the great waters to the northeast—possibly, I thought, in lands still held by the British—and many of their councils were contemplating war.

Keenly aware of Preying Eagle's presence, I felt glaringly awkward, especially when serving anyone near him. His resonant voice disturbed my concentration, causing me to falter more than once, but even as I knelt in front of his leggings, he never seemed to see me. Making matters worse, I respected his opinions. They were carefully thought out and sensible, inspiring fresh respect for his shrewd intellect and judgment.

By contrast, Kicking Horse, who was eager to plunge into war, overwhelmed me with attention, as he did during our Bible readings. If he could not catch my eye by standing or sitting near places I must pass, he pestered me—tickling my arms or neck with a shaft of dry grass while I knelt, tapping my shoulder as I walked by, or tunelessly whistling.

In one way, Preying Eagle's disregard relieved as much as saddened me. It set me free to concentrate on God's purposes and stilled my heart as none of my own efforts did. Even as I searched for defects that would turn my heart away, the stories Red Woman, his grandmother, told revealed traits in him that deepened the admiration I felt. Each night, I asked the Lord to remove my feelings, and each day his treatment of others, both young and old, increased them. Fortunately, these contradictory emotions no longer maddened me. They had been the hallmark of our relationship since its inception and, through constant practice, I had grown adept at setting them aside.

After I had been wandering a long while through these memories, Two Doves leaned toward me to ask, "What are you thinking, little one?"

"Nothing important," I replied. How could I admit I was pining for her son?

"I have been troubled by sadness in your eyes. Running Deer and Elk Dog Boy have also noticed and are concerned. The Moon of Yellow and Falling Leaves is almost upon us. Are you longing for your people?"

No," I confessed without much enthusiasm. "It is just the rain." I did not mention I had been grieving for Father. They considered it ill-mannered to speak of the dead.

"It may be the rain this day, but what was it yesterday and the day before? You have even missed several stitches in Little Turtle's leggings—this is not like you."

"Perhaps," teased Red Fawn, "she dreams of a handsome warrior."

My ridiculous habit of blushing confirmed my friend's guess, but as I continued concentrating on my stitches, Two Doves changed the topic. "Preying Eagle wants you to make a shirt to guard him against the winter cold. Are you willing?"

"Yes," I replied, though I could not lift my eyes. "That would please me."

"Good. Hides-in-Shadows, call Elk Dog Boy. Bid him to tell Preying Eagle that Eyes-Like-Water needs him."

My friend promptly did so, leaving me to confusion under my mother's watchful gaze; and before the latter rose to retrieve a pelt, Preying Eagle was dripping rivulets of rainwater onto our hide-covered floor.

As he stood immobile, I stretched the large buckskin across his shoulders. They felt cool and damp from the rain, and their familiar tone beneath my fingers set loose an inescapable flood of memories. Fighting hard to subdue my thumping heart, I marked the length of his arm; but though I carefully avoided his eyes, I could feel them closely trailing mine. I needed next to encircle his neck, but while I tried, he playfully straightened as he had by the falls, taking me so by surprise that I glanced upward. The warmth in his dark eyes set my hands aquiver, making me doubt the stability of my legs.

Observing the whole, his mother insisted he let me take an accurate measure, but even as she scolded, I heard laughter woven into her tone. He must have heard this also, for while his gaze flushed my skin a vivid pink, he lowered his head only enough to keep my legs from giving way.

Hurriedly noting his neck's circumference, I returned to my needlework, industriously attacking it until the heightened drumming of rain announced he was ducking outside. Only then did I venture to raise my head, but I immediately wished I had not. All five women were exchanging secretive looks, just as the elders had the first day while Preying Eagle spoke, but I felt far too vulnerable at that moment to ask them why.

CONSTRAINED BY THE limits of my mother's dwelling, only our extended family gathered inside for the reading of the Word that evening. The rain-soaked ground was too muddy for us to sit outside. Hides-in-Shadows and I had come to a new ease with our translating and, having finished Genesis several days past, we had begun to read the Gospel of John. When she told them that the Word became flesh, they saw another reminder of The Old Man's promise to return, and they heartily approved Nathaniel's honest nature.

He had always been one of my favorite characters and the verses about him unavoidably reminded me of Captain Anderson, who shared his given name. I wondered if he was still at the outpost, if he had tried to find me or if I had greatly overestimated his regard.

John chapter three produced dramatic responses: they inquired along with Nicodemus how they might be born again. Having made only the briefest reference to the crucifixion, I was unsure how to answer. I decided to let the text suffice, underscoring the clear inference in verse six: to possess a certain nature, you must be born from someone who also possesses that nature.

As astute observers of animals, employing various characteristics of each to teach their children about life, they readily understood this concept. A fawn inherited the nature of a deer, a calf the nature of a buffalo, a kit the nature of a fox, and so forth. Using this analogy, I explained that we receive God's nature when we are born of His Spirit, just as we received the nature of men when we were born of our mothers.

A handful of men, my adopted father and brothers among them, began fervently expressing a desire to be born of God.[47] Soon, most of the group was doing so. I felt overwhelmed by their fervor and unsure of what to do until the very text again guided me. We read that God gave his Son so we could live eternally and that men fell into one of two categories: those who loved and came to the light and those who hated it.[48]

The last verse provoked a tremendous response: "He that believeth in the Son hath everlasting life. He that believeth not the Son shall not see life, but the wrath of God abideth on him."[49] Running Deer, Preying Eagle, Two Bears, and several of their uncles and cousins leaped to their feet, proclaiming their belief that the Creator sent Jesus and their determination to walk in His path. My remaining brothers, mother, aunts, and two friends followed suit, as did Old Man and Red Woman.

Having heard about baptism and its purpose earlier in the chapter, they began asking, much like the Ethiopian eunuch, "What is to keep us from dipping under the water?"[50] "Nothing," I replied, seeing no reason why they should not be assuming their repentance and belief was genuine, but this whole gathering and their passionate vocal reactions was unlike any church service I had ever attended. It astounded me to the point of inaction. Who would baptize them? This was something of which I had never thought.

What would happen if they did not fully understand God's plan, I fretted—but then, did James and John, Andrew, or any of the disciples who received baptism into repentance understand precisely what would follow? Did Peter apprehend it fully while he voiced, "Lord, to whom shall we go? Thou hast the words of everlasting life. And we believe and are sure that Thou art the Christ, the Son of the living God"?[51]

I told Running Deer what I had in my heart to do. If he considered it appropriate, I would baptize him, and then he could baptize the rest of the gathered people, as I did not feel it was my place as a young woman. He heartily assented, and we immediately trudged through the mud to the lake where he, receiving baptism first, baptized the other professing men. They, in turn, baptized their believing women, conscientiously asking each if she understood the solemn commitment she was making to turn from her own ways and follow the Creator's path for the duration of her life.

The joy I felt was so intense, I could not decide between laughing and crying. I did both plentifully, astounded by the work of God! The men, so unlike my reserved father and grandfather, sang and danced in open jubilation. They reminded me of David when the Israelites carried the Ark of the Covenant into Jerusalem. It was a remarkable and inspiring sight, nothing like my traditional worship, but this people were unlike any I had ever met. Watching Preying Eagle and his father and brothers' elation and my mother and friends' more subdued but obvious joy, formed one of the happiest moments of my life. Mud clung to everybody's soaked clothing, but in our exultation, no one cared.

How can I adequately describe the events that transpired during the subsequent days? What had happened that evening spread like a fire throughout the village. We performed little work that was not essential, for a great portion of the people wanted to profess their faith in Jesus Christ and receive baptism. Every night, weather permitting, much of the band gathered for the reading of the Word, asking questions, absorbing God's instructions, insatiably desiring more of Jesus.

As we continued through the book of John over the next several weeks, they came undone when they heard that Jesus was beaten and then sacrificed on the cross. I reminded them of passages we previously read that foreshadowed this event—the animal sacrificed to cover the first man and woman after they had sinned in the garden, the ram provided to Abraham as a sacrifice instead of Isaac, and the prophecy that the snake would bruise His heel while He crushed the evil one's head. We read Psalm 22 and

Isaiah 53, passages predicting Jesus' betrayal, beatings, and death, though their two authors, David and Isaiah, had lived 1,000 and 700 years respectively before either event took place.

They were furious with Judas, whose disloyalty and betrayal they found appalling. Moreover, they pronounced all those who killed Jesus worthy of death. I reminded them that Jesus Himself could have slain them on the spot but chose instead to die for us all, as the Creator had planned from the beginning. He did not ask His father for their deaths but willingly gave Himself in their place, asking instead that the Father forgive them, for they did not know what they did. In addition, according to the Word, to which their own hearts testified, we were all worthy of death—which was the real cause of His. We all killed Jesus by our sins.

Their grief was profound, contrasting sharply with their euphoric baptisms. Each returned to their lodges in silent sorrow. However, as we read the next night of His glorious resurrection, their mourning once more erupted into joy and they again broke out in exuberant adoration of our great and glorious Creator and Friend!

SEVERAL MORNINGS afterward, the women of the village were gathering squash and pumpkins. The believers among them often asked me questions while we labored, desiring clarification of some point they hadn't understood or wanting to know about things that we hadn't addressed during our Bible readings. Mostly, they wanted to hear about their special role as women. In answer, we read the latter half of Proverbs 31, which concludes: "Favor is deceitful and beauty vain, but a woman who feareth the Lord, she shall be praised. Give her the fruit of her hands, and let her own works praise her in the gates." [52]

Swallow Woman arose, obviously offended, and walked away in a huff. Hides-in-Shadows and I followed, wishing to ameliorate the situation. She had listened to the Word but had not yet received baptism, and we desired to remove any barriers to the Gospel I had inadvertently built.

"Your book says I am useless," she spat, "but Preying Eagle wants me, not you! Go away! Our people talk—all say they do not want you! Return to the white man!"

Hides-in-Shadows looked so pained, she might not have translated Swallow Woman's exact words, but it was too late. I had understood them devastatingly well.

Choking back my feelings, I tried to explain, "Everyone can see the Creator made you beautiful. There is no shame in this, but outward beauty cannot last. We all grow old. He wants to make our hearts beautiful."

I showed her passages in the Scriptures about Sarah and Esther, famed for their loveliness and used greatly by the Creator. We also read the verses about Sarah's inward beauty, precious in the sight of the Creator, which came from her deep reverence of Him. She seemed appeased and returned to the women, but, crushed by her words, I fled to seek solace in my family's empty dwelling. Not long afterward, Elk Dog Boy came looking for me.

"Black Elk and Little Turtle found a white man while hunting," he announced. "We think from his hand talk he is looking for his white woman."

My mouth fell open. "Is he my false uncle?"

Before I finished the question, Two Bears was at my side, escorting me to the middle of the dwellings.

"Lord," I prayed as we approached the place where they detained him, "please let him be anyone but Henry!"

All nations whom Thou hast made shall come and worship before Thee, O Lord, and shall glorify Thy name. For Thou art great, and doest wondrous things; Thou art God alone.

Psalm 86:9-10

Chapter 10

"CAPTAIN ANDERSON!" I CRIED, breaking into a happy trot as I recognized the haggard-looking officer. As onlookers cast me curious glances, I quickly tamped down my glee and hurried instead to my adopted father.

"You know this man," stated Running Deer. The Captain's undisguised relief making clear I was the woman he came seeking.

"Yes," I replied, barely able to suppress a smile. "He is my friend."

"Ah. He has been looking for you. Do you wish to speak with him?"

"Yes."

When they heard my reply, Preying Eagle and Two Bears stepped forward, apparently thinking I needed their protection. I bit my lip, struggling to control a strong impulse to laugh. They accompanied the Captain and me to their mother's dwelling, where the two of us recounted the past months' changes in such rapid English that Hides-in-Shadows would never have kept up.

He had traveled to the outpost the next day, as planned, but had delayed leaving until late afternoon. When he came across the horseless coach and searched among the dead bodies, alarm, relief, and bewilderment launched successive campaigns against his reason, until he spotted the arrow lodged in Stump's heart. The light was too faint for him to follow the many scattered hoof prints, so he continued the short distance to the fort, cherishing the unlikely hope that I was there.

Presenting himself to his superior officer, he reported his discovery and Monroe's alleged Indian troubles, including his speculation about the true culprit. His commander swiftly granted him permission to search for me the next morning, which he did as soon as light permitted. The rain, however, had obliterated much of the days-old trail. Here and there, he caught traces of it winding into the foothills, but it took unpredictable turns and finally gave out in the deepening woods. Unable to neglect his responsibilities further, he returned to the outpost, daunted but not hopeless, and asked for further leave to follow the river into the hills.

"What about Henry? Is he looking for me?"

"I don't know," the Captain replied. "I delayed for that purpose, but he raised no alarm, and I haven't returned since. What did happen—were you abducted?"

"No—rescued. Stump and that half-witted man robbed the coach. What they planned to do when they unexpectedly found me, I will leave to your imagination. Stump strongly intimated that Henry wanted only my money and had instructed him to kill me when we returned from our honeymoon."

Captain Anderson raked his fingers through his hair. "I had not wanted to frighten you, Miss Callen, but I had a strong hunch that your father had been poisoned."

"Poisoned? You can't be serious!"

"I wouldn't jest about such a thing."

"No, of course not," I admitted. "The idea is just so horrible."

"After you left, I spoke to the liveryman who attended to him. He wouldn't come right out and confirm my suspicions, but neither could he deny them. Didn't you wonder about the suddenness and intensity of his illness?"

"Yes, I did, but no one besides Henry could have done it, and though he never liked me, I thought he cared for Father. Why else would he have asked us to come see him?"

Sitting opposite me, Preying Eagle observed my distress and grew agitated. Two Bears, who sat behind me, watched the reactions of my friend.

"You gave me the answer to that question a few minutes ago. You didn't think it odd that Horace heard from Henry so soon after inheriting your grandmother's estate? The two of you presented his only obstacles. Once he'd reestablished the relationship, he had only to kill your father and marry you to have everything. Your wealth offered a desirable bonus."

As I lay my head in my hands, Preying Eagle sprung to his feet and Two Bears immediately followed his lead.

"I'm all right," I assured them, "my friend told me some horrible news."

Still wary, they sat back down and Captain Anderson continued. "I am especially sorry to point out that your father fell ill shortly after we began showing a more personal inclination toward each other. Henry needed to act quickly or lose his opportunity."

"Oh, how dreadful!" I moaned. "But how did he do it?"

"I'm not sure. He—or Pinckney—might have sprinkled bits of a poisonous plant into your father's vegetables. He has an extensive garden with a knowledge of botany to match."

Can we bring him to justice?"

"That will be difficult. We have reason to suspect him, but since his henchmen are dead, how do we prove his guilt? The woman you overheard in the general store might be able to identify Mrs. Lawsons' pianoforte, but that doesn't prove your uncle burned them out."

"But he rode over the northern slope minutes after the blaze."

"Your testimony would at least demonstrate that he had been there, but as for your father's death, Henry is shrewd. He will have removed any evidence—perhaps has even torn out and burned the plant—and justice moves slowly out here. The judge will not repeat his circuit for quite some time, and Henry has gotten rid, one way or another, of anyone who stands in his way or is a threat to him."

I could only shake my head in frustrated sorrow.

"But let's talk of you, Miss Callen. Can these two understand what we're saying?"

"No, not a word."

"Do you have anything you want to gather together before we leave?"

"Leave? I can't."

"Are you a prisoner then—some kind of slave?" His voice became tense as he looked at Two Bears. "You can't want to remain among these savages."

"You are quite mistaken to think them savage. As we can both attest, Henry and his ilk deserve that label, but these people are honest and kind. I've been cared for as a daughter."

"You do look well, but if you are free to go, whatever could induce you to stay?"

"The Lord has been doing wondrous things here, and I am happier than I've ever been. Anyway, where would I go? I could presume on friends for a while but don't wish to impose and, penniless, I have nothing to offer a husband. Here, I'm well-loved and of valuable service."

"Are you certain, Miss Callen, they understand nothing?"

"Maybe the chance word, here or there, but even that is unlikely."

"I thought that you and I…"

To my relief, he trailed off. I suspected what he was about to say and had no idea what to answer. He had taken so long to find me that I had given up hope he was looking, but my reprieve quickly concluded. He plunged ahead, barely breathing between sentences.

"I don't care a jot for your fortune, Miss Callen; I have plenty. When I've finished my duty, we could settle far enough from Monroe that we need never encounter your uncle; or if you dislike living out here, we could move back East. My family will love you and, if you wish, we could engage lawyers to fight Henry's governorship of your inheritance."

"Captain Anderson ..."

"Don't you think it's time you call me by my given name?"

"All right. Nathaniel..."

"May I call you Alcy, instead of Miss Callen?"

"Yes, I'd like that very much." I took a deep breath, considering my reply. Was this not precisely what I desired less than three months ago? If the people felt as Swallow Woman said they did, perhaps I should accept his offer. Only, who would read them the Word? Hides-in-Shadows was not proficient enough to manage the difficult bits.

"Henry can have the money. You do me honor, Nathaniel, by what you suggest, but I'm quite changed." Had I not suspected God intentionally placed the approaching month on Running Deer's heart? Capt...Nathaniel's timing certainly made it easier for me to leave. "Can you honestly say you love me?"

"I wouldn't speak of marriage lightly. I contemplated it a great deal in Monroe and more while searching for you. Alcy, I'm not a man who is easily carried away by passion or given to pretty speeches, but you are a fine, well-educated woman, easy on the eyes, and I've never found a more pleasant companion. "Our marriage would offer every promise of happiness, and I was sure you were of the same mind in Monroe. Given time, we will overcome the strangeness the past months have put between us, and I'm confident we will grow to love each other deeply."

It was a very reasonable, even generous, proposal from a man steadfastly ruled by his head.

"Are you asking me to marry you because I said I have no place else to go?"

"No," he replied firmly. "I decided to do so that day we rode in the carriage with Henry, but when you told me you were only seventeen I resolved to wait a year. Meanwhile, I'd planned to put my regimental affairs in order, purchase property and build you a suitable home."

I felt moved by his forethought. He was undeniably very dear, and I had prayed earnestly and often that the Lord would bring about this very end.

"Must we talk about this in front of them, Alcy? Can't we get some privacy?"

"They are afraid you might take me against my will."

"That's preposterous!"

"You and I know that, but they…"

Running Deer interrupted, throwing back the door flap of our dwelling, so now all three of my protectors stood or sat close by. When Two Doves brought in a meal of rabbit and the squash we had picked previously, he told her to send Elk Dog Boy to find Hides-in-Shadows.

"I see I'd never have succeeded were I so inclined," Nathaniel quipped as I rose to serve supper.

"No," I replied, enjoying the security my family offered. Had he been Henry, I would have had nothing to fear.

"They don't frighten you?"

"I've never felt safer. Can I give you an answer tomorrow, after I've taken some time to pray?"

"Yes, certainly, I would expect no different under normal circumstances, but given your current surroundings, I can't see what there is to pray about."

"Much has happened in the past several months."

We heard Elk Dog Boy calling from outside, and Running Deer invited him to enter. When Nathaniel saw Hides-in-Shadows, his surprise and curiosity were obvious.

"She was brought here as a child," I whispered, "and has been my interpreter and tutor."

Running Deer instructed Hides-in-Shadows to sit beside Nathaniel, with whom she was fascinated, though she tried to conceal it. He was the first man she had seen since childhood who shared her looks, so much so I wondered if they could be brother and sister. Remembering that he was from Boston and her family had been homesteaders, I dismissed the idea.

My adopted father told him they had nothing to do with the events in Monroe, and though they were not afraid of battle, they preferred peace— they did not intend to attack the white village unless they were provoked. Nathaniel took this all in, wanting to gain as much information about them as he could to report to his commanding officer.

"The trouble is the arrow in the man's chest," explained Nathaniel. "He worked for Miss Callen's guardian, who will insist it proves Indians robbed the coach."

Hides-in-Shadow looked puzzled. "What is miskallin?" she asked, unsure how to translate the word.

Nathaniel turned toward her quizzically. "This is Miss Callen," he replied, indicating me with his hand.

When she told this to Running Deer, he frowned and waved his hand dismissively. "These words mean nothing. We know her name. Do white men stand by while a woman is shamed?"

"No, but a judge can't rule that this happened unless Miss Callen testifies. I will convey what she has told me, but it would be far better if she tells them herself."

"You have something to say?" Running Deer asked me.

"I wish to ask my friend what happened to the valuables stolen from the little man who was my traveling companion. The slow-witted man rifled through his pockets and took several items, including a watch. Unless someone else arrived before you did and robbed him, it should still have been in his possession. I can guarantee my brother took nothing but the horses."

"Your brother?"

"The warrior sitting behind you."

Glancing over his shoulder, Nathaniel grimaced. "Returning the coach horses would demonstrate his peaceable intent. Do you think you'd be able to identify that watch before my commanding officer?"

As my family began to grasp where his question headed, concern filled their eyes. Each began looking at the others, but none of them looked pleased.

"Certainly," I assured Nathaniel. "If you think that will prevent trouble, I will gladly testify to everything I saw and heard that day."

"Excellent! Then we will leave right after we are finished eating."

My guardians engaged in a heated discussion that I understood only in part. Primarily it concerned Nathaniel's trustworthiness. Preying Eagle questioned his motives for taking me away.

"I will not leave without Running Deer's permission," I told Nathaniel. "If he gives it, I will go."

"Permission? You told me you were free."

"I'm as free as any daughter. Out of respect, I'll await his consent. I won't repay his care by disregarding his wishes."

Nodding with pleasure as Hides-in-Shadows translated, Running Deer asked, "How far is this fort?"

"Most of an entire day of hard riding," replied Nathaniel.

"Will you bring this woman back when she desires to return?"

"Yes, certainly. I would not keep her against her will. However," he added, glancing at me meaningfully. "I am just as determined that she stay there if she chooses."

"She already knows she may remain there if that is her desire. Daughter, you trust this man and are willing to go with him?"

"Yes."

"Good. Your older brothers will go with you until you are close to this place of the long-knives. Tonight your white friend will stay in the guest lodge, and you will leave in the morning. Let us go. It is time for reading the Creator's Book."

Captain Anderson did not look pleased with our delay as we walked to the center of the village, but as he had no alternative, he accepted it. I felt quite the opposite. I was reeling from the suddenness of our departure and its likely consequences.

When our discussions were over, Running Deer requested that I accompany him to the lake. "I have much to speak that is grave and we must clearly understand each other. What this spotted long-knife says troubles me. We do not know these white men and their ways. If you go, you may benefit our people, but how can I protect you? Are you certain that this man is worthy of trust?"

Running Deer's concern touched me. Over these several months, I had come to see why the people held him in such high esteem. Like his eldest son, he held that balance so few men achieve of strength with gentleness, justice with mercy, fervor with restraint, and gravity with humor.

"Yes, I will be safe with him."

"He appears to be a good man, and all noticed your delight with him," he noted, a faint smirk teasing his lips. "You restrained your smiles, but they danced in your eyes. He did not try to hide his. Did his uncle ask your father for you?"

"No."

"It is the Moon of Yellow and Falling Leaves. I do not ask you to make your decision now and have forbidden anyone to persuade you. Your own heart must tell you where it rests. The long-knife walks in the path of the Creator and is of your people. He has been searching for you long and has come to take you with him. If he wants you for his woman, he can send horses for your bride price later, and we will send him ours in return. You are not bound; I give you permission to accept him and remain in his place if that is your choice."

Before I could reply, he shook his head and put his hand up to say I should stay silent.

"It is not the time for answers. Preying Eagle and Two Bears will wait near the path to the long knives' village until the sun takes three rests. This Captain must return you or bring horses. We will know your answer when we see them. Our people will pray that the Creator makes His desires known to you and keeps you safe from evil."

As we walked toward the village, my mind was awhirl. I felt as if the detour I had taken had suddenly rejoined the main road, routing me away from the most significant and fulfilling part of the entire journey. Were I to refuse Captain Anderson's offer, my late father would think I had lost my senses, and my grandmother, had she known Nathaniel, would certainly agree. Even Running Deer seemed to think it fitting that I return to my own kind.

My stomach knotted sharply. Nathaniel's proposal had seemed surreal—not his words or sentiment but that he voiced them with Preying Eagle watching from just beyond his shoulder. Their expressions offered a clear contrast between both the men themselves and the two separate lives that lay before me. Nathaniel's face had been open, attentive, and encouraging; Preying Eagle's vacillated between his familiar dark squall and a house with all its shutters closed up tight. If I remained with this people, I would undoubtedly face the bleak prospects Hides-in-Shadows expected. Marrying any other warrior was out of the question.

Nathaniel had been confident of my answer, and all he had said about our relationship was true. With one simple syllable, I could secure an admirable husband with whom I could grow old, raise children, and enjoy safety within my own culture; yet, I would rather die single in the center of God's glorious will than to have all these apart from it. If there was one thing I had learned in these past three months, it was the utter dependability of the Lord. I could trust Him no matter what circumstances came my way. They were all the same in one sense: as long as He held me I was fine, and nothing could separate me from His love.

"Lord, I want to live out my years doing your bidding and being of use to others, whether here or elsewhere. If You sent Nathaniel to return my life to its former course, then so be it. I only ask You to show me Your will."

Lay up for yourselves treasures in heaven, where neither moth nor rust corrupt and where thieves do not break through and steal: For where your treasure is, there will your heart be also.

Matthew 6:20-21

Chapter 11

PREYING EAGLE and Nathaniel were arguing when I joined them in the meadow at dawn, each holding the bridle of a horse in addition to his own.

"Alcy, this stubborn Indian insists you ride this pony, bareback, rather than the saddled horse I brought for you."

This was an unpromising way to begin our journey. I felt deeply tired or deeply sad; it was hard to tell which, maybe both. I mounted Preying Eagle's paint, dumbfounding Nathaniel and settling their dispute. The former did not look the least surprised, only pleased and subtly triumphant.

I hated to say farewell. Hides-in-Shadows had been verging on tears as I placed my Bible in her hands—the outpost or Nathaniel would have one I could read. I only hoped she could translate easily enough for the people to fully understand the Creator's way. Two Doves carried herself as regally as she always did, but her face looked older than usual. Elk Dog Boy and Little Turtle seemed glum and Running Deer decidedly grave.

As I was about to urge my milk-splashed pony into line, Old Man gripped her bridle. His eyes, peering piercingly into mine, spoke silently of his sorrow, but the words he whispered were of Red Woman, his wife.

"She does not come from her lodge to say goodbye."

The hurt that I felt must have shown, for he discreetly moved his finger to the corner of his eye, letting me know that grief, not anger confined her to her dwelling.

"I trust the Creator will lead your heart," he added, but I somehow understood what he really meant was "guide you to come back to us."

From the first day that he questioned me before the elders, we had formed a special bond; and afterward, he confided he had been asking the Creator since childhood to return His Book to them. Everything in me longed to leap off the pony and throw myself into his embrace, but the people frowned on public displays of affection. Instead, I merely nodded, hoping he was as adept at reading my expressions as his eldest grandson had been during those days by the waterfall.

My mount fell in line behind Preying Eagle's dapple-gray, Nathaniel rode behind me, and Two Bears brought up the rear with the coach horses. Preying Eagle's assumption of command irked Nathaniel, but as Two Bears' presence lent strength to his brother's claim, my friend had no choice but to submit. Even so, tension hung heavily in the air between them, and I could think of nothing to dispel or ameliorate it. Whenever we reached an area wide enough for two to ride abreast, Nathaniel quite naturally coaxed his horse forward; we had much to discuss about the past months apart and our hopes for the future. Preying Eagle just as swiftly did the opposite, slowing his mare so that he could take the space. The one time Nathaniel almost gained the spot, Preying Eagle veered off the trail to lead us through the trees, once more forcing my friend to drop back. Eventually, Nathaniel gave up, and we each became engrossed in our private thoughts.

Why Preying Eagle acted so unreasonably, I was hard-pressed to guess. He quite obviously did not need to speak with me: he rode beside me in stony silence. More likely, he felt it his duty to protect me; his experience with Stump had not recommended men of my kind.

Whatever was his motive, I was glad for it. Nathaniel expected an answer to his proposal, but I felt awkward giving it within Preying Eagle's hearing. Furthermore, I was still unsure of how I should respond. My head clashed virulently with my heart, and God seemed wholly silent. Only in fleeing Henry had I needed to make such a grave decision alone, and that was provoked by the instinct to survive. Yet, I recalled what Father and Grandmother did if they did not receive specific direction from the Lord: they followed the dictates of their God-given sense, or failing that, they waited. Waiting was not an option and the sensible choice was plain, but why could I not quiet my heart?

Perhaps the trouble was my conscience. To accept Nathaniel's proposal felt selfish and unfair. He deserved a woman who loved him unreservedly. Yet, if Father, Grandmother, and he were correct, the indisputable affection I felt toward him now would deepen. Already, I had noticed endearing qualities that I had forgotten: the twinkle in his eyes, his ready smile, and his frank and even temperament. I rarely wondered what he was thinking, and, unlike my adopted menfolk, he sought my wishes and opinions. Moreover, he had not asked if I were in love with him or espoused a passionate love for me; he asked only if I were willing to become his wife.

Grandmother said that real love only developed over years, and I had excellent reasons to believe her. She had two laudable marriages. Watching the obvious exchanges of affection between Grandfather and her had always made me feel secure, as if the strength of their love and commitment made the whole world safe.

As my eyes fell on Preying Eagle's scar, I began pondering the real purpose for this journey. He had only done what was right under the circumstances, and I prayed I could make this sufficiently clear. I wondered what the man to whom I would give testimony was like. Nathaniel held him in high esteem and had also mentioned, the day I left Monroe, that his wife would offer me an eager welcome. Would she do so now, after I had spent months with people she would likely consider savages? I did not even know what I looked like now, other than chance reflections I had caught in the lake.

While Allison and I were preparing for our coming out ball last year, we had spent hours in front of Grandmother's large dressing table and mirror. Could it be possible that only a year had passed—it seemed like an age! Grandmother's maid had coifed our hair perfectly, and our dresses, of the most beautiful white silk, were sewn to exhibit the loveliest aspects of our individual figures. We did not have any mirrors in the village, and though I wore the better of my two dresses, it had not only faded to a charcoal gray but was more threadbare than ones I cut up for rags back East. My complexion must be far from the fair hue Henry had often complimented. My hands were the color of his maple desk and no longer of a fine, soft texture.

Was it any wonder the handsome warrior riding before me rarely looked in my direction? The contrast between Swallow Woman and I must be vast. Even while she was on hands and knees, digging for wild potatoes or scraping the hair off a pelt, she looked graceful and perfectly groomed.

AFTER RIDING STEADILY until the sun hung far past its zenith, we dismounted on the crest of a hill. Below it, we could see the outpost road, and I guessed it was from this height that Preying Eagle had watched Stump and his cohort attack the coach. Nathaniel had been correct, after all, about the distance between the village and Monroe. From here, we would need to travel an additional hour, making the journey well over eleven altogether.

Pulling off the fur-lined moccasins I had lately taken to wearing, I reluctantly exchanged them for the confining ankle-boots in my saddlebag. They were quite dear to me, a continual reminder of the woman who made them, but though they were wonderfully practical, they would not suit the society to which I was returning. In addition, they inevitably brought to mind those days by the falls—days I needed to thrust from my mind were I to marry Nathaniel. God led me then and would lead me now, and putting away Two Doves' gift did not equate to putting her out of my heart.

As I cut the thongs that kept my braids from unraveling, the memory of Preying Eagle weaving them flushed my cheeks; and as I wound my loose hair at the nape of my neck, I wondered if he, too, was remembering. One upward glance answered my question. His face was impassive, and as his eyes met mine, I could not detect the least amount of warmth. At first stern, they became severe as he watched my transformation from Eyes-Like-Water to an orphaned young white woman with significantly altered prospects.

Suddenly grasping my wrist, he led me into a small clump of pines, turned my palm upward and dropped into it two new strips of soft hide. My breath caught in my throat as his fingers closed over mine, and I hoped he might give me some small inducement to return.

"When three suns have slept, you come to this place," he said firmly.

"Our people need you to read the Creator's book."

"Alcy!" called Nathaniel. "We will soon lose the light!"

Preying Eagle pulled me back into the open and helped me onto my tall army mount, his hands lingering about my waist as if he might say something more. Instead, he turned abruptly and strode over to the dapple-gray.

"How far to this white man's outpost?" he demanded.

"Not far," answered Nathaniel. Although I translated only the words, I felt embarrassed by their tone. He had sounded impatient almost to the point of hostility, creating an unpleasant context in which to bid my brothers goodbye.

As we wheeled away, I looked over my shoulder to gain the last glimpse of them both. A trace of a smile played in Two Bears' eyes as he lifted a hand in fond farewell. His elder brother's face looked unmovable as iron. Mine, I am sure, betrayed me, for leaving them felt like death.

THE FORT WAS small and housed fewer people than the one in which Father and I had stayed on our journey. The sentries gawked curiously when we rode through the gates and up to the commander's office, but none of them questioned Nathaniel.

"Come in," the Major answered Nathaniel's knock. He was a tolerant-looking man in his middle years with a large mustache and intelligent eyes. I liked him almost as quickly as I had liked the Captain. When he saw who we were, he hurried around his desk and warmly clasped my hand. "So this is Miss Callen! You gave this young man quite a scare when he arrived and confirmed that you had not. My wife, Paulette, and I would like you to stay with us and our three children if that suits you."

"Oh, yes sir," I replied. "Thank you."

"Then would you like to freshen up or tell me right away what's happened during the months you have been missing?"

"I would like to freshen up if that's not inconvenient."

"Yes, of course. It will thrill my wife to have another woman living here."

His statement was intended kindly but was awkward to deny or affirm. Before he had a chance to notice my embarrassment, however, he had already walked over to the door. As he ordered a young man to call his wife, I longed suddenly and intensely to see Elk Dog Boy, who often performed similar duties.

"She will be here in a moment and show you to our home. You must have had a harrowing experience."

I wondered what notions they all formed. "It had its moments of horror."

Mrs. Young, who entered as I answered, was every bit his equal in warmth and appeal. Her light chestnut curls framed large blue eyes that held a genuine look of welcome that relaxed me instantly.

"Miss Callen!" She swept over and took my hand. "It's a pleasure to finally meet you. Nathaniel, why didn't you bring her to me first?" As she scolded I detected a slight French lilt. "You men! Anyone can see she's tired, no? And I dare say hasn't had much to eat today. Come. You can freshen up and we will talk over dinner. George, will you and Captain Anderson be joining us shortly?"

"Yes, my love," replied the Major. "In about half an hour."

Sliding her arm through mine, she led me through a door in the fort's structure a brief walk from Major Young's office and into a comfortable, albeit small, sitting room. Two girls, about five and fourteen, popped their heads through a door in the opposite wall. Both had their mother's brown waves, but only the youngest had her blue eyes.

The latter ran up to me immediately, took my hand, and began swinging it back and forth. "Are you the lady Uncle Nate's going to marry?" she asked. "Every night, we've been praying for you with Mama and Papa."

"I'm an old friend that he thought was lost, but as you can see, the Lord has been answering your prayers. I'm perfectly well."

"But," she shook her head in confusion, "If you were not lost, why have we been praying for you?"

"Tennie, help your sister get a basin ready for Miss Callen, and some towels. She is tired, and I dare say does not want to be quizzed." The little

126

girl hesitated, looking as if she much preferred to ply me with uncomfortable questions, but either reason or the desire to please her Mother won out.

"Yes, Mama," she replied, with the bob of a little curtsey, and scampered off through the door by which she had entered.

"I am sorry, Miss Callen. We have been praying for you for the past few months, and she adores her uncle Nate. He is not really their uncle, of course, but the children are very fond of him. He is an exceptional man, the kind one does not often run across, and one of George's closest friends."

"She's a dear, but please call me Alcy. And I agree with you both about Nathaniel. He's one of the finest men of my acquaintance."

Nicole, the older girl, had liquid brown eyes and a graceful, somewhat diffident manner. She quietly informed her mother that my accommodations were ready and then hauled a kettle to the other room.

"If you will follow my daughters, Alcy, you will find everything you need, and the girls will give you privacy." She emphasized the last few words for their benefit, so after filling a basin with the hot water, they slipped back into the kitchen.

The room in which they left me was neatly furnished, housing both a large and a small bed, a dresser with a washbasin on top, several sweet dolls, and a wooden gun. Washing with warm water felt wonderful, but as I lifted my head, I felt startled by the face that stared back at me. The sun had turned my skin nearly as brown as Two Doves', making my greenish-blue eyes appear larger and more luminous by contrast. I was not sure I liked the alteration, perhaps only because I looked so unfamiliar. Less tangible was the change in my expression—the sheltered girl who had fled Monroe had been replaced by a capable young woman.

Both my hosts' warm welcome and their little girl's questions showed they were aware of Nathaniel's intentions and quite confident of my response. I had much to look forward to if this were a sample of our future. The trust and friendship of his commander spoke highly of him, as did the affection of the entire lovely family.

I wondered what his father and mother were like. They were both living, though probably older than either of my parents would have been. He was nearly a decade my senior and the baby of his family. His older sister, he had told me, had not lived in Boston for many years, having met and married a New Yorker while on holiday one summer. Only his maiden aunt, of whom he was very fond, remained with his parents. Had he considered what they might think of my life's recent events? They might deem me unfit to bear the family name, much less their grandchildren.

A knock on the door awoke me from my musings, and the older daughter informed me that her father and Captain Anderson had arrived. In their company stood the owner of the little wooden gun, a boy of about eleven with deep brown eyes and a strong cleft chin like his father's.

"Miss Callen, this is my son, Aaron," Major Young introduced us. The boy somehow managed to look shy, curious, and warm all at once, bringing to mind the black-eyed village children.

The meal was a pleasant affair that included many old favorite dishes and plenty of engaging conversation. George and Paulette had met in Lancaster, Pennsylvania, where she spent the summers with her aunt. It was less than a day's ride from Philadelphia and, as they visited there occasionally, we discovered we had many common experiences and even one shared acquaintance.

The children asked a myriad of questions about the village, which I happily answered, hoping to persuade the entire company that not all Indians are savage. We left the details of my experiences in route, however, for the Major's office, as they were not fit conversation for young ears. Afterward, the men returned to the office, and Paulette and I chatted while we washed plates. Noticing the dark circles beneath my eyes, she suggested that I rest, an idea that I welcomed, but I first had something else I was very eager to do.

"Paulette, could I impose on you for some paper, ink, and a quill? My friend, Allison, wrote me several months ago, and I haven't been able to respond to her."

"But of course! When you are finished, Aaron will take it to my husband's office and George will include it in the post."

Having been supplied with all the necessary equipment, I had only to decide which of many things to write.

Wednesday, October 8, 1817

Dearest Allison,

Congratulations on your wonderful news! You pay me a great honor by asking me to become your child's godmother; however, as you read this letter, you'll see why I can't presently give you a response.

I hardly know where to begin, and I know one event will grieve you greatly: on July 29th, Father went home to the Lord. I miss him more than I can say. The rest seems too fantastical to pen, but I will give you a brief account.

My uncle was horrid! He tried to force me to marry him after Father died, but I escaped. While doing so, a warrior carried me off to live among his people, many of whom have come to saving faith in our Savior through hearing God's Word. You surely think I'm joking, but I promise you I'm not.

An officer with whom I had become well-acquainted in Monroe, found me yesterday, proposed, and is awaiting my answer. You and John would like him very much. He loves our Lord and is one of the finest men I've ever known. My hesitancy is twofold, and you'll laugh while you read it: I don't want to leave the Indians, and the warrior who rescued me confuses my heart.

You are no doubt shocked. He quite clearly does not feel the same toward me, and now that I've committed my thoughts to paper, the answer I should give is obvious. It is absurd that I have been wrestling with the decisions at all.

As I will now have an address to which you can write, please do so often. I've missed you so much. And yes, now that I've sorted everything out, of course, I will be your child's godmother—providing I can perform my duties from a distance.

Please give my love to John, your mother and father, and your brother Thom. Your friend always,

Alcy

Sinking into the boy's bed, which he had considerately vacated for my visit, I thought about how much I missed Allison's whole family and wondered if Nathaniel would mind going through Virginia on the way to Boston. It was not likely. Virginia was quite a bit farther south than this fort or Pennsylvania, so we would need to make a significant detour.

The last thought reminded me of my people, and I began longing to see them. My people? Whether in thought or address, I had always referred to them as Preying Eagle's people or simply *the* people. Thinking of them as mine increased my yearning for them manifold. I would greatly miss watching their faces as they listened to Hides-in-Shadows' translations. They were not the people of my flesh but had become the people of my heart, and though I had always considered my stay with them temporary, a terrible homesickness seemed to swallow me whole.

Perhaps Nathaniel and I could visit them before we traveled east, or better yet, he might allow me to return to them until his term of duty was over. If Wooden Legs and Joking Woman would excuse Hides-in-Shadows from her chores, we could study English more intensively to ensure she accurately interpreted for them when I left.

Just the possibility started joy bubbling in my heart, but as I thought more rationally, the bubbles quickly burst. I could not put that sweet boy out of his bed for any length of time, and unmarried I could certainly not travel east with Nathaniel. It made more sense for us to wed immediately, and then my place would be at my husband's side.

"Alcy Anderson." I tested the name on my tongue and liked the way it sounded. "I am Mrs. Nathaniel Anderson," I said aloud, picturing myself at his side.

"Lord, I can't delay giving him my answer any longer. I've come to a decision and hope it is Your will. If not, please tell me plainly—it will affect many lives besides my own. I do not understand why You have been so silent. I'm not asking for a yes or a no, only that You answer."

Snuggled in the luxurious mattress, sleep came quickly and deeply, and I awoke at twilight, refreshed and at peace. "Preparations are in the heart of man," I recited, wholly sure now of my reply, "but the answer of the tongue is from the Lord."[53]

A man's heart deviseth his way: but the Lord directeth his steps.

Proverbs 16:9

Chapter 12

NOW THAT I had my answer, I did not want to keep Nathaniel dangling or expose him to any more awkward moments with his friends. He had been wonderfully patient. I spent the remainder of the early evening listening to the children tell stories, mainly about their beloved Uncle Nate, until we began preparing the table for dessert.

Tennie pulled me along with her to each plate she set and squeezed my hand before letting go. "You sit here, Miss Callen," she whispered, motioning to the place I occupied earlier. "I like you. May I call you Auntie Alcy?"

Who could resist such friendly frankness? "I like you, too, Tennie, and would be happy for you to call me your Aunt, but first…"

Just then, the men came in and took their places at the table. Paulette's apple tart rivaled old Lisbeth's, and afterward, Nathaniel asked me to take a turn around the stockade's catwalk. The air was crisp and the breeze just strong enough to stir the senses as it floated clouds across the slenderest crescent moon. Darkness draped the distant hills in solitude, as if this place were the farthest extremity of the earth; and unlike the constant hum of the village, only bits of the sentries' conversation punctuated the silence.

Once we were out of their hearing, the Captain slowed his pace and took my hand. "They are a lovely family, aren't they? I knew you and Paulette would take to each other. George has reminded me about a settlement farther east than Monroe—no more than five hours from here, where land is plentiful, and as it was established several years ago, it will have more amenities suited to a gentlewoman's taste. We can visit it before my duty is up if you'd like, or we can go back East before making any decisions. My father's business holds a place for me should we decide to remain in Boston, and the family owns a small country house across the Charles that would suit a newly married couple ideally. We may use it as long as we like. You have only to say the word, and Mother will increase the staff in readiness for our arrival. Naturally, whatever we decide, I would like you to meet them as soon as possible."

"You've thought of everything," I replied, looking up into his warm amber eyes. "I'm greatly honored that you want me for your wife, Nathaniel. Of all of my acquaintances, you are one of the men I most admire. I'm also certain you will make a most wonderful husband—but I cannot accept."

"You…you are refusing my offer of marriage?"

"Yes." I looked down, hating the bewildered disappointment I'd caused. "Had you asked me three months ago, I would've consented with joy, but I'm too changed. You deserve a wife who loves you differently than I do."

"Be sensible, Alcy. We have been away from each other. The regard you once felt for me will rekindle as we reacquaint ourselves. I'll give you all the time you need."

"I'm sorry, Nathaniel. My regard for you has not lessened in the least— my expectations have increased."

"Meaning exactly what? Am I to believe those savages somehow raised you to a standard beyond me?"

"No, that's not what I mean at all. They…"

"You surely don't wish to return to them after seeing how welcome you would be here?"

"I was horrified sick when I found myself in Preying Eagle's hands, but the Lord comforted my soul and has directed my behavior. He prepared their hearts amazingly for the Gospel. All they needed was someone to tell them. You witnessed with your own eyes the throng that turns out for our nightly Bible readings, and many have committed their lives to Him. We had a mass baptism that reminded me of the accounts we read in Acts."

"I understand how thrilled you are and am grateful He allowed you to be a part of it, but be sensible. You were not born to that kind of life. As my wife, you would live in the way to which you have become accustomed—the way your father intended you to live. They will work you like a horse. You have already grown too lean."

"I do work harder than I've ever done and don't expect you to agree with my decision; but I would far rather have few, difficult years on earth doing the Lord's bidding than many comfortable ones spent pursuing my own pleasure. Honestly, Nathaniel, if I were to die there tomorrow I'd die quite happy. God has graciously fitted me into His plan, and I wouldn't trade these last months for any amount of time elsewhere."

"Alcy, do you think God can only use you among a tribe of Indians? You make marrying me sound like a choice between serving Him or not. There are people in Boston who need to hear the Gospel and in the local settlements as well. I would hope you would serve Him wherever you reside."

"Yes, of course, but for reasons of His own, He has chosen to place me in the village. My people cannot read His Word without me. How can I abandon them?"

"Your people? Alcy, you will never be one of them. God created you a white woman of genteel birth."

"Perhaps you are right," I shrugged, thinking of Swallow Woman. "They may always look at me as a foreigner. They are, nonetheless, the people I choose. The village is my home and where I wish to stay."

"You are very young," he groaned, shaking his head, "and no doubt impressionable, but I've never thought you stubborn and foolish. What of the marriage you want and children?"

"The Lord may not plan for me to marry, but if He does, He can provide a way that won't prohibit me from staying there. The one and the other are not mutually exclusive."

"Alcy! You surely wouldn't consider marrying one of those warriors!"

"I might."

"That's indecent! You can't seriously consider raising a passel full of half-breeds. Think about what your father would say!" He paused for a moment, apparently contemplating a plausible explanation for my refusal, for he asked, "Is there something you're not telling me? You were alone with 'your brother' for the better part of a week. Did he force himself on you?"

"No!" I answered, reddening from his unexpected allegation. "He was thoughtful and considerate—even gentle."

Nathaniel dropped his gaze, unable to look at me, and turning toward the catwalk tightly clutched its railing. "I see. That explains much—his high-handed manner, your ready acceptance of it, even your refusal to act in your own best interest. I'm a conceited fool. When you grew eager to accompany me here, I assumed I knew your answer, but you came to protect your child's father."

He raised a hand to silence my reply as if he needed to get the words out uninterrupted.

"I understand how terrified you must have been. As a soldier, I have seen people do things to survive that they would never normally consider. Tell me plainly, Alcy, though I ask you to please spare me the details. It will not make a difference. I will still marry you, as promised, and we will raise his child as mine. But," he moaned, "may the Lord give him your light eyes!"

I could hold my Scots-Irish temper no longer. "You are quite far off the mark! Preying Eagle treated me with a respect that excelled many gentlemen of 'polite society,' though I can't say the same of you at this moment! Your assertions are base and offensive, and your arrogance indefensible. Not only is he your brother in Christ, but he is also clear thinking and intelligent, skilled at all he turns his hand to do. If he wanted me, I would thank my Father in heaven for the privilege of bearing his children."

Nathaniel looked down, red-faced and struggling to regain his composure. "Of course, you are correct. I had no right to say the things I did. You must be sensible that it smarts to be rejected in favor of someone who has so little to offer you in the way of stability, worldly goods, or position in life."

"Honestly, Nathaniel, what he has is all I want," I replied, somewhat mollified. "During these last months, I've learned what is truly valuable cannot be purchased and that real security comes only from God. I sincerely appreciate your offer, even your willingness to raise another man's child, but you're not in love with me. You regard me highly, as I do you, and we fit well into each other's plans. At one time, this would have been enough; it is no longer."

He did not bother denying the accuracy of my statement but turned to reason. "Alcy, do you not realize we will be at war with them in the decades to come? Settlers are coming this way by the scores, many believing it our manifest destiny to take this land. Pastors are encouraging their flocks to drive out the savages as Israel drove out the Canaanites. They will kill your husband and sons and you will die hungry and old before your time. Have you considered these things?"

"Should I determine my course because of other men's covetousness? My husband and children, should I ever have any, I will trust to God, to whom the battle belongs."

Moonlight dimly silhouetted his profile as he leaned rigidly against the parapet. For a long time, he stood silently staring at the stars that had begun shining over the hills once the wind picked up.

"You are right," he stated with sudden decision. "I stand ashamed of my arrogance. This is not the reunion I'd envisioned between us. Will you forgive me?"

"Of course," I replied, my ire dying away. "Your friendship means much to me. Must you tell Major Young of the village's location? If Henry got wind of it, he might cause problems for them as a means to gain his ends.

This tribe has never encountered a settler, let alone been a threat to one."

"What about the family of the auburn-haired girl?"

"She was found wandering the woods as a child, dazed from exposure and lack of nourishment. If not for them, she would have died."

"That warrior of yours could do a lot of damage if we had to fight him, and that other one, too."

I smiled, reminded of my first impression of Preying Eagle. "He's not my warrior, nor is he the reason I'm returning. He is my brother, nothing more—and wouldn't you fight fiercely to protect your family?"

"Yes, certainly. Alcy, I will do nothing to put either you or them at risk, but you know I must tell the Major what I have learned. As a soldier under his command, I would be irresponsible to do otherwise. However," he twinkled, "I can honestly say they are soon moving to their winter camp, and I haven't an inkling of that location."

I smiled at his complicity. "You are forever protecting me from Henry one way or another."

"Ah," he sighed. "I'd hoped to see that smile across my breakfast table. I'll miss it greatly."

"You make me wish my answer could have been different."

"It's getting chilly. We should go back to the Young's so you can get some sleep. The Major wants to talk with you early tomorrow morning. He's interested in the things you overheard in Monroe in addition to wanting to hear your account of the coach's robbery."

As we walked through the door, his friends' eager faces betrayed their hopes of happy tidings, but they were too tactful to ask us questions. Ours showed there were none. Bidding each other goodnight, we made an early end to the evening.

SHORTLY AFTER SUNRISE, Nathaniel escorted me to the office where Major Young and a man named O'Fallon listened to my testimony.

"And these Indians never held you against your will?" asked the Major.

"No sir, they took me in as a daughter. I wish to return to them as soon as possible."

The Major's head shot up in surprise, and he looked at Nathaniel for confirmation.

"You... you...," he faltered, "are quite sure you are not making too hasty a decision, Miss Callen? Your trials have been severe, but you must not allow them to addle your thinking. Nate led us to believe that you and he..."

"Miss Callen has refused my proposal."

"She is not of age," Mr. O'Fallon pointed out. "She cannot make such a grave decision without consulting her guardian."

Seeing horror cross my face, Nathaniel hastily argued, "We can't return her to her uncle—plus I gave her adopted father my word that we wouldn't hold her against her will. Frankly, we don't want trouble from this tribe. Our regiment would be no match for them."

"How large?" O'Fallon inquired.

"I saw only one of many bands. The people numbered in the hundreds."

"Miss Callen," began Major Young, "would you consider residing here until you are of age? At that time, no one could dispute your wishes."

"May I ask you a question, Major Young?"

"Yes, go ahead."

"Did you bring your family to this outpost because it is the place above all others you desire to live and raise your children?"

"No, I was assigned here; but, I beg your pardon, I cannot see the relevance of the question."

"I, too, am submitted to a commander, and He has assigned me the task of reading the Bible to these kind and peaceful people. I can't refuse Him any more than you could decline your orders."

"Well, put that way I can hardly argue with you, but a capable man or..." he looked at the Captain, "a couple would be far better equipped for such a work than a defenseless, well-bred young woman."

"God chooses the weak things in this world to confound the mighty so that no flesh can boast in His presence."[54]

"Perhaps so, but the whole notion is extraordinary. Under these unusual circumstances, you are free to go whenever you would like, but your parting will grieve my wife and children. We had hoped to make you one of our number, at least temporarily. We will relay this information to the circuit judge and now have several witnesses who can testify that you are quite unmistakably alive. I do not think we have enough evidence to prosecute your uncle for your father's murder, but he will not gain your fortune. The judge can have it tied up under pending investigation until you come of age. At least you can take a small measure of satisfaction in knowing you prevented him from achieving his goal."

"Thank you, sir."

"Major Young, may I escort her back to the village, as we discussed?"

"Yes, certainly. You may leave anytime Miss Callen is ready. Captain, would you consider staying with these Indians for a while? You could gather information helpful to our dealings with them...and be available should your young lady have a change of heart."

"Yes, sir, gladly. We will leave as soon as possible."

AFTER THANKING THE Youngs for their hospitality, we began the journey. Paulette kindly offered me a shawl and a warmer dress, as the morning was quite cool, but I refused, not wanting to take anything from her that she could not easily replace. Had our situations been different, I would have liked to become better acquainted with her, but I would not likely visit the outpost again and was certain she would not call at my home.

Home! My heart soared in anticipation of returning there by nightfall. When I first came to the village, I never imagined I would think of it that way, but being at the fort had made me acutely aware it was exactly where I belonged. Would they be surprised to see me so soon? Precisely when did the Moon of Yellow and Falling Leaves end? The moon was new a few days ago and most of the trees were beginning to color gloriously. Now that I was sure where my heart rested, I could not wait to become one of the people, a foxglove uprooted from a formal garden and grafted into a vine flowering wildly over the hills.

Swallow Woman's warning crept over my heart like a dark shadow, but I knew she was not entirely correct. My mother, youngest brother, grandparents, Hides-in-Shadows, and Red Fawn certainly wanted me; and I had good reason to hope that my father, three other brothers, a few of my aunts, and the many believers did as well. If the rest of the people felt as she said, I hoped their hearts might open to me over time.

As we rode out of view of the outpost, I asked Nathaniel to stop so I could don my warm rabbit-lined moccasins and undo my hair. Mutiny had risen in my heart when Preying Eagle insisted I wear braids, but I now felt wholly different. The weight of the heavy coil pulled uncomfortably at the nape of my neck, unnaturally elevating my chin; and as I remembered the expression his eyes had then held, hope began stirring that it might be there again. Winding the lengths of soft hide around my braids, I yearned to be home with the fervor of a young rabbit longing for the warmth and security of her warren.

"You seem very far away, Alcy. Of what are you thinking?"

My immediately deepening color gave him all the answers he needed.

"Ah. My rival."

"He's far from that," I smiled a bit sadly. "He spoke more to me yesterday than he has the entire time I've lived in the village. Please don't divulge any of what I've told you. I meant to hide it in my heart but blurted it out in anger."

"Your secret is safe with me, but you have only to note his overbearing manner to suspect what he feels toward you."

"I am one of his responsibilities, nothing more, but he takes them seriously."

"Doesn't the other brother? I never noticed him acting overbearing."

"Preying Eagle is the eldest, so the weight falls on his shoulders—and Two Bears has a much easier nature."

"You know them better than I do, but I had the distinct impression he wanted me off his territory."

"They have narrowly prescribed methods of courtship, and he engages in none of them—quite the opposite."

"So, your feelings toward him haven't any bearing on your decision to stay?"

"No," I shook my head. "I would be quite a fool to base so momentous a commitment on so dismal a hope, and in one way I'm thankful he is indifferent. It has helped me sort out God's will. If Preying Eagle wanted me, I might always wonder if selfish desires rather than the Lord led me to return; and when things become difficult, I might regret my choice. As it is, I will face adversity assured of God's plan, knowing He will uphold me whatever may come. Besides, there is a very beautiful girl from the village who has set her cap for him, and no doubt she will succeed."

"Even in your ragged clothes, I doubt she is prettier than you, Alcy. I've always thought you a handsome young woman, but depriving you of all your finery has made you surprisingly more so."

"Nathaniel, you're very dear," I laughed, "and half-blind. You will make a most wonderful husband to some fortunate young woman. This girl is so graceful they call her Swallow Woman for the beauty of that bird in flight."

"Oh—you mean the interpreter. I'd assumed you meant an Indian woman."

One of my eyebrows arched involuntarily. "No, but I agree the description suits her as well. Her name is Hides-in-Shadows."

"What an extraordinary thing to call a young woman. Why on earth would anyone name her that?"

Answering this and many more questions about her history occupied the next quarter-hour, and by its end, we had arrived at our intended meeting place. I held my breath, anticipating Preying Eagle's reaction to my swift return, but was sorely disappointed. Two Bears and he were nowhere in sight. Nathaniel, who very considerately did not point this out, helped me off the cavalry mount. Perhaps they felt as Swallow Woman implied; and yet, their father had specifically commanded them to wait.

"Nathaniel," I ventured. "Could we have come to the wrong spot?"

He shook his head definitively. "No. There is the little clump of pines to which your warrior took you yesterday afternoon and the peak that lines up with them. The other does the same on the side opposite."

My stomach sank. We waited over an hour—possibly two—each check of Nathaniel's timepiece diminishing my confidence, when suddenly they emerged from the tree line. Each had a deer slung over the rear of his horse, and they had slung another over the back of my pony.

For the briefest instant, Preying Eagle looked startled and then hastening his mare forward leaped to the ground before she had stopped. His eyes, sweeping over my braids as he closed the gap between us, held enough pleasure and approbation to satisfy my susceptible heart. Whatever Swallow Woman felt, he was glad I was coming home.

He even greeted Nathaniel affably, expressing thanks for my quick and safe return, which I translated happily. However, when I asked if he would grant permission for the Captain to accompany us to the village, Two Bears and he exchanged frowns.

They consented, heaving the dead deer onto the Cavalry mount's saddle so I could ride the paint, underscoring both Preying Eagle's authority over me and my allegiance to him. This annoyed Nathaniel but so warmed my heart that three of our four-member party commenced the journey home with better dispositions than those we had brought with us. Once the fourth checked his irritation and fell into line, the trip passed by quickly and without incident.

Excitement bubbled up inside me as I spotted the familiar promontory marking the ascent to our camp. All of my family came out to greet us, along with many dear others. Hides-in-Shadows beamed and then seeing Nathaniel did as her name suggested, while Red Fawn almost danced with glee. Running Deer managed to convey deep satisfaction, though he said nothing outside of the usual courtesies, and my mother's joyful countenance will remain etched in my heart forever. Her brother, Many Feathers, met us with a small contingent of warriors I did not recognize and urged the Captain to remain with us until we broke camp.

When we had retired to Two Doves' dwelling so our family could enjoy each other's company unreservedly, Red Woman embraced me. Tears ran down the furrows in her wrinkled cheeks, and her husband and sons quizzed Nathaniel about our talk with Major Young.

AFTER SUPPER, MY Father announced, "We will walk," and escorted me to the precipice. As we gazed down upon the hills, ablaze with the colors of fall, he asked, "Where is this place of the white man?"

I pointed in the direction we had come.

He nodded then became still for several long moments before concluding, "It is too close. We will change our winter place."

When he lapsed into silence again, I thought about asking where we would go but decided to keep quiet. He seemed pensive as if he were working out something in his mind. After a long while, he turned to face me.

"The Moon of Yellow and Falling Leaves has come. Has your heart found its rest?"

"Yes," I replied, certain of my answer. "My heart rests here."

"Good," he again nodded. "I could not have parted with you easily."

While I was grateful for this unexpected disclosure, I felt suddenly vulnerable. I had respected and admired him almost from the start, but Father's empty place in my heart was too tender to let Running Deer claim without knowing his feelings. He had been consistently generous, considerate, and protective, but his face—like his eldest son's—invariably revealed little or nothing of his thoughts. Now that he had made them clear, I hoped my demeanor conveyed my affection. I was far too in awe of him to voice it.

"We are concerned that one day we may find ourselves in conflict with the long knives," he told me gravely. "Your heart will own much pain."

"The Creator brought me here. He knows if this will happen."

"Even so, 'No one can serve two masters; he will hold to the one and despise the other.'[55] You must choose."

As I walked down the path beside him, I contemplated both his words and Swallow Woman's cruel assertions. They had not accurately reflected any of the hearts that mattered most to me. Perhaps she was also mistaken about others.

"You are very quiet. You cannot do this?"

"I am troubled by something I heard from a young woman shortly before Captain Anderson arrived. She said many of the people hoped I would return to the white men. I fear I will always be a foreigner, never one of the people."

Halting, he took hold of my shoulders and looked at me intently. "Do not disquiet your heart on this account. Hides-in-Shadows told me all when you left. Swallow Woman eats her own bitterness. Preying Eagle is not blind. She has desired him from childhood, but he has never wanted her. She is like her mother, who was also beautiful in form and face when she was young, but they have small hearts. No one who has watched or listened to you agrees with her."

Impulsively, I rested my forehead on his chest as I would have my own father, and he gently rested his chin atop my hair.

YOU HAVE NOT YET experienced the cold and hungry Moon of Difficulty or the cruel battles that take place with our enemies," warned Two Doves once I returned to our dwelling. "Are you certain your heart has had time to decide?

"Fighting will not end among any people until there is an end to greed. Leaving you yesterday felt like death. Leaving you again would tear apart my heart."

"It would tear mine also," she smiled. "Now, stand up. I want to see if this fits you." She held up the beautiful spruce-colored dress she had shown us all on the day of the downpour.

"This is for me?" I asked, recalling how eager she had been to please the recipient. "It is beautiful! I cannot wait to put it on."

She helped me out of my old dress, cast it aside, and would have done the same with my petticoat; but though I removed it, I could not let it go. Its tattered remains held too many fond memories. I stroked the soft folds of the doeskin, cherishing it more than the finest silk, for every quill and stitch held my new mother's love. Taking her a little by surprise, I hugged and kissed her warmly, unable to contain my happiness.

"Preying Eagle has given me two more doeskins from his kill this morning so I can make you another, but we must cure them first."

"How can I ever thank you for all that you have done for me?"

"You have," she responded, "by returning to us. My heart always desired a daughter and the Creator has answered my prayers."

Just this past July, I had asked the Lord how He could have allowed all that had happened. Now I asked Him why He had been so kind. I certainly had done nothing to warrant such love.

As we gathered that evening for the reading of the Word, I heard many mutterings of approval concerning my attire and could not resist glancing in Preying Eagle's direction. His face displayed unconcealed pleasure, as it had the first day he examined Stump's dapple-gray mare.

An unfamiliar warrior sitting closely by his side looked startled when our eyes met fleetingly. He was neither as handsome as my eldest brother nor as tall as Kicking Horse, but he bore himself with an unmistakable air of confidence. I quickly looked to the ground lest he think that he, not Preying Eagle, had drawn my attention, but not before noticing that his comment to the latter had produced a deep scowl.

As Running Deer stood to address the people, all our eyes turned his way. "The Creator sent this woman of pale skin and eyes like water to bring us back His book. She promised to serve our family and obey me as a daughter obeys a father. She has done this well, working beside the other women without complaint, helping wherever she found a need, caring for our old, and loving our young. You have all seen her worth. As you each have a part in her, I have asked her to tell you where her heart rests."

The commitment I was about to make was daunting, yet a profound peace had settled in my heart that I knew was from the Lord. My mother's warm dark eyes gave me much-needed courage to speak before so large an assembly in a tongue I had not mastered, and I hoped the words Hides-in-Shadows helped me adapt from the book of Ruth would express all that was in my heart.

Approaching the fire, I tossed upon it my gray dresses and worn-out shoes, pledging while the flames consumed them: "As my white woman's clothing turns to ashes on the ground, so my life as a white woman goes down into the earth. Where you go, I will go; and where you lodge, I will lodge. Where you die, I will die; and there I will be buried. May the Lord let nothing but death divide me from this people."[56]

As I listened to their vocalizations of acceptance, my cautious heart felt fortunate and full. In my preoccupation with Nathaniel and my own decisions, I was unaware of how many had grieved, assuming I would remain at the outpost. That evening, when I knelt to read the Word, I looked into faces full of warmth and relief, smiles and affection. Three moons ago, I was bereft of family and cut off from friends. Tonight, I had become one of the people.

There is no one who has left house or parents or brothers or wife or children, for the sake of the kingdom of God, who shall not receive many times more in this present time, and in the age to come, eternal life.

Luke 18:29

Chapter 13

"SPOTTED LONG-KNIFE is looking for you," Elk Dog Boy told me when I set down our family's waterskins the next morning. "I go too," he added a bit sheepishly, "to keep you safe."

We wended through the trees to the meadow where Nathaniel tended the cavalry mounts.

"Good Morning, Alcy! Judging by your escort I have gone up in the trustworthiness department."

"You cannot blame them," I laughed. "They have a very bad impression of white men. Preying Eagle's report about Stump and mine about Henry confirmed the tales they've heard. I'm glad that they met you. You're the only white man they don't think is a savage!"

He grinned, knowing it to be true. "The color of that deerskin suits you."

"Thank you, it's much warmer and more comfortable than my others. Two Doves has been wonderful to me; it's been so long since I've had a mother's care or guidance."

As he watched Elk Dog Boy take a seat several paces beyond my shoulder, his eyes crinkled against the rising sun. "Do you remember the conversation we had in Henry's carriage before your father became ill? I asked you what you desired for your future."

"Yes, I had not wanted to ride home alone with Henry."

"Yesterday, I often thought of your answers. Except for the husband and children, whom," he teased, "you are passing up of your own free will. God has given you the desire of your heart."

"Nathaniel, I cannot have it both ways—unless, of course, you are also wanting to burn your white men's clothes."

"Your eyes twinkled exactly like your father's just then."

"Did they? People usually say I have my mother's looks, but I'm glad to carry some of him with me, even if it's only a twinkle. When Preying Eagle was unconscious, I often thought about that conversation. God has been very gracious to me. How far away is the settlement you plan to live in once your duty is over?"

"That's why I asked to speak with you. I've been thinking and praying about something this morning, and I'd like to know your thoughts before proceeding further. Do you think your elders would consider allowing me to come back in a few months?"

"I don't know. They show you much respect."

"After the ignorant things I said a couple of nights ago, I'm embarrassed to admit how much the Lord has been stirring my heart. I marvel at their hunger for the Word. They are like fledglings waiting with their mouths open wide. I'm beginning to suspect God is calling me to help nurture them. Would you object?"

"By no means—I'd like that very much! But is this because of me?"

"No, though I admit your presence lends this village more appeal. Should God confirm my inclinations, I see no reason to rule out our marriage, do you?"

"No," I shook my head, "but I'm not sure Running Deer would grant us permission. He is concerned that I will not know where I belong should aggressions rise between us and the soldiers at the outpost. Marrying you would greatly complicate that choice."

"Do you need his permission?"

"Yes. I implicitly embraced their customs in my pledge, and here a father's rule over his daughter is absolute. Had I known you would feel this way last evening, I might have held off, hoping they would extend a welcome to us both. It's too late now."

"I'm as surprised about this as you are and not prepared to live here permanently—at least not yet. How," he nodded toward my youngest brother, "can he stand to wear nothing but a breechcloth? Should the Lord bring me to that point, I will keep my own clothes, thank you. Walking around like that, especially when it's this cool, is out of the question."

I struggled to restrain a fit of giggles. "I'm sorry. I simply can't imagine you with long red braids."

"Neither can I."

"You will not like what they call you—The Spotted Long-knife."

He pulled his brow together sharply. "Why?"

"Your sword, I guess. They called Major Young 'The Elder of the Long-knives,' so perhaps the last refers to all the military. The spots are your freckles. None of them have any, so they stand out as a distinguishing feature."

"Well," he shrugged, "I'll take the designation as a degree of acceptance. If I was to live here, would you reconsider your answer?"

I smiled, wondering what God was planning while trying to sort out how I felt. "That would clear away the fundamental obstacle."

"Fair enough. If it's God's will, He can bring your new father around to the idea."

Heading back toward the village together, I asked him something that had long been troubling my heart. "Nathaniel, if the righteous triumph over the wicked, why did Henry triumph over my father?"

"He didn't—at least not from God's vantage point. God certainly could've prevented your father's death. The Word clearly says He has numbered every hair on our heads, and that we need fear only Him who can dispatch both body and soul to Hell.[57]"

"Then doesn't that imply He will protect us?"

"Read the entire chapter when you have a chance. Shortly before that verse, He tells His disciples they may die for Him. Primarily the passage urges us to hold back nothing, not even our lives, but to trust He will use both our lives and deaths for His own great purposes. Henry only destroyed your father's earthly tent, his temporary covering, and he succeeded because God's purpose for Horace on earth had been completed."

"Are you saying He planned for Henry to kill him?"

"God doesn't want anyone to sin, but He gave Henry free will and knew what he would do with it before He created either of them. You know the verse: 'All things work together for good to them that love God, to them who are called according to his purpose.'[58] Had Horace not died, none of the events for which we've just been praising God would've happened—at least you wouldn't have been involved. These people would have remained unknown to you, and your new loved ones might still be lost in their sins."

"I just wish Father hadn't suffered so."

"So do I, but I'm sure he would tell you if he could that his suffering is not worth mentioning compared to the wonder of seeing Jesus face to face. Now that he has tasted heaven, where do you think he would prefer to be?"

"Heaven."

"And from that perspective, don't you think Horace would gladly have lain down his life so they could gain salvation?"

"Yes. You are quite right. Sometimes, I've felt angry with God about it, but looking at it that way turns his death into a commencement of sorts—both for him and God's plan to bring the Word to this people."

"Best of all, it's the truth—or God is false. 'Precious in the sight of the Lord is the death of his saints.'[59]"

"I hope they'll let you return. You are much better at explaining these things than I am, and they have so many questions."

"Ask the Lord to guide me and direct their hearts."

145

"I will."

When we arrived at my mother's lodge, we found the door closed, which was unusual for this time of day, so I called for permission to admit Nathaniel. The flap flung open, and Preying Eagle ducked out so rapidly that I stepped backward to avert a collision. Instead of nodding briefly, he drew closer, until I could see nothing but his scarred chest. Startled, I looked up and noticed an entrancing smile slowly spreading from the corners of his eyes to the rest of his handsome features.

What happened to Nathaniel in those moments, I had no idea. Before I gave him or Elk Dog Boy another thought, they had disappeared, I assumed into our dwelling.

Running Deer emerged in minutes and bid me accompany him, but Preying Eagle blocked my way, bringing about the impact I had barely avoided. My heart thumped wildly as my palms, flung out to maintain my balance, came in contact with his bare torso, and his hands warmly grasped my waist.

Presuming he had miss-stepped, I tried afresh to follow his father; but he barred my way a second and third time, letting me know his actions were entirely intentional. When I again glanced up and found mischief in his grin, my knees began to weaken; but he refused to budge until I reciprocated with a smile.

Once released, I scurried after Running Deer, hoping he might attribute my heightened color and odd breathing to the hasty steps required to catch up. His eyes assessed me quizzically, but he continued the measured stride he usually employed when pondering matters of consequence.

"While you were at the white man's outpost, I have given something Two Doves told me much prayer and consideration. She says your heart longs for a warrior. Is this so?"

All hope of returning to my normal hue evaporated. "Yes," I responded, incapable of giving artful answers to any of the awkward questions he often posed, as if God Himself were calling me to account.

"Good," he nodded. "I will exchange horses with a warrior and allow him to take you."

Too stunned to reply, my color became the least of my concerns. If he meant his eldest son, I would happily comply, but after months of indifference, those few playful moments were hardly enough to make me secure.

"How many summers have you lived?"

"Seventeen."

"Good. This is a healthy age to bear children. Until your heart rested, I would not permit any of our warriors to spread his blanket over you. Now that you have become one of us, I will allow them to do this."

Them? There will be more than one?

"Do you understand what this means?"

"Yes. Hides-in-Shadows told me."

This explained why Kicking Horse had never waited outside our dwelling. Sharing his blanket would be deplorable, but I felt aghast at yielding him a husband's rights! My pledge was less than twelve hours old and twice already I was sorely tempted to regret it.

"Good," he nodded. "I have given two warriors consent. They both have shown courage in battle and skill in hunting. One is esteemed for his good judgment and restraint—I wish you to accept him, but you may choose between the two."

I breathed a little more easily. My father's choice could not be Kicking Horse; he did not fit the description. I was certain, though, that he was the other. His interest was plain, his uncle had paid several unexpected visits to my father, and both my parents had seen me return his smile.

Running Deer's choice might well be Preying Eagle—or even Nathaniel, who I assumed had just been speaking with him. Whoever he was, I knew not only my father but also the whole village would expect me to accept him, and my pledge made turning back impossible. Were I to break my word, I would unearth their confidence in everything I had said and spoil the very purposes for which I had returned.

"*Lord,*" I prayed inwardly, "*when You directed me to commit myself to this people, You knew what my father would require. Please help me keep my promise and trust You to direct his heart.*"

"Are you unwilling?"

"No." I shook my head, though I felt as if I were flinging myself from the promontory. "I will accept the warrior you have chosen."

He abruptly stopped, as though surprised by my prompt acquiescence. Gently pulling me towards him, he tenderly confided, "Your trust and obedience please me. You have once again proven yourself a worthy daughter of our people."

His earnest praise overwhelmed my heart, uncovering my intense longing for his love and approval. I wished he might never regret taking me into his family.

"Spotted Long-knife," he continued, "wants the elders' permission to return to us. Do you want this?"

"Yes."

"Is he the warrior your heart desires?"

I was unsure of what to say. I could not lie, but if Nathaniel were his choice and I told him no, he might think I wanted Kicking Horse. Had I not just asked the Lord to help me trust Him? Feeling once more I was leaping from the precipice, I took a deep breath and answered, "No."

"Good. He would grieve us by taking your heart away. You would always be a white man's woman, raising his white sons next to ours. The warrior I have chosen will fill your belly with his sons, mingling your blood with ours. He will bind you to us as long as you live, though food becomes scarce and battles rage. This is what I want and also what our people want."

I felt so deeply touched, I could not immediately answer. He—and the people—wished me bound to them unalterably!

"I am glad our Creator entrusted me to you," I whispered. "Give or withhold your consent to whomever you will. I will be guided by your wisdom."

He caressed my cheek in the manner of his eldest and then strode away. I felt profoundly grateful for his care but reeled from the magnitude of his decree and all its implications. Inhaling deeply, I determined I would not give way to fear. My heavenly Father had led me to this point and was wholly worthy of my trust.

"But Lord," I mumbled, "if You are willing, please let his choice be Preying Eagle!"

"RUNNING DEER IS A wise and thoughtful father," Hides-in-Shadows remarked as we dipped our water sacks into the lake.

"I am fortunate he adopted me," I replied, wondering if he had apprised her of the content of our conversation. She did not pry into my feelings and I did not volunteer them—they were far too jumbled to express—so we walked to the village in silence.

Returning to my family's dwelling, I was relieved to find only the soothing presence of my mother. "You have honored your father greatly with your trust," she smiled. "He returned from your walk very pleased."

"I am in awe of him," I confided. "His wisdom and forethought astounded me from the first. The Creator was exceedingly kind when He put me into your care."

"He blessed us as well. I, too, think Running Deer is remarkable and have always considered myself honored to be his woman. He was much like Preying Eagle at his age." Glancing at me meaningfully, she added, "We noticed on several occasions that Kicking Horse has gained your attention and everyone sees he desires you. He is a fierce warrior, greatly respected for his courage."

I appreciated Two Doves indicating whom I should expect but had no more idea what to reply than I had earlier with her husband. To accept his attentions filled me with dread. "I did not purposefully encourage Kicking Horse. He took me by surprise several times when I was new to the ways of our people."

"I am glad to hear this," she replied, "for he is not our choice for you. Running Deer gave his consent only because you seemed inclined to smile at him. Many young women are."

"I dread the thought of sharing his blanket. He is not easily put off."

"You can duck out whenever you wish to be away from him. It is your right. And the spotted long-knife—your heart does not desire him?"

"He has been a very good friend," I answered plainly. "At one time, I thought he would make me an excellent husband. He is so like my father was—perhaps too much so, and too like me."

"Heat and cold must come together to enliven the wind. It is the same with husbands and wives. If they are too much the same, they have little friction but also little excitement—like the calm lake rather than the rushing river. Some women like the lake; I prefer the river."

I wished to speak of Preying Eagle, but if her son were not my father's choice, it would be awkward for me to divulge my desire.

"There is another warrior who gained your father's permission..."

Our menfolk entered the lodge before she could finish, accompanied by Red Fox, the unfamiliar warrior whose eyes I had met last evening. Curious to learn why he had come to our village, I listened to Running Deer introducing him to my mother; but heeding my friend's warning about her flirtatious cousin, I dared not raise my eyes.

As I knelt to serve the circle of buckskin-clad knees awaiting breakfast, I felt a rough warm hand deliberately touch my own beneath the dish; and when my eyes shot up and found Preying Eagle's, I barely managed to corral my pleasure and relief. A quick glimpse toward Running Deer showed he had noted the exchange as well and looked pleased, but whether with my self-control or delight in his son, I could not tell. What anyone else observed or thought, I lacked the temerity to discover.

Shortly after the men left, my aunts and cousins joined us, along with a friend of Quiet Woman's named Cries-at-Night. She kindly offered to teach me how to weave the beautiful chokers that established her reputation as a skilled artisan.

While awaiting her instruction, I resumed sewing Preying Eagle's hunting shirt, which Two Doves had helped me design and cut before I left for the outpost. We had dyed the buckskin green, like my own, and embellished the seams with fringe to keep away insects as it moved. Similarly, while the breastplates, chokers, and anklets my aunts wove were highly ornamental, they primarily offered protection to vital spots during battles.

"Why are there strange warriors in the village?" I asked Quiet Woman curiously.

"They come from allied bands to find suitable wives among our untouched daughters."

I glanced furtively at Red Fawn, knowing how much she dreaded this possibility. She was uncharacteristically quiet and kept her head low.

"Their band lives farther to the south," continued Quiet Woman, "and is very powerful. A closer alliance with them will add to our strength."

"They arrived shortly after you left with the spotted long-knife," Two Doves chimed in, "and will stay in our village until we journey to the winter place."

"How," I asked, "can they choose a woman in so brief a time?"

Joking Woman, Hides-in-Shadows' mother, shrugged. "One woman is as good as another to many warriors. As long as she cooks his food, makes his clothes, and warms his bed at night."

"The courting must be swift," explained Quiet Woman, "but all will delay as long as they can. The warriors look first among the elders' daughters."

"The wise ones will seek modest, hard-working women, not only those who please the eyes," Joking Woman added, looking hard at Hides-in-Shadows.

It had not occurred to me until that moment that one might select her. I felt greatly threatened by the thought, yet I knew she longed to be married and could not selfishly wish her otherwise.

Cries-at-Night chuckled, "Many mothers are tiring themselves out, praising their daughter's skills and finding clever ways to display their fine work. Some craft their efforts as artfully as we perfect our weaving."

"They have good reasons," responded Quiet Woman, looking intently at Red Fawn. "These warriors are proven in battle and sons of respected elders. The fortunate young women who gain their notice will rest securely at night and never suffer want. All mothers wish this for their daughters."

"But what if the young woman loves her family deeply," asked Red Fawn, trying to maintain an even voice, "and does not want to leave her village?"

"If she loves them as deeply as you say," answered her mother, "she will help them form an alliance that may keep them alive. There are many rumors of an enemy moving into our allies' lands above the large water. They may enter into our lands next."

"If our daughter refused such an honor," declared Cries-at-Night, "my husband would put her out of our dwelling. She would shame her family and proclaim herself disobedient and foolish—then who would want her? She would die alone and childless."

Red Fawn looked as if she wanted to cry, but she bit her lip to keep it still.

Hoping to allay her fears, I asked, "Will a warrior ask for a woman who does not display a desire for his attention?"

Cries-at-Night shrugged her shoulders. "If the warrior offers many horses or the daughter does not please her father, her desires may not matter."

"You are full of questions, little one," observed Quiet Woman. "To make a necessary alliance for his people, a father might accept horses for his most obedient and beloved daughter. And as you said, the days for deciding are few."

"Raise your water-colored eyes to a warrior you find handsome," laughed Joking Woman, "and you may warm his buffalo robes before the new moon rises. You, too, are the daughter of an esteemed elder."

My aunt's affectionate teasing hit me like a well-aimed kick. Concerned for my two friends, I had not imagined I might be in the same danger.

Ever perceptive, my mother added, "A warrior's interest rarely takes a woman entirely by surprise. She will know she has attracted his attention if he visits her family's lodge, but if she does not even raise her eyes to look at him, he will usually pursue a more receptive woman. However, once she has gained his attention, she must be all the more careful that she does nothing he may misinterpret. Her father may prefer another warrior for her, but benefiting his people will weigh heavily on his heart."

Catching my mother's warning, I asked the Lord to help me avoid Red Fox.

WHEN MY FRIENDS and I set out for our evening firewood, we found our favorite place curiously full of young women gathering theirs. We quickly learned the reason. In the adjacent field, the strange warriors were helping our valiant men prepare their younger brothers and cousins for the risks entailed in the upcoming journey. Thankfully, the stranger I most feared was far too absorbed elsewhere to notice my arrival. Following his gaze, I saw Swallow Woman walking slowly and deliberately along the edge of the woods, swaying under a large bundle like some ancient princess.

Between flirtations and sport, the atmosphere crackled with excitement. The strangers elicited smiles from untouched women, and our warriors, employing the same tactics, proclaimed themselves rivals.

Whoops and laughter, teases and taunts, showered the glade as warriors hailed their younger cousins' accomplishments or marked their failures. These youths reciprocated in kind, cheering whenever a warrior won an untouched woman's attention or jeering if she turned away.

My heart went out to Little Turtle. He struggled to keep his face impassive while helplessly watching a stranger garner the attentions of a girl he had long wanted. Only proven warriors—already established as able providers and protectors—were eligible to marry. He was permitted neither to declare his interest nor ask her to wait.

"That warrior keeps watching you," Hides-in-Shadows whispered to Red Fawn.

I had noticed him also and remembered meeting him with Many Feathers.

"His father and he visit my father often," she replied shyly. "They stay late in our dwelling each night talking about the Creator's path."

"That is wonderful!" I blurted, regretting my outburst as her lip began to tremble.

"They talk much of the alliance, also. His name is Stands Apart."

"Do you like him?"

"He is confident and direct as you can see, but he makes me uncomfortable. He is not like his father, who jokes with me often. He holds himself aloof, carefully assessing all he sees."

"He's wearing a courting blanket!" warned Hides-in-Shadows.

Expecting Red Fawn to retreat toward the village or at least lower her eyes, we were both astonished when she evenly met his gaze. A beautiful, if not altogether genuine, smile graced her sweet face. Seeing it, he crossed the field and wrapped her in his blanket, but not before she tossed us a look of helpless resignation.

"Will they force her to marry him?" I asked my remaining cousin. "She is not like that young woman who might have shamed her family."

"My father says Many Feathers has been waiting to see if anything came of their talk about Jesus before he permitted him to court her. This morning settled that—he baptized Stands Apart and Spotted Eagle in the lake. Whether they will insist she accepts him, I don't know, but she seems to have taken what her mother and Cries-at-Night said while we were sewing very seriously."

While I sadly watched the stranger guide our friend away, Hides-in-Shadows tugged my elbow and a slow smile began dimpling her cheeks. "You also have not escaped a warrior's notice," she whispered, nodding toward the far field.

Surreptitiously, I glanced up and spotted Preying Eagle watching me from atop the dapple-gray mare. When we locked eyes, he urged her to a full gallop, sending my heart into my throat as he suddenly plunged over her far side. I stood breathless, dreading the thud of his body against the hard earth and terrified that the mare might trample him to death. Instead, his hand swept under her belly, plucking his rifle from the grass before he swiftly regained his seat.

Wheeling her, he rushed directly to the place where I remained standing, transfixed, whooping and waving his rifle when I broke into a relieved smile.

"WHERE IS RED FOX?" asked my father while Two Doves and I served our menfolk supper.

A satisfied smile played about Preying Eagle's lips. "Feasting in Talks-With-Bitterness' dwelling."

"My clever brother," Two Bears snickered, "drew that long-winged bird straight into the fox's open jaws."

Running Deer looked amused, Little Turtle looked as if the comment reminded him of the girl he had likely lost today, and my mother looked as pleased as I felt. After ladling generous bowls of stew for my father and Nathaniel, she handed me a surprisingly scant amount for her eldest. Fearing my friend's presence left us in short supply, I tossed her a questioning look, but her only answer was a playful glint.

When I offered Preying Eagle the meager portion, he not only deliberately touched my fingertips but also refused to support the bowl until he caught and held my gaze. He had to be my father's choice! Why else would he openly garner my attention, first in front of the other young warriors and now before his watchful family?

Two Bears refused his dish, puzzling me as much as my mother's variance in portions. "Hand it to him," he nodded toward his older brother. "He will pass it to me." His eyes twinkled as Preying Eagle shot him a curious glance, and I did as he instructed. "You see," he teased, "our sister obeys very well. The warrior who takes her will gain a fine woman."

Boldly, Preying Eagle enclosed my whole hand beneath Two Bears' bowl, while Elk Dog Boy pointed to a repair I had made on his leggings. "See the good stitches she makes. Her warrior's clothes will not come undone in the middle of a hunt."

I smiled to say thanks, but feeling uncomfortably conspicuous, darted Running Deer a cautious glance. Busy with his supper, he did not appear to have noticed, and I rose to fetch a bowl for Little Turtle.

My mother's aim became clear as she continued ladling out tiny portions, and one brother after the other told me to hand them to Preying Eagle. Though their obvious collusion delighted my heart, they asked for so many helpings I feared their stomachs might burst.

"What is all this laughter?" Demanded Running Deer. "And what are you doing to your sister? Let her eat so she can translate!"

His sons fell silent until they noticed the upward tugging at the corners of his mouth; and Nathaniel, who had caught on despite the language barrier, looked at me with a mixture of resignation and congratulations.

"Spotted Long-knife can translate!" Elk Dog Boy suggested.

Running Deer cast my friend a speculative glance. "You will do this?"

"Yes, certainly," Nathaniel nodded, "though I will need either Alcy or the red-haired girl to translate."

I interpreted for my father, substituting the appropriate names, and it was decided not only for the evening but also for the duration of Nate's stay. Recalling Two Doves' warning, I wondered if Running Deer did this to keep me from a prominent position while our village entertained the strangers. Whatever the reason, I knelt contentedly behind our men folk with my mother, relieved to be away from Kicking Horse's torments and out of view on such an emotionally volatile day.

That night, I lay on my bed wondering if I had dreamed it all. If so, I hoped never to awaken.

THE RISING SUN intensified Preying Eagle's attentions, making them as clear as they were frequent. His warm dark eyes followed me wherever I went, caressing my heart and setting it ablaze. Although Two Doves' demeanor did not alter as we sat alone in her dwelling, she introduced a subject that halted my needle mid-stitch.

"On the day you came to us, Running Deer forbade Preying Eagle to speak with you beyond the normal courtesies. He also forbade Hides-in-Shadows to translate that conversation. I have ached as I have watched the grief this has caused you, but now he has given me permission to tell you all."

So that was why he ignored me, and she had been aware of my feelings from the start! I remembered that she had caught me stroking the blanket I had shared with Preying Eagle and wondered how obvious my feelings were to everyone else. "Have I shamed you and my father by acting foolish over him in the eyes of the village?"

"No, your admiration is only natural and what the people expected. He spared you from an evil fate and all our young women see he is desirable. After so many days alone with him..." she shrugged, "how could you feel otherwise? Most are sure of nothing, but your aunts and I have watched what happens when he draws near. Your eyes go down and your color comes up.

"I told Running Deer before you left with Spotted Long-knife that your heart had made its choice. You proclaimed it while you were measuring him for the shirt you are sewing. This was why I wanted Elk Dog Boy to fetch him."

She was as good at hiding her thoughts as her husband and sons, but what about Running Deer? He, alone, last night, had not joined in the family's conspiracy to force Preying Eagle and me to enjoy further intimacies. "And Running Deer? Why did he forbid Preying Eagle?"

"For your sake, little one. The day Preying Eagle returned to us with you, he announced to the elders that he wanted to take you. Your faithful care while he slept surprised and pleased him. You could have taken the horses and left him to die. He described your modesty, your eagerness to serve him, and your gratitude when he began teaching you our ways.

"All these we have now witnessed for ourselves and are proud to call you our daughter, but as you stood before the elders, Running Deer saw uncertainty in your eyes. All our sons have made good choices from childhood, but a warrior's desire for a woman can cloud his judgment. Many young women who have left their families lament their decisions after it is too late. He did not want this for either of you."

All at once, many confusing things fit together: the promise in Preying Eagle's eyes and his words between the dwellings that afternoon we arrived, his territorial behavior with Nathaniel, even Swallow Woman's jealousy— the whole village must have learned of

155

his intentions. Judging by his conduct, his father likely lifted his prohibition yesterday morning while they talked in our lodge.

"Preying Eagle does nothing by halves," she continued. "Only by forbidding his attentions could Running Deer free you to listen to your own heart. Our eldest is our choice for you, and you are our choice for him, so twice the match blesses us. We have met no other woman we would like half so much to bear our grandchildren, and your marriage will keep your dwelling close to mine, assuring us of much time together. As for Kicking Horse, that hothead will mind his manners—your father or brothers will always be close."

I could feel myself profusely blushing, but I did not care. With dizzying speed, I had gone from the spinster's life I envisioned at the outpost to living out my days with the warrior of my longings. I felt free: free from the fear that Running Deer had some other choice in mind, free to respond to Preying Eagle's newly overt attentions, and free to allow my heart to run away with joy.

Kicking Horse could not have missed Preying Eagle's unconcealed attentions or my open responses, but neither of these deterred him. Both warriors still looked askance at Nathaniel, whose familiarity with me cast him as a rival. Kicking Horse, whose confidence knew no boundaries, sneered derisively when he was in Nate's proximity, never doubting which one of them would claim me as his spoils.

Although my father allowed Nathaniel and me remarkable freedom to associate with each other, Hides-in-Shadows and he saw much more of each other than I saw of either of them. She was, by necessity, almost always at his side.

Joking Woman, alone, was not pleased with the arrangement. Her daughter's new preoccupation sheltered her from the attentions of the wife-hunting warriors; but as I observed Hides-in-Shadows' radiant expressions, I guessed my friend minded neither this seclusion from their notice nor the alterations to her duties.

Nathaniel, ironically, had come to this village for a woman whose heart he could never have and stumbled over another whose heart would never be her own again.

To Him that is able to do exceeding abundantly above all that we ask or think, according to the power that worketh in us, unto Him be glory in the church by Christ Jesus, throughout all ages, world without end, Amen.

Ephesians 3:20-21

Chapter 14

WHILE TWO DOVES and I were talking, Elk Dog Boy ducked into her dwelling to say that a warrior was waiting for me. I warily emerged, unsure of which approved suitor to expect, and found my answer a few paces away.

He stood straight as an oak in his best clothing, his gleaming black hair ornamented handsomely with eagle feathers. I felt utterly enthralled. The courting blanket he had slung over his shoulder removed any doubt about his intent, and his eyes were lit with anticipation that matched my own.

When he drew me into his blanket, we neither embraced nor spoke of marriage, but he asked a myriad of questions for which he had no answers during his months of waiting. Where was my home? How had I escaped my father's false brother? Why had I tended him while he slept? Did I find their ways difficult? How was my life here different from the white world? Did I miss the people who shared my blood? Why had I not married Spotted Long-knife as they all had expected, and why had I chosen to become one of his people rather than remaining with my own?

I answered these as best I could within the limitations of my ability to speak the language, and, in turn, he told me he had struggled harder with Running Deer's prohibitions than he had while counting coup for the feathers he wore. When he had seen the ache in my eyes under the pine trees, he had been sorely tempted to answer the question he read there, but rather than break faith with his father, he devoured his own heart and trusted our Creator would return me to him.

On the first day we arrived in the village, he had been astonished to discover the importance of the book he accidentally tossed into the river and became determined to know its contents. An inner lack, an unmet need that he sensed but could not express, had made him feel restless and often alone. He was amazed when others confessed this also, even his father, once they realized they had been longing for Jesus. Since meeting the Creator, peace and joy replaced his agitation and unrest.

He felt awed by the Creator's work on behalf of his people and deeply grateful to have played a small part by rescuing me. When I asked him why he had, he shook his head, confessing an odd and overwhelming impulse had prompted him. It was not normally their way to interfere with strangers.

Once we returned to our mother's lodge, we visited with Running Deer and Two Doves awhile, giving me a tiny glimpse of life as his woman. Only since my pledge had his father allowed him to visit our dwelling while I was present, apart from our earliest Bible readings or the elders' councils. Watching the easy friendship between him and Running Deer and the affectionate respect he paid his mother did nothing to lessen the happy expectations I had formed by witnessing our parents' interactions.

Hides-in-Shadows called from outside, asking if Nathaniel and she might gain admittance, and my father yielded readily. When she saw Preying Eagle and I sitting side by side underneath a blanket, her face shone with delight. Nathaniel looked mildly surprised, but his nod and understanding smile signaled that he understood the implications and genuinely wished me happiness.

FOR THE NEXT few days, I did not see Preying Eagle anywhere. I missed the lingering warmth of his eyes and wondered where he might be. Hides-in-Shadows was unusually pensive, leaving me to my thoughts, which often drifted to the irreversible break I would soon make with the people of my birth. Regardless of the quality of his character, they would regard my marriage to him as an unfathomable rejection of my own race for a society they disdained. Worse yet, they would likely make the same assumptions Nathaniel voiced on the catwalk. I had only to remember his or Mr. O'Fallon's look of horror to realize this and had once employed the same false standards myself. It was frustratingly unjust.

When Nathaniel joined us, Hides-in-Shadows immediately perked up, leading me to wonder if she had been thinking of him. This sunk my mood even further. Stirring her heart so hopelessly seemed crueler than her despair of marrying. Even if he returned her feelings, she surely knew Wooden Legs would never allow him to take her away. My new people also had their prejudices.

"Nathaniel," I began when my thoughts had made a full circuit. "Why do we tend to lump others together? We have only to look at the diversity of our own kind to see the logic is faulty."

"It is easier that way," he shrugged. "A man doesn't feel as guilty if he stops thinking of people as individuals. If we label a whole group savage, we feel justified fulfilling our manifest destiny at their cost. Unfortunately, it's what happens in any conflict. When my father and grandfather fought in our War for Independence, they didn't ask 'Are these Englishmen of good character?' before firing their muskets."

He reached for our water sacks, but both Hides-in-Shadows and I quickly pulled them away. By helping us, he might degrade himself in the eyes of our warriors.

"Yes, but our governments were at war," I countered. "This tribe was not part of Tecumseh's massacres. They are not even of the same tribe. Why should they be stained with his guilt?"

"Your thinking is more idealistic than practical, Alcy. Weren't you frightened sick when you found yourself with Preying Eagle, even though he'd done you a very good turn?"

"But that is my point, Nate. I could see him only as a savage. God prepared the harvest here, but were I not forced into the situation I'd never have recognized it. I've been rethinking my fundamental assumptions about what it means to be civilized and have concluded it is character and not breeding that counts. Henry had refined his manners exquisitely but they didn't extend to his thoroughly savage heart. Father would have liked Running Deer if he could've looked beyond his prejudices. They are very much alike."

"Man looks at the outward appearance, but God looks upon the heart,"[60] chimed in my red-haired cousin, who loved the verse.

"Yes, exactly!" I exclaimed. "I've thought of sending for help from churches back East but am afraid they'd insist these people become farmers and dress like white men. How much of what we call Christian is our tradition, unrelated to Scripture or morality? I'm sure my grandmother, a delightful and devoted Christian, would proclaim our peoples' worship 'heathen' because they neither stand still nor sing hymns."

"What is wrong with it?" asked my friend, a look of concern creasing her brow.

"Nothing at all," Nathaniel reassured her. "It is just different from what Alcy and I are accustomed to in church. David danced with joy before the

Lord and the only person censured in the Biblical account was his wife."

"Why?" asked Hides-in-Shadows, "What did she do?"

"She mocked him for his exuberant display. As a result, she was never able to conceive."[61] Nathaniel surprised me by blushing as he added the last.

"I don't want to be like the Pharisees. They put burdens on men they couldn't bear and kept them from the Kingdom of God. I wish you could have witnessed the mass baptisms, Nate. They were extraordinary! I've never seen such ardent expressions of joy or worship."

"I was busy looking for you," he smiled.

The conversation ended as we ducked inside my mother's dwelling. Two Doves and I busied ourselves with needlework while Hides-in-Shadows translated a discussion between Running Deer and Nathaniel. I would miss him a great deal when he left and wished he did not have to return to the outpost at all.

A few hours and many topics later, Elk Dog Boy again informed us that a warrior awaited me. I hurried out eagerly, having missed Preying Eagle greatly during the days apart, only to feel my stomach drop. Looking as splendid as he had the first day I met him, Kicking Horse stood tall, an arrogant smile twisting his lips. As I stepped into his outspread blanket, his predatory eyes made me feel more like a prize than a woman whose heart he desired, and I wondered if his rivalry with Preying Eagle had prompted his attentions. He had known nothing else about me when I first arrived.

I attempted to duck out immediately, but he held the blanket in such a way that I could not escape without causing a struggle. Hides-in-Shadows, who had also emerged from our lodge, headed toward her mother's dwelling. Glancing back over her shoulder, she looked as if she was undecided whether to stay or go.

"Please come," I called. "We need you to translate."

"We do not need words," Kicking Horse replied as she returned. "Go! Leave us—now!"

She did not leave, and I did not respond, allowing him to assume I had not understood. I hoped that Running Deer, or even Nathaniel, would step out of the lodge.

Kicking Horse began bragging that his courage and skills were unequaled by any warrior in our tribe and that every unmarried girl in the village felt jealous that I was his choice. Then as he paused for a response I did not immediately give, the expectation in his eyes changed to impatience.

I hoped to bring home my point quickly but also to avoid insult to either him or his family. "I am aware," I began, "of the honor you are

160

paying me. All who esteem valor above everything speak of you with the greatest respect, but my heart is not free. It belonged to Preying Eagle when I came to this village and is still his. I was ignorant of the people's ways and regret that I led you to believe I desired your attention. Please forgive my ignorance and release me."

I was doubly glad Hides-in-Shadows had stayed. There were nuances to my sentiments beyond my ability to articulate in their tongue, and he continued to hold the blanket fast.

"Running Deer should have told this to my uncle," he spat, "when I sought permission to spread my blanket!"

"He knew only his son's intentions and left the choice to me. Everyone in our village knows that you are the desire of many young women. When he saw that I returned your smile, he thought I might prefer you."

"It is as you say," he replied, somewhat mollified, "but you have made me look foolish!"

The man's conceit had been his undoing, but I had no idea what to reply. Fortunately, Running Deer came out of our door. Kicking Horse immediately slackened his grip on the blanket, and I ducked out from under it. The two men exchanged greetings while I retreated to our dwelling, but Kicking Horse did not come to our Bible reading that evening.

THE SUNSET WAS particularly beautiful the next day as I walked home with my bundle of sticks, looking all around for the man who held my heart. I supposed he must be hunting, as Little Turtle and Two Bears were absent also. While ducking inside our lodge to see how I might help my mother, an intriguing sound, reminding me of a bird's song carried over the wind, soon caught my attention. My father must have noticed my curiosity for, catching my attention, he motioned with his head toward our door-flap.

I stepped out and closer to the sound, but it seemed to move, luring me farther away from the safety of my mother's dwelling. When I reached the path to the lake, I hesitated. It was too far from the village for me to walk alone, especially as night was quickly falling; but when I glanced back, I found Two Bears watching me with an amused and satisfied expression. He shooed me forward with his hand, arousing pleasant suspicions about what lay ahead.

The fallen foliage crushed beneath my moccasins emitted its distinctive fragrance, and the blustering wind picked up bright orange and yellow leaves and swirled them about. Climbing a slight rise through elms and apples, I began to think my imagination had been playing tricks. The tune had become so faint, I thought it might only be the wind whistling through the treetops, but then the notes started up again—only paces away.

Curiosity compelled me around a bend within sight of the water, where I spotted a solitary figure leaning against a hickory tree. He was blowing into a kind of flute, carved on the end to resemble a bird's head. Silhouetted sharply by the sleepy sun, it appeared its beak was producing the alluring song.

I stayed rooted where I was. His blanket obscured his form and the tree cast a shadow that hid his features; but before I had decided to move nearer, he slipped toward an increasingly secluded area. Once he disappeared altogether, I would have turned back had I not recalled Two Bears shooing me forward.

After timorously taking a few more steps, my heart suddenly leaped. The warrior emerged from the shadows, engulfed me in his blanket, and peered keenly into my eyes. Softly brushing my hair with his cheek, he whispered words in an impassioned tone that I instantly recognized.

"Come dwell with me!
I am a warrior,
well known among our people.
I have riches that will be yours also,
respect that you will share.
I will surround you with strength
and defend you from our enemies.
When you hunger,
I will bring you food.
When you are cold
I will provide skins for your clothing.
I will fill you with children,
offering you great joy.
They will bind you to me until death
and care for you in old age.
Come dwell with me!"

The traditional response Two Doves taught me expressed my feelings perfectly:

"I am yours altogether."

Attaining the answer he desired, he began whispering delicious sentiments that needed no interpreting—until Elk Dog Boy burst upon us.

"At last!" he exclaimed, showing no surprise that we were wrapped closely together. "Father is waiting."

As we headed to our parents' dwelling, we saw Two Bears and Little Turtle approaching with a string of horses, among them the brown and white pony on which I had already ridden. Leaving me with them, Preying Eagle swiftly returned with his father and offered him all the horses but the paint. He passed her rope to me, elucidating his odd behavior many weeks ago. All the while, he had been planning this day. Afterward, Running Deer bid me water his new horses and pasture them among his own large herd, from which he selected horses for Preying Eagle to formally seal our engagement.

IN THE EARLY morning hours, we packed up all that had been our lives for the past twelve weeks. The whole process fascinated Nathaniel and me as we helped take down dwellings and stretched their covers between their poles. The latter we harnessed to gentler horses, forming triangular sledges on which we fastened our belongings.

Our band was decreasing by six women, all accompanying new husbands toward the rising sun and then south along the edge of the great waters. Two were significant to me: Swallow Woman, whom I would not miss, and Red Fawn, whom I hated to see go. Happily, though, Stands Apart, her husband, and his father planned to return to us soon.

After bidding Red Fawn a tearful goodbye, Quiet Woman and her youngest, Chirping Bird, joined Two Doves and me while Many Feathers led the warriors ahead of us to look for enemies and game. My father kindly included Nathaniel among their number, but Little Turtle, not having tasted battle, was among the hunters who rode beside the women and children. Old Man and his remaining childhood companions brought up the rear.

Judging by the sun, we headed southwest. Preying Eagle, Two Bears, and Little Turtle had been scouting that area for migrating enemies while they had been absent, and happily, had not found any. For someone who had always lived on the outskirts of a bustling city, the wilds of this land were wondrous to behold. Several of the beautiful vistas were familiar because Preying Eagle and I had passed them on our way north to the summer place or en route to the outpost, but with such a large party, the warriors had chosen a less direct, more easily traveled course.

While Quiet Woman absorbed Two Doves' attention, Hides-in-Shadows rode up alongside my pony. She began shyly asking me about Spotted Long-knife: how long I had known him and what I thought of his character. My answers brought her obvious pleasure, but when she asked if I thought he might return someday, I did not want to offer her false hope.

"I am not sure," I admitted. "What do you think of your first white man?"

"He is surprisingly polite. I thought white-skinned men were thieves or murderers."

I could barely keep a straight face; she sounded like a Pennsylvanian girl describing an Indian. "They do not all have two heads and eat their children," I teased, but as a look of horror crossed her face I hastily added, "There are as many kinds of pale-skins as there are men. Have you never known of any thieving or murderous brown-skinned men?"

By then Chirping Bird, Red Fawn's talkative little sister, had sidled up to us. "The Horned Warriors steal an untouched girl each summer," she informed me. "One that has just entered womanhood. They sacrifice her, believing her death will fertilize the earth."

"That's dreadful!"

"Do you not remember? A few suns back, Spotted Long-knife and Hides-in-Shadows read about them in The Book."

"I am sorry, Chirping Bird; I do not know who you mean."

"The enemies of the Israelites—the ones who made children pass through fire."

"Ah." I realized she meant the worshipers of Molech and decided not to confuse her by explaining they were from another place and time. Lacking ships and written records, they did not grasp history's far reach or know that other continents existed. Living so similarly to the nomadic early Israelites, they assumed the characters in the Old Testament were their ancestors. Of course Adam, Noah, and at least one of his sons were. "Do they live nearby?"

"Close enough that I have not slept too well lately. I became a woman during the Moon When Ponies Shed."

"The beginning of summer," my red-haired cousin clarified.

Two Doves and Joking Woman interrupted our conversation to point out the way to our last winter place and then resumed their discussion.

"Do you want Nathaniel to return to us?" I asked her once Quiet Woman had engaged Chirping Bird's attention.

Hides-in-Shadows did not need to reply; the color beneath her freckles answered for her. Instead, she asked, "Why do you call each other such odd names? I have already forgotten your white name because it has no meaning. It is just a series of sounds. No one has difficulty remembering our name for you. They just look at your eyes. Why do they call him Nathaniel Anderson?"

"Our names had meanings once, but many are lost to us now. They told what village the person lived in or identified the child's father. Nathaniel likely had a forefather named Ander. What about names like Two Bears or your father's name Wooden Legs—you cannot know what to call them from looking."

"That is different but in a way the same. Two Bears has killed two bears, which are the most ferocious of all creatures. Have you never noticed the huge claws he wears?"

"Yes, they are grotesque."

"To kill one bear is notable, but to kill two is astounding!"

"Did Elk Dog Boy kill an elk and a dog to earn his name?"

"No," Hides-in-Shadows laughed. "That would not be unusual enough. He is called Elk Dog Boy because he shows exceptional skill with horses."

"Horses?" I felt lost.

Her face dimpled deeply. "Long ago, when Old Man's father could barely walk, our people saw their first horses, but they did not know what they were. They looked like elks but allowed men to lead them like dogs—so we called them elk-dogs. His father's cousin was the first to capture one."

"Does my father run like a deer?"

"He did when he was young, and my father's legs are remarkably strong. He was not happy to learn the Creator takes no pleasure in the legs of a man.[62] They have always been his pride."

I could not suppress a smile while asking my next question. "Surely, Little Turtle did not gain his name by killing a little turtle, and he certainly does not look like one!"

"Oh, but have you not noticed he is slower than his brothers and goes inside himself often?"

I nodded, admitting I had. "What about Preying Eagle?"

"He used to pester Old Man, asking him why the Creator did this or that. So since his heart, like the eagle, seemed to live between heaven and earth, Grandfather named him Eagle Boy."

"How did he become Preying Eagle?"

"In games, he developed a distinctive style of swooping down on opponents as if they were prey—just as he did to the white men who attacked you. Many say the Creator destined him to find you and bring us His Book. I believe this also."

She became lost in thought, so we rode awhile in silence before she asked, "Does setting aside your white life never trouble you?"

"Sometimes—especially lately. I have given much thought to something Running Deer said. I meant every word of my pledge to the people, yet he wisely realized that I might one day be tempted to leave. Marrying your cousin will irreversibly bar the way. I could not abandon him or our children, nor would Preying Eagle allow me to take them. Sometimes I am tempted to bolt before it is too late."

Her delicate brow furrowed deeply. "But it is already too late. You are already his."

Her words took me by surprise. "I do not understand."

"The day Running Deer and he exchanged horses you were bound to him until death. He cannot release you unless you are impure, like Joseph planned to do with Mary until the angel stopped him. White men do not do this?"

"Engagements are entered into seriously but can be broken by either party."

"But what of the vows they have made?"

"They are not made at engagement but on the day of the wedding."

"Then what is 'engagement'?"

"When a man asks a woman to marry him and the woman accepts."

"Then if they have said they will marry, they are bound."

I could not argue. Not only did I lack words to convey the difference, but I also agreed with her. Once a person gave his word, he should keep it. The points she brought up, however, offered me a possible answer to a question I had about the biblical text she mentioned. Mary and Joseph had not married, so why did Joseph need to divorce her quietly?[63] Perhaps they, too, considered betrothals permanently binding. That would clarify a few passages about divorce in the New Testament and some confusing instructions in Deuteronomy.[64] It also offered a reason why believers are called Jesus' bride before the marriage supper has taken place.[65]

"You have become silent," she noticed. "Does this worry you?"

"No, I was just thinking."

"Do you wish Running Deer had not given you to him?"

"No, not at all. I have wanted to marry Preying Eagle almost since I met him, but the speed with which everything has taken place magnifies my fears."

"What scares you?"

After considering a moment, I answered. "Preying Eagle himself. When I am left to my thoughts, worry sometimes creeps into my heart. I fear the chasm between our cultures runs too deep for us to truly become one and the very qualities that attract me to him also fill me with alarm. I felt similar to this while watching our warriors racing swiftly over the hills.

The quick beat of their horses' hooves shook the ground, filling my ears and making me yearn for such exhilaration. I longed to feel the wind on my face, whipping my loose hair far behind me as it did theirs. Yet, I would not dare mount one of those half-wild creatures: it might rush me headlong into danger. Your cousin is like his namesake. He inspires me with awe, but I cannot predict what he will do. Sometimes, I fear he is unknowable."

"Even the eagle is known by his mate."

"Yes, but that is because they mate with other eagles. I am a sparrow, used to flitting about in a kitchen garden, not soaring from the heights."

"My father says the Creator clothed you the hide of a white woman but gave you the heart of an Ally. You have the courage I have always lacked, else," she shrugged, "you would have stayed at the outpost."

"I am glad I have his good opinion, but that is not at all the way I see myself. From a little child, I have been inclined to fret, which is the opposite of courage. As for deciding to stay, it was more a need than a choice—if I had left, I would have surely died from grief. Even so, I feel wholly out of my depths."

"I do not understand this expression."

"I feel as if I have waded into a river too deep for me to keep my footing; yet, however vehemently my fears argue otherwise, I am certain the Creator bade me enter it. In Skippack, I could maintain the illusion that I managed my own destiny. It was not true, of course, but the familiar and the predictable lulled me into believing it. Here, my vulnerability faces me at every turn—but this is good. It propels me continually into the arms of our heavenly Father. If Preying Eagle and I are already bound for life, why has he not taken me?"

"He waits for his father to choose the day," she answered. "Usually, the wedding is soon, as it was with Stands Apart and Red Fawn, but some betrothals last longer."

We lapsed into silence again for a while, something obviously weighing on her mind, then after a while, she began again. "The white world seems foreign and dangerous, though I am born from it. I do not think I could live there."

"You would be fine, as I will be, if the Creator one day chooses that path for you."

Coloring deeply, she looked down, announcing clearly what had prompted her questions, but as we rounded a tall bank of spruces, my attention was arrested by the sight of our warriors on a distant ridge. Their very stillness was striking, like tautly pulled bowstrings ready for release.

I will betroth thee unto Me, forever. Yea, I will betroth thee unto Me in righteousness and judgment, and in loving kindness and in mercies. I will even betroth thee unto Me in faithfulness, and thou shalt know the Lord.

Hosea 2:19

Chapter 15

"WHAT COULD BE down there?" I whispered.

"Buffalo," answered Two Doves, "fat from the long summer's grazing. The herds often travel the river at this time of year. An enemy would not leave themselves exposed for so long."

"Soon our warriors will begin the hunt," Joking Woman joined in. "We will eat well tonight!"

My two younger brothers and their friends urged their horses to the ridge. Someone, I could not make out who, gave a signal and they sped as one man down the other side. We also nudged our mounts forward in unison and, cresting the hill, could see many hundred buffalo grazing leisurely in the valley.

As they began to stampede, their hooves pounded the earth so loudly, they nearly obliterated the hunter's frenzied cries. Preying Eagle, his bow taut, raced over the trembling earth. Leaning perilously over the side of his mount, he shot an arrow that went straight into a bull's vital spot, flipping the creature's hindquarters over its heavy, snub-nosed head.

"Look!" exclaimed Two Doves. "There, at the back of the herd. Elk Dog Boy has brought down a calf!"

As the warriors wove in and out of the beasts, they were engulfed by such huge clouds of dust that we could distinguish only Nate and those with highly unique mounts. Preying Eagle emerged slightly as he brought down two in succession.

"Why does he kill so many?" I asked his mother.

"He is getting covers for us to make your dwelling," answered Two Doves. "We will have much scrapping and tanning to do."

"He is magnificent!" I sighed, apparently aloud. Unable to understand English, his mother turned to my friend. "What does she say?"

Hides-in-Shadows considered for a moment. "She said Preying Eagle is like a great sun rising in the east, capturing all eyes."

Joking Woman laughed. "Wait until she sees how much more work a buffalo requires than a doe! Will he capture her eyes then?"

Two Doves smiled. "We will have much meat this winter. This unexpected herd is a blessing from our Creator. Let us go."

We moved forward into the carcass-strewn valley. To my new people, explained Two Doves, a kill this size not only signified a full stomach today and tomorrow but for many months to come. We cut the meat we would not roast into strips so we could dry them in the sun for jerky or grind them with chokecherries to make pemmican. Old and young alike searched for markings on arrows or lances that identified the buffalo their men had brought down, sliced along the giant spines, and pulled the hides away to expose the meat. This, we cut into manageable pieces, salvaging every part—if not to eat, then for some other purpose—the sinews, horns, bones, everything.

While we worked, Red Woman regaled me with stories, often smiling so broadly that the creases in her face nearly swallowed up her eyes. The new ones often made me laugh and the old ones I treasured up in my memory, hoping one day to accurately tell them to my own grandchildren.

By the time we began roasting ribs over the fire, our empty stomachs were growling for notice. I had found the day's work gruesome but was pleasantly surprised by the taste of the meat. It was much like beef and more to my liking than venison.

Two Doves and I made soup for Running Deer's parents, who were too old to chew well; and after we had eaten our fill, Preying Eagle enclosed me in his blanket. We sat within it near the fire while warriors described their part in the hunt or recounted brave acts they witnessed. Many Feathers told us he killed an enormous bull with his lance, the traditional way of their fathers. This was more dangerous than shooting an arrow from the safety of a horse's back, and his courage greatly impressed the younger warriors.

Wooden Legs embarrassed my white cousin, as they had begun to call Nathaniel, by bragging about the cows he had killed. Proud fathers whose young sons had felled their first calves marked the occasion by giving horses to poorer families, and all who brought down many buffalo gave meat or robes to those in need. Leaning against Preying Eagle's warm shoulder, I felt quite foolish over the fears I confessed to Hides-in-Shadows. God certainly had given me the desire of my heart; when would I stop allowing fear to steal my joy?

"I have gained many hides to make your lodge today," he whispered in my ear. "My buffalo robes long for your warmth."

His eyes smoldered in the firelight. Understanding, now, that our union was irrevocable, I shyly confided, "I long to warm them."

"I go then," he murmured, "to my father." Leaving his blanket to protect me from the chilly night, he circled the fire toward Running Deer.

Nathaniel joined me shortly afterward with something weighing on his mind. We walked together, carefully keeping in view of the community to avoid scandal and aware our common language guaranteed privacy.

"I told you before, Alcy, that I wished to return to your people for a longer visit once my commitment to the Army is over. Do you think they might accept me living among them?"

"They might."

"I still have no intention of going native, as you have," he grinned. "In the dark, I wouldn't have been able to tell you from one of their women had I not known your features so well. I'd like to stay for a large portion of the coming year."

Hides-in-Shadows, who had walked up behind him, struggled to keep her dimples from twitching.

"That would be wonderful! Ask my father. Preying Eagle and he are over there by the fire talking with some other elders."

"I am ashamed," he confessed, "when I recall what I intimated about you and him at the fort and fully expect the two of you will be very happy together."

"I will be even happier if you are to return to us."

Hides-in-Shadows' expression echoed my sentiments; and as the two of them set out toward Running Deer, Preying Eagle stole up behind me.

"I am coming for you soon," he whispered in my ear.

Turning, I smiled up at him, uncertain if he had quoted Jesus by chance or design.

"What was Spotted Long-knife wanting?" he asked.

"To live here for a while."

His eyes grew somewhat guarded. "Do you want this?"

"Yes," I answered frankly, "though I wonder if sharing the Scriptures is all that is stirring Spotted Long-knife's heart. He looks differently at our fire-haired cousin than he ever looked at me."

As we followed them, Preying Eagle remained thoughtfully silent and then asked, "Does she know he desires her?"

"I'm not sure that even he knows it yet, but their hearts show plainly on both of their faces. Why haven't any warriors spread their blanket over her?"

"She is like a green twig—easily snapped—not strong enough to raise a warrior's sons."

"I think it is that very vulnerability that has unlocked a tender place in Spotted Long-knife's heart."

Preying Eagle grinned down at me, patiently waiting for me to realize I was speaking in English, so I translated my thoughts as well as I could.

"Do you think she would be willing to leave our people to live among the white men?"

He shook his head definitively. "No. She is much afraid and Wooden Legs would not be willing. We have heard of their greed and deceit. What father would allow his daughter to live among such people?"

I laughed. "I am one of them!"

"No, he replied, quite seriously. "You are one of us, The Creator gave you their skin so you could get His Book and bring it to us."

"There are many God-fearing and kind people among them. What if Spotted Long-knife decided to live with us?"

Preying Eagle shrugged. "That would be different. Her brothers would make sure he treated her well."

"And will Two Bears and Little Turtle make sure you are good to me?" I teased, stopping before our family's dwelling.

He raised my chin with his hand, rubbing his thumb softly across my lips. "They will not need to—I will make sure of this."

THE NEXT MORNING, we staked the hides and meat strips in the sun to dry. Two Doves, Red Woman, and I scraped the hair off the ones we intended to use for my dwelling and left it on a few that would be blankets. Afterward, the dazzling sun did the primary work, leaving us to a day of fun.

Elk Dog Boy and Little Turtle joined a column of youths opposite another long line. Each opponent had wrapped a buffalo robe around his arm for protection and stood waiting until we heard one shout: "Let us grab them and kick them in the face until they bleed!"

One column rushed the other in mock, yet serious, battle with the object of kicking their opponents down. I hated to watch, fearing my brothers would be injured: the game seemed to lack all rules of fairness.

As several large youths ganged up on Elk Dog Boy, I glanced at Two Doves. She stood where she was, watching impassively as the three pummeled him together. Later, when I asked Preying Eagle why neither he nor Two Bears had intervened, he explained that the beating Elk Dog Boy had taken was more valuable than the blood he had lost. He would be better prepared to protect himself the next time, an essential skill for a life of war. No wonder, I thought, the warriors were so fierce.

Two teams gathered around two burning piles of brush for the second game, about one hundred paces apart. Each youth then grabbed two brands from the fire, hurling or using them as flaming clubs against their opponents. They did this to intimidate each other until one team ran to their pile in fear. It was brutal and brought to mind Nathaniel's taunts about raising my children among them; and yet, I would rather they be realistically prepared for this life than coddled. Instead of giving way to fear, I was learning to practice what my late father had taught me: to trust God to take care of the many things I could not control.

While we watched the games, Nathaniel told me Running Deer had accepted his idea and promised to take it before the elders, as it would affect everyone.

Giving him a sidelong glance, I teased, "Did he agree to act as your go-between with Wooden Legs?" I expected him to stammer and go red, which he did, but he also responded quite tersely.

"You are certainly jumping your fences. Have you forgotten that I proposed to you only a short while ago?"

"I can't help observing, sir," I smiled, "that you never blushed like that over me."

Not one to argue with the obvious truth, Nathaniel confessed. "You must think me shamefully fickle, Alcy. I never expected to feel anything like this—no wonder I couldn't entice you to accept my offer."

I had not expected him to seriously entertain any ideas about my friend—at least not yet—but I was delighted. "A girl like Hides-in-Shadows is a rare find. She's trustworthy and sensitive to the needs of others. There is no other woman I could recommend more highly, but she will not allow you to court her against her father's wishes."

"Do you think he might permit it?"

"'Nothing is impossible with God.'[66] The people haven't known you long, but they regard you highly, and your valor during the hunt demonstrated both your courage and your ability to provide well. They refer to you as a warrior, which is an absolute requirement. I'm not sure, though, that they'd allow you to take her away."

He looked down toward his boots and frowned. "Then that would be the end of it. I won't take a wife and return to her only when it's convenient.

I've known men like that, trappers mostly, and have thought them to be scoundrels."

"What of seafaring men whose voyages take them away for the better part of the year? Many women would prefer the few months they can be together to a life without them. Doesn't the army separate many families?"

"Yes. That's precisely why I've waited until my duty was over to consider marrying. I suppose the idea is foolish, but my normally dispassionate reason gives way with her entirely—and I abhor the thought of her marrying one of these men."

"The gain is all on the side of inquiring, and you'd be asking permission to court, not marry her. The rest of it, you can work out if she is of the same mind."

That night, after he read the Word, Nathaniel accompanied Running Deer to the assembled elders, asking them to consider his proposed regular and lengthy visits. When they discovered his purpose, they readily agreed, and, taking courage, he asked my father and Preying Eagle to speak with Wooden Legs about his other inclination. Preying Eagle was eager to do so. My father was more reluctant but agreed, asking me to accompany them to translate and answer questions about Nathaniel that they could not.

Wooden Legs had already been watching their interaction during discussions about the Word and given the match consideration. He respected Nathaniel and also liked him, but when my father asked if he would consider allowing Hides-in-Shadows to live among the white men, he became obstinate.

"I would fear for my daughter if she went away from the love of her family and friends," Wooden Legs explained. "Hides-in-Shadows is not like the other women of our village, or even like Eyes-Like-Water. They are hard oaks; she is the soft willow whose heart drinks too deeply. It breaks when others do not bruise, perhaps because of the great hurt that caused her wanderings. And yet," he quipped, "when this long knife is near, she becomes Glows-Like-Embers. What do you say?" He addressed me. "You know her heart. You know this white warrior and his character. You have lived among his people and have also embraced a people who were not your own."

I felt honored that he asked my opinion. Warriors did not usually seek a woman's counsel, but as I was his adopted niece, he considered me a close relative.

"Hides-in-Shadow's heart rejoices when he is near," I answered, "and you could not find a man among any people who would care for her better than Spotted Long-knife. As for living among his people, white men are as varied as brown. Some are caring and some unkind, many are both. My cousin will have adversity wherever she lives. As David told us, 'Many are the afflictions of the righteous, but the Lord delivers him out of them all.'[67] The Creator will be with her wherever He sends them."

Always pragmatic, my father asked, "If you consent, what bride price do you require?"

"The customary horses," Wooden Legs shrugged, "and a fire-stick."

We bid him good night and looked for Nathaniel, who we found pacing impatiently nearby.

"This one," Joking Woman jerked her head toward him as we left her dwelling, "is trying to wear a rut in the grass."

"So, what did he say?" asked Nathaniel eagerly.

"He has promised to ask the Creator for His guidance, nothing more," Running Deer replied, "but he has watched his daughter's face when she looks at you."

"When can I expect his answer?"

"When the Creator speaks to his heart. Be anxious for nothing."

As my father, in his usual brevity, had said all that he thought was needed, he walked away, leaving a restless Nathaniel to his own thoughts and prayers. Preying Eagle guided me to our family's dwelling in the camp, and as I lay gazing at the plentiful stars through our smoke-hole, Hides-in-Shadows crept in to join me. Wooden Legs and Joking Woman had asked her if Nathaniel's desire was hers also, which she promptly confirmed.

"Can he honestly want me?" she asked.

"Yes, very much, but he realizes there are obstacles to the match."

"Oh, my heart feels like a sack with too much water, so full of joy it may burst. He is the most astounding man I have ever met. He knows the Creator's Word as if he has written each verse on his heart and was so daring in the hunt. I cannot understand why he would choose me. Surely, such a warrior could take any untouched woman. Are there few in his village?"

"No, there are plenty—not at the outpost but in Boston, and he will be sought after if he returns to the place unmarried. You are the woman he desires. He sees all the lovely, tender qualities I saw in you from the first day. He also thinks you are quite beautiful."

"He has said so?" she asked.

"Not in those words, but when I told him about Swallow Woman's beauty and grace, he quickly concluded I described you."

Sighing, she lay back in the grass, her thoughts drifting up in the stars until another crowded them out. "Is it frightening?"

"What?"

"This village he lives in?"

"I have never been there, but if it is like Philadelphia, it is very large—much, much larger than our band—and quite different. I was very happy back East. Only when I came out here did I find the white man's world unpleasant, and that was due to my uncle. Spotted Long-knife will care for you well and his family is bound to love you if they are remotely like him. Truly, you have nothing to fear."

"Sleep!" my father commanded us, and she withdrew to her family's lodge.

TWO DOVES GENTLY shook me awake before sunrise the next morning, her voice tinkling with happiness. I felt as if I had just lain down, so busy were my dreams about Nathaniel and Hides-in-Shadows.

"What is it?" I asked. "Did they say yes?"

"You must get up quickly. Running Deer is waiting for you."

Hastily making myself presentable, I ducked outside our dwelling to find a dark, blanketed figure.

"You will walk with me," he commanded.

My searching eyes found Preying Eagle's sleeping form while Running Deer led me from the drowsy camp to the top of a hillock closer to the rising sun. He lifted his arms in praise to the Creator and then watched the dawn paint the valley below before breaking his silence.

"Preying Eagle is eager to dwell with you and says your desires match his. Is this so?"

I wondered if I would ever become accustomed to his blunt questions about the most intimate components of my life. "Yes."

"Good," he nodded. "Before this sun sleeps, he will take you."

Astonished, I blurted, "Does Two Doves know?"

With a twinkle in his eye, he again nodded, and I realized my question was foolish. He always consulted her before concluding family matters, and his decision explained the lilt in her voice.

"Go, your mother is waiting to prepare you."

These unexpected tidings reminded me of something Jesus had told the disciples: no one but the Father knows the day or hour appointed for His return. I ran happily down the hill, searching for Two Doves among the shorter shadowy shapes that were already moving about.

"Running Deer was waiting until we sewed the cover for your dwelling," she explained. "A warrior and his woman need privacy. Preying Eagle assured your father he knows a lonely place he can take you."

I suspected I knew our destination well.

"Is your heart troubled by what he will expect of you?" Taking a porcupine tail from her bag, she brushed my hair until it gleamed.

"No. I am only afraid I may disappoint him."

"You are certain to disappoint him at some time," she shrugged, "as he will you. Never mind this. Only the Creator is perfect, but He fashioned you for my son and has taught you well from His Book. Preying Eagle wonders if he will disappoint you also. Running Deer has warned him he must play you as he would his flute. Pleasant notes are coaxed to life with gentleness and restraint. I have been Running Deer's woman for twenty-five summers, and he makes my heart sing louder now than he did at first."

After ornamenting my hair, she led me to our gathering relatives and friends. Preying Eagle wore the deerskin shirt I had sewn for him, which fit admirably, and I wore an ornate new dress Two Doves had designed for this occasion. I hoped Preying Eagle would think me attractive, and, judging by the warmth of his eyes, I believe he did.

Since we had made our vows on the evening we became betrothed, the ceremony consisted of simple admonitions given by Running Deer and translated for Nathaniel's benefit and mine by Hides-in-Shadows. We exchanged rings made from buffalo horn, which our father related to the story of Adam who, upon awakening, recognized Eve as bone of his bone and flesh of his flesh.

"So it was with Preying Eagle," he announced, as he relayed my husband's thoughts regarding me the night he awakened from his deep sleep. "Looking into the eyes of this woman, he recognized a part of him."

I marveled, learning he had felt this way, and remembered my musings as I bathed in the pool the next day.

"And we, too, believe the Creator fashioned Eyes-Like-Water for Preying Eagle," continued Running Deer, "and compelled him to snatch her from her enemies so we would have His Book."

All the people nodded their agreement, and he declared us married. Just as if I had been born to them, Two Doves and my aunts had prepared a feast and Running Deer gave many gifts in my honor. I was glad Nathaniel witnessed our marriage, not only because of our friendship but also as a safeguard for the future, lest anyone assume that our union was not legitimate. Hides-in-Shadows looked radiantly happy beside him, translating the many stories and jokes told by our guests; and his uncharacteristic self-consciousness betrayed the feelings he harbored in his heart.

TURNING EAST AFTER our farewells, my husband and I rode high into the forested hills and stopped once we were out of sight. He grinned in answer to my quizzical expression and pulled me atop his mare, surrounding me with arms both possessive and affectionate. I felt like I had come home.

"I am yours altogether," I sighed. Resting my head between the firm mounds of his chest, my newfound understanding heightened my enjoyment of the sentiments he murmured into my hair. As we weaved carefully through trees and around boulders, the roar of water in the distance set my heart dancing. This lovely spot recalled the days when I thought myself his slave. He was now thoroughly the master of my heart.

After building a fire in our room of cedars, he freed my hair and became captivated by its length and texture; and while he worked free the fastenings of my dress, his eyes melted away all of my concerns. We reveled in unfettered freedom, Solomon's Song perfectly expressing my thoughts.

> My beloved is mine and I am his.
> The fresh green grass will be our wedding bed
> in the shade of the cedar and cypress trees.
> My beloved is bright and ruddy,
> standing out among ten thousand.
> His hair is black as a raven;
> his mouth is most sweet.
> Yea, he is altogether lovely.
> I am my beloved's,
> and my beloved is mine.[68]

How precious is the intimacy designed by our Creator to seal our hearts as husband and wife! I deeply appreciated the Lord's protective admonitions that had kept me pure[69] for this night of wonder. To share such delicious familiarity with another man would have been profane, like offering myself to a foreign god. Who can fathom the perfection of His ways?

Lying nestled against my husband, my thoughts returned to the story his father had related. "When did you recognize me as your woman?"

"As my father said—when I awoke."

"Immediately?"

"Yes. No. Sleep-mist wrapped my head, and my thoughts strove hard against each other. The knife you held cast you as my enemy, but I could not drain the life from your eyes. You made sense only when my blood escaped the bandage and your brow began wrinkling with concern."

"Did you know then?"

"Yes and no," he repeated. "Your composure surprised and pleased me. You looked no older than my little cousin, yet only at first did you shrink from me. And," he grinned, "while your fingers danced little steps across my back, I grew determined to gain you as my woman. You?"

"When I first saw you, I was terrified; but when you awoke, I became confused. You were unlike anyone I had ever known. I wondered if Eve felt the way I did when she met Adam—stirred by unfamiliar longings and wonderfully safe. That is why I was so surprised when your father said almost the same thing of you this morning."

A wolf began howling, as it had while we stayed here before, and I told him of the simple weapon I had fashioned against it.

"That was good as long as you jabbed at it. Wolves fear their prey's sharp horns, but a lone wolf would not have attacked us. Like most men, they are cowardly without their pack. This wolf is not alone."

Startled, I raised up on my elbow, thankful this never occurred to me that horrid night.

"Listen…you can hear a slight difference in each tone and direction. That is his brother, and there is another…and another. They howl to reassure each other that they are still there, as my cousins and I do when we raid—only we make birdcalls. I am a gray tree owl."

"Will they attack us?"

"No. Those are not the howls of hunger. There is much game in this forest less challenging than a warrior," he smiled, "or even a woman with a sharp stick."

Secure in his arms, I drifted off peacefully, thanking God for His wonderful grace toward me, His handmaiden.

THE AIR WAS too brisk for bathing when the chirping birds awoke me the next morning, so I took the opportunity to watch my husband sleep. Running my fingers over the scar from Stump's bullet, I reflected with both sadness and gratitude that he had received it because of me. I kissed it softly, again and again—this blessed wound that had bound me to him more firmly than my petticoat had bound his chest.

How many things in life were like this? At first, they fill us with dread, but we later recognize them as initial steps toward greater joy. I would never willingly have caused him pain, but neither could I wish that lovely scar away. Were it not for his wound, I would have left him.

Months ago, while assessing his strength, I had trembled with fear. Now I relished the tone of his muscles under my palm. In so many ways, he reminded me of Jesus. He rescued me from trouble while I was unaware he existed; [70] and though he had reason to slay me, instead he wooed my heart. Long before I knew he loved me, he planned and provided for our union, setting me free so I could come to him of my own will. [71] He even advocated my case before his father,[72] urging him not to regard me as an enemy but as a beloved child.[73]

As my wanderings returned to his handsome face, I found him watching my investigation. His eyes held a vastly different look than they had the night of their first opening, inflaming my cheeks as I recalled last night's intimacies. I was truly his altogether.

We spent two lovely nights in this most beautiful of places, our enjoyment of each other heightened by our ability to communicate with words. Listening to his heart assured me again that the fears I expressed to my cousin so recently were, as most fears are, unfounded. Indeed, as she had suggested, I began to know him in a profound way reserved only for his mate.

He taught me how to interpret the sounds and movements of birds, to learn which animals had left tracks in the soft ground near the river, and to note the damage they did to grass or leaves where the soil was hard. Learning I had become lost in these woods, he showed me how to orient myself by moss, which grows on the northern side of trees, and to inconspicuously mark my way were I eluding an enemy. I prayed I would never have to use the last.

Alas, with a mutual sense of regret, we resumed our journey by a more direct route, and I knew we neared our destination when my husband stopped and reluctantly bade me mount my own pony.

No good thing will He withhold from those who walk uprightly. O Lord of hosts, blessed is the man who trusteth in Thee!

Psalm 84:12

Chapter 16

THE ASSEMBLING CAMP was as remarkable as the packing camp had been. Dwellings sprang out of the earth in unison, each facing east and tilted as a precaution against the driving winter storms. Nestled within protective heights, it was warmer than the summer place had become, and a thinner, leafless forest allowed the sun to reach us throughout the day. A large bank of evergreens offered an additional buffer against winds from the north, and the river that bordered us to the west was rapid and deep, qualities that insured the ice layer, if it froze, would be thin.

As Preying Eagle and I wound our way through the village, we found an unfamiliar lodge had been erected beside my mother's dwelling, devoid of color or the characteristic smoke-stained peak. Our family, who rushed out to welcome us home, explained that it belonged to me, for they considered a couple's dwelling the wife's property. All the while my husband and I had been getting to know each other more intimately, Two Doves, our aunts, and several other women had been tirelessly sewing together the hides we had scraped after the buffalo hunt. I need only to tell my husband which designs I desired him to paint.

"Is your dwelling dry and comfortable?" asked my mother as we washed our clothes in the river.

"Yes, it is perfect," I sighed, "though it seems large as a cave without you, father, and Elk Dog Boy." Having had my own room most of my life, I relished the privacy, but I would never have said so for fear of hurting her. "I lack sufficient words to express my thanks and surprise."

"We wished to thank you," smiled Quiet Woman, her round face alight with pleasure. She had been slow to warm to me but over the months had become my favorite aunt. "We are happy that we no longer walk in darkness."

"I only read the Book," I shrugged. "Our Creator brought it to you. I am grateful He allowed me to come along with it."

"You also brought joy to our hearts, little one, by choosing to stay with us."

Before I could reply, Joking Woman nudged me with her elbow. "And how do you like sharing your dwelling with my nephew?"

"Exceedingly well," I replied, coloring deeply at my aunts' knowing grins. Two Doves looked pleased and Hides-in-Shadows a bit befuddled.

"Do you still think," prodded Joking Woman, "that he is 'like the sun rising in the east, catching all eyes'?"

"No." I shook my head and then broke into a delighted smile. "The sun is not worthy to be compared to him."

They all broke into peals of laughter, and Joking Woman, who had spotted my husband walking on the upper bank, loudly called him. Waving him over, she repeated every word; but rather than modestly deny them, as Father or Captain Anderson would have done, he raised his eyebrows and tossed me a meaningful grin.

"I have found my woman most enjoyable."

Breaking into a fresh fit of giggles, none of my aunts could immediately reply, but once Joking Woman recovered, she said, "I will bet a buffalo robe that she will give us little help picking cherries when they ripen—her belly will be so large she will not be able to climb a tree!"

"I will gladly help you win that wager," declared Preying Eagle, tossing me another grin before he turned and strode away.

Since I could not bid the earth to swallow me, I buried my head in my work, understanding much better why my red-haired cousin had hidden so often in the shadows.

AS THE MOON reflects the sun, so I shared in the esteem offered to my husband and was granted a new ease with other warriors. Their wives made a sport of raising my color, for which I amply, albeit involuntarily, rewarded them. In Grandmother's home, no one even alluded to marital intimacies much less discussed them openly. Although I found their intensely personal attention embarrassing, I appreciated what it signified: their reserve toward me had crumbled, allowing them to accept me as one of them.

Apart from this teasing, they treated me with increasing respect, less like a daughter or niece and more like an equal, though I still had so much to learn. My efforts after the buffalo hunt had proven to my credit, dispelling lingering suspicions that I might become a drag on the tribe. A drain on one family was a drain on all, and though they pardoned a lack in vigor in the elderly or very young, they deemed it inexcusable for a healthy woman.

Preying Eagle and all from our band who had embraced Jesus grew rapidly in their understanding of His ways. Since the tribe did not have a system of writing, they committed whole chapters to memory, employing a method they had long used with their histories, both tribal and personal. Elder family members told a story to a young boy and expected him to repeat it aloud the next night. During any given day, I was asked to read or repeat sections of Scripture or check verses to refresh someone's memory. They put my abilities in this area to shame, though I could not remember a time in my life when the Word had not been emphasized.

I admired their unquestioning obedience to the Lord and wondered if their stricter authority structure made this easier than in my former society. While I was a child, my parents had required me to obey, but they allowed and even encouraged me to voice well-thought-out objections, provided I did so respectfully. Among my adopted people, a child who disagreed with his parents' decision kept silent, and the whole village enforced his obedience. Eventually, he concluded for himself that his parents' love and vastly greater experience warranted his trust. On balance, adults treated children with dignity, never holding them up for public ridicule, and cultivated individuality rather than conformity.

They were so starved for the Creator's Word that my voice grew chafed before they were ready to quit listening. The historical sections became particularly beloved, as the ancient Hebrew way of life was so similar to their own. The same was true about the Psalms, especially those concentrating on victory over their enemies or mentioning quivers and arrows. In some of these, they grasped nuances that I altogether missed, and their insights, in turn, led me to a richer understanding.

Conversely, their way of life led to many misunderstandings. Many shared Chirping Bird's notion about the Amalekites and believed the Assyrians were a second brutal tribe that lived far to the south, many days beyond Red Fawn's new band. They were quite certain the rider of the white horse in John's Revelation was one of their own people—after all, he carried a bow and arrow—and they pictured buffalo being sacrificed on The Temple altar.

Sheep gave me the greatest difficulty. They had simply never seen one. When I drew one and imitated the sound it made, they said: "Ah, buffalo calf." They could not fathom a herdsman acting like the one depicted in John 10. No man, however skilled with creatures, could lead buffalo around or would put them in a pen. Furthermore, if one could do so, only the craziest of men would sleep in the opening as I explained the Hebrew shepherds did.

"He would be trampled to death," reasoned Old Man.

Unable to breach the misunderstanding or argue with his obvious sense, I became increasingly sympathetic with the ancestor who first named a horse an elk-dog and prayed that Nathaniel would quickly return.

As fall turned into early winter, severe winds threatened the warmly smoldering embers in the center of my dwelling. Preying Eagle entered the village with a large party of triumphant young warriors leading several strings of horses. Their bearing proclaimed they had won a great victory, but though I ululated loudly along with the other women, I was uncertain what had taken place.

"Why are we making this commotion?" I asked my ginger-haired cousin.

Hides-in-Shadows cocked her head. "Are you not relieved they have come home safely?"

"Yes," I assured her, "but where have they been and how did they come across such a quantity of horses? When Preying Eagle did not return to my dwelling, I assumed he was hunting."

"No—raiding," she answered.

"You can be proud of him." beamed Two Doves. "He has led his party to great success, and look at Little Turtle! He can now begin a herd of his own." She pointed to my middle brother, who pulled a top-quality black-socked buckskin stallion and a chestnut mare.

"Have they fought a battle?"

Two Doves shook her head. "Preying Eagle is much too cunning for that. They snatched these horses from under their enemies' noses. See—not one warrior bears a wound or a scar."

My heart dropped down to my stomach. She surely was not telling me my husband was a thief! "But why have they done this, and why is everyone rejoicing?"

Both of my companions gaped at me. "You especially, little one, have cause to rejoice," replied his mother. "Your husband has shown great prowess and leadership. You can rest satisfied and secure tonight, glad you are the woman of a clever and wealthy warrior."

"Little Turtle has also given you a reason to be proud," joined in Hides-in-Shadows. "He has demonstrated stealth and skill in elusion—very important for a warrior. You are not pleased?"

I did not know what to say, but my husband, his torso erect and his head held high, spotted us in the crowd and urged forward his dapple-gray mare. Women, pressing against my back to see what he intended, sharply sucked in their breath as he leaned down to offer me a woven grass rope. Straining against the other end of it was the most beautiful horse I had ever seen. Her black coat gleamed as brightly as his well-oiled locks.

"He is giving her to Eyes-Like-Water!" whispered Cries-at-Night.

"Why?" sputtered Chirping Bird. "The mare is fine—fine enough to give to his father or one of his uncles."

As he gazed down from the back of his mount, Preying Eagle's eyes, shining with proud anticipation, drove away all other thought. My knees felt the now familiar weakening, and the honor he had paid me struck me dumb. He was too wonderful for words.

"My cousin," he nodded toward Hides-in-Shadows, "said you longed for a spirited mount."

Every eye seemed riveted on my reaction, but though I opened my mouth, I could form no words. What was I to say to such a gift—stolen, perhaps, from some other warrior's adoring wife? By accepting her, I would publicly endorse what seemed plain theft. By rejecting her, I would humiliate and dishonor my husband, a grave offense in any village and sure to carry exceedingly severe ramifications here. Peter's verses concerning husbands [74] skipped hastily through my thoughts, but I was not sure how to apply them. Asking the Holy Spirit to convict Preying Eagle's heart without my censure was one thing but partaking in his sin was quite another.

"I have never seen a finer horse," I murmured, stroking her strikingly intelligent face. "I am unworthy of such honor."

Satisfaction suffused his whole countenance, so swelling my heart I was once again speechless, but as soon as he wheeled to lead her to his herd, I fled to my dwelling. Unwinding my braids, I retrieved some sweet-scented buffalo fat his mother had given me, rubbed it between my palms, and had just finished working it into the dry ends of my waves when he ducked under our flap. His skin was still damp from dipping into the cold river and his eyes shone with pleasure as he stepped forward to entangle his hands in my loosened locks.

Shyly, softly, I spread kisses up his chest to the base of his neck, hoping he would not mention the mare until the Lord had directed both my heart and words, and as he leaned forward to ease my reach, he returned my affection with such boldness that he chased his gift completely from my thoughts.

"When the sun wakes," he whispered, nestling sleepily against my back, "I will teach you how to handle such a mare. She will carry you like the wind."

The persistent excitement his voice carried chilled my hopes for a longer reprieve, but as I was asking the Lord if I should speak or remain silent, my ever-perceptive husband pressed for a response.

"When you become this still," he informed me, "I know something unsettles your heart."

Worn out from the rigors of the day, I took the coward's way out by remaining so silent he assumed I had fallen asleep. The next morning I was no less exhausted. Guilt had robbed me of genuine rest, and though I stole away to gather firewood before he woke, my ears kept constantly alert, dreading his footfall.

As I passed my husband's herd, I spotted the black mare standing close to his roan and impulsively laid down my bundle. She was a bit skittish, nickering lightly as I pulled up a handful of grass and slowly approached her from the front; but once she had accepted my offering, she allowed me to stroke her mane and neck. Last night's fires had exaggerated none of her fine qualities. As I became absorbed by the desire to ride her, warm arms slowly encompassed my waist, pressing me back against a fresh-smelling hunting shirt.

"Go ahead," whispered Preying Eagle, nuzzling my neck in the privacy of the barely awakening sun. "Climb up on her back."

"I dare not," I murmured, more to myself than to him.

"I am here," he assured me. "I will not allow her to speed away with you."

Summoning the nerve I could not find last night, I answered, "If I do, I will find it too difficult to give her up."

He laughed softly into my hair. "She is yours. No one will take her from you."

I did not want to disrupt the intimacy of the moment, enjoying the weakness his nearness spread through my limbs, but I knew if I did not, the courage would be hard to rouse again. "I cannot keep her," I whispered.

Perplexed, he turned me around, "Why not? She is fit for Many Feathers. Did you pretend the gratitude you showed me last night?"

"No," I leaned my forehead against his chest, unable to meet his eyes. "I have never seen a more magnificent creature, and the honor you pay me touches me more deeply than I can express."

"What then?" he asked, impatience edging into his voice. I tentatively stroked his chest, trying to recapture his tender mood, but seeing my attempt to do so was proving futile, I confessed. "The Creator's Book tells us not to steal."

"I did not steal her; I took her in a raid—from an enemy."

"The Creator tells us to love our enemies. How can you love an enemy while you are taking what is his?"

His face hardened and he brushed my hands away. "Your words are upside down. I take what is my enemy's to weaken him, as the war-chief did who raided the tribes of the Philistines."

"But King David and the Philistines were at war."

"We are at war—and if we do not weaken our enemies, they may kill us! They have already killed uncles and cousins; I am bound to avenge their deaths."

"What we gain while defending our village is one thing, but the Word says, 'love your enemies, do good to them which hate you.'[75] You are my husband, and I want to please you in everything, but accepting her puts me at odds with my convictions."

"Pah!" he spat. "I am a warrior and you are my woman—you do not question what I do! I will not act like a white man to please you."

Before I could reply, he stormed away, leaving me wholly shattered. I hoisted my abandoned bundle onto my back and trudged back toward my dwelling, growing more indignant with every step. He had brushed aside Jesus' words as carelessly as he had brushed away my hands. How had I allowed emotion to sweep me into this untenable union? He had treated me more like a servant than a wife—dismissing my feelings and chastising me for differing with him! His arrogance was insufferable!

Even as these thoughts stomped through my head, my heart felt convicted. What had he expressed that I had not expected and implicitly agreed to when I had accepted his horses? His father had required unquestioning obedience; had I expected my husband would require less? His rebuff hurt my feelings and his dismissal pricked my pride, but had I not done the same to him by rejecting his gift? Perhaps we were not so different after all.

Jesus had said, "Blessed is he who is not offended by me,"[76] but I could not remember the context. I shook off the words, horrified by what they implied about my husband's faith. Thus far, he had followed the Creator zealously; so though he thought himself wholly in the right, he would surely come around given a chance to think.

"But what if he does not?" my heart questioned keenly. "What will become of me if Preying Eagle rejects the Scriptures—I am bound to him until death!" My head in my hands, I cried for the Lord to soften his heart, if not toward me then at least toward His Word, and for Him to make me like Sarah, who obeyed her husband, calling him lord.[77] With a rueful chortle, I remembered how fervently I had prayed that Preying Eagle would not sell me. God had granted my desire and even given me a legitimate solution for my longings, but what had really changed? Only my title was different. "I am still his property and now will never escape unless the Lord provides me a pair of wings!"

Memories of Father scolded me sharply: "You are borrowing trouble again, Alcy. Let the …"

"Eyes-Like-Water," Elk Dog Boy called outside my lodge. "Running Deer says you are to come to Two Doves' dwelling."

"Oh Lord," I muttered, "forgive me for my rebellious pride and please help me to speak as You would have me speak. There is something to what he said about David's raids. Am I wrong?"

Braving my husband's displeasure had been horrible; facing Running Deer's disapproval filled me with dread. Taking my Bible, I ducked into Two Doves' dwelling to find Preying Eagle, Hides-in-Shadows, and the entire council waiting. My mouth felt as dry as my palms felt damp. Running Deer was talking to my husband in hushed tones, but neither of their faces conveyed anything.

"Tell us what you told your warrior about raiding," began Many Feathers, Two Dove's intimidating elder brother.

I stole a nervous glance toward Preying Eagle. "If it seems good to the elders, I will read you all the passages I can find that might have a bearing, and you can decide for yourselves what is right for our people. As the Creator and Hides-in-Shadows can witness, I have never desired for you to become like white men, only that you follow Jesus. I hold my husband, my father, and all of you in the highest esteem, and trust the Creator, who has placed me under your authority, will direct your hearts."

"You have spoken well," nodded Many Feathers. "We want to hear what the Creator says."

Once Wooden Legs had asked the Lord to bring each passage to mind that He wanted them to examine and to tune their hearts to His, I read the verses in Luke I had quoted to my husband. Next, I turned to Paul's instructions to repay evil with good and make every effort to live in peace with all men.[78] Conversely, afterward, I read the chapter that described David's raids on the Geshurites, the Gezrites, and the Amalekites while he was living in Ziklag[79], and several narratives about the Israelites plundering their enemies. They all listened in contemplative silence, pensive and inscrutable.

Preying Eagle did not return to my dwelling until late that night and left at first light. All the ensuing days he repeated the same pattern so that I saw him only if the elders called me to reread passages. They mulled over each for what felt like an eternity, praying gravely and fasting. I wished Nathaniel were present to give the benefit of a soldier's perspective, steeped in Biblical wisdom and coupled with experience less sheltered or limited than my own.

The hostility felt by many warriors and their women grew palpable as the controversy spread. Since that first bewildering night, I learned that raiding was a regular and deeply entrenched part of their existence, enriching the band while providing opportunities for younger cousins to hone their skills before their lives depended on them. To abandon this practice threatened their survival, particularly since other tribes would continue to steal. Most feared they would lose their herds without any means to replenish them.

"When the Creator gave our people horses," Red Woman explained, "He greatly enlarged the territory in which our warriors could hunt and increased our chances of victory in battle. As the horse goes, so goes our people. Of all creatures, only the buffalo shares such significance."

Every morning I awoke feeling ill, yearning for my husband's former tenderness and wondering how I would get through the day. Talks-With-Bitterness and her ilk were angry that I had meddled in their way of life and accused me of bringing disharmony to the village. At first, they simply whispered among themselves or turned their backs if chores brought us together, but once they suspected Preying Eagle had withdrawn his favor, they spat or shouted that I should return to my white home. I felt acutely miserable, withdrawing to my dwelling as often as possible; yet, in clear conscience, how could I have followed any other course?

Night after night, I lay awake asking myself the same question: had God directed my heart to this people, or had I abysmally mistaken His will? At the time I had returned, I had little to entice me from a worldly perspective—I knew nothing of Preying Eagle's intentions and had much to gain by marrying Nathaniel. True, I hated to leave my adopted family, but the confidence I had felt in God's direction was the lone element that had brought me back.

What would I do if the elders rejected the Scriptures in favor of their traditions? My brief, intensely happy marriage was already failing miserably; continuing here would be thorny and probably futile. What was I to do?

It was far too late to change my mind—Running Deer had seen to that by tying me irrevocably to his son.

All my efforts to find a solution brought me to the same conclusion: I had no other option than to trust my heavenly Father. He was as capable of making His will clear to them as He had been of making it clear to me. "The king's heart is in the hand of the Lord, as the rivers of water; He turneth it whithersoever He wills."[80] On the other hand, to presume that I alone understood how this people should walk in the light of Scripture was grossly arrogant. King David, a man after God's own heart, might side with my husband on this issue; and yet, Jesus' words were plain.

During that dismal time, my small circle of friends, which happily still included Two Doves, sustained me. Hides-in-Shadows had been present with the council whenever I was, in case I found translating difficult, and had related the details to my mother and aunts. Although I was uncertain they agreed with my position, they each made clear they understood my feelings. They too had husbands or fathers they had thought wrong at times and had also felt utterly powerless.

"YOU ARE HAVING difficulty concentrating," Quiet Woman gently scolded while instructing me in the art of weaving breastplates. "Shall we wait until your heart is not so occupied?"

As my tears began wetting the horsehair in my lap, she put her work aside and enveloped me in her warm, comforting arms.

"I feel sick with grief," I sobbed. "Preying Eagle no longer wants me. During the past five suns, he has entered my dwelling only to sleep. He does not touch me and barely speaks; and when I awaken, he is gone again."

"When he is there, do you poke and prod him to talk with you?"

"No, I have been trying to win him without a word,[81] as Scripture directs, but even this does not seem to help. He is not cruel—just silent and unapproachable!"

"You do well, little one," she soothed, stroking my hair as if I were Red Fawn. "Give him time. When a warrior is sorely troubled, he retreats to a cave to seek his own answers. Do not let his struggles disturb your peace and never attempt to follow him there. A ferocious bear lives in that cave and will attack if you try to enter. When your husband is ready he will emerge, and you will find joy with him again. While you are waiting, trust his heart, and trust the Creator who joined you together."

As a jewelry smith fits gold nuggets into perfect silver settings,[82] so my aunt's words fit the hollow places in my heart. They freed my mind to follow her instructions and my fingers to weave the slender bones in place. With every linkage, I asked the Lord to mend my marriage and make it impenetrable to the enemy of our souls.

The following day, the council called the whole village together, and Standing Bull addressed the people. "This is a hard thing the Creator has put before us. So you will know that Preying Eagle's woman has not placed her words in the Creator's mouth, Hides-in-Shadows will both read and translate for you. Listen to the Creator and judge what is right." My cousin then stood before the assembly and read several passages the elders deemed most pertinent to their decisions.

Fireheart, the husband of Talks-With-Bitterness, sprang to his feet. "Who can listen to this?" he sneered. "This is the white man's book. This woman owns a trickster spirit. Her white fathers sent her to weaken us so they may drive us into the setting sun. She thinks we know nothing of her lying people, but she is wrong. She has caught Preying Eagle with her foreign eyes and would ensnare all our hearts."

Several other warriors sprang up also, proclaiming they agreed. Their vehement speeches tore at my soul, and when they became threatening, my husband, father, brothers, and other men of my family rose to their feet, joined by most of the believing warriors. I felt so ill, I thought I might need to excuse myself. How had everything gone so wrong? Standing Bull, whom the council chose as their spokesman because we were not related, called me forward to answer Fireheart's accusations.

"No one sent me; I chose this people in good faith. Ask Preying Eagle—he will tell you I was unaware he was watching the day he rescued me." Turning toward the elders, I pleaded, "Do with me whatever seems good to you—only do not turn away from the Creator or fight among yourselves on my account."

What was I saying? The words had leaped from my mouth as if they possessed a life of their own. Perhaps Major Young had been right to wonder if my mind was addled.

Standing Bull bade us all to sit down. "We have all heard that the Creator's Son did not bring peace but a lance.[83] This sun, we have seen this is so. He, not this woman, has directed our hearts, and His Book has caused this conflict. How can we contend with Him? Are His ways not higher than ours, and is not our wisdom foolish to Him? What does raiding gain us? We take our enemy's horses and he takes ours. He kills our father and we kill his. Let us obey the Creator's Words and He will reward and protect us."

Kicking Horse called out, "Does the Creator ask us to cower like women?"

"No," answered Standing Bull. "Many people of the Book were also warriors. We will fight valiantly to protect our women and children, our horses and our dwellings, but we will not take what does not belong to us."

"What of the horses we took in the raid?" asked my quiet brother, Little Turtle, whose tender conscience warred with his desire for a herd.

"Let every warrior decide for himself."

With these words, the assembly concluded. Individual warriors met the council's decision with a mixed reception, mostly according to their commitment to the Word. Preying Eagle left immediately, towing the black mare.

SENSING SOMEONE'S presence in my dwelling the next night, I awoke to find my weary husband adding sticks to our embers. "Are you all right?" I asked cautiously, concerned to see a dark gash on his forehead.

"It is nothing—a small nick."

His voice sounded guarded, and I was unsure what to expect after a week full of strain. Feeling his eyes following me closely, I rose, removed my tattered petticoat from the saddlebag, tore off and dampened a small piece of it, and bent to gently cleanse the cut. His hands slid up about my waist, traveling around my back to pull me against his firm chest.

"I am grateful to the Creator," he murmured thickly, running his lips across the base of my throat and up to my ear. "He has given me a woman with courage to speak the truth,"

Relaxing against him, I welcomed his affection and returned it with joy.

"I am grateful I belong to a warrior who risks his skin to do what is right."

My heart brimmed with thanksgiving. My heavenly Father had answered my pleas for this man I loved so deeply and arranged for Running Deer to permanently bind me to him. I hated to consider what I might foolishly have done, had I been free to leave.

The next morning I awoke tired but happy, my husband's arm settled possessively about my waist and his warm, even breathing in my hair. I felt delightfully settled and secure, but as I extricated myself to fetch our morning firewood, my stomach felt unexpectedly queasy.

Many waters cannot quench love; neither can the floods drown it. If a man would give all the substance of his house for love, it would be utterly despised.

Song of Songs 8:7

Chapter 17

AS CRISP, COLD gusts whistled through the leafless trees, the small fire in my dwelling so darkened the smoke-hole that it no longer stood out as a newlyweds' home. We celebrated Christmas in much the same way my family always had in Skippack: thanking the Creator for sending his Son to redeem us, reading the Scriptures, and exchanging gifts, as this was also their custom on joyous occasions. God's Christmas present for my red-haired cousin, however, took us all by surprise.

The weather had been teetering between snow and sleet for several days when we heard Crow Feather shouting from his guarding place. A crazy white man, he yelled, was trying to tug fifteen horses up the ice-covered hill. Scrambling up to watch his struggle, many began speculating about his identity and the reason that compelled him to make such a foolhardy climb, until a blast of wind blew off his hat, fanning out strands of brownish-red.

"Spotted Long-knife—he has returned!"

The cry echoed throughout the village as warriors picked and slid their way down to help him up the slope. When Hides-In-Shadows and I heard the name, we also clambered up the crest. Her pretty face dimpled deeply, though her mother scolded. "Do not give him too many glances and smiles. Make him work for you—and be sure you tie the hide!"

Having no idea what Joking Woman meant, I turned to Two Doves, who explained this was a sort of chastity belt made from buffalo pelts. "Many mothers require their daughters to wear them while they are wrapped in a warrior's blanket." Seeing my surprise, she smiled. "I did not think it necessary for you, Preying Eagle owns my trust, but if I had known that it was Kicking Horse waiting that evening outside my dwelling, I would also have made you put it on. Wooden Legs and Joking Woman like your friend, but they are unsure of his white ways."

Controlling the impulse to burst out laughing was becoming an important social skill.

Hides-in-Shadows ran home to change into her most beautiful dress and tuck an abundance of escaping curls back into her reddish-gold braids.

She looked lovely when she returned, quite pink in the cheeks from hurrying and from the cold, but she was too late. The warriors had led Nathaniel around the slope into a hidden ravine, which provided a less perilous way to enter the village from the south. Engulfing him in a swarm, they asked why he had come and what errand could be so urgent that he did not wait until the ice thawed. If he understood any of their questions, he revealed nothing, and my cousin found it impossible to edge her way in to translate.

Preying Eagle, who had already guessed my spotted friend's intent, provided a place for his horses among our herd and then lead him through the village to the guest dwelling. Over supper in my lodge, the Captain confided that he had missed our red-haired cousin sorely, increasing his conviction that he could not do without her. Preying Eagle nodded, offering advice and the loan of his courting blanket, but he gravely shook his head when Nathaniel declined his flute.

"Wooing a woman takes skill," I translated for my husband. "She may shy away if you approach her too directly or rush to offer her your horses. You have been away, and memories are often treacherous. You lay awake while the sun sleeps, remembering my cousin's smiles and perhaps her scent while she bandaged you." He smiled wickedly, knowing perfectly well he described neither Nathaniel nor Hides-in-Shadows. "You recall the fine texture of her hair and how she felt when she lost her balance and fell against you."

I felt myself turning bright red, but his brothers' snickers egged him on.

"When your brother's loud snoring robs you of sleep," he continued, "you imagine how she will feel close against you and what she will say when you disclose your heart. Soon you cannot separate the woman and the dream, so you must first make certain your memories are correct. Talk to her of weather, talk of your family, talk of everything but the desire you have for her. Once you accept Wooden Leg's horses, you cannot change your mind. You have bought and cannot sell her."

When Preying Eagle's brothers broke into a chorus of laughter, poor Nathaniel looked unsure if my husband advised him in earnest or had made him the butt of some inscrutable joke.

In the pause that followed, Two Bears joined in. "A cousin of ours badly wanted a certain daughter of another band. His heart, he claimed, sang while he watched her dancing with the other untouched women. He urged his uncle to gain permission for him to court her, which her father granted, and straightaway took her to a private spot."

"While he made his pledges of protection and provision," chortled Little Turtle, "he kept smelling rotting squash and scolded himself for taking little care to select an appealing place. Only after she accepted his horses did he learn he had been smelling her!"

"Another cousin," continued Two Bears, "spread his blanket around a woman who attracted him, but even when he spoke of serious matters, she did nothing but giggle. He did not want a silly wife, so he courted a less beautiful but more sensible woman."

Elk Dog Boy looked as if he might burst. "Why are you telling him this? We all know our cousin—she is not silly and does not smell foul!"

"Not to us, little brother," shrugged Two Bears, "but to Spotted Long-knife—who knows? You will learn. We all laugh, but he needs to see if he likes her up close. He will have to share her buffalo robe until an enemy snatches away his hair."

What more they discussed, I could not say; I quit listening once Two Bears mentioned scalping. His tone had been so casual—as if he depicted the natural, well-accepted fate of any warrior, and I read nothing to contradict him in his brothers' good-humored expressions. With eyes still crinkling with laughter, Preying Eagle suggested we ask the Lord to guide both the couple and her parents or to close the matter in all their hearts.

THE NEXT MORNING, Joking Woman pulled me into her dwelling where I found her red-haired daughter in a dither. Hides-in-Shadows had been waiting for and dreaming of this day, fearing it would never come. Her mother and I gave what brief answers we could to her bundle of questions, urging her to calm herself, but even as the words left our lips, I knew we were asking the impossible.

Before she decided whether fear or joy would win the day, we threw back the door-flap and saw Nathaniel patiently waiting. Hides-in-Shadows lifted her gaze to merry amber eyes and a reassuring smile.

Nathaniel did not have the least idea of how to conceal his love for her, and this was precisely the antidote she needed to calm her fears. Her youngest brother, following at a respectable distance, told us later that neither of them stopped smiling the entire time they walked along the riverbank.

During the next few days, Nathaniel divided the bulk of his time between the dwellings of Joking Woman and Two Doves, discussing the band's conclusions about raiding and revenge or his plans for the future. If the elders would consent, he wished to take up residence in our village for most of the coming year, making occasional excursions to the white man's world for supplies and news of his countrymen.

Only a blind man could have missed my two friends' feelings for each other. They spent each evening side by side—one listening to or answering questions and the other translating or gazing up admiringly, and after six days, Running Deer decided they had waited long enough.

"Fetch your white cousin," he commanded me, "and bring him to Joking Woman's dwelling."

As we sat down by his fire, Wooden Legs openly studied Nathaniel while Running Deer presented his proposals. Nathaniel waited quietly, trying to understand the largely one-sided dialogue until he needed me to convey his desire to take Hides-in-Shadows east to meet his family. To this, my uncle slowly shook his head and severely pulled down the corners of his lips.

"We have known Spotted Long-knife several moons," my father broke in. "He has faithfully done everything he has promised. All knew he wanted to keep my daughter at the white man's outpost, but he brought her back to us as he had pledged. His request is reasonable. You took Joking Woman from her family and never returned her; Spotted Long-knife asks only for a short visit."

Wooden Legs remained grave, and Joking Woman cast her eyes toward the fringe on her skirt. Neither had an answer. They felt God had arranged their daughter's union with my spotted cousin, but the qualms they had voiced after the buffalo hunt remained. After what seemed an interminable silence, Wooden Legs nodded his head, and relief spread across Nate's face like a bright rainbow after a storm.

As the couple ambled afterward toward the river, I wondered if Nathaniel's proposal would sound as unconventional to Hides-in- Shadows as my husband's had to me. Regardless, she was already his altogether.

THE FOLLOWING DAY, all the women who were stooping to collect firewood stood erect and gaped. Spotted Long-knife not only toted a white man's fire stick along the path to the village, but he was also leading three times the customary number of horses for his bride's price. Joking Woman's overlooked daughter had become the most highly valued young woman of their tribe. Nathaniel would have gladly doubled these to have her, for he knew her worth far exceeded rubies.84 Blushing from his extravagance, she shyly accepted his horses and led them back up the path to her father's herd.

In a village with less than six hundred persons, no one could keep anything secret. In hushed tones, her aunts and cousins, friends and acquaintances, described the scene to their relations. If the past months had gradually increased her standing among those who were grateful she could translate the Creator's Book, Nathaniel's gift caused the whole band to recognize her worth. No longer did they refer to her as the girl who hid in the shadows. They called her Valuable Woman.

WITHIN TWO DAYS, the smoke-hole of my dwelling was no longer the cleanest in the concentric circles of the winter camp, and my cousin took her turn blushing deeply as her mother teased. The warriors joked similarly with Nathaniel, but her brothers communicated a sterner message. If he mistreated their sister, they would track him down, wherever he took her, and bury him in a grave so shallow that coyotes would dig up his body.

Besides the new status of a married woman, Nathaniel gave his wife several Christmas presents. One filled her with irrepressible joy; the others with dread. The first was a Bible of her own, which she clasped to her chest as if she feared it might escape. The others were dresses with bonnets to match, underscoring their imminent departure from everything, save her short-haired warrior, that she held dear.

Paulette had arranged for a dressmaker to sew one in a lovely peacock green to offset the red in my cousin's hair and another, a more practical traveling dress, in deep brown. Two Doves and I tailored them further to fit her petite figure, narrowing the waist and bodice, which needed to fit tightly since women were no longer imitating the late French empress.

Nathaniel gave me Christmas presents as well: a quill and a book of blank pages in which I began recording my extraordinary experiences as one of the people.

As Valuable Woman and I worked throughout the village, I taught her everyday pleasantries exchanged in polite eastern society, explaining why people left cards, the correct attire for differing social events, topics to avoid, and proper ways to address the dignitaries she was bound to meet as part of her husband's influential family.

"I fear I will embarrass him," she confided. "There are so many things I must or must not do to keep from shaming his family—far more than we require here."

"They desire your good opinion as much as you desire theirs. Just follow Nathaniel's lead or his mother's and aunt's, and you will find your footing—just as you helped me gain mine."

"Yes," she nodded, more to herself than to me. "The Creator will be there also to lead me. I want to make Spotted Long-knife proud."

"Who?" I teased.

"Oh!" she blushed. "I mean Nathaniel."

Two things she lacked, without which she could not enter polite society: she had not learned to write and needed an English name. Her little sister had called her Yin-yah, a mispronunciation of her given name, and her whole family had so adopted it that she could not remember the original. Neither Nathaniel nor I could produce any names sounding remotely like this, so the nick-name was of no more use than the strange-sounding translation of her village name.

Working diligently to read and form letters, she soon mastered the necessary social correspondences and began to sign them Anna Mary Anderson in honor of Nathaniel's favorite aunt who, he told us, shared his wife's gentle nature and pixie-like sparkle.

WHEN WINTER BEGAN blanketing the pines with ice, a chilling suspicion began wrapping itself around my heart.

"You must eat more," Valuable Woman urged after we had served our husbands. "You will weaken if the winter grows long."

"I do not know what is wrong with me," I confided. "Ever since the discord over raiding, I have felt ill. I thought it was just nerves, but though that all ended a moon ago, I have not improved."

Her brow creased tenderly, "Perhaps you are not drinking enough water. The winter sun can be drying."

"Maybe so—it does come and go. I will drink more and see if that helps. Sometimes I feel fine, but at others, I feel so tired I could collapse."

"What does this mean—collapse?"

"Fall down. In this instance onto my bed."

"It is probably nothing," she soothed, though the crinkling of her brow deepened. "You are not yet used to working in the cold."

"We have needed much more firewood lately, and then there is the water! I thought I had been growing stronger, but I hide in my dwelling after hauling our sacks, exhausted. Worst of all is the butchering. I cannot stand the stench and go running for the bushes." I hung my head and began picking at my finger-nails. "Preying Eagle has noticed—he drops his kills at Two Doves' door as if he were womanless. What must she think of me?"

My friend's eyes were full of sympathy, but her prolonged silence declared that she, too, would feel ashamed.

"Have you spoken with her?" she finally asked.

"No—I am afraid she will think me unfit for her son."

"I will haul your water until you are feeling better," she suggested. "No one need know, and perhaps whatever is ailing you will soon pass."

197

"You cannot. I do not haul my water only; I haul hers! I appreciate your offer and will miss you desperately when Nathaniel takes you east, but it might sink me more deeply if she discovered you helping. I will keep doing the best I can and, as you said, hope it will pass. Please pray it will."

It did not pass, and I often noticed my mother and aunts whispering when they thought I could not see. Sometimes they frowned; sometimes they smiled oddly. Had they been more like Talks-With-Bitterness and her lot, I might have thought those smiles smug, even disapproving, but these women had amply demonstrated goodwill, affection, and loyalty.

Unable to bear the tension any longer, I brought my sewing to Two Dove's dwelling. Our menfolk had gone hunting, and Valuable Woman, colluding with me, promised to keep my aunts engaged.

Once I had greeted my mother, we stitched in awkward silence. She seemed as if she was waiting for me to speak, as if she already knew I had something I wished to tell her, but I could not find a way to bring the matter up. If my disclosure did not invoke her disdain, I was certain it would make her worry.

After a while, she cautiously ventured, "You are growing too thin, and I have noticed that you often feel poorly."

Her tone held such unexpected solace that my trouble poured out in a relieved rush. "I am an unworthy daughter," I confessed when I had finished, "and an unfit woman for your son."

A gentle smile lit up her face "On the contrary," she replied, "we are all very pleased. As for my son's prey, our whole family has benefited from his frequent hunting. Not since I carried Elk Dog Boy have we so often had fresh meat, and when I felt as you do, Red Woman dressed my husband's kills."

As I tried to work out her meaning, my face must have looked as blank as the little-stitched doeskin in my lap.

"Since my son took you as his, none of your aunts nor I have seen you go into the Women's Lodge."

Retracing my memories of the past weeks, I realized she was right. So much had happened lately—getting married, that horrible week of conflict, preparing my friend to go to Boston, and trying to pull my weight while ailing. I had not given the Women's Lodge one thought.

"You are right. My last stay ended just before going to the outpost. That was nearly two moons ago. Do you think I might…?" The freshly sprouting hope was too fragile to put in words.

"…be carrying my grandchild?" Two Doves smiled serenely. "Yes— everything you have told me declares it so."

Awash with wonder, I impulsively hugged her. "Oh—thank you! I thought something was terribly wrong inside of me."

"Not something wrong, little one," she laughed, "something very right. But do not thank me, thank our Creator—and my son."

Scrambling up, I was about to run and tell Preying Eagle when I reached the door-flap and stopped short. "Oh. He is not here. He went hunting with our brothers."

"They will be home before nightfall, but he already knows. That is why he has been so determined to provide you the best food."

"How? I have said nothing to anyone but Valuable Woman."

Two Doves looked at me tenderly. "A child growing within a warrior's woman so soon after he has taken her offers proof of his strength. His hands search for signs our eyes might miss. He has been tending mares for many years, first his father's and then his own, and knows the signs that announce she will foal. Joking Woman will be pleased—she has already won her bet!"

As our news spread from dwelling to dwelling, warriors congratulated Preying Eagle for his evident virility; but Nathaniel looked so sheepish, I guessed he was remembering his comments about half-breeds the night I refused him. Valuable Woman looked down at her own belly in obvious question, embarrassed that she had not made the connection between my symptoms and condition.

"You will bear a warrior," announced Quiet Woman. "Preying Eagle is one of four brothers, his father one of three, and Two Doves the only daughter of her mother."

"I do not care if it is a boy or girl," I shrugged, "only that it is healthy."

"No," corrected Joking Woman. "You must pray for a warrior. Many are needed to fend off our enemies."

"Hope for a daughter when you grow older," Cries-at-Night advised. "You will tire more easily and need help with your chores."

"While the small one grows within you," added Two Doves, "think often of your favorite warrior of old. This will help you choose qualities you desire for the babe and compose your lullabies. When you sing them, they will set a pattern for him to follow as he grows. When I carried Preying Eagle, I thought of my great grandfather. He was the mightiest warrior of my girlhood band and the wisest. Preying Eagle is much like him."

Choosing David, I meditated on his Psalms, singing them as I sewed garments for the babe, and about the time crocuses forced their lance-shaped tips through the late winter snow, I regained my former vigor.

THE BUDDING TREES heralded the sad departure of my dear friends. Dressed in one of Nathaniel's gifts, Valuable Woman asked me to coif her hair and then completed her ensemble with gloves and a matching bonnet. Her errant curls had finally become assets, charmingly framing her face as they peeked from under the bonnet's brim, but the smile she returned to her admiring husband cast little sparkle into her eyes. As we watched them ride away—no longer Spotted Long-knife and Valuable Woman but Captain Nathaniel and Mrs. Anna Mary Anderson—I watched her catch her quivering lower lip and imprison it between her teeth.

Missing their departure by only hours, Elk Dog Boy galloped swiftly into the village, loudly raising an alarm. He had ridden northeast with Runs-Like-Antelope and Black Elk, scouting the way to our summer place, but when they had spied a war party advancing toward us, they immediately dispatched him with the news.

While our believing women gathered to pray, their husbands and sons prepared hastily for battle. The farther they could meet the enemy from our village, the less they endangered their families.

In his heightened state of agitation, my husband looked so fierce that he frightened even me. He had so altered his appearance that I might not have recognized him were I not present while he donned his paint. Vivid memories sprang up of the night I had first looked into his eyes, casting a horrifying specter some unfortunate warrior would face today.

Far more chilling was my fear that Preying Eagle might encounter an opponent of equal hostility and strength. I prayed fervently for God to grant him victory and bring him safely back to raise our unborn child, about whom there could now be no mistake. I felt definite movement beneath my broadening waist and rounding belly.

Men I regarded as extended family, always restrained and respectful, often gentle and frequently humorous, looked altogether fearsome. They carried highly decorated war shields, clubs, and lances, shoved freshly sharpened knives into weathered sheaves hanging from their belts, and slung bows and bags of arrows between their sinewy shoulders.

Each carefully chose his horse for its ability to perform in war, a different form of mental and physical exertion than hunting or riding. Preying Eagle painted his roan, which had proved steady and unafraid to head into a fray, with the same designs he painted on himself.

Only now did Two Doves' solemn warnings on the evening I chose this life sink into my heart. I had lost an uncle during the latest war with England and had read of many conflicts in Europe or New Spain, but nothing had prepared me for the dread I felt.

These were not handsomely uniformed gentlemen marching once or twice in a lifetime after some elusive glory, nor were they indentured pawns of a greedy emperor or king. They were unnerving depictions of what lay ahead of every man I cherished, save Nathaniel, not only today but many times every year for the remainder of their lives. Only the oldest and most infirm would stay behind.

Once they had all mounted, Many Feathers addressed the assembled people. "When the young herdsman, David, saw his people's tallest and fiercest enemy boasting against them, he declared that lances or clubs have no power to save.[85] The battle belongs to the Lord."

Deafening whoops resounded from the warriors while we womenfolk ululated excitedly. My husband, drawing his mount up beside me, leaned down to caress the back of my neck.

"Follow my mother and Elk Dog Boy's lead as you would mine. Little Turtle gains his first taste of war today. I trust the Creator will protect you and give us victory, but His ways are not always the same as our wishes. You must prepare your heart. An alert warrior will notice the child you carry and the unusual color of your eyes, which might work to your favor or disadvantage. You are young and pleasing to look upon. If he is merciful, he will take you as part of his spoils and raise my child as his own. Welcome him."

As I took in what he meant, I grew cold with fear. Not once had this hideous possibility entered my mind, and perhaps it was just as well—it might have turned me from the Lord's purpose.

"No!" I replied, shaking my head. "I would rather welcome death."

He lifted my chin and looked piercingly into my eyes.

"An enemy will not reach you unless I am dead. Stay alive, if not for yourself than for the sake of my son. You see how it is between Many Feathers and Quiet Woman. She carried Black Elk when my uncle saw and claimed her. Go to her dwelling tonight. She will tell you." Drawing my temple against his, he ran his thumb tenderly over my cheek. "A cruel warrior will not be merciful. He will delight in making what is beautiful ugly and destroying what his enemy most treasures. Decide quickly how to use your knife."

"We go," my father called, and the renewed ululating of the surrounding women drowned all chance to reply. As I watched Preying Eagle's straight, strong back disappearing into the ravine, I hoped it was not the last I would see of him, that he knew how very much I loved him, and how happy he had made me. Were I to die today, I would not have chosen differently.

NONE OF US COULD have forced a morsel down our throats, so we prayed with one another instead of eating our evening meal and read Our Creator's words. He had not left His throne, and we entrusted our lives, as the Israelite tribes did before us, into His hands. With so much at stake, this was far from easy. I returned to Him continually to lay down fears that I kept picking back up, amazed all the while by my mother's tranquil faith. She had a husband and three sons whom she could lose today; still, she remained in an attitude of prayer, encouraging and instructing me by her example.

"May I enter?" I later called outside of Quiet Woman's dwelling. Of all my aunts, I loved and respected her the most. She had a sensitive and warm heart coupled with wise counsel and strength.

"You are welcome here, little one," she called, but when I ducked in and saw my young cousin, Chirping Bird, I hesitated.

Quiet Woman warmly smiled. "Come. Sit down. Preying Eagle told me he would send you. We can speak freely. My daughter is well acquainted with the fates that may befall a woman and she also knows my heart."

I had so many fretful questions that I did not know where to begin, so I related all that my husband had told me.

"He fears you are unprepared for what may shortly come. Your strong attachment to him is plain, but your wits, not your heart, must guide you."

"But how can I do as he bids me?"

"You must. If the enemy reaches our village, it is as he has said—our menfolk are already dead. They will look for things they can carry—useful goods, jewelry, well-made clothing. They will replace their dead children with our young sons and daughters and take our choicest women for wives or slaves. The infirm and ugly they will cut down where they find them. Hide well. If you are fortunate, no warrior will find you. If one does, pray you will stir his desire."

"I would rather he gave me to his wife."

"No, little one, you would not. Your willingness may soften even the most callous warrior, but what charms do you possess that will work on a woman? She will snatch away the son you bear to raise as her own and work you so hard you will fall down in a heap. When you are broken and too worn to be of further use, she will cast you out like an old cook-pot, leaving you to starve or be eaten by dogs."

Quiet Woman was not prone to exaggerate, but I could not believe what I was hearing. "Surely the woman's husband would interfere?"

"You would regret it if he did. She would suspect you are crawling under his covers while she sleeps and would beat you until you can no longer stand. A woman's slave is her property—her husband will not tell her how to use it—and even if she suspects nothing, she will still beat you. She will beat you because she has burned her family's supper, beat you whenever her husband treats her harshly, beat you if his mother owns a sharp tongue and she can say nothing in reply. No, my little one, do not wish for this."

I was too stunned to reply.

"In every family of every village," she continued gently, "you will find a woman born to another tribe. It is the way of war. If a warrior finds your hiding place, do as your husband told you—welcome him."

"I could not."

"I know, little one. This is how you feel tonight, warm and surrounded by those who love you. I felt the same, but you may feel differently tomorrow."

"But how," chimed in Chirping Bird, "can I show I am willing?"

"Smile," replied her mother, "even though you will prefer to spit! Reach up so he can grab your arm and easily hoist you up behind him."

"Is this what you did with my father?"

Quiet Woman simply nodded, but something in her expression conveyed how deeply it had cost her. Surely, God did not bring me here only to have me snatched away, and yet I knew what my husband had said was true. God's ways are not always the same as our wishes. Had not the past six months offered ample evidence of this? Never, in my wildest imaginings, had I wished a savage to whisk me to his village. As I thought how blithely I had dismissed Two Doves' concerns the evening I burned my dresses, I resolved to take Quiet Woman's counsel to heart.

"Preying Eagle said I must decide quickly how to use my knife. I have never killed anyone and am not sure I can."

Quiet Woman smiled indulgently, as if I were a very young and ignorant child. "If you fought off one warrior, another would claim you. Do you have the strength to fight a war party? He meant the knife for you. If a warrior finds you, you must quickly assess his temper and act accordingly."

"For...me?" I stammered, horrified by the suggestion. "But his child...I could never..."

"Then you must do what I have already described. Let the warrior know you are glad to warm his buffalo robe—and pray he is not cruel."

I sat before her dumbly, wondering how anyone could do such a thing and shoving the alternative out of my mind.

"But he might have killed Preying Eagle," I mumbled, as much to myself as to her. "How could I..."

"Warriors display the trophies they gain so everyone may see their valor. You will recognize your husband's hair by the tokens he has woven into it—but even if you see them hanging from the warrior's lance, you must still encourage him."

"I do not think I can," I muttered. "I could not bear…"

"You *will* bear it because you *must*. It is the only way to preserve Preying Eagle's child. In time you will grow grateful. When this people attacked my village, my younger sister and I hid deep in a gully under a clump of bushes. Many Feathers burst upon us, his lance raised high, then he looked down at my large belly and his fierce expression changed."

"She is too modest," my little cousin grinned, "to tell you that he thought her beautiful."

"I will never forget my first glimpse of your mother," Quiet Woman confided. "She had been carrying Preying Eagle for about as long as you have carried his son and held herself as elegantly then as she does now. Next to her, I felt like a waddling goose. You know she is Many Feather's sister and is just as clever. She kept pushing Runs-Like-Antelope toward me, whispering that I was his mother."

My aunt paused, smiling at her memories. "He had just taken his first steps and began following me about, tugging at my dress or grasping the fringe of my hem for balance—and his big eyes began tugging at my heart. He looked so little and helpless."

"What of Many Feathers?" I asked.

"I hated him."

"Did he not know? How could you hide your feelings that well?"

"I am sure he expected little else. But I forced myself to smile, which showed him my intentions, and treated him with the deference due to any valiant warrior. I tried to hate Two Doves also, but with little success. I felt so alone and she welcomed me with such kindness that I could not long resist."

"When did you stop hating him?"

"Cleverness and patience run in their family. Whenever I hear Two Doves speak of their great-grandfather, as she did recently to you, I think he must have been just like Many Feathers. He allowed me several moons to mourn my husband, which I did deeply; and he, too, was grieving. His first woman died while she was bringing forth Runs-Like-Antelope. By the night his mother placed Black Elk in my arms, I felt only gratitude. He had spared Black Elk's life as surely as he had spared mine."

"I have always thought you love my father deeply," stated Chirping Bird.

"As I do. When I noticed how gentle he was with Black Elk, even treating him with affection, my hatred lessened to acceptance. He is a just man, as inclined toward mercy in everything as he was with me. He was also young and handsome—more handsome, though our young guest will not believe it, than Running Deer or Preying Eagle. I began to miss his warmth during nights that he hunted far from the village, and by the time I bore him Red Fawn, my former life was a pleasant but distant memory."

"Did you ever learn," I asked, "what happened to your sister?"

"Yes—you know her well. She is Cries-at-Night, Standing Bull's woman, the one who helped you make Elk Dog Boy his choker. The women of our family have always been known for our weaving and we brought our skill with us. She, like you, had recently wed a warrior she loved and grieved him heavily. Standing Bull's two sons were already hunters, too old to offer the comfort Runs-Like-Antelope offered me, but she soon had a growing belly to console her. You know the wives of Ugly Arm, Two Lances, and Fireheart. They are also from my tribe. All but Talks-With-Bitterness are happy, and that one can never be pleased."

"I cannot imagine life here without you. You have been like another mother to me."

"And you have become like a daughter, especially since Stands Apart took Red Fawn away. Now that I *know* the Creator rather than know about Him, I see His kind hand. Could I choose, I would not wish my path had been different."

As I slowly walked back to my dwelling, I tried to imagine myself making Quiet Woman's choice and could not, and yet I saw the practicality of her advice. I was thankful that she had told me her history. In addition to providing me hope should the unthinkable happen, I enjoyed getting to know her better.

I was also grateful that I had not been aware of this hideous prospect while at the outpost. I would have found it much more difficult to reject Nathaniel's offer; and yet, I would not have traded the last five moons as Preying Eagle's woman for any amount of time elsewhere. Not only that, I could not wish Valuable Woman to be deprived of her husband. She was infinitely better suited to be his wife than I was, and God had obviously arranged their marriage. As I thought of them, a twinge of anxiety pricked my heart and I prayed fervently they had traveled a different route from the war party.

NEAR DAWN THE next morning, an agitated hunter shouted from the watching place. "Warriors—in the pass!"

Tossing aside whatever we held, we ducked out of our dwellings, snatching whatever weapons were nearby, and dispersed in all directions. I scanned a pack of youths and hunters for my youngest brother as Two Doves grabbed my wrist and pulled me toward the ridge of evergreens.

My feet felt like lead beneath my cumbersome mid-section, and I feared I might slip until a firm hand grasped my upper arm. It compelled me toward the ridgetop and thrust me between the trees. Only then did I glimpse my helper—Elk Dog Boy—who then placed an arrow against his bow quicker than I had regained my footing. Both Two Doves and he fixed their attention on the mouth of the narrow ravine.

"They will enter the village there," explained my brother. "The incline is slick from last night's frost. Their horses will not like it."

While I stood struggling to catch my breath, fears about Preying Eagle tore at my heart; but before these gruesome images had fully seized it, the young look-out began urgently shouting.

"They come!"

Two Doves tightened her grip on Running Deer's old war club while Elk Dog Boy's nodded toward the watching place. We could just make out the tips of a row of bows assembling there.

"Hunters," Two Doves whispered. "They will greet the enemy with a rain of arrows. Where is your knife?"

As I lifted the blade, she touched my arm cautiously. "Don't forget what Quiet Woman told you—use it only if you must."

I had not forgotten one word, but before any warrior could reach me, he would need to cut down my beloved little brother and mother, who considered herself too old to be spared. How was I to welcome their killer?

The Lord hath made all things for himself: yea, even the wicked for the day of evil.

Proverbs 16:4

Chapter 18

MY HEART SO pounded, I thought it might burst my chest until we heard the youthful watcher's next cry. "It's Many Feathers! Standing Bull! Wooden Legs! Preying…"

My legs nearly buckled when I heard his name, but Two Doves was still holding her breath. He had called neither Running Deer nor my two other brothers. At last, he spotted them bringing up the rear, and we added our joyful ululations to the others resounding from every direction. Cousins and friends crept out from unexpected places and ran to the spot where moments ago the hunters had trained their arrows.

When my husband's eyes met mine, I could not squelch the joy that broke across my face and reached out my arms as he urged his mount forward. He hoisted me up behind him and tried in vain to pick his way through the throng. Pressing my face into his hunting shirt, I murmured thanks to our Father above for bringing him back safely, but when I opened my eyes and sat up, I was startled to see a frightening, unfamiliar warrior staring fixedly at me.

He wore his hair in a peculiar fashion, shorn close on each side with a thatch on top that stuck straight up, giving the impression of a horn sprouting out of his head. Recalling Chirping Bird's story, I pressed harder against my husband but then remembered I need not be afraid; my mounding form proclaimed that I no longer qualified for the Horned Warriors' strange sacrifice.

Once we had greeted our menfolk, Standing Bull, who urged us toward the center of the camp, astonished us with a tale that could have come from the book of Joshua. "We allowed the enemy to see us atop the ridge—the one where we had watched the buffalo grazing. When they saw our great numbers and knew they had lost the advantage of surprise, they accepted our invitation to talk.

"We had no wish to slaughter them, our delegation explained. The Creator had shown our people a better path. If they would leave their weapons as we would leave ours, we wanted to share the Good News from His Book, but the Creator put great fear in their hearts.

"Except for this warrior," Standing Bull motioned to the stranger, "they all fled, suspecting our invitation was a trick. We trailed them until they left our territory and have returned unharmed—as you can see. The Creator has given us a weaponless victory."

We could barely contain our euphoria. Warriors danced exultantly before the Lord, and women and children joined in praise for His deliverance. Later, someone dubbed the strange warrior Listening Man, as this was why he had come to the village; but when Wooden Legs offered him a place in Joking Woman's dwelling, my aunt left for the lodge of her eldest son.

"Why do you ask me to serve this evil one?" She spat when her husband followed her there. "His people killed our little girl—can you have forgotten? This very warrior may have dashed her head on the ground. I will not return to my home until that evil one is gone!"

"Woman," chided Wooden Legs, "what happened to your whispers in my ear about loving our enemies as the elders considered the raids?"

Joking Woman vehemently shook her head. "This is different! I will always hate them. There is no helping it."

"Then," her husband replied softly, "I will ask the Creator to free you. While bitterness still eats your heart, live with Smiling Fox, but you will still serve us."

Listening Man was as eager to hear and take part in the Gospel as many of our people had been. As days turned into weeks, the believers among us grew to love him for his eager devotion, all except Joking Woman and Chirping Bird.

The younger made every effort to keep out of his sight, ducking in and out of dwellings and hiding behind trees whenever she noticed his distinctive thatch approaching. She was convinced he had come to select a sacrifice for his tribe's fertilization ceremony, which she would suit perfectly. At night, she often lay awake listening for him to creep into Quiet Woman's dwelling and carry her off. After asking Wooden Legs to explain her odd behavior, Listening Man assured us that neither she nor any untouched woman needed to fear this fate. Years ago, a young war-leader named Petalesharo intervened on behalf of a stolen girl and persuaded his tribesmen to abandon the heinous ritual.

Joking Woman's aversion ran much deeper. As she adamantly rejected his overtures of friendship, she refused the healing God offered her heart, breaching her intimacy with both the Lord and her husband. She grew increasingly miserable until we happened across the parable of the unforgiving servant during an evening reading. When she heard that he, though forgiven a huge debt, violently demanded payment from a man who owed him little, she gasped so sharply that every eye turned in her direction.

As the Master in the story asked, "Shouldest not thou also have had compassion on thy fellow servant, even as I had pity on thee?"[86] tears streamed down her usually jovial face. She begged Listening Man to forgive her, and to the gathered people, her simple confession became a flame to dry kindling. Neighbor approached neighbor, asking forgiveness for long-held grudges until few hard expressions could be spotted in the village. That very night, Kicking Horse and my husband became friends.

RETURNING TO THE summer place was glorious. The blooming trees and wildly flowering meadows swathed the dull winter countryside in pinks, blues, and yellows. Blossoms and buds had replaced the brightly colored leaves around the lake where my husband courted me, and rain had drenched the drying grasses green.

While replenishing my water sacks, I thought of Valuable Woman and all the hopes we had shared with each other there. They had sprouted like this changing landscape, altering our lives forever. Next to the waterfall, I thought this the most beautiful place on earth.

As the spring rains increased to summer thunderstorms; so my longing intensified for my sweet, red-haired friend. Nathaniel and she had been gone for less than four months, but it seemed forever. Everyone treated me with special consideration for the life I carried on behalf of our tribe, but I missed our sisterly closeness and ease of conversation.

In one way, though, she benefited me by leaving. Communicating constantly in my adopted tongue spurred me to think in it also, helping me express myself more naturally. She was so far better at translating the Scriptures, especially abstract concepts, I looked forward to relinquishing that task; but for now, I was the Lord's provision and prayed He would increase my abilities.

Preying Eagle took great delight in my changing form. He never tired of laying his hands or head upon my burgeoning belly, which provoked our child to kick with gusto. The longer I was his wife, the more thankful I became that God had arranged our marriage. We were different outwardly, but the things we cared about deeply were identical, often bringing to mind Wooden Leg's description of my heart.

I now realized how much of me I had imprisoned beneath all the layers of convention in Skippack; and rather than hate their way of life, as Nathaniel feared I might, I felt it set me free. Only an awesome God could have known how to fulfill the secret longings He had placed within me when He formed me long ago. To Him be the glory forever and ever!

BEFORE THE MOON of Cherries Ripening was upon us, our believing elders began debating about The Dance. Many felt we should not participate, as the Scriptures prohibited self-mutilation, and they were unsure they should worship our Creator with those who did not keep to His path. Others felt we should bring the Good News to our kin who were still in bondage to darkness. Knowing nothing about it, I could offer little worthwhile guidance.

After listening to all the opinions voiced, Old Man took a firm stand. "Jesus worshiped at the Creator's Dwelling with those who tried to trap him. Did they all genuinely worship the one true Creator? Some were like we used to be: wanting to worship the Creator and waiting for His Son. The disciples also continued going to this place after He rose from the dead, telling their tribesmen of Jesus' resurrection. How can we do otherwise?"

"What my father says is true," conceded Running Deer, who had feared some of the younger believers might be led astray. "Only, let us make a pact together that none of us or our sons will disparage Jesus' sacrifice by fastening himself to the pole."

Standing Bull pressed my husband to attend. Since his young cousins held him in high esteem, they watched what he did and followed his lead. Preying Eagle, however, felt reluctant. He judged me too near bearing to make a long journey on horseback and was concerned that his son might come while he was away.

The Dance itself would last only a week, but we lived the farthest east of our tribe, and a band as large as ours would need to move slowly. Besides this, he had lately been performing the heaviest tasks among those the warriors disdained as women's work and did not want them added to his mother's burdens. While we were discussing the matter together, Two Doves and my two youngest brothers ducked into my dwelling.

"Go, as Standing Bull suggested," Little Turtle urged Preying Eagle. "Father goes also and says we must stay to protect the women left behind."

Two Doves laid her hand on my stomach. "Your son has not yet dropped all the way down. He is first to open his mother's womb and will take his time."

"We will do our sister's heavy hauling," volunteered Elk Dog Boy.

Little Turtle shot him a distinctly displeased sidelong glance, to which Two Doves responded, "If your sister's water sacks are too heavy, her pains may come too soon. Do you want her to push out your brother's little pot-bellied son before he is ready?"

Little Turtle looked as if something foul passed under his nose, but he shook his head. "Why does Father not let me go? Our little brother can do the lifting."

"And our women?" asked Preying Eagle. "What if raiders come?"

Little Turtle compressed his lips and nodded briefly before exiting my dwelling. He already knew his father's reasons and that they were sound, but my husband's agreement with them helped him subdue his fervent desire to rebel. His mother and younger brother ducked out also followed shortly by Preying Eagle who, grabbing the few possessions he needed, caressed my cheek warmly and trotted toward his herd.

For once, Two Doves was wrong. In the middle of the second night after my husband rode away, my back began to ache, and muscles I was not aware existed began forcefully contracting my lower abdomen.

Shaking the figure sleeping next to me, I whispered, "I think the baby may be coming."

Forcing herself awake, Two Doves felt for the involuntary tightening in my belly and kept her hand there until it relaxed.

"Yes, little one. He comes. I will help you to the Women's Lodge."

"Oh," I inhaled quickly, "the pain! Just let me lie here until it goes away."

"It will not go away for long. Come," she gently prodded. "The walk will help him press further downward."

I could think of nothing I desired less but also knew there was no chance this baby would retreat. With great effort, I managed to turn over and Two Doves helped me to my feet, and by the time we crossed the short distance to Quiet Woman's dwelling, water was rushing into my moccasins.

"He is impatient—this little pot-belly," my aunt clucked. You should have meditated on Two Doves' great grandfather. You go on to the lodge. I will wake Joking Woman."

I smiled, though I knew she could not see, and thought how glad I was that my mother and aunts had made me walk and walk before dawn every day since we had moved back to our summer camp. My steps were slower and more difficult now, but modesty compelled me onward. If we did not reach the Women's Lodge, I feared I might bear my babe in full view of the village.

Once inside this special dwelling, my mother and aunt guided me to an upright pole embedded deeply into the ground and then, after spreading straw over a buffalo robe at its base, helped me lower myself to kneeling there with my legs wide apart.

"Grasp the pole, little one," Quiet Woman explained, "and when the pain comes, bear down. Your son will do the rest."

Nodding acquiescently, I tried to relax between the ever-quickening waves, muttering very short prayers as I pulled against the pole. These women were so uncomplaining, so used to facing life's difficulties with calm. I refused to shame myself by crying out in fear.

This odd position combined with the babe's weight to create considerable pressure, and my body began struggling forcefully to expel him. I felt an unrelenting urge to bear down and push hard, pulling mightily against the pole, yet the babe did not come.

"He is as eager to be out as you are to have him out," Two Doves assured me, gently wiping the perspiration from my face. "Another push—maybe two."

Panting, I tried to gather my strength but was overcome by another urge to push, more powerful than the last. Coupled with my body's immediate compliance, the babe slipped out onto the straw.

Two Doves cooed at the scrunched-up face so loudly protesting his expulsion. "He is a boy and a big one! Preying Eagle will be proud."

As I caught my breath, I watched her gazing at him tenderly in the early morning light that had begun filtering through the smoke hole. She examined every part of his tiny form, pronouncing him perfect; and as she placed his tiny wet body in my arms, I felt instant and overwhelming love.

"Oh, how beautiful you are," I crooned as he attempted his first meal. He was red and wrinkled and had a surprisingly thick thatch of straight black hair. "I think he already resembles Preying Eagle."

"Yes," smiled Red Woman, "and Running Deer and Old Man before him. Their blood runs strong."

"What will Running Deer name him?" I asked, already aware that this honor would fall to my husband's father.

"We will see," shrugged Two Doves. "We will just call him Little Potbelly for now. When he distinguishes himself from other boys, his name will emerge."

Quiet Woman cleaned him while my mother used a feather to tickle me under my chin. "Let yourself laugh," she encouraged. "This will force out whatever remains inside you."

I found this difficult, having never been particularly ticklish, but complied and was surprised by how readily my stomach cooperated. It began contracting again, though not as painfully as before, and once the afterbirth was expelled, Red Woman scooped it into a bag and carried it outside.

Quiet Woman, meanwhile, was busy greasing Little Potbelly and rubbing him with star puffball spores. When she handed him to me, he smelled as wonderful as his delicate, warm skin felt—altogether delicious.

Beyond the door-flap, Red Woman began scolding someone. "Put down that knife—do you want to bring him an early death?"

We listened while her equally agitated husband answered. "That is just women's superstition!"

"Why do they argue?" I asked Two Doves, who had ducked her head out and then back into the lodge.

"She has hung the afterbirth in the tree, as her mother taught her—and her mother before her. Old Man and Little Turtle have taken it down. Old ways die slowly," she shrugged. "Has he finished eating? Old Man will want to see him."

"Yes, here he is," I answered. "I am exhausted."

"Rest well, my little one," she smiled, stroking away the hair that clung damply to my forehead. I will bring back Little Potbelly when he is hungry. Preying Eagle told me that you neither cried out nor struggled while he was considering whether he would take your life. Who, but the missing rib of my valiant eldest son, would show such courage? You have shown it this night as well."

I smiled up at her, grateful for her approval, but wondered if she would regard me so highly had she known how petrified I had been. "God's grace alone kept me from screaming in terror. I was too frightened to move."

"Courage is not a lack of fear, little one, but what you do when fear faces you."

IN THE DAYS that followed, many women who stayed away from The Dance streamed by my dwelling to see the baby who was half-white but wholly one of the people. Joking Woman brought him a rattle she had fashioned from the stomach of a hedgehog, Quiet Woman an intricately beaded frock of the softest doe-skin, and Two Doves a beautifully decorated cradleboard. Water and wood appeared at my door flap every day and also a steady supply of food.

Little Turtle carried his nephew around so frequently that Elk Dog Boy became impatient for a turn, so I saw my son only when he was hungry. Though I missed him, I was thankful for the time to rest and regain my strength—he was a good but frequent eater, waking me several times a night.

As I lay deeply sleeping, I dreamt that Listening Man was in my dwelling, squatting quite near to my face. His distinct thatch of hair stood in clear relief against the starry sky streaming in from my smoke-hole, though his face was lost in his shadow. As my eyes adjusted to the night, darker and lighter areas on his face gave the illusion of war paint, but all I could make out was the glint of his eyes.

"Listening Man—when did you…?"

Before I could finish, he clamped a hand over my mouth and spread an unpleasant grin over his face.

"No sound!" he grunted in a language similar enough to our own that I understood him and tilted his chin toward three other thatch-haired warriors standing in the shadows. As they stepped forward, I saw that one was holding my Bible and another my infant—with a knife poised over his belly. My limbs felt so heavy, I could not make them move, but as the warrior hoisted me onto my feet, I realized I was not dreaming.

Afraid for my son, I stepped unresisting through a hole they had slashed in the back of my dwelling and wove silently behind them between dark lodges to the forest's edge. A tall, thatch-haired youth stood beneath a pine, keeping their horses ready and quiet, but my captor did not pull me up on his mount, as I expected.

Guiding me by the arm he still gripped toward a speckled pony tethered to his blanket roll, he gestured for me to climb up. I did, darting a glance toward the cruel-looking warrior who held my son and then back to the sleeping village.

It looked so peaceful that I wondered afresh if I was dreaming, and as often happens, odd aspects of this nightmare conflicted with each other or made little sense. Why had the raiders left other dwellings undisturbed, and why could I make out large forms dotting the hill where we kept our herds? Had our warriors raided a village, they would have stolen the best horses and stampeded the rest to thwart a chase. My slowly stirring mind jerked awake as our sentry's fate became sickeningly apparent: he lay in a motionless lump near the speckled pony's feet.

As we plunged into the dark, Little Potbelly began to protest, but his captor clamped a swift, large hand over the tiny, wrinkled face. I dug my heels into the pony, charging up beside the man I had mistaken for my friend, and promised to cooperate if he would let me hold my son. He was about Running Deer's age and seemed to be the leader.

Snapping something I could not understand, he pointed to the babe's captor, who assured me Little Potbelly was alive by turning him so the starlight reflected off his open eyes. When we increased our speed, though, my son renewed his wailing, and his cruel captor startled him into silence by grabbing his tiny ankles and dangling him in the air.

"Give him to me!" I cried, frantically snatching at the air as the reckless warrior swung him out of my reach.

"We have the woman," he sneered. "We do not need this sniveling potbelly."

Grinning as the babe's face twisted in a frightened shriek, he slung Little Potbelly over his head as if he might hurl him into the bushes. "Give her the potbelly!" barked the leader. "We are safely away, and her warrior will not be able to follow until several suns have passed."

The cruel one let go, dropping my son in mid-air so that I had to lunge to catch him. I had never known such heartlessness. Holding Little Potbelly tightly, I thanked the God of all things for keeping him safe. The past twelve moons of adversity and wonder had taught me more profoundly than all the prior years that He was entirely trustworthy and His methods truly perfect. He was not absent or asleep, and by His grace, I hoped not to give way to fear.

That morning, Quiet Woman had dressed Little Potbelly in the frock she had embellished, so I began picking at the beads, hoping their color would show brightly in the morning sun.

I hated to destroy the lovely design—she had created it so painstakingly, and her stitches were so small and tight that they seemed impossible to weaken without calling my captors' attention. Managing to work several loose, I intermittently slipped them to the ground and hoped they fell too lightly for the warrior traveling behind me to hear.

Low-lying branches aided me also: they offered a ready supply of leaves into which I could dig my nails while pushing them out of my way and an excuse, when they would not budge, to veer into and trample the soft, low growth along the path.

WHEN AT LAST the sun began sending faint shoots over the horizon, we picked our way down a well-hidden gully and dismounted to rest.

"Why have you stolen us?" I asked the older warrior. He appeared less rash and far kinder than the one who had carried my son.

"One of our warriors, Two Crows, lived for a while in your village. When he returned to us, he said your white-man's book offers your warriors great power. We want this also."

His reasonable tone aroused hope that I could appeal to his fatherly instincts. The warrior he called Two Crows was surely Listening Man. Was God answering his plea to bring his people the Gospel?

"Why did he not come?" I asked. "He is like a brother to me. I would have been happy to see him."

The older warrior pulled his lips sharply downward, but before he could answer, the warrior who had dropped Little Potbelly cut in. "He returned to us weak—like a woman—talking only of love. He would not steal you, but we did not need him."

In the scant light, he looked even more menacing than he had by night. Three ugly scars slashed each side of his face, from hairline to mouth, in too deliberate and perfectly balanced a pattern to have been made by an animal's claws.

A third warrior, stone-faced and slightly older than the scarred one, nodded in agreement. From their similarity of features, I guessed the fourth, who carried my Bible, was his brother.

"We have our sacred bundles and our holy men," the fourth man added. "We need no love to defeat our enemies."

Assuming they were confused, I told them, "Love is not a weapon, nor is The Book. It prevented our warriors from slaughtering you between the ridge tops."

"Bah!" the scarred man spat. "Your medicine deceived us—your warriors are cowards—afraid to fight!"

"Then why do you wish to be like them?"

His deepening color warned me I had struck a nerve and should press no further. "A wolf does not wish he were a coyote! When the vultures have eaten the flesh off your warriors' bones and your choicest women grow heavy with our sons—then we will gain a *love* for your people!"

The stone-faced warrior and his brother snickered while the older man and youth remained politely silent.

"Your book possesses chants and incantations for power," the older one explained. "We want these and also to discover what sacrifices and gifts this god requires. You will read them to us, and we will know how to gain this god's protection."

"It has neither chants nor incantations," I answered. "Only songs of praise and instructions for following the Creator's path. The Book will not protect you or harm us if you possess it—the Creator has promised He will never forsake us. As for sacrifices, they are not like your spirit bundles and can never win His favor. He offers it freely to everyone who wants Him to adopt them."

The older man's face remained placid, but I could tell he was pondering my words. "How," he asked after thinking for a while, "do we get this adoption?"

"By turning from your own ways and gods to love and serve Him only."

"Why do you listen to her?" scoffed the scarred man. "We are warriors! We serve no one!"

"The Morning Star makes us strong," the stone-faced warrior added. "We have their book—it is enough!"

"If a woman steals a warrior's flute," I asked, "will he love her and do whatever she bids?"

"No!" retorted the tall youth. "Women were created to please warriors and warriors were created to please themselves! If she wishes to gain his attention, she must prove herself yielding."

"So it is with the Creator," I answered. "We cannot command Him to do what we please, whether we possess His Book or not."

The oldest and the youngest both became pensive, the stone-faced man appeared uninterested, and the other two screwed up their faces with disgust.

"She talks like Two Crows'" the scarred one sneered. "Why listen to her?"

"Hush," the leader grunted. "Yellow Arrows—hand her the book so our ears may taste it."

The fourth warrior retrieved it from his pouch and handed it to me.

Flipping to John's Gospel, I read, "'As many as received Him, to them gave He power to become the sons of God, even to them that believe in His name, which were born not of blood, nor the will of the flesh, but of God.'[87] The Creator wants you as His sons, but he will not force you to love Him. As sons imitate their fathers, His children imitate Him. Two Crows imitated His Father, the Creator, when he refused to do evil."

Not knowing what to reply, the leader looked down at my son, who was beginning to fuss. "Take the potbelly and lie down with him. We resume our journey when the sun reaches the lowest tree branches."

I did as he commanded, turning my back toward them while I fed Little Potbelly, but I could not sleep. After a time, they began talking freely.

"You heard what she said," declared the one they called Yellow Arrows. "This book will not give us power. Let us collect a war party and attack their village before they know it is missing."

"You are a woman," mocked the scarred one, "if you fear her menfolk. We have defeated them often."

"That was before this spirit lived among them," replied the older man. "I was part of our delegation in the valley. The woman's words make little sense, but this book gives them power, and they own fire sticks like the white men."

"My cousin has seen one of these fire sticks," muttered the stone-faced warrior. "They blow holes right through a man."

The older man nodded. "Even a small boy walks carefully when he faces a mountain lion."

"Go home and cower in your dwelling!" the cruel one spat. "Yellow Arrows and I will raise a war party."

"I understood little of what she said," broke in the youth, "but as she read this spirit's book, my heart grew warm with its power. We should return her to her people."

"You are not a warrior," scolded Yellow Arrows. "You have no part in our council."

"Let him talk," the older warrior commanded. "He is my sister's son."

"We cannot take her back," argued the stone-faced man. "She will tell them who stole her, and they will make reprisals."

"Let us surprise their warriors," advised Yellow Arrows, "as they ride back from The Dance."

The older one grunted. "You sound like one eager to taste death."

"Better to die plunging my knife into an enemy's heart," the cruel man jeered, "than to cower like an old dog."

They were silent for a while as if settling down for rest, and I soon felt the warmth of a cook-fire and smelled brewing chicory.

"There is nothing to tie our tribe to this woman's disappearance," the leader put forward. "I find her appealing. She shows courage, and my woman needs help with her harder chores. Her warrior cannot have owned her long; she has lived too few summers. I will help her to forget him."

My skin began to crawl. I was not so naïve as I was with Henry and understood exactly what he implied.

"Wagh! You are too old and your belly too round to please a woman," mocked the scarred man, thumping his own hard-muscled abdomen. "If you wish her to forget him, hand her to me!"

The hair on the back of my neck stood up as my every nerve stood on end. I lay waiting for the older man's reply, but no one spoke for such a considerable time that I began to suspect they had fallen asleep. I started to exhale, relieved my fate would not yet be decided, until the leader grumbled, "We will gamble for her."

I felt ill. Gazing down at Preying Eagle's baby, my memory flooded with all that Quiet Woman had confided. *"Lord, You control all things. Please restore me to my husband—but if we must belong to one of them, please let it be the leader."* Even as I asked, I fully felt my petition's irony: I was now begging for the very thing I found revolting only moments ago. Still, the older man would surely be kinder and a better father to my son; and his wife, though she might beat me pitilessly, would provide a buffer from his attentions.

"What will you wager?" the leader inquired.

"Two fox pelts," mumbled the stone-faced man.

"Two? Make it four!"

"I wager a colt," announced the cruel warrior, "but if I win, I also claim her book!"

Again, the leader was quiet, as if he were contemplating the cost of its loss. "Agreed," he decided. "Yellow Arrows, you have said nothing. You do not want her? She is healthy and pleasant to the eyes. She will bear you fine sons."

"I have taken a woman recently and do not need another, but I will wager a pelt for the potbelly. He is strong. If my woman does not want him, I will give him to my sister."

"My son?" I thought, feeling as if the man had kicked me in the stomach. *"No, Lord—You surely would not let them separate…"*

"Agreed," the leader announced decisively. "Cuts-His-Face, what do you wager for him? She will not be happy if they are parted."

"Bah!" the scarred warrior spat. "I do not care if she is happy!"

"Unhappy women are a misery," the old one cautioned, "and this one possesses a skilled tongue."

"Hmph! I will also wager a pelt, but not for her sake. I will enjoy teaching him to hate his people. If she wants to keep her tongue, she will learn to keep it silent. A mute woman would have much appeal," he added, rousing chuckles from his companions. "Perhaps I will remove it for sport."

As laughter erupted, I felt like I could no longer breathe. How, in so short a time, had their hearts moved from a desire to hear God's Word to molestation and mutilation? I forced myself to remain calm, recalling that Sarah had twice braved similar situations.[88] "You are her children," Peter had written, "if you do well and let nothing terrify you." I repeated the words again and again, but they did not long stave off my terror. A sharp victory whoop announced who had won me: the man I most feared.

My stomach heaved, as it had the night I mistook Preying Eagle for Nathaniel, only I was sufficiently acquainted with this savage to know that he deserved that title. Still, however horrid my circumstances were, they could not change God's faithful character. *"Oh Lord...please..."* I felt such dismay I could barely form thoughts. *"Lord, save us—and help my faith not to fail."*

"Here is their spirit-guides book," said Yellow Arrows, as casually as he might offer a bowl of chicory.

A sharp thud sounded behind me, and then a sudden sucking in of breath. Maybe, I hoped, an arrow had flown into the ground at the man's feet or an angel had appeared to save me. I was sorely tempted to turn and see, but my hopes were dashed just as suddenly. The next sound was paper tearing, repeated again and again until the cook-fire crackled wildly.

"Now you see how much I fear their spirit-guide!" proclaimed the triumphant warrior. "He has *no* power!"

As the acrid smoke burned my nostrils, my heart felt far sicker than my stomach. I could do nothing but helplessly weep while the two brothers stamped rhythmically around the leaping flames, every step carefully placed to laud their frightening friend's audacity.

The older man grunted sullenly but his tall nephew sounded chagrinned. Although he was powerless to thwart the victor's mocking, he abruptly got up and strode from the gully. At least, fully absorbed by the burning, they paid no attention to me.

My reprieve was short-lived. The boastful winner stepped over my stock-still form, squatted down, and cocked his head while examining my face. Overwhelmed by the smell of his greased thatch, I could barely keep my nose from wrinkling, but he stared at me so intently that he noticed when my eyelid momentarily twitched.

"She is not asleep!" he announced, grabbing my jaw and turning it so he could better peer into my eyes, now opened widely. "I am Cuts-His-Face! You are mine to do with as I wish. That old man will protect you no longer."

When he noticed my tear stains, he roughly thrust a hand into my hair and yanked my head upward, twisting it so the others could see.

"Where is her bold talk now?" he scoffed, pointing to the damp streaks.

Still suspending my head, he directed my eyes toward the smoldering fire.

"Where is your book?"

"Burned," I murmured, trying hard not to wince as he again jerked my head around so I could face him.

"Your spirit-guide could not save it and he cannot save you!"

As my neck began to quiver from the strain of being twisted like a puppet, he cocked his head from one side to the other. A slow grin curved his lips while he watched me try and fail to control my trembling, and then he let go of me without warning, bruising my cheek as it hit the hard ground.

"Shall I carve her face," he asked his friends, as I numbly stared at my soundly sleeping baby. "Or shall I thrust it into the embers that ate her book?"

No one replied, but all except the tall youth gathered behind him to witness my shame. With his knife, he lightly traced the pattern of his scars across my cheeks, brightening the eyes of the stone-faced warrior and his brother, but the older man shook his head.

"Wait until we finish our game."

Deeply grateful, I thought he might be trying to help me—from the first, he had seemed the kindest—until he casually continued.

"Wait until we arrive in our village and cut her there so all can watch. If you slice her face too deeply or burn it severely, she may become weak and die along the way."

"Cut her now!" Yellow Arrows argued. "Our hunger for her pain is strong—but do not cut too deeply. Then, smear the wounds with dirt. They will fester and swell by the time we reach our people. Then, when you slice them deeply, all can watch her writhe and scream. You will prove her god has no power."

While I listened to Yellow Arrows plan, my tremors became uncontrollable. His tone was feverish—and all at once, I understood why my husband had told me to use my knife. I could not now, even if I wanted to. It lay in my dwelling, beside my bed, and I needed to stay alive to protect his son.

Rolling me onto my back and tilting my face from side to side, Cuts-His-Face considered their suggestions and then suddenly seemed to come to a decision. His eyes gleamed while he angled his knife over my face and lit as it bit into my unblemished cheek. While he watched the blood trickling into my hair, his own ugly scars twisted with satisfaction.

"Where is your god now?"

Seizing a handful of gritty soil, he forcefully rubbed it into the slashes until my face burned so badly I was afraid I might cry out. Salty tears, streaming unbridled into the fresh wounds, sent me into violent spasms, further filling his eyes with glee. Afterward, he pointed his knife toward my sleeping infant.

"Did his father take delight in the softness of your face?"

I nodded weakly, my mouth too dry to speak, my heart too terrified to imagine what this pitiless man was planning.

"If he comes for you, he will not know you. You will run to him, unable to call his name, but he will turn away in disgust. Even your potbelly will cry in horror when he opens your eyes and sees your ugly face. Who, then, will give you this "love" you crave? You will beg me to keep you, lest you fight dogs for food. *I* am your god now!"

"Come," urged his friends when they grew bored of watching. "The sun is awake. We want to finish our game."

Cuts-His-Face seemed reluctant to end his torment, but when his friends became insistent, he smugly smiled and swaggered back to the game.

I turned over toward my baby, making certain he had not been harmed while I was squirming away from the sharp blade. Never, through all the days of fear with Henry or even from the tortures I imagined by the falls, had I felt such terror, and I possessed no strength to fight it. My teeth rattled from shuddering, whether from pain or fear, I could not tell and did not care.

"Why," I cried silently, *"did You allow this to happen?"* Would Little Potbelly shriek when he awoke and I leaned over him—and what of Preying Eagle? Touching my wounds, I wondered if he could love me disfigured beyond recognition. *"Oh, God—You alone can help me."* As I lay shaking, I almost forgot the others, so absorbed was I with misery, until their leader let out a sudden whoop.

"The potbelly and your pelts are mine!" he boasted.

"No!" I sobbed silently. *"Lord, don't let them do this. Don't let them take my son!"*

Compared with his loss, the painful throbbing in my face seemed nothing. I had been confident the Lord would cause Cuts-His-Face to win him also. Had I not read a hundred times that the decision of a lot is from the Lord?[89]

Now not only would Little Potbelly never know Preying Eagle, but he would also think another woman was his mother. *"Why, Lord?"*

At once, I thought of Cuts-His-Face's plan to make him hate his own people and of my earlier plea for the leader to win us. The older man had disappointed me, but I was still sure he would be a kinder father. He also seemed less bent toward hate. This, at least, offered me a slight measure of consolation.

Curling tightly around Little Potbelly, I wept until exhausted, and then something inexplicable happened. I began to feel hope. God was not asleep, just as He had not been sleeping when Preying Eagle snatched me away from Stump. Not even Cuts-His-Face could limit His love and power, and I would no longer arrogantly dictate to Him the outcome of my circumstances.

Job also lost his children, every one, and his pain was far more prolonged than I hoped mine would be; yet, he clung to one hope. "I know that my Redeemer liveth and that He shall stand at the latter day upon the earth; and though worms destroy my skin and body, yet in my flesh shall I see God."[90]

Bow down thine ear to me; deliver me speedily: be thou my strong rock, for a house of defense to save me.

Psalm 31:2

Chapter 19

FOR THE SECOND time in twelve hours, a hand clamped over my mouth. My eyes flew open, but the face peering into mine was not scarred and scornful but troubled and smooth. Gesturing that I should stay silent, the tall youth removed his hand, pressed a bit of cool, dampened leather against each of my sore cheeks, and softly wiped them free of grit.

I lay perfectly still, feeling like a small child: wary of further pain but aware he meant to help. Surely, I thought, darting an anxious glance over my shoulder, he did so at his own peril. Neither the vicious warrior nor his friends would be pleased to catch him frustrating their goal.

Following my eyes, he curved his lips up faintly, shook his head, and drew out a small pouch that hung inside his hunting shirt. He dipped a finger into its contents, gently dabbed it on each slash, and then looped the little bag around my neck. Motioning that I should tuck it into my dress, he tossed a cautious glance at his sleeping kinsmen.

"When they awake," he whispered, "wipe it away."

As grateful tears dampened my lashes, he shook his head again, quite adamantly.

"No—make yourself take courage! Fear is like the scent of roasting meat. It rouses their craving for your pain. This sun you are safe. Cuts-His-Face waits to shame your god before the village. When he arises, bring your lips up, so." He demonstrated with the corners of his mouth. "Offer him welcome."

He read revulsion in my eyes, for he once more soberly shook his head. "Your old life is lost. You must face what lies ahead. Even a brutal warrior grows tender toward a woman who admires him, and he will not ruin what he regards as his. You may yet find some happiness."

The suggestion made me ill, but he meant it kindly. Doing my best to quell my feelings, I hoped he could read my gratitude as easily as he had my fear; and once he returned to his kinsmen, I fell into an exhausted sleep.

"GET UP!" COMMANDED Cuts-His-Face, roughly poking a toe into my ribs. "We go!"

I rose on my hands and knees, shielding my son from my cruel master's foot while wiping away the ointment with the corner of his small blanket. A brief scan of the horizon announced their reason for haste: the sun had already climbed well into the treetops.

As I guided my horse into line, I began freshly assessing my situation. The older man needed me to care for Little Potbelly until we reached the village. Once he took the babe away, I would have only one reason to keep myself alive: the hope that his wife might allow me to serve as my son's wet nurse, as Moses' mother had for him. If she were near the older warrior's age, as I expected, she would be past bearing children and unable to perform this essential duty herself.

Cuts-His-Face looked no less threatening in bright light, and as hostile as he was toward the Gospel, I could not imagine him allowing me to share it. Nonetheless, I pondered the tall youth's advice—so similar to Quiet Woman's—and attempted to smile when my new master glanced in my direction. The corners of my lips would not budge. Instead, I submissively lowered my eyes, keeping my pony close behind him.

We traveled steadily and without incident, though to make up the time we had lost oversleeping, the leader kept up an unrelenting pace. Other than making it difficult for Little Potbelly to settle for his meals, this worked to my advantage. Cuts-His-Face had no time to further his torments.

When we reached a more open terrain, my respectful behavior began yielding alarming results. He began pestering me in the manner of my former suitor, Kicking Horse. I could not understand why he bothered. He already owned me. Why should he try to gain my attention? Perhaps he was simply bored or the challenge appealed to his vanity.

Whatever his reason, he set my good sense at war with everything else within me. Encouraging him might diminish or even avert his cruelties for a time, but they would surely intensify in duration and brutality if I raised expectations that I did not carry through. As Two Doves once told me, a warrior's pride was a formidable foe.

Quiet Woman had submitted to Many Feathers and over time had grown to love him, but Cuts-His-Face shared none of my uncle's admirable traits. Besides, her situation and mine were very different. Preying Eagle was very much alive. Breaking faith with him would scar me far worse than slashes with a knife. Perhaps this was Cuts-His-Face' aim.

Whatever his goal, I was bound to receive his attentions. My only choice lay between receiving them whole or as he promised—mutilated beyond recognition. In safety and conceit, I had been heartily offended when Nathaniel suggested I traded my virginity to Preying Eagle in exchange for kind treatment. Now, I realized, only the grace of God would keep me from sinking so low.

As I stared at my captor's naked back, I thought of Shadrach, Meshach, and Abednego, who chose the fiery furnace rather than unfaithfulness to God.[91] My dilemma differed little from theirs: the Creator, alone, could deliver me from this evil. On the day of torture, He would give me the courage to stand firm.

The older warrior interrupted my thoughts, sidling up beside me and holding out his hand to receive *his* new son. However, when he saw a blanket slung across my front, he assumed the babe was feeding and trotted ahead to retake the lead. I breathed a deep sigh of relief. Not only would my babe's garment betray what I had been doing, but in my hand lay a bead I had just loosened. Sliding it to the ground, I cast a nervous gaze at the dark clouds gathering over the horizon. A sudden downpour might wash away or alter the location of every bead I had dropped along its path.

Working another free, I asked my Savior for His aid. He had commanded a violent wind to cease when the disciples feared drowning; He could certainly blow the clouds off course. He did not. They seemed instead to follow us tenaciously, but once again, I had reason to be glad that He, not I, rules over all. By the time the sun had pulled up its covers, the clouds were so thick they obliterated both the stars and moon, forcing us to stop well before we reached the Horned Enemy's village.

I settled with my son a slight distance from the others but dread of the morning stole my sleep. However long a reprieve the blackness provided, it would only delay my fate. Yellow Arrow's feverish proposition still rang in my ears, and each time I closed my eyes, I saw Cuts-His-Face's eager expression. Had I slept in my bed just last night? It seemed like weeks ago.

I felt someone curl up behind me, smoothing a hand over my backside. It could only be Cuts-His-Face. Without his permission, the others would not dare make use of me. As his hand slipped over my hip and down my stomach, I thought my panicking heart might halt. I breathed in deeply, evenly, hoping he might leave me alone if he thought I was asleep. Apparently, he did. Rising on one elbow, he pressed his chest against my back, craning over my shoulder to peer down at my face.

"Let her rest," the older warrior ordered. "He little potbelly will wake her soon enough. Without enough sleep, she will not produce much milk."

Cuts-His-Face did not budge, as if he wrestled with his leader's wishes. I prayed the starless sky hid my eyes, unnaturally scrunched together, and that he could not detect my nostrils flaring from the smell of sweat and bear grease. Finally, he yawned and rolled over.

I lay listening for a long time, lest he too feigned sleep, and then inched far enough away that I could not feel his warmth. Wondering if I could sleep at all, I watched the moon emerging slowly from a cloud and then closed my heavy eyelids. The next thing I heard was a dove gently cooing.

Could it be near dawn? I did not remember falling asleep, but only the sun coaxed most birds to sing.

As I closed my eyes, a quavering whistle startled them wide open. It descended and then trilled only feet away, and even I knew gray tree owls do not make nests in low-lying scrub. While scanning the brush, my heart thudded so wildly I feared it might wake Cuts-His-Face. He had turned onto his side, so close that I could hear his even breathing.

A dark shape, barely perceptible, began to distinguish itself from a sparsely growing bush. It looked frightening, painted black from hairline to nose, creating the impression of a disembodied mouth and chin. While it signaled for me to remain silent, a second form, painted unfamiliarly, parted the leaves. A bare arm grasped the hem of Little Potbelly's blanket and quietly tugged him into the shadowy scrub.

I exhaled for the first time in moments, relieved the soft sounds had not awakened the warrior behind me, but then I heard the dull thud of a well-placed kick.

"Cuts-His-Face, wake up," I heard Yellow Arrows whisper. "Listen! I have heard two owls—a bad omen."

"You are an old man," grumbled Cuts-His-Face. "Go back to sleep."

"Where is the woman?" asked the war party's leader.

"We are here," I whispered, wrapping my excess buffalo robe in a bundle around the arm I kept against my chest, hoping it might pass for Little Potbelly in the darkness. Hearing my voice, he began whimpering in the thicket, so I rose on an elbow, pretending to pull him toward me to nurse, and began soothingly singing. The ceasing of his cries was as well-timed as its start had been ill, giving the impression he had gained what he sought, but the older man was not satisfied.

"The calls were too many," he murmured, "Wake Tall Man. He may earn his first eagle feather tonight."

"Wagh, you sound like frightened women," mocked Cuts-His-Face. "Her warrior cannot yet know that she is missing. Go back to sleep."

Yellow Arrows returned to his place, and since all appeared normal, the older warrior resumed snoring. Intently staring into the shrubs in front of me, I prayed my son would remain quiet. If he awoke a second time, I might not fool our captors so easily. After what seemed like hours, the black face assumed its position between the branches and signaled for me to move toward him—quickly!

As I did, he blurred past me, piercing the air with a sharp cry. "Whump," I recognized the sound of a war club brought down behind me, and the answering crack beneath it. Frenzied whoops and grunts filled the air as I reached safety behind a wide tree trunk; and before I could turn to see what had transpired, my four assailants lay dead upon the ground. The first thing I saw was Little Turtle straddling the tall youth, his war ax raised.

"No!" Before reason restrained me, I sprang from my hiding place, and in that split second, the tall youth knocked my brother backward and pounced on him with his knife.

Wrenching me back to safety, my husband snapped, "What are you doing?" I had never heard him sound so harsh.

"He…he…has been helping me," I sputtered.

A quick command halted Little Turtle, who had once more gained the advantage over his tall adversary. Running Deer and Two Bears leaped forward, tightly binding the youth's wrists and legs. Rustling the brush heedlessly now the danger had passed, Elk Dog Boy emerged from the woods' edge, holding Little Potbelly.

My heart turned over. This was the first time I had seen my husband in over half a moon. He was even more strikingly handsome than I had remembered, despite the paint—or maybe because of it. Hurtling myself against him, I sobbed with relief that we were safe and with horror that my impulsive cry had almost killed our brother. With my head buried in his chest, I awaited his well-deserved censure, but he did not give it. He just held me, unwilling to let me go; and were it not for our fussing son, I would have gladly remained in his comforting arms forever.

When his little brother held up the babe for his inspection, the moonlight reflected on a broad row of white teeth. He enfolded his offspring in the secure, loving grip with which he held my heart, and I thanked God for giving me to this man who had now rescued me not once, but twice.

Running Deer held Little Potbelly next, his deft hands inspecting him from head to toe. "He is strong like his father," he announced proudly as a tiny fist gripped a prodding finger.

Carefully snatching the babe away, Two Bears held him a few inches from his chest. "And big for one just born."

I was grateful for a quiet moment to talk with Little Turtle. "Can you forgive me?" I asked. "My rash cry almost killed you."

"I am safe," he shrugged, looking a little embarrassed. "I am glad the Creator stopped me from causing an unjust death."

When Preying Eagle bade me mount the speckled pony, I felt relieved. This had been the most terrifying day of my life, and the horn-like top-knot dangling from his lance made me shudder. Picking our way carefully through the dark, we made camp only when we were a good distance away.

Little Turtle explained how they found us. My son's cry had awakened him as our shadowy forms passed Two Dove's dwelling. After noting the direction we headed, he awakened Elk Dog Boy and Standing Bull's two youngest sons, stopping only to tell Two Doves and Cries-at-Night before they set off. Their friends rode toward The Dance to alert my husband, and my brothers pursued us. As the sun rose, they followed my markings, pocketing the beads along the way.

"You would have been proud of her," Little Turtle told my husband. "The war-party chose their way with care, but she left so many signs that tracking them was easy."

Reaching the gully as the horn-haired war party was leaving; my brothers noted their number and watched to make certain they continued southward. Then Little Turtle cut east alone, hoping to intercept his father and other brothers, whom he presumed would be riding swiftly toward the village. Standing Bull's sons had driven their ponies as hard as they were able to go, had met up with the band returning home, and informed my menfolk that we had been stolen. When Little Turtle reached them, he led them southwest, avoiding half a day's pursuit, and at the gully, they picked up Elk Dog Boy's well-marked trail.

I was awed by how well my little brother had hidden. Not once had anyone suspected his presence, and not once had I been left without someone in pursuit. How like God! Even as I despaired of life, He had already arranged my rescue. When would I ever learn to disregard the whisperings of my fears and trust in Him completely?

AS WE LAY DOWN to rest, Preying Eagle curled around one side of our tiny son and I curled around the other. Our father and brothers slept nearby; the tall youth bound between them tightly enough to prevent an escape but not enough to cause him pain.

"I am grateful to the Creator," Preying Eagle murmured. "This tribe is our most formidable foe." Across the darkness, he reached for my cheek, but when he found and caressed it, he felt me wince. "Why do you pull away from me?"

Although I could not see his expression, I knew his brow was knit together, trying to peer into my heart. "They…they…gambled for us," I explained, dreading the ugly scars the morning light might reveal. "The winner scored my cheeks with his knife, from hairline to mouth, in a pattern to match his own so that all would see he owned me. The tall youth applied salve to them while the others slept, but they are still quite tender. I should apply more."

Drawing the pouch from my dress, I massaged into each a dab of the healing mixture. Preying Eagle lay so still, I could almost feel his tension, like a storm-cloud about to burst.

"The warrior lying behind you?" he asked. His voice was flat and tight.

228

"Yes. His three-feathered thatch dangles from your lance. His companions persuaded him to wait until we reached their village to complete the work, so he could boast that our God has no power."

Softly, gingerly, his fingertips felt the barely scabbing ridges.

"You may not think me pleasant to look upon when the sun rises. He intended to mutilate me so severely that even our son and you would turn away in horror."

"I should have cut out his eyes and staked him in a fire while he still breathed!"

His tone was chilling, as if he were capable of doing such a thing, had done so before and might again. I could not help shuddering. Could my husband, so tender toward me, also act like a savage? No! I pushed the thought away. He was surely fierce in battle, but not merciless. He had given vent to his feelings nothing more.

Lifting Little Potbelly, he lay him down on my other side, and then pulled me firmly against his chest, running a hand down my back, my hip, my upper leg, as if he was reclaiming his territory. Sheathed in such possessive tenderness, the past day's anguish poured out in a torrent.

"He reminded me of a hungry mongrel refusing to let go of a meat scrap. His hate was so vehement. Why?"

Gently, my husband entwined his hand in one of my braids. "He could see from your health, your clothing, and your ornamentation that you were the treasure of a warrior. By assaulting you, he assaulted me."

"But why? Did he know you?"

"No, but his people feel much shame. They cowered because of the great fear of us the Creator placed within them, and he boasts to hide his fear. He knows they cannot defeat us, so he attacks where we are vulnerable."

"What do you mean?"

"You. My son. By harming you, he damages me deeper than a blow from a club or lance and can then boast that I could not keep you from him."

"That is exactly what he said," I sighed, "only of the Creator."

"He walks Satan's path and spouts the same lies."

I lay still, thinking for a few moments about the parallel he had drawn. It was like the sudden flicker when sparks meet dry wood, casting light into a dark place.

"You have grown silent," Preying Eagle murmured. "You are in pain?"

"No. I was just mulling over what you said." Alit with new understanding, I lifted my head to look into his face, but his features were lost against the dark grass. "It is just as you say—Satan and Cuts-His-Face use the same tactics! Satan knows the Creator's Book—he quoted it to Jesus. So since he knows he cannot defeat God, he aims to destroy what

God loves most. Then, once sin has disfigured our hearts, he declares us too repulsive for God to love, so that we hide from Him."

Lying back down, I felt Preying Eagle nodding against my hair. "You are mine," he murmured. "That cruel one could not make me stop wanting you. Think of Red Woman. Her teeth are gone and her eyes disappear into her wrinkles, but Old Man sees only her beauty. I will not quit wanting you until I quit breathing."

Happy and secure, I snuggled closer against him, but something else kept nibbling at my heart. "Why did the Creator allow this to happen? They destroyed His Book."

Preying Eagle grunted but did not answer right away, and when he did, I at first doubted he had understood the question.

"The day I brought you to our village. I told the council I was determined to take you as my woman; but when Father refused his consent, I burned with anger. I insisted Two Bears and Little Turtle go hunting with me. I wanted to be far from him, far from the council, and from you—who were everywhere, tormenting my eyes. After Two Bears watched me smolder for several suns, he asked if I believed our father's heart was good. 'Of course,' I answered, irritated that he would ask me such a foolish question, until he added, 'Then why are you angry?'

"Not until you burned your white woman's dresses did I grasp how well my father understood you. I thought only of my own desire, unaware you could not accept my horses until you accepted my people; we are inseparable. We are like this with our Heavenly Father—our ignorance makes us angry. Perhaps He is answering the tall youth's secret cries, as he answered mine, or maybe He removes our tough crust."

"I am not familiar with this word."

"When my mother taught you to gather the wild grain that grew in the field beyond the fir trees, did she make you rub them hard between your palms or on a rock?"

"Yes," I nodded.

"Before a hard chafing, the grain's useful part is trapped. We are the same. Hardship rids us of what is dead and useless. As for His Book," he shrugged, "the Creator will supply our need."

Curled safely in the crook of his body, as our little one was curled in mine, I pondered all he said until waves of exhaustion dragged me under.

WHILE THE SUN began stirring, so did my little one, rooting for his breakfast. Preying Eagle, eager for a well-lit glimpse of his son, rose on his elbow and watched him over my shoulder.

"He has a healthy appetite," he observed, petting Little Potbelly's hair while the tiny cheeks sucked in and out. When I felt his body become unexpectedly rigid, I knew his eyes had traveled to my face.

"Are they horribly ugly?"

"No," he reassured me, tenderly running his fingertips along the scabbed ridges. "They feel more distinct than they look. This warrior kept a sharp blade, so his cuts were clean. They will always sorely remind me that I left you vulnerable."

Pressing my lips into the hollow of his palm, I pleaded, "Do not punish yourself. Were you to make the decision again, based on what we knew when you left, I would hope you would choose the same. If you must be angry, be angry with the Creator, who knew they were coming but did not tell you."

A slow smile broke across his handsome features as he gently tilted my head so he could see my eyes. "You are leading me back to what I said last night about the Creator's heart."

Nodding, I returned his affectionate smile, and he began nuzzling my hair with his cheek.

"After your time of healing is over," he whispered, "I will show you my love has not lessened."

"We go!" Running Deer cut in. "This one," he nodded toward the tall youth, "wishes to come with us."

As we stood up, my father and brothers' mouths dropped open. None of them was yet aware of yesterday's torments. Then, as they turned toward their young prisoner, their shock changed to accusing glares. Preying Eagle related all that I had told him, his account of the youth's aid softening them somewhat, but as they struggled with anger and grief, tension dominated the first part of our journey.

While we traveled, Running Deer described the joyous outcome of the festival, exposing the timing of Satan's assault. Many Allies who heard the Gospel left their bands for our village so that they, too, could listen to the Creator's Book. By destroying both The Word and its translator, the enemy of our souls hoped to also quash their budding faith.

Sadly, the Good News had also caused grievous division, just as it had in our band that past year. Raiding their enemies had been only the first of several issues; another was retribution. Our warriors considered it a solemn duty to avenge the death of a family member, but Paul, in Romans, clearly taught the reverse. "Vengeance is mine, saith the Lord. I will repay."[92]

Abandoning these inbred traditions was very difficult, even for those inhabited by God's Spirit. Not only did it war with the instincts they shared with all mankind, but they feared discarding them might dishonor their dead. I was thankful the Scriptures produced these results while working on their hearts, quite apart from anything I did or said.

With each breaking issue, the faithful paid a price for rejecting traditions that conflicted with Scripture, as my Celtic ancestors had a millennium ago when the Truth freed them from worshiping tree spirits. Many preferred bondage to what was familiar over freedom from the law of sin and death, dividing families as they left us for other bands. Indeed, it was precisely as the Word declares: "The light has come into the world, and men loved darkness rather than the light because their deeds are evil."[93]

On the way home, we met trickles of our returning people. Talks-With-Bitterness's two elder daughters and their husbands, all devoted to the Truth, told us their parents had gone to live with Swallow Woman's new band. They also brought us joyful tidings: Spotted Eagle and his clan had decided to align themselves with us. Stands Apart had only to retrieve Red Fawn from their village, where she was recuperating after the birth of their son.

When Two Doves saw us coming, her face lit with joy, but it darkened into a scowl when she noticed my scabs. I wondered uncomfortably how she might reassess my courage when she learned how terrified I had been. Watching her weave through a small crowd, as she had last summer when I entered her village, I realized how wholly my feelings had changed. I had been frightened of the people, frightened that I would fail the task God set before me, frightened that the warrior who bewilderingly stirred my heart would cast me off to the highest bidder. Today, though I echoed her restrained decorum, my heart began to sing: "*O magnify the LORD with me, and let us exalt His name together. I sought the LORD, and He heard me, and delivered me from all my fears.*"[94]

How wonderful it is to know His power, not only to save but also to release us from the inner struggles that bind us up tightly—"Let everything that has breath, praise the Lord!"[95]

Firing his gun above the crowd, Preying Eagle proclaimed he had a son. I would have loved nothing more than to retreat to my dwelling with my husband and our little potbelly, but we had too much to tell that concerned the whole band. Little Turtle and Elk Dog Boy became heroes that day, gaining admiring glances from many untouched women; and when the tall youth's help became widely known, they stopped regarding him with such suspicion.

"As the stones Joshua heaped by the great river[96] reminded his people the Creator had saved them," announced Running Deer, "let my daughter's scars remind us that He saved her from a great evil."

I felt awed by the change perspective made: first, changing my scars into a monument to God's saving power, and second, in regard to our burnt Scriptures. Only the pages were lost, Wooden Legs reminded us. Our various clans had already committed most of the New Testament to memory. Until God supplied us with another Book, each family would take turns reciting their portions. During the ensuing weeks, Jesus turned this, as He does all things, for our good.[97] No one needed to translate, as they naturally had memorized the Scriptures in their own tongue, leaving me time and energy for my newborn. More importantly, the Word became thoroughly something of the people, losing all lingering association with the white man.

Once we could politely separate ourselves from the assembly, our immediate family went to my lodge, and Wooden Legs took the tall youth to Joking Woman's dwelling to learn what he knew of Listening Man.

While I listened to Two Doves describing her grandson's birth, I was swept into a virulent wave of homesickness. I wished my white parents could have met him. Picturing Father as he had been in life for the first time since his death was like welcoming home a longstanding and very beloved friend.

Glancing up, I found Running Deer regarding me with love and pride and thought of a verse from the book of Joel that Nathaniel had shown me before he left. I could not see why it reminded him of me—it was God's promise to restore the crops Israel lost to locusts[98]—until he pointed out that I, too, had suffered severe losses, not of food but family. In this village, God had given me a mother and father, uncles and aunts, even a grandmother and grandfather who genuinely loved me, and answered my longing to be of use to Him. The tenderness in Running Deer's eyes, the joyous faces of Red Woman and Old Man cooing over my wee one, and the pride in my new mother's voice underscored how correct he had been. I would always hold my late family very dear, but God had truly restored to me all that I had lost. To Him be the praise forever and ever!

We were under great pressure, far beyond our ability to endure, so that we despaired even of life. Indeed, in our hearts we felt the sentence of death. But this happened that we might not rely on ourselves but on God, who raises the dead.

2 Corinthians 1:8b-9

Chapter 20

MUCH TO THE joy of the entire village, Nathaniel and Anna Mary returned in the Moon of Shedding Geese, almost four weeks after my son's birth. She was radiantly happy and just becoming aware of her own budding little one. Joking Woman, Wooden Legs, and her brothers could barely contain their excitement as the new couple rode into camp in their wagon, but neither could any of the rest of us.

His family had loved her, as we were confident they would, welcoming her into their home and hearts. His mother and aunt guided her into their society, as my mother and Valuable Woman had done for me. They regretted only one thing: the Lord confirmed He desired for them to live among her adopted people. Who can argue with Him and win?

My friends had brought us a new Bible, aware that the "Word of the Lord endureth forever,"[99] but paper and leather do not. Between the dunking mine received last August and wear from continual use, they were concerned it might now be in tatters. The timing could not have been better, and though the people grew confused when Nathaniel described a printing press, they jubilantly thanked the Lord for swiftly answering their prayers. How like the Almighty to supply our need before we were aware of it! My friends had purchased the new Bible several months before my abduction. In addition, they gave me a copy of Scott's Ivanhoe, as they knew I loved to read but had no way of buying or borrowing books. I tucked it away for nights that Preying Eagle was away.

I could not imagine a happier time. All my closest friends had come back home, including Red Fawn, whose son had been born a few weeks before Little Potbelly. We worked side by side each day, as we had when we were all untouched, and in the evenings, our families talked for hours, catching up on our experiences over the moons of separation.

Nathaniel thought my son was adorable, though I mercilessly pointed out that the plan he proposed on the catwalk would never have worked. Little Potbelly never would have passed for his. He, in turn, teased me for

234

making such a poor effort to forget what I had already forgiven. How wonderfully God had altered our plans.

Our chores, themselves, were the same that we performed a year ago, but while we worked, Red Fawn and I wore our little potbellies snuggled in cradleboards on our backs or hung them from trees to rock in the gentle breeze. My son's huge eyes appeared to soak in everything, reminding me often of his watchful father, while Red Fawn's son usually slept. Both were happy and warm, enclosed as tightly as they had been within us during the last few weeks preceding their births. Our conversations, however, were distinctly different, centering often on the dissimilarity of our marriages produced by the varying mixtures of our cultures.

My red-haired friend wrinkled her freckled brow. "Spotted Long-knife insists that I voice what I think," she confided, "as if I were another warrior. And if I do not know what I want or understand what he does, he demands that I question him!"

"He wants you to understand their ways," shrugged Red Fawn.

"Even when I understand perfectly, he asks me to offer my opinion—especially if my face announces doubt or tells him I think he is wrong."

Red Fawn's eyes opened wide. "I would not dare challenge Stands Apart. He might feel insulted, but his ways are so like any warrior's, there is little for me to question. What about you," she looked at me. "Do you find living with Preying Eagle difficult?"

"I would if Running Deer had not taught me what to expect. Truthfully, though, I find our people's ways more freeing than restricting. I am less anxious, less concerned about aspects of my life I cannot govern, not only those in Preying Eagle's care but also those beyond his or the elders' control."

"I have been afraid you might feel oppressed," Valuable Woman confided. "Spotted Long-knife's sister would if she had married my cousin."

"Sometimes," I smiled. "But learning to trust my husband has taught me much about trusting Jesus. Often, I have wondered why He would place me on this or that path that I did not care to walk, but I am learning to relax and leave my life in His care."

Without thinking, I began rubbing my fingers over the ridges on my cheek. I did not know what was in the salve that Tall Man gave me, but the scars had healed so nicely now that they were barely visible.

"Yes, but He is the Creator," Red Fawn persisted. "When my father gave me to Stands Alone, I submitted. I know my father well and respect him well, as do all our people. But with Stands Alone I sometimes bite my lip. I have grown to love him, but he does and says things differently than my father would. They cannot both be right. How do I place my confidence in him when my heart shouts he is wrong?"

"I have found this hard also," I sighed, remembering an incident a few weeks before Red Fawn had returned, "but it is very much the same, especially because I so often do not understand."

"Ask us," replied Valuable Woman. "We will be happy to tell you anything we can."

"You are not always here, and neither was Red Fawn until recently."

"What did Preying Eagle do?"

"On a night that I was particularly weary, Little Potbelly would not stop crying, though he was dry and well-fed. I was afraid he might wake our neighbors, so I began to hoist his cradle-board onto my back, hoping a walk might settle him. Without a word, Preying Eagle swept him from me and ducked outside. I thought he was helping," I shrugged, "so I drifted off to sleep."

"I would thank the Lord for such a husband! I have slept very little since our son arrived."

"I did, but a few moments later Little Potbelly's wailing woke me up again and Preying Eagle, empty-handed, ducked back inside our dwelling. When I asked what he had done with our son, he told me he left him hanging from the hickory tree."

"What did you do?" asked Red Fawn.

"I stared in disbelief as Preying Eagle lay back and closed his eyes."

Valuable Woman cocked her head. "Did Little Potbelly keep crying?"

"Yes, so loudly I feared he would wake the whole village. I bolted outside, but when I tried to unhook him from the tree, Preying Eagle grasped my hands and ordered me to leave him there. As I listened to Little Potbelly's wails, I kept imagining how scared he must feel—alone in the dark—and it took all my resolve to do as my husband demanded."

Red Fawn asked, "Did you?"

"Yes, but I lay between our buffalo robes wide awake with anger, wondering how Preying Eagle could be so cruel! I knew he was tired also, but he surely did not think a few paces and a wall of buffalo hide would be enough to muffle the cries. Then Little Potbelly began screaming so loudly that I half-feared warriors would flood from their dwellings, armed against an attack."

"Did they?" Valuable Woman smiled as I paused to take a breath.

"No, though I do not know how our near neighbors slept through it. After a while, Little Potbelly stopped; so Preying Eagle retrieved him, laying him down beside me, and curled up around my back."

"So all was well," concluded Red Fawn, as if she could not see why I was bothered by my husband's behavior.

"Not in my heart. I wanted badly to shove Preying Eagle away. How could I feel affectionate toward a man who had proved so callous? But as he reached across my shoulder and began stroking our son's head, those verses about Sarah began pricking my heart."

"Which?" asked Red Fawn. "I do not recall them."

"The ones in 1st Peter that say God praised her for 'calling Abraham lord.'[100] I argued that our situations were different, that her husband was 'the friend of God,'[101] not a man who punished an infant for crying. Even as I did, though, I knew I was wrong. Abraham gave Sarah much better reasons to be angry than Preying Eagle had given me— twice—and all to protect his hide!"[102]

"What did he do?"

"He told her to say she was his sister," answered Valuable Woman, "so a fierce war-leader would not kill him to gain her."

"Did he—this war-leader—take her?"

"Yes," Valuable Woman nodded.

"What did Sarah do?"

"She deferred to Abraham, trusting God to intervene on her behalf."

"Did He?" asked Red Fawn.

"Yes—on both occasions—and commended her for quietly hoping in Him."[103]

Red Fawn tilted her head, eager to know how I had reacted. "So you stopped feeling angry?"

"Not right away, but as I began to recall the many times I thanked God for your cousin, I felt ashamed. He had just rescued me from Cuts-His-Face. Should I rebuff him because our thinking differed?" My cheeks grew warm as I recalled his promise to love me until his last breath, but as close as I felt to my friends, this was too private to divulge.

A bit sheepishly, I confessed, "I also thought of the first night I spent by the falls with Preying Eagle, before I knew him, and of the anger I had felt toward God. I had not understood what He was doing, just as I could not understand what my husband had done, but you have seen how His plan has unfolded. I have found more joy here than I ever could by following my own wishes, and I began to see that my problem with my husband is the same I have with God. I did not truly trust him. I thought I knew better than he, just as I had thought that God had made a horrid mistake by allowing Preying Eagle to carry me off."

"But the Creator is not a man—He knows everything," Red Fawn protested. "I obey Stands Alone because I have no other choice, but sometimes I feel as you did—angry in my heart."

I smiled, nodding in complete sympathy. "It is not a question of whether they are right but of whether God's design for marriage is good. If Quiet Woman gave you a belt to bead and told Chirping Bird to weave a choker, what would you think if your little sister grabbed the belt instead?"

"I would not like it. If my mother gave me the belt, she would expect me to complete it."

"But Chirping Bird may think she beads prettier patterns."

"It would not matter," replied Red Fawn, sliding me a sidelong glance, announcing she had caught my point. "Mother would hold me, not my sister, responsible for its completion. But we are talking about lives—what if our husbands are wrong? As our cousin just told us, Abraham nearly forced Sarah into another warrior's bed."

Shuttering, I pictured Cuts-His-Face's gleaming eyes. "And how did Sarah escape?"

"God saved her!" Valuable Woman piped up. "He warned the war-leader in a dream, forbidding him to touch her."

"Exactly! Sarah's trust was not in Abraham but God—not only to guide her husband but to provide a way of escape if he failed."

"Ah," sighed Valuable Woman, "that is how those verses tie together."

Red Fawn and I looked at her blankly, unsure of what she meant.

"They appeared to me like a string of poorly matched beads—one not going well with the other. First, Peter says she called Abraham lord and with his next breath tells us 'we are her daughters if we do not give way to fear.' It makes sense now. Her courage came from her trust in God, allowing her to submit without fear. But what happened between you and Preying Eagle—you did not finish your story."

"I turned towards him once Little Potbelly was asleep, and all the tension just seeped away. However inscrutable his reasoning seemed, he was worthy of my trust; and if he erred, I trusted the Holy Spirit would correct him."

Both of my cousins exchanged knowing glances, reminding me of their mothers. "Did he explain why he did it?" asked Red Fawn.

"Not then, but just before sunrise Little Potbelly began crying again. Preying Eagle repeated his actions, bringing him in only once he stopped wailing, but my hardest test came after Preying Eagle had left for the far field. Little Potbelly started up again while I was lighting the fire for our early meal, and I was sorely tempted to give him what he wanted. I knew just how my little one felt—my empty belly had been growling painfully."

"What did you do?"

"Hung him in the tree as my husband wanted. As soon as I walked away, he stopped crying, so I was quickly able to retrieve him."

"Too bad Preying Eagle was not watching," smiled my red-haired friend. "He would have been pleased."

"Someone must have seen. Shortly after I had fetched our morning water, Running Deer called for admittance. He never comes to my dwelling if I am alone, but this morning he grasped my shoulders and told me how much my obedience had honored him. I am still unaware of how he knew of it," I shrugged, "but I felt grateful and unexpectedly rewarded for my choice."

"Perhaps it was our Heavenly Father," offered Valuable Woman "It reminds me of a verse I recently read that says He sees in secret and rewards those who obey in secret.[104]

"I know who told him," divulged Red Fawn. "I overheard Two Doves telling my mother but did not understand what they were talking about. It was Standing Bull's sister. She had been displeased when she heard Preying Eagle wanted to marry you. She was afraid you would bring us all grief and strongly warned his father to forbid him. When he did not listen to her, she told Two Doves she thought him foolish; but after observing you that morning, she asked for his forgiveness. Do you understand why Preying Eagle did it?"

"Yes," I smiled, recalling the warmth in his eyes. "He explained everything to me later that evening." The details were far too personal to recount aloud, but I cherished their memory:

"You deeply please me," he had confided, pulling me close. "Your stiffness last night announced that you were angry, and yet you turned to me in welcome."

Resting my forehead against the hollow of his chest, I confessed he might feel differently if he could have listened to my thoughts. I was ashamed of my defiance and felt all the more wretched when he began tenderly stroking my hair.

"You are not right in this," he murmured. "You were angry because you desire to protect our son, but your obedience revealed what lies in your heart. You chose confidence in my judgment, though it fought against your own. This is doubly important because you do not yet know our enemies' ways. Your life and our potbelly's might one day depend on you swiftly obeying—with no explanation—and your trust clears my mind to overcome my opponents. If my heart is questioning whether you are safe, my eyes will be searching the trees or rocks, and an adversary will cut me down quickly.

A warrior is better off without a woman than with one who will not obey him."

His description gave me hope that I might one day be like the wife of Proverbs 31,[105] whose husband trusted her with his heart.

"Little Potbelly must learn not to cry," he explained. "He might draw raiders to the village or alert an enemy to the place you two are hiding. When any infant in the village gains a habit of wailing, his parents train him in this manner."

Not until Little Potbelly grew older did I fully grasp the relationship between respect, trust, and obedience. My son's quick submission allowed me to guide him easily, keeping him from many troubles and contributing to the harmony in my dwelling. While he was still young, he often complied only outwardly—as I had that evening—but over time he learned that Preying Eagle and I were worthy of trust, reminding me of something Jesus told his disciples. "Ye are my friends if ye do whatsoever I command you. Henceforth, I call you not servants...I have called you friends." Initially, I obeyed Him to please my parents; later I obeyed because I loved Him myself and saw clearly that He is trustworthy and true.

WHILE PRAYING ABOUT living with us last fall, Spotted Long-knife had assumed he would act as a sort of pastor for our band. Seeing the elders effectively shared this role, he limited himself to privately clarifying texts for them and publicly answering unanticipated questions. While back east, he had learned about a Cherokee leader, named Sequoia, who had invented an alphabet for his people, and he longed to do something similar.

Failing this, he planned to transliterate our language into sounds that corresponded roughly with the English alphabet. Then, we would need only to teach them what letters made each sound. Meanwhile, however, our band redoubled its effort to memorize the entire Bible, each clan taking responsibility for one book, according to size. Our huge family, which included Old Man, Red Woman, and all their offspring's families, took the sixty-six chapters of Isaiah. Spotted Eagle's took the Gospel of John, eagerly wanting to gain a grasp of this vital portion of Scripture we had finished studying before he and Stands Apart joined our number.

Valuable Woman and I taught English to anyone willing to learn, guarding against the danger that something might happen to Nathaniel and the two of us before the translation was finished. Preying Eagle, much to his credit, became one of my first students. The only words he knew previously were "I love you" and "you are so wonderful," which he heard often as I slipped back into my former tongue while expressing intense emotion. He attacked English with the same discipline and diligence he exhibited in all aspects of his life.

Along with him, we taught Red Fawn and Stands Apart, with whom Preying Eagle became fast friends, leading him in the path of Christ. To provide practice pronouncing the odd sounds for them all, we spoke only English when we three couples were together, and by our first anniversaries, Red Fawn, her husband, and mine could engage in simple conversations and understood much of what Spotted Long-knife, Valuable Woman and I said, leading to an event I never anticipated.

For it is God which worketh in you, both to will and to do of his good pleasure.

Philippians 2:13

Chapter 21

DURING THE WARM days of autumn, Preying Eagle and Stands Apart returned with an agitated hunting party. Hearing excited whoops echoing off the cliff face, Valuable Woman, Red Fawn and I left our bundles and climbed the short path to the lookout. What I saw both shocked and unnerved me. They were towing eight bedraggled white men, strung together with ropes around their necks. All but one was on foot, scrambling to keep up with the mounted warriors ascending the hill. The other lay over a saddled horse, perhaps wounded. I thought this harsh treatment appalling and immediately ran down the path to intervene on my countrymen's behalf.

Nathaniel had left that morning for the outpost, so Valuable Woman followed to help me translate; but when we reached the village edge, Preying Eagle purposefully intercepted us. "She goes," he ordered, nodding toward our red-haired cousin. "You, take our son to your dwelling and do not come out until you are called." A jerk of his head indicated the path that wound in the opposite direction.

His forbidding tone chafed, and I could not understand why he was excluding me. He surely knew I would be interested in their fate. Crossing the short distance to my lodge, I recalled his regret over killing Cuts-His-Face too swiftly, plunging me into both a fierce attack and defense of his character.

Like a rapidly growing weed, my disapproval soon extended to the whole hunting party, until I recalled the day Nathaniel first entered our village. My menfolk had restricted his movements, but they had not mistreated him. Surely, these prisoners had done something to warrant rough handling.

Inside my dwelling, I waited and waited, feeling much like a little girl banished to the nursery and then forgotten. Did Preying Eagle think I might interfere with the council? Now that I considered this, would I if I deemed their decisions unjust or cruel? My conscience began pricking me with questions I had no desire to answer; such as, why I assumed my judgment was superior to that of our aged men.

"I am certainly better equipped to understand my own kind," I parried, but my conscience refused to support the claim. Indeed, it further provoked me—asking why I so readily kicked against my husband's direction whenever my sensibilities tilted a different way. I wondered how long a woman must be married before her husband proved himself worthy of her entire trust, but the answer to that question was exasperatingly clear. The problem was the same I had recently confessed to Red Fawn and Valuable Woman and lay not with Preying Eagle but my own heart. Fingering this weed to its roots, I found a desire to manage everything as I saw fit.

"Lord, neither my husband nor the council need *my* guidance—You are quite able to lead them. Please prune this foul spot from my heart, for my efforts to rid myself of it have proved futile. I continually fall into the same error in thinking." Thankful that He is faithful to cleanse us from all unrighteousness when we confess our sins,[106] I set aside my discontent and picked up my mending.

When Two Doves brought me a bowl of stew for supper, she informed me that Valuable Woman would read the Scriptures that evening; and before I could ask her why, she ducked outside. I feared my cousin might become overburdened. She tired more easily now that she was carrying a little one. Mindful, however, of the Lord's earlier reproof, I trusted the elders had good reasons.

When Preying Eagle came to escort me to the central fire, he cupped my face in his hands. "Stay behind me and do not raise your eyes. I do not want these men to see them." His eyes looked even darker than usual, holding the same turbulent clouds they had when he noticed the bruising on my arms peeking out of the pool.

"Have I displeased you?" I asked, unsure what had stirred them.

"No," he replied, tenderly stroking my cheek as he had done so often before. "You please me deeply."

"How is the wounded man?"

"He will recover."

"Why did you bring them here?"

"It is not for you."

He stated this so flatly that I knew he would discuss them no further, but I wondered what his answer meant. Did he indicate I had overstepped by asking or was he saying they had not come for me? The latter was a possibility that I had not considered, but it might explain many things.

THE FOLLOWING MORNING, Valuable Woman came to my dwelling to relate her concern. "My heart aches for that young man," she confided. "Someone has stolen his wife." She glanced up at my slight scars, blushing for fear that her choice of words revived horrid memories. "During a recent visit to the outpost, he learned that Nathaniel and his wife lived here. They came hoping we might know or have news of her. He seems to love her very dearly."

"What did he look like?" I asked, considering the possibilities my husband had raised last evening.

"He is young—no older than Two Bears. His eyes are light like yours but as blue as the sky and his hair reminds me of late summer corn tassels."

I sighed with relief. The description sounded nothing like Henry. "Did he say where he was from?"

"That island—the long one—between Boston and Philadelphia, where Spotted Long-knife's sister lives."

"New York?"

"Yes, that is it."

"What is the talk in the council?"

"I am surprised Preying Eagle has not told you. He is the one who urged our warriors to capture them."

"I am surprised also. I would have imagined him sympathetic, not only because I am white but because of Cuts-His-Face."

"He says the old one is a lying snake and the young one like a hare, playing tricks."

I disliked learning my husband's opinions through his cousin. It churned up the old unsettling suspicion that I would never truly understand him; yet, he was not a man who acted or spoke without reason.

Sensing my displeasure, my friend admitted she had probably said too much; so out of love for her, I did not press further. We asked the Lord to have mercy on both the man and his lost wife and to restore the latter as He had my son and me to Preying Eagle.

That evening was a repeat of the last one, but late the next morning, the council sent my husband to fetch me to them. "Stay behind me," he ordered, "and keep your eyes down, as you have for the readings."

While I was ducking under the flap behind him, the hair on my neck stood on end. The menfolk I regarded with such esteem were discussing methods of execution. Many Feathers noticed our arrival and commanded his sons to bring *the* prisoner, not prisoners, and they immediately left, needing no further description.

Once they had stood the man in the center of the council, Running Deer addressed him. "Stone-Eyes, tell us again about this woman you seek."

While waiting for my father to finish, I idly considered his name for the young man. Eyes-Like-Sky would seem more fitting from the way my friend had described him. Then, as I opened my mouth to translate the question, I heard Valuable Woman speak. With my eyes fixed to the ground, I had not known she was present and assumed they had asked me here for this purpose.

"We have told you already," an older, exasperated voice replied.

Something about his tone, or maybe his inflection, was exceedingly familiar.

"She is young, seventeen—no eighteen now. Her hair is dark, but not black—like the woman who kneels behind that warrior—and about her size, but her eyes are the color of the sea."

Such cold shudders ran up my spine that I clutched my husband's sheltering back. How was this possible? My friend had told me the man was young and blond.

"What is 'sea'?" Valuable Woman translated for Old Man.

"Big, big water," replied the prisoner. He sounded as if he was addressing a considerably stupid housemaid.

Unthinkingly, I dug my fingernails into my husband's flesh until I felt his muscles tighten; and when I let go, he sprang up.

"Fasten him to the post!"

Depictions of the tortures they had discussed swam in my head. I was familiar with the execution post, but happily, no one had occupied it during the past year. The prisoner clearly understood the portent of my husband's verdict, for he began pleading for mercy.

"Coward!" Preying Eagle spat, but the inflection in the white man's voice was so like Father's, I felt an unexpected wave of pity.

"You know this man," Running Deer stated as they dragged him away.

"Yes," I nodded. "He is my father's false brother."

"Preying Eagle said so. He brought you here this morning to confirm it, lest we separate the flesh from his bones unjustly. You are certain? Do you wish to look him in the face?"

"There can be no mistake," I replied, chiding myself for a lack of common sense. I should have realized immediately why my husband had kept me secluded. The angry clouds in his eyes announced it. "But I would like to see him, in case I am wrong."

The elders and other warriors nodded their approval and voiced their assent. I felt ashamed of the error in judgment to which my arrogance had led me, not only toward my husband but also toward all these esteemed men. They had not kept me away to tilt unfairly against my countrymen; they had been protecting me from unnecessary risk and anguish.

"What would you have us do to him?" asked Many Feathers.

"I do not know," I replied artlessly, shaking my head. "I am torn and my mind is unclear about the answer Jesus would give. On one hand, He was kind to the woman caught in adultery, though her guilt was plain. On the other, I am convinced my uncle has been the death and torment of many. Spotted Long-knife is certain he murdered my father."

"The decision rests with you and your warrior. We pray the Almighty will guide your hearts."

"Oh, Lord!" I prayed inwardly, as my husband escorted me to see Henry. *"I desired to govern these men's fates, but now that I am given that task, I do not have the least idea what to do."* I felt panicky at the very prospect of facing him. "Oh," I pleaded with my husband, "what should I say?"

"Say what is in your heart. He cannot harm you. Red Fawn's brothers have tied his hands behind the pole."

I looked at my uncle, stripped nearly bare and sweating profusely despite the chill November air. Unlike me, he was thoroughly acquainted with the grisly reprisals he might suffer from my husband's kind—he had even imitated them on more than one occasion. I had not thought myself capable of pitying him, but his terrified stare somehow roused my heart.

"Uncle Henry."

Recognizing my voice, his eyes shot upward. "It *was* you in the tent." Taking in my scars, the babe on my back, and Preying Eagle's protective proximity, he leaned back against the post and smugly twisted his lips. "Oh, this is rich. You escaped me to become a savage's broodmare. Not so pure and unwilling after he tortured you, eh? Where was your dear Savior hiding?"

As I engaged his eyes, I expected to feel fear or hatred. Instead, I felt pity. "Uncle Henry, even while you mock Him He is waiting to embrace you. Grandmother and Grandfather prayed for you continually while I grew up. Have you no fear of Him, even while facing death?"

"Answer for yourself," he scoffed, casting another glance at my husband. "Why fear a God who can't keep a white woman from serving the needs of an animal? You would have been better off with me." His eyes raked over my body, stirring hideous memories.

"No look!" my husband ordered, knocking Henry's head back against the post so hard I was afraid it might crack. When my uncle's eyes returned to mine, they were dazed with pain and blood trickled from the lip he had bitten.

"He did not inflict these scars, Henry, nor did anyone from this village. He rescued me from your foreman's assault." As surprise washed over his features, I remembered he did not know this. "I have freely chosen to live here and joyfully accepted this man as my husband. The Lord has blessed me to overflowing, and these people have turned with one heart to the God you spurn. Only His influence has kept them from killing you already. Have you not the sense to call upon Him for mercy?"

"If I do, you will free me; and if not, he will kill me." He nodded toward Preying Eagle. "Is that it?"

"No. I do not refer to His mercy on earth. You will pay for your crimes."

Henry spat violently, splattering my cheek and braid; and Preying Eagle grabbed his hair and jerked him upward, pressing his knife against my uncle's trembling throat.

"Please," I implored him, gently tugging at his hand. "I do not care that he has done this. Let Spotted Long-knife take him to the outpost. The men he has murdered are all white. Let white men judge him in their court."

"What of your father?" Preying Eagle asked.

"He would want his brother to be given every chance to repent. God will avenge my father's death."

"He is the man?" Running Deer asked, attracting my attention to the gathering crowd. I was grateful Valuable Woman and I had few pupils; I had found my uncle's words profoundly embarrassing.

"Yes. What will you do to the others?"

"You have spoken well. They are white, let a white men's council decide. Spotted Long-knife returns in four suns. We will keep them until then."

"This one," Preying Eagle declared, "will remain where he is."

Running Deer's nod sealed the pronouncement, but he noticed I looked pinched. "What creases your brow?"

"The wind grows increasingly cold. I am afraid he will become ill from exposure."

"He deserves no better!" my husband cut in.

"What would you have us do?"

"Whatever my husband wishes," I answered, instantly regretting my hasty protest. "May I feed him and bring him water—perhaps a blanket if it gets cold?"

"Why?" Preying Eagle demanded. "Why do this for a man who would take you by force and then drop you off a cliff?"

"Jesus said, 'If your enemy hungers, feed him; if he thirsts, give him drink.' Surely, I have no greater enemy."

247

"Then do as Jesus says," he relented. "But no blanket!"

AS THE DAY WORE on, Henry's manner changed from insolence to wariness. He did not rise when I brought his supper but shrank back like a cur expecting to be kicked. Since his hands were tied behind the pole, feeding him was unexpectedly awkward. I needed to lift each morsel to his mouth, shuddering when my fingers brushed his lips; but he held his head so much like Grandfather had when he was ill, my aversion quickly diminished. I spoke little and he said nothing, but his eyes looked bewildered while I carefully dabbed dripping broth from his chin.

Later that night, as the wind whipped through nearby trees, Preying Eagle recounted his part in the story. His hunting party had come upon and trailed the group of white men closely for several hours, surrounding them when they bedded down for the night. Because he and Stands Apart understood rudimentary English, they were able to grasp bits of the conversations, including Henry's directives to the young man from New York.

A soldier had said Captain Anderson and I married and had taken up residence with a tribe in the high hills northwest of the outpost. A helpful sort, he also mentioned the dates of Nathaniel's next scheduled visit to the fort, so Henry's party planned their foray to coincide with his absence. Learning our people were friendly, they intended to pose as homesteaders searching for a missing wife. Then, once I had been located, they would buy or abduct me.

Henry would have stayed behind, hidden at their camp, had one of the miscreants not stumbled upon a young hunter in my husband's party the next morning and forced a confrontation. Lacking another alternative, Henry receded into the background, and the yellow-haired New Yorker proceeded to relate his story.

"I wondered why you suspected he was my uncle. He looked so pathetic while I fed him this evening. I could not help imagining my grandmother caring for him when he was a little boy."

"Your heart reminds me of the stew you made tonight for Red Woman—everything is boiled together until nothing is distinguishable. You fear him and then you pity him. I have kept you from his snake ways, yet the sadness in your eyes accuses me of cruelty. You are all upside-down. I do not understand you."

"I cannot help seeing my grandfather when I look at him. They are so alike."

"He is a wolf wearing buffalo skin so he can creep into the herd. His sins have tied him to the post. He does not deserve your pity."

Preying Eagle loved me plainly and deserved more appreciation than my contradictory emotions offered. "I did not mean to make you feel accused, nor do I think you unjust. Quite the opposite, I am very grateful for your protection."

BY MORNING, LACK of sleep had hollowed dark cavities under Henry's eyes. Between bites of breakfast, he asked, "What will they do to me?"

"Captain Anderson does not return for several days."

"Please tell me," he pleaded. His voice sounded hoarse and yesterday's arrogance was noticeably absent. "Alcy, wondering what to expect is driving me mad. What kind of torture?"

For the first time, I recalled he had not understood my conversations with my husband and father.

"They will not torture you. It is enough to keep you tied here."

He looked uncertain but added after silently watching me for a while, "This is your doing, isn't it?"

Unsure what to answer, I said nothing.

"You always were soft-hearted."

Hot tears stung my eyes. His tone was so like Father's.

"Surely, you do not weep for me?"

"You surprised me; that is all," I replied, embarrassed that he had seen them.

"I would have treated you well, had you been willing. You would have lacked nothing."

My husband was correct: my emotions were so confused that none were properly separated from the others. This man almost certainly murdered my father; and yet, learning that he had felt more than antipathy toward me oddly mattered. Perhaps I was unable to separate him entirely from the rest of my beloved family. Whatever the reason, my feelings took me in too many directions at once to pay them any heed.

"I would have lacked what I wanted most—a partner with whom I could follow Jesus and a husband whom I could trust."

He looked like he might protest until I spoke more plainly, "Stump informed me of your...arrangement, Uncle. I cannot be so easily deceived this time. Captain Anderson will take you and your men to the outpost and charges will be brought against you there."

249

"On the word of Indians and Indian lovers?" he sneered, contempt again bolstering his courage. "Have you forgotten how important I am considered in this territory, Alcy? They will free me, and I will personally burn this village to the ground."

"Look around you, Uncle. You would not dare. We are several hundred strong. I have been to the fort and met with their commander—you will find no help there. He is a close friend of Captain Anderson, and his wife is a friend of mine. He has learned much about Monroe from us."

Apprehension stole into his stony eyes.

"The Captain knows my people well and will vouch for their veracity—more, I might add, than anyone can do for you."

THE NEXT DAY WAS chilly, but by the time I brought his evening meal, the sun had carved deep furrows in Henry's brow and blistered his bare flesh. He shook uncontrollably when the cold air blew against his fevered skin, spilling the water that I held to his lips.

"Alcy," he pleaded, "help me."

"I will not go against my husband's orders. If you want to leave this post, pray the Almighty will move his heart."

Slumping over, he muttered, "What is that verse, the one my father quoted so often—or was it your grandmother and Louise?"

"It was probably all of them if your childhood was like mine, but you haven't given me enough to go on."

"About sin exposing you."

"'Ye have sinned against the Lord and be sure your sin will find you out.'"[107]

"Yes," he muttered in a barely audible whisper. "'Your sin will find you out.'"

"I used to hate hearing it. When I was naughty, I always managed to get caught."

"Perhaps that made the difference."

I had to strain to hear him and became uncertain whether he spoke to me or himself.

"No one believed me capable of the things I did—not even your father. He had no idea how wretchedly I used him, even as he lay on his deathbed; but you always suspected me." He turned, engaging me with his bleary eyes. "How?"

"I'm not sure. Perhaps you let down your guard, considering me no threat, or perhaps the Holy Spirit showed me your true nature." As the wind picked up, his teeth rattled. "Here," I said, holding the soup to his lips. "This will warm you for the moment."

"Pray for me."

"I do, Uncle, and will continue."

I began fearing for his sanity during our Bible reading. He wailed loudly and indecipherably. Little Turtle told us it unnerved his fellow prisoners, who were certain we were torturing him. At one point, Preying Eagle walked over as if to strike him, but he just stood staring instead, looking as if his heart were at war.

"If it is this cold now, how will the Moon of the Frost be?" I asked my husband as he laid more sticks on our embers inside our dwelling.

"We will make camp farther south and not so high up, like last year, but I do not think we will return to the same place. Many in the council think we should move toward the sun's resting place or up into the colder forests. I agree." He waited a short while for my response, before asking, "Why have you become so quiet? Are you thinking of your uncle again?"

I nodded my head, embarrassed he had caught me. "His skin was burned badly today. He must feel as if he is freezing."

With a deep groan, he lay back, gazing first at the bright stars shining through our smoke-hole and then long and hard at me. "Put on your clothes," he abruptly commanded. "We will bring him a robe, though he does not deserve it."

When we arrived at the post, he did not need our help. Running Deer and Valuable Woman had already brought him blankets and were telling him of our Savior's death as a substitute for his. We retreated silently between the lodges but stopped as we heard him begin to weep.

"He says he is too far gone for forgiveness," my cousin's clear sweet voice informed my father.

"Ask him if he deserves the mercy Eyes-Like-Water has shown him, bringing food and water to the murderer of her father, who also wished for her shame and death."

When Henry heard the question, his weeping became profuse, but he did not answer.

"Why does she do these things?" continued Running Deer. "Because you have treated her kindly? No. All know what you are. It is the Creator, dwelling in her heart Who shows you mercy. He welcomes you through her, murderer that you are. She is just His water skin, pouring His mercy out for you. Before the Creator lighted our path, I would have slit you from throat to belly and let my dogs feed on your entrails."

"Why do you not?" my uncle muttered.

"Because the Almighty makes me bring you blankets instead. He has robbed me of my sleep with your moaning, and my woman will not stop praying for you. How can I forbid her?" He paused, watching Two Doves approach with a bowl. "Here," he held the bowl to Henry's lips, "she wants to warm your insides."

Looking up at Valuable Woman, Henry murmured, "Please thank his wife for the soup and also for her prayers."

I could not restrain the tears that streamed down my face, though I was not sure I cried for Henry or Father, who had never stopped loving him. What Running Deer said was true—it was not in me to show my uncle mercy, nor was it of myself that I began deeply desiring his salvation. Yet, I found it had somehow become the desire of my heart.

Preying Eagle swiftly left the shadows. As starlight glinted off his knife, my breath caught in my throat, and Henry drew back from his looming form like a frightened animal.

Cutting Henry's bonds, he ordered, "Tell Tall Man to bring his salve to the guest lodge," then switched to English. "Stand up. Make sleep with your white warriors."

Henry's legs did not at first cooperate, having lain useless for several days; but with effort, he rose and hobbled to the guest lodge between Running Deer and Preying Eagle, looking up at them now and then as if afraid it was a trick.

Be not overcome of evil, but overcome evil with good.

Romans 12:21

Epilogue

ON THE FIRST OF Nate's visits to the outpost the following spring, he learned that old Judge Abbot had hanged Henry and three of his men. The encounter with our warriors had scared the young New Yorker into testifying against all four. Ample townspeople added their voices, and the jury not only convicted my uncle of murdering the Lawsons but also those former employers whose portraits hung in his gallery.

Sadly, no one could say whether he responded to our Savior's repeated attempts to embrace him, but I rather think he did. While Nathaniel was escorting the prisoners to the outpost, Henry asked him for a Bible and, according to Major Young, refused any defense at his trial.

I returned to the outpost also, but not until my twenty-first birthday. In a sharp twist of irony, I, as next of kin, gained Henry's fortune in addition to Father's on that day. Valuable Woman loaned me a dress and bonnet for the event and coifed my hair.

When I ducked out of her dwelling, Little Potbelly, whom we had begun to call Walks-in-His-Grandfather's-Shadow, stopped to gape at my attire. "Look, Grandfather. Momma is hiding under a white woman's headdress."

We each looked at the other for a moment, too surprised to speak. My second son just stared from his cradleboard. Later, when his grandmother asked why he had been so surprised, Walks-in-His-Grandfather's-Shadow said that I would fool no one with the disguise—white people had fire hair and little spots like Valuable Woman, or yellow hair like her daughter Abigail. When Two Doves informed him he was half-white, he just laughed, pulled up his shirt, and flung it off.

"Look, Grandmother!" he cried, smacking his palms against his stomach. "I am not half white—I am all one color!"

When I stood before the judge, both Major Young and Nathaniel vouched for my identity, and Asbury, to whom we had written in Monroe, arranged to send funds periodically to the outpost. The money enabled Nathaniel, whom we gave power to act as my agent, to track down as many rightful heirs of Henry's victims as he could find and restore what Henry had stolen. Next, he contracted a printing of the Gospel of John in the Allied tongue and one of each subsequent book that he translated.

1834

I HAVE NOW LIVED through as many Moons of Yellow and Falling Leaves with the people of my heart as I had lived with the people of my birth. Much has changed and much remains the same, but I would not trade them for twice as many comfortable years elsewhere.

Five years after our daughter was born, Ol' Hickory, hailed as the hero of the campaigns against the Indians, took office as President of the United States. He implemented many policies that grieve our people and the Allies' Great Councils talk much of war. Our band prefers peace, but we will not stand idly by and watch the destruction of our families. We take comfort knowing God, Who planned the end from the beginning, will grant us the grace to glorify Him through whatever He sets in our paths.

When Preying Eagle and I were newly married, I often marveled at how ideally suited we were to each other. My wonder has only increased as the passing years have afforded me further insight. Becoming one flesh only began in the room of cedars. Whether gazing into the bright faces of our children or considering the babe I now carry within, I realize that Running Deer and Two Doves were right. Bearing Preying Eagle's sons and daughter has tied me to my new parents, my new people, and my husband more profoundly than I had imagined possible. Our children not only blend our blood but our joys and sorrows, hopes and fears, our futures and pasts. I am no longer the pale-skinned adopted daughter of one respected leader or the light-eyed wife of another. I am a mother of our people's children, a single white bead woven inseparably into the richly colored design of our tribe.

While living in Skippack, I would have answered anyone who asked why the Lord had made me, "to glorify and worship Him," but never did I anticipate the wondrous way He would unfold my life. When my daughter asks how she can know the Creator's plan for her, I tell her simply to do what He has said, taking one step of obedience after another. He alone sees the end from the beginning, and our paths emerge in the light of His Word.

As we look back over our lives, we may not see anything we consider significant that the Lord has accomplished through us. Our perspective is not His. Ruth never knew that her devoted service to Naomi placed her in the lineage of the Messiah, nor did Esther set out to save her people from annihilation. Faithfulness in the small things Jesus sets before us brings about His great plans. During those first few days in the power of my fearsome warrior, I leaned against the smooth-barked tree near the waterfall and declared that I had no people to save. I could not have been more wrong. The Almighty gave me these beloved people and saved them from eternal destruction.

Over the years I, too, have had a change of name, but it has happened gradually. Less often have the people called me Eyes-Like-Water and more often The-Woman-Who-Brought-Us-the-Book. They honor me with this name; yet, I know I did not do this any more than my courage kept me still when I first looked into my husband's opened eyes. I simply did not resist my Lord's plan by insisting on my own. I did nothing for God; He did what He wanted with me. By abiding in Him we bear fruit, for apart from Him, we can do nothing.

And the Spirit and the bride say,

"Come!"

And let him that heareth say,

"Come!"

And let him that is athirst come.

And whoever will,

let him take the water of life freely.

He which testifieth to these things saith,

"Surely, I come quickly!"

Revelations 22:17 and 20

Even so, come quickly, Lord Jesus!

Light Bird's Song

Preview of the second novel in the People of the Book series

1839

PACING WOLF restlessly shifted atop a small rise, just beyond the range of a dozing sentinel's arrows. Hidden in the tall, coarse grass beneath the canopy of an ancient crabapple tree, he took in the size and number of his enemies' lodges. He was eager to exact his vengeance. The grass felt prickly and cold, even through his deerskin shirt; and his breath, swirling up as he warmed his fingers, clung damply to his high cheekbones.

Wiping them irritably, he spied a faint pale wisp drifting aloft above a smoke-hole and tilted up the edges of his mouth. He would not need to wait much longer. Hidden within the layers of a lodge-cover, a woman was coaxing her dying embers to flame. Her dwelling awoke like a living thing, glowing welcomingly against the chilly night sky.

The earth had been like her this year, stirring early to arouse all that depended on her care. Unseasonable warmth had helped him cover twice the ground he could have in snow and kept the moccasin impressions he followed fresh. All the while he tracked them along the riverbank, he had thought their wearer's carelessness odd; and when they met the hoof prints of a small war party, he began to grow suspicious.

They led me to this village too easily, Pacing Wolf concluded. *This warrior is overconfident or he intends to incite us.*

The surrounding lodges looked flat, like black peaked mountains painted across an unbleached buffalo hide, but as the first shoots of light streaked purple across the horizon, they began to take a conical shape. A nearby bird greeted the morning, and a sniffing dog poked its nose through cold ashes from last evening's cook-fire. Mothers would soon search their larders for food, and daughters would scavenge firewood below trees that sprang, like the one that hid him, from the bottom of the hill on which he lay.

Before finishing the thought, a light peal of laughter interrupted his thoughts, and he shifted to a thinner spot between the sprouting branches. Beside a lodge on the village-edge, a newly lit cook-fire cast light on a figure that he quickly passed over. Surely, such a pleasant sound had not arisen from a silver-haired grandmother's shriveled throat, but as he followed the old woman's lively gestures, an attentive young companion stepped into the fire's glow. Her neck was like a doe's: long and slender, and while he watched her cross the meadow, her graceful form stirred his senses.

Every step that brought her closer increased the beat of Pacing Wolf's heart until he inwardly trotted to and fro like the restless animal whose name he possessed. Conforming each muscle to the twisting lines of the thick, gray trunk, he drank in the cold air slowly, evenly, tamping down the urge to hastily rush out.

As Light Bird drew within feet of the ancient crabapple, something—she could not say what—pulled her to an abrupt halt. She stood perfectly still, as if sniffing for a predator's scent, but could detect nothing amiss. Concluding her imagination was playing tricks, she started plucking up twigs for firewood, but as she began crawling among the tree's roots, the skin on her arms began to prickle. She froze, listening intensely while her eyes darted this way and that, but she heard only the wind rustling branches overhead.

Suddenly, a dark shadow knocked her over with such force she could not scream. Hard-muscled arms pinned her own against her ribcage and rolled her within a thick buffalo robe before she could draw a breath. Twisting and turning frantically, she tried to squirm out of its dark folds; but her unseen assailant hoisted her off the ground, slung her over his shoulder, and bounded effortlessly up the hill.

Rescue me, Lord, from the evildoers; protect me from the violent, who devise evil plans in their hearts and stir up wars every day.
Psalm 140:1-2

Endnotes

1 Proverbs 3:5-7
2 Ecclesiastes 9:4
3 Isaiah 40:8
4 I Corinthians 11:8
5 I Corinthians 11:8
6 Genesis 2:24
7 Ecclesiastes 10:19
8 John 11:25-26
9 2 Samuel 15:1-4
10 2 Corinthians 6:14
11 Acts2:1-10
12 Austen, Jane; *Sense & Sensibility*
13 Luke 10:25-37
14 Luke 10:37
15 Proverbs 3:7
16 Psalm 27:1
17 Ecclesiastes 4:11
18 Matthew 6:34
19 Matthew 6:34
20 Genesis 37-50
21 Psalm 139:16 - NIV
22 Isaiah 46:10
23 Matthew 6:34
24 2 Timothy 2:4
25 Colossians 3:22
26 Titus 2:9-10
27 Psalm 139:16
28 Matthew 6:34
29 Esther 4:14
30 Ibid 4:16
31 Mark 9:24
32 John 12:25
33 John 12:26
34 I Peter 3:1-6
35 I Peter 3:16
36 2 Corinthians 6:14
37 Psalm 103:13-14
38 Psalm 94:18-19
39 Psalm 118:1
40 Matthew 6:30
41 Romans 8:38-39
42 Romans 8:31
43 Romans 12:21
44 Proverbs 31:17
45 Daniel 7:9-11
46 Proverbs 13:21
47 John 3:3
48 John 3:19
49 John 3:36
50 Acts 8:36
51 John 6:68
52 Proverbs 31:30
53 Proverbs 16:1
54 I Corinthians 1:27-28
55 Luke 16:13
56 Ruth 1:16-7
57 Matthew 10:28
58 Romans 8:28
59 Psalm 116:15
60 I Samuel 16:7
61 2 Samuel 6:20 and 23
62 Psalm 147:10
63 Matthew 1:18-19
64 Deuteronomy 21:23-24
65 John 3:29 and 14:3
66 Luke 1:37
67 Psalm 34:19
68 Song of Solomon 2:16, 1:1617; 5:10-11,16; 6:3
69 I Corinthians 6:18
70 Romans 5:8
71 Ephesians 1:4
72 I John 2:1
73 Ephesians 1:5
74 I Peter 3:1-2
75 Luke 6:27
76 Matthew 11:6
77 I Peter 3:6
78 Romans 12:17-19
79 I Samuel 27:8-9
80 Proverbs 21:1
81 I Peter 3:1
82 Proverbs 25:11
83 Matthew 10:34-35
84 Proverbs 31:10
85 I Samuel 17:45
86 Matthew 18:33
87 John 1:12-13
88 Genesis 20:2
89 Proverbs 16:33

[90]Job 19:26
[91]Daniel 3
[92]Romans 12:19
93John 3:19-20
[94]Psalm 34:3-4
[95]Psalm 150:6
[96]Joshua 4:6
[97]Romans 8:28
[98]Joel 2:25

[99]I Peter 1:25 [100]I Peter 3:6
[101]James 2:23
[102]Genesis 20
[103]I Peter 3:4
[104]Matthew 6:2
[105]Proverbs 31:11
[106]I John 1:9
[107]Numbers 32:23

Author's Note

A River too Deep is a work of fiction, though it incorporates historical figures and events to anchor the setting. I have intended to accurately reflect early 1800's Allied culture, avoiding erroneous stereotypes, glorifications, or denigrations, and by using English translations of indigenous concepts and labels. Although objectionable in general, the terms savage and Indian are used by Anglo Americans throughout, as is Negro on one occasion, to authentically reflect the era.

The tribal response to the Gospel is based on a recent verifiable account within a Pacific Island tribe with similar mores and structure. Unfortunately, during the novel's time frame many sincere missionaries employed repellent efforts to conform individuals to European habits of farming and in-school education. I am thankful that Native Americans from all tribes are now coming to know Jesus and pray not only that they will feel free to worship Him in ways that do not divide them from their rich heritage, but also that the rest of the body of Christ will embrace rather than misunderstand these differences.

If you enjoyed this novel, kindly consider leaving a review on Amazon or the site where it was purchased and on Goodreads. Writing is far easier for me than making readers aware my books exist, and reviews make a huge difference.

Lastly, you have taken the time to meet me (nothing could reflect my heart more fully than this series). Now I would like to meet you. If this might interest you also, please drop by my Facebook author page. I have met many new and cherished friends this way!

Meet the Author

Sydney Tooman Betts currently resides with her protagonist-inspiring husband at the foot of the Blue Ridge Mountains. While single, Ms. Betts (B.S. Bible/Missiology, M.Ed with an emphasis on teaching reading) was involved in a variety of cross-cultural adventures in North and Central America. After marrying, she and her husband lived in Europe and the Middle East where he served in various mission-support capacities. Her teaching experiences span preschool to guest lecturing at the graduate level, and she has been privileged to serve as Sunday School Superintendent, Children's Church Director, or Women's Ministries facilitator in several evangelical denominations. Before penning the first novel in this series, A River too Deep, she wrote several stories included in an adult literacy program.

Made in the USA
Middletown, DE
15 December 2023